DIVERSION

DIVERSION

Dwayne Morrow Mystery #4

DARIN MILLER

ISBN: 978-1-7368666-9-6 (Paperback)

Library of Congress Control Number: 2022916015

Any references to historical events, real people, or real places are used fictitiously. Names, characters, and places are products of the author's imagination. No portion of this book was created through use of artificial intelligence (AI), nor may any portion be used to train AI.

Front cover photography by Nicki Miller.

Printed by Kindle Direct Publishing, in Columbus, OH, USA.

First printing edition 2022. Current printing edition 2025.

www.darin-miller.com

DARIN MILLER
Dwayne Morrow Mysteries

This one's for Gina.

"Life's earthly burdens
Now have passed
At home with God
She's free at last..."

—*Nancy Jo Miller*
November 19, 1987

TABLE OF CONTENTS

CHAPTER ONE

"I don't think he even noticed us," I muttered, guiding my rental car along Orin Way. A jacked-up truck on oversized knobby tires roared past, mostly in my lane. The driver, a craggy-faced, middle-aged man with a jaw so square it literally had corners, flipped a bird in my direction before laying on his horn. I tried to respond in kind, but my unfamiliarity with the Fiesta's controls only led to my ineffectual punching of the steering column. I started for the power window, willing to fly my bird higher and longer than his, but when I couldn't find that control either, I gave up. I missed my Optima.

Melanie's fingers tickled the short hairs at the base of my skull. "I thought you didn't want to be noticed," she said. "Silly me. I thought we were merely guests. Had I known, I might've been able to arrange a spotlight for you, maybe some backup singers."

I cocked my head and shot her a quick glare. "You know what I mean."

"Dwayne," she sighed, massaging the bridge of her nose. "It was his *wedding!* What did you expect?"

I shook my head. "I don't know."

She narrowed her eyes and sighed. "You're a real piece of work, do you know that? It was like pulling teeth to get you to go. You told me yourself you didn't want to detract from Matt and Sheila's special day with any bickering. And now, because Matt didn't pay enough attention to you, you're *pissed?* Sometimes, I don't get you at all."

We fell into silence as my house appeared on the horizon. It was five o'clock in the afternoon, but I hadn't slept at all the previous evening; I was

1

quickly grinding myself into tight-lipped irritability. I didn't want to discuss my ongoing difficulties with my older brother anymore.

"Do you think it was all right to let Jasmine go with Nola?" asked Melanie. "I'm starting to feel like I'm taking advantage." It was a subtle attempt to lighten the mood by swapping topics, but I was still feeling pissy.

"Of course," I said tightly. "You've used her before. You pay her."

"Well, yeah, but not with—well, not when she had so many kids to watch."

"'So many?' Mel, it's *three kids*."

"I know," she said, staring vacantly through her window. "Still—"

I turned into my driveway, a long tongue of dirt and loose gravel. I knew what was bothering Melanie—or perhaps I should say whom. Scott Nichols was one of those three kids, and after the last tumultuous week, she wasn't quite ready to stop being suspicious of him. Scott had come into our lives after his mother had been murdered, and for a scary moment, it looked as if the sixteen-year-old had actually committed the crime himself. Of course, it didn't help matters when he had asked Jasmine to hide a handgun for him before being arrested at the scene of a subsequent murder. Everyone's faith in Scott Nichols had been shaken except mine, and now that he had been vindicated, I was growing weary of defending him. Still, I held my tongue because I knew my mood had been fouled by sleep deprivation. We could always discuss it when I was more rational.

"It'll be fine," I said. "Billy could use the distraction, anyway."

Billy Garrett was our reporter friend Brady's ten-year-old son. He had been born with spina bifida and ambulated on braces and crutches or in a wheelchair, depending upon the terrain. His mother had been killed in a traffic accident years before, and whenever Brady needed daycare, he turned to the Caudills, whom he had known since his own childhood. Brady was currently in the hospital, recovering from a gunshot wound he had sustained the previous evening. I made a mental note to call and check his condition, see if it was any less critical than it had been before we had left for the wedding. I couldn't stand the thought of any more victims from the train wreck that had brought Scott Nichols to my door.

I parked beside my two-story whitewashed farmhouse and got out of the small car, stretching my legs and wincing as blood flow returned in a wave of pinpricks. Melanie's fingers snaked through mine as we moved towards the porch. She had been awake as long as me; her eyelids were beginning to droop as well.

"At least with Jasmine gone, we can nap without guilt," she said, stifling a yawn.

Dexter, my eight-year-old black cat, yowled his greeting as I pushed the door inward. He was well beyond his feeding time and was most definitely unamused. If I was getting the feline-to-English translation correctly, he was threatening a report to PETA if I didn't clean up my act. I disarmed my security alarm while he continued to complain noisily.

"Okay, okay," I relented, kicking off my stiff dress shoes and passing through the living room into the kitchen.

"I'll check the hospital while you feed your mammal," said Melanie, heading for the cordless phone in the hallway.

"Thanks," I called, pulling a plastic container of dry nuggets from the cupboard below the microwave. Dexter circled my ankles while crying, making the feeding process as difficult as he possibly could. He nudged the container at precisely the right moment, resulting in a food pile that was three times his normal amount. "Hell with it," I muttered, scritching his back and tucking the container back into the pantry.

I wandered back into the living room and debated the merits of straightening up a bit as Melanie conducted her phone call in the hallway. Several days' worth of newspapers had collected beside the couch, and there were empty glasses on the coffee table. Dirty socks poked out from beneath the couch and every surface was obscured by a thin layer of dust.

Near the fireplace, a trail of cat sick lay on the hardwood floor like an elongated comma, and I groaned. Anyone with a cat will testify that hairballs and trails of half-digested food are somewhat commonplace; after eight years of coexistence, cleaning up the mess was still my least favorite responsibility. Cleaning the litter pan was a close second.

Melanie appeared in the doorway, her face considerably brighter. "Brady's doing better," she said. "He woke up a little while ago. The doctors say they expect him to make a full recovery."

"Well, that's a relief," I said, plopping down on the couch. Housework could wait. "You should call Nola."

"I already did," said Melanie as she eased down beside me. I slid an arm around her shoulders. "She's going to dilute the story for Billy, but at least now she can tell him his dad won't be home for a few days, but he *will* be coming home."

I leaned my head backward against the overstuffed cushion and closed my eyes. It was nice to have a moment without worry. Melanie snuggled against me, and I could smell the subtle scent of perfume I had given her the previous Christmas. As much as I wanted to strip off my button-down shirt and slacks and dive into bed, I didn't want to disturb this perfect moment. Sleep got tired of waiting for me to change my clothes, and I drifted away.

I awoke with a jolt, nearly toppling Melanie onto the floor. The house was quiet, and the room was dark. Dexter was perched on the back of the sofa, staring down at where we had slid sideways onto the cushions. I glanced at the digital display on the television tuner. It was a little after nine.

What had awakened me?

4

I tried to sit upright, but Melanie was laying on my legs and mumbled something thickly incoherent when I moved them.

I was in the middle of a yawn when the doorbell sounded again.

This time, I gently shook Melanie's shoulders while I eased my legs out from underneath her. She looked up at me with one groggy eye, her blonde hair tangled and lopsided. *"Hmmph?"*

"Company," I said as I stood up. She mumbled something else before sliding face first into the divot I had left behind in the cushions. I finished my yawn while padding toward the front door, absently trying to smooth my rumpled shirt. I snapped on the porch light and peered through the peephole.

"Oh, my God!" I said as a slow smile crept across my face. I opened the door wide. *"Gina!* I wasn't expecting you!"

My sister's crooked grin turned into an outright chuckle as she clasped her hands over her mouth. "Nice 'do, little bro," she said, reaching out and tousling my hair. I glanced at my reflection in the glass of the storm door and saw that my hair was standing completely on end. I pulled back and self-consciously tried to mash it back to my head. Gina giggled.

"Well, don't just stand there," I said, smiling broadly. "Come on in."

"Didn't you pay your electric bill?" she asked as she entered the darkened living room. I made the circuit, switching on lamps as I went.

"Very funny," I said. "Melanie and I were napping."

"So *that's* what you call it," she said, easing the strap of her purse from her shoulder and dropping it beside the sofa. Sometime during our exchange, Melanie arose from her slumber, and her head appeared over the back of the couch. Gina's cheeks flushed, and she smiled sheepishly. "I didn't mean that the way it sounded, I was just—"

Melanie grinned as she pulled herself off the couch. "It's all right," she said. "If I'd have had my way, we *wouldn't* have been napping."

I shifted on my feet while my girlfriend and sister reveled in my discomfort. They had never met before, and this wasn't exactly the introduction I had envisioned.

"If you'll excuse me," said Melanie, easing toward the hallway, "I'm going to see if I can get this wild mess under control." She jabbed at her own lopsided tower of hair before disappearing. A second later, her footsteps receded up the stairs as she made her way to the master bathroom.

"She's cute," said Gina, perching on one arm of the sofa.

"Why, thank you. I certainly think so," I said. I couldn't keep the smile off my face for long. "I can't believe you're really *here!* It's been years! And *look* at you!" I took her delicate hands and pulled her to her feet, spinning her around and giving her the once-over. She wore faded Levi's and a lightweight cream-colored sweater. Her silken black hair flowed around her slender shoulders as my 360-degree examination quickly degenerated into something closer to ballroom dancing. She giggled again, and we hugged fiercely.

"I suppose it'll be your wedding next, huh?" She eased back onto the arm of the couch.

"Slow down, Cochise. Mel and I have only been seeing each other for the past half year or so."

"*Ah*," she said, nodding. "I see you and Matthew share a distaste for commitment."

"Not fair. It wasn't Matt who didn't want to get married. Sheila's first trimester mood swings made her believe Matt was only asking because she was pregnant, and she told him she didn't want to get married just for the sake of it. She was so touchy he had to wait for the time to be right. Thank goodness the time came before the baby did."

Gina sighed. "I can't believe we are about to have a niece or nephew."

"I can't believe Matt actually scored."

We grinned at each other and were about to continue our dissection of our brother's personal appeal when Melanie reappeared, her hair pulled back in a plastic clip. "I called Nola and told her I was on my way," she said. "And apologized, of course. I didn't expect Jasmine to be there this late. Do you mind if I borrow the car?"

"Of course not," I said. "Do you want me to ride with you?"

"No, I don't think that's necessary. Why don't you stay and catch up with your sister? I can either stop by on my way back through, or if you aren't planning on going anywhere, I could just return the car in the morning."

"Morning will be fine," I said. We exchanged a quick smooch. "Be careful."

"I will," she said, pocketing the Fiesta's keys. "Maybe Tuesday evening we can find you a replacement vehicle."

"I guess so." I couldn't decide which I hated more, the rental car or the prospect of three to five years of car payments.

"It was very nice to finally meet you," said Melanie, taking Gina's hand.

My sister nodded her head and smiled graciously. "Same here. I hate that you have to run off so quickly. We haven't had a chance to chat. I want to hear if my brother's been behaving himself."

Melanie laughed. "Of course not, but then again, that's kinda why I like him. Maybe we could do lunch sometime. How long will you be in town?"

"A couple more days anyway. I figured I'd pester Dwayne until he can't take it anymore, then I'll travel south and do the same to the parents."

"Good. I'll look forward to it."

"Bring your daughter," suggested Gina. "We'll have a regular girls' day out. Shopping, eating, and more shopping."

"Sounds like a plan."

I followed Melanie to the front door and collected another smooch. "I love you," I said, pulling her into my arms.

7

"Love you, too," she said, giving me a quick squeeze before hurrying to the car.

·····•••⌒⊙⌒•••·····

I glanced up at the clock on the mantle and was startled to see that it was after two in the morning. Gina and I had abandoned all pretense of civilization and had camped out amongst throw pillows in the center of my living room. Donatos Pizza had already come and gone, and Dexter was showing an inordinate amount of interest in the empty box, hoping with each subsequent pass someone might have refilled its content. We had just finished perusing my collection of family photos and had exhausted talk of the good ole days.

"I'm surprised Mom didn't insist you follow them to Lymont immediately after the wedding," I said, taking a swig from a can of Pepsi. "You know how she is. She hates it that you're hardly ever home."

Gina smiled. "I'll be hearing enough of that when I get down there," she said. "She's still waiting for me to marry and settle down, preferably in Lymont."

"You'd go crazy," I said. "You've never been satisfied staying in one place."

"I've spent years trying to explain that, but Mom doesn't understand the appeal of travel. I have experienced so many different things, so many different cultures. There's no way you can gain that kind of insight from a textbook or the internet. I mean, I *know* she's proud of me, even if she doesn't understand the way my head works."

"She'd *better* be proud of you. I don't know any other Midland Valley students who have won awards for their photography."

She waved away my comment and made a sound like a leaky tire valve. "They're just pictures. It's not like I'm solving murders or anything. I saw the news this morning. I guess you just caught another one."

"I didn't do it single-handedly," I said. "And it was really more dumb luck than actual deductive reasoning—"

"Oh my, yes. Dragging out all the ten cent words, eh? So, tell me, is this a passing phase or is this your future?"

I shifted my numb backside on its cushion. "I think it's my future. I don't know. I guess it is for me like globetrotting is for you."

She nodded. "It's important to choose a profession you truly enjoy. A person spends too much time on the job not to enjoy the work. What about your consulting business?"

Despite my aspiration to become a full-time detective, my real bread and butter was still my systems consultant business. I had no formal training but had educated myself via the internet, books, magazine articles and plain old trial and error. I was pretty proficient with computer hardware and a regular pit bull with network issues. Best of all, I was cheaper than all the certified guys, and word of mouth had lent me a comfortable, if somewhat irregular income.

"I'll keep it up as long as I have to," I said. "The money's better, and the work's not all bad."

"So, tell me about Boggs Investigations," she said, rolling her eyes. "Is it everything you imagined?"

I laughed to myself. She had no idea. "Doug Boggs is the same little militant no-neck who went to school with us. I don't think he's matured past fourteen."

"Honestly, not many of your classmates stick in my mind because you were four years behind me. It frankly wasn't cool for me to acknowledge any of you even existed."

"Thanks."

She grinned and playfully swatted at Dexter's tail. He hissed his disapproval. "Still, Doug Boggs *does*, but not so much because of him as his mother. My God! I worked in the office, remember? I can't tell you how many times that woman came over to raise holy hell with Mr. Adams because of the grief you guys gave her son. I've never seen a grown woman dress like that—all fluorescent colors and none of the good ones. Eventually, we developed an early warning system so Mr. Adams could escape through the teacher's lounge."

I laughed. "She hasn't changed a bit. She's Doug's office manager, and I still have to deal with her on a semi-regular basis."

"Sounds like fun."

"Well, right now, I'm suspended, so I guess it doesn't matter."

"*Suspended?* How could you be suspended? Especially after that latest case you solved."

"I was kind of acting on my own. Doug dismissed the case because he didn't think we were capable of handling it, but I felt sorry for the teenage boy that was involved. He didn't have any family left, and the people around him were really screwed up. Anyway, I apparently ruffled one of Doug's many feathers somewhere along the way, and I got myself released from duty for three weeks."

"What a little shit," said Gina, automatically siding with me even though she knew none of the details. It's one of the many great things about siblings. "I ought to kick his ass."

"While I appreciate the sentiment, I don't really think it would help anything. I can't get my PI license until I put in the prerequisite number of hours in training. And besides, I have a consultant job lined up for tomorrow morning. It should hold me over pretty well. Enough about me, already! Tell me something new about your life. Anybody special?"

Gina smiled. "Nope. There *have* been a few of interest, but it never works out. Most guys aren't willing to abandon their own careers in favor of mine. The very concept seems to threaten them."

"That's too bad."

She shrugged. "It's not so bad. I'm thirty-eight years old. I've visited 147 countries and seen the full spectrum of economic wealth and poverty. I've witnessed religious rituals that were astonishing—a few that were frightening, but *nothing* you could have gleaned from documentaries on TV. And don't look at me like I'm some old maid. I've had affairs that would make you *blush*, little brother. The only regret I have is that I never had children, and honestly, it's only half a regret. I know that a child would severely impede my ability to fly on a moment's notice, and I don't know if I'd be willing to give that up. Kind of selfish, huh?"

"Not at all. Maybe that's just the way it's supposed to be."

"Most days I see it that way, too. But every now and then, that damn biological clock can pound like a sledgehammer."

I rested my back against the frame of the sofa. There wasn't much I could say. I had turned thirty-four the previous December. Sometimes I could hear my *own* biological clock ticking. I had a difficult time envisioning myself as a father, but I hadn't entirely dismissed the idea. My relationship with Melanie's daughter gave me hope I wouldn't be a total failure. Still, although guys can produce offspring until the day they die, I didn't want people asking me if I was my own kid's grandpa. I suddenly felt pressured to produce.

A cell phone rang that was not my own.

Gina twisted sideways and snagged her purse from beside the couch. "Hold that thought," she said, fishing the bleating instrument from a pocket in her leather bag. "Yeah," she said into the speaker.

I struggled to my knees, allowing the blood to flow back into my lower extremities. I had been sitting yoga-style far too long for someone who doesn't practice the art. I chased Dexter out of the empty pizza box and collected it and the paper plates we had used, carrying them into the kitchen. Gina's conversation was mostly one-sided; she did most of the listening and supplied an occasional monosyllabic reply. She began pacing the room, and I slowly became aware of a heightening tension in the air. I couldn't hear a word she was saying, but the set of her shoulders shifted, and what I was seeing bothered me. I tossed the trash into the wastebasket and eased back toward the living room. She had just disconnected from her call.

"Everything all right?" I asked pensively.

She offered a smile that was too quick. "Of course. Why?"

I glanced at the cell phone. "I don't know. It just seemed like that call upset you."

"Well, only in the sense that I have to go."

"What?"

She tilted her head. "I'm sorry, Dwayne, but that was an old friend of mine, Chloe. She and I have traveled together on a couple of occasions, and she's in a little bit of a jam."

"Should you call the police?"

She uttered a strange, high-pitched laugh. "Don't think *that's* necessary. It's just a little personal problem, and she had heard I would be in town for Matt's wedding, and—" She shrugged.

I frowned, disappointed the evening was coming to such an abrupt end. "Can't it wait 'til morning?"

"Unfortunately, no," she said, and she was already pulling her things together. As she reached the door with her car keys in hand, she turned and paused. "Don't worry, little brother. I'm not going anywhere for a few days. I'll give you a call tomorrow."

"Promise?"

She smiled and cupped my face in her hands. "Promise."

12

It was a promise she wouldn't keep.

CHAPTER TWO

Monday morning brought thick fog and the threat of rain. I attempted my three-mile run but was still too sore from the events of the previous weekend to hit my stride. I settled for a pace that approximated an urgent dash to the restroom. I felt ridiculous, but by the time I returned to my house, the knots in my back had loosened, and I felt pretty damn good. I still had time for a leisurely shower before heading off to Total Care Landscaping, my latest upgrade project. Despite my temporary suspension from Boggs Investigations, and despite the drizzle that started falling a few hundred yards before I actually *reached* my house, nothing was going to adversely affect my mood this day. My big sister was in town, a paycheck was on the way, and life was good.

The phone was ringing as I emerged from the shower, and I dripped across the hardwood floor to retrieve the handset from my nightstand. "Hello?"

"Are you about ready?" It was Melanie.

"Oh," I said, a little disappointed it wasn't Gina. I had already completely forgotten that I had no transportation until Melanie showed up with my rental. "Yeah, I will be by the time you get here."

"You don't sound very happy to hear from me. Did everything go all right last night?"

"Oh, yeah, sure," I said. "I'm sorry. I just thought maybe you were Gina. She got a phone call late last night and took off to rescue a friend."

"Nothing serious, I hope."

"I don't think so," I said. "She told me she'd call sometime today so we could get together again later."

"I told Jasmine about the shopping trip, and she was really excited. You don't think she'll cancel, do you?"

"Nah," I said. "She wouldn't do that. She's looking forward to the opportunity to get to know you better."

"Good," said Melanie. "The feeling's mutual. I'll be there in about fifteen minutes."

"See ya."

I pulled a pair of khaki Dockers out of my closet and a white, short-sleeved ribbed shirt and proceeded to get dressed. Dexter waited patiently while I ran a brush through my dark hair, trying to find order where there was none. I eventually opted for a dab of gel, which at least tamed the wild ends. I made a mental note to grab a haircut at the first available opportunity.

As I was feeding Dexter his breakfast, the phone rang again. I damn near skipped across the room, sure that it must be Gina, and could barely contain my disappointment as I recognized the Caller ID. It was Doug Boggs. "Oh, it's you."

There was a momentary pause while he debated a reaction. Eventually, he plodded forward, his voice buoyant beyond believability. "I read about the Dotson case in *The Dispatch*."

Shit. Well, that was that. He was calling to make my suspension permanent. He had more or less forbidden me to take the job, and I had done it anyway. I could argue the point if I chose, but I was having difficulty mustering the desire. Mine and Doug's working relationship had been strained so often we both had stretch marks. Maybe it would be better if I

15

hired on as a security guard elsewhere, put my hours in with a company that wasn't held hostage by a hillbilly version of Tammy Faye Baker as an office manager. A life without Loretta Boggs—*ah!*

"—and I was thinking of you."

I belatedly realized I had drifted away from the conversation. Doug had paused and was obviously waiting for a response. I opted for noncommittal. "I see."

Doug laughed, a big donkey sound that ricocheted all over the scale. "I figured you'd be more interested than that. You can start tonight. Why don't you swing down by the office and—"

"Wait a minute," I interrupted. "Am I hearing you correctly? Are you trying to give me an assignment? I thought I was suspended."

Another big donkey laugh. "Oh, I think you've learned your lesson by now. So, what I'll need you to do is—"

"Huh-unh. No way. You're letting me off too easy. What's *really* going on?"

Doug paused again, trying to find a new way to bulldoze past the facts, but the hamster that turned the wheel in his head was apparently fatigued. He sighed. "Because Gildy Parsons asked for you. She saw the stories on the news and—"

"And you thought you'd take advantage of all the free advertising for Boggs Investigations."

"Well—I don't necessarily see anything *wrong* with that."

"Well, that's too bad," I said. "Because I'm not available. I picked up an assignment with Total Care Landscaping that's going to keep me tied up for a couple of days."

"The Parsons case wouldn't begin until tonight—"

"Doesn't matter," I interrupted. "My sister is in town, and I hardly ever get a chance to see her. She's only going to be here for a few days, and I fully intend to capitalize on the free time that you forced upon me."

"Aw, come on, man," said Doug, his voice affecting the same whiny quality I remembered from high school. "This case is really too good to pass up, and I think it's just the kind of thing you've been looking for. Can't you at least—"

"Sorry, Doug. I don't even want to know about it. My priority is family at the moment, and I can't imagine anything that would change my mind. Why don't you send your mother? I understand she did a real bang-up job on that last assignment you gave her." Even as thick-headed as he was, Doug couldn't possibly have missed the sarcasm in my tone.

"I *told* you, Gildy Parsons asked for you," he said, his sniveling tone still grating on my nerves. "Besides, I don't think Ma wants to take another assignment so hot on the heels of her last one. She said that chasing people all over town may not be her cup of tea. She told me to give it to you."

I raised a suspicious eyebrow. Loretta Boggs recommending *me?* Had hell frozen over when I wasn't paying attention? I heard a wimpy toot from the driveway, and I realized Melanie had arrived in the rental Fiesta. "Sorry, Doug. Can't help you. Mel's here, and I've gotta go."

"But—"

I disconnected, cutting his pleas short. It was beyond satisfying to finally have a little power to flex in our lopsided arrangement.

······•●◎◯●•●·······

I dropped Melanie off at her apartment before heading north to Columbus, where I stopped at Microcenter to collect the various components I needed for my job: Six Intel processors, compatible motherboards, solid state hard drives, and an appropriate number of memory chips. Armed with everything I needed, I cut across Bethel Road into Hilliard, where Total Care Landscaping was located on Avery Road.

Sue Slattery met me in the reception area with a cup of coffee and a fresh doughnut. She was a short woman with apple cheeks and auburn hair that was boyishly styled. Her grin was perpetual, and I found that encouraging. She was a first-time client, so I had no idea what demeanor to expect. Some of my clients were real jerks, and I simply wasn't in the mood to deal with attitude when my own was so very upbeat.

"Nasty day, huh?" she said, tilting her head toward the large picture window that overlooked the parking lot. The earlier drizzle had settled into a steady rain, but I was barely aware.

"Doesn't bother me at all," I said. "Unless, of course, your systems are out in the parking lot."

She laughed. "Nope. Three of 'em are right out here. The other three are in the offices back there. I'd start out here. Nancy and Tina are out, so you won't be underfoot at all."

"Sounds good," I said. "Lead the way."

Overall, the day went pretty well. All the data files from the system were stored in the company's cloud, so data loss wasn't a concern. I replaced the motherboards and processors, adding memory to each system. Then, I performed clean installations of the latest version of Windows Professional, acquiring patches and fixes from Windows Update as I went. Next came the individual programs upon which Total Care relied to function, including activating new versions of Office I had downloaded. Finally, I connected the data files from the cloud and tested each system extensively. When everything seemed in good working order, I asked Sue to take them for a test drive.

"Wow," she said, her fingers flying over the keyboard. "I can't believe the difference in speed."

I beamed proudly. "Uh-huh. I also added shortcuts to your most frequently used programs to the Quick Launch toolbar by the Start button. If you don't like them, I can always delete them."

"No, no," she said quickly. "That's good. Nancy can never remember where half the damned things are in the Apps menu. Oh, this is just great. I can't wait until you get around to mine."

She looked at me hopefully, but it was already four-thirty. I grimaced. "There really isn't time to do another system today."

She shrugged. "I suppose that's what I get for being unselfish and starting you out here. Oh, well. I've suffered with the damned thing for three years. I suppose one more day won't kill me."

"I can do yours first," I offered.

She grinned. "Deal. Until tomorrow?"

I was already packing my tools into my black leather carrying case. "Tomorrow."

The rain continued into evening, and traffic crawled like snails. Still, my mood could not be sullied by such mundane things, and I entertained myself with the radio on the ride home. It was almost five-thirty by the time I arrived. I hurried inside and checked my answering machine to see if Gina had called, but I only had one message, and it was from Doug.

"Listen, buddy, I've been thinking. Maybe I haven't been entirely fair with you. I'm willing to give you double your normal salary on the Parsons case if you'll pick it up. I'm sure it'd be right up your alley if you'd give me a chance to lay it out. Give me a call."

Right up my alley. How ironic. To date, *all* my assignments for Boggs had involved loitering in alleys, noting the activities of various lowlifes. Not this time. Huh-unh. I deleted the message.

Dexter was delighted at my somewhat timely return, and he followed me around the house, chirping his approval. I fed him—on schedule, for once—and was about to do the same for myself when I heard the crunch of gravel in the driveway. I hurried to the living room and peered out through the large picture window overlooking my lawn, hoping Gina had decided to drop by in lieu of calling. Instead, it was a familiar silver Mazda carrying Melanie and Jasmine. Jasmine emerged from the passenger side clutching two large, brown paper sacks. I stepped out onto the porch.

"Hope I didn't overstep my boundaries," called Melanie, fighting with a seatbelt that simply didn't want to retract. She clutched a white plastic bag in her hand. "It's Chinese. I brought enough for four..." She scanned the driveway, but there was only my lime green rental vehicle to see.

I smiled. "That's sweet of you," I said. "But Gina hasn't called. Apparently, her business with her friend is taking longer than she expected."

Jasmine bounded up the stairs to the porch. "Hey, Dwayne," she said as she passed, her eleven-year-old arms straining to maintain a grip on the oversized bags. "Kitchen table?"

"Yeah, that's fine," I said, holding the door for her. "Thanks, kiddo." I lingered on the porch, waiting for Melanie.

"She hasn't even called?" asked Melanie before leaning in for a kiss. "You don't think anything's wrong, do you?"

"Nah," I said, following her into the house. "I'm sure she'll call sooner or later."

"Well, in the meanwhile, cheer up," said Melanie, making herself at home in the kitchen. She retrieved metal utensils from the silverware drawer to replace the plastic sporks AAA China had sent and crossed to the refrigerator for beverages. "I don't have to work tomorrow, and I thought we could spend a quiet evening together, just the three of us—*four*, of course, if your sister shows. I thought maybe we could rent a movie or something."

I stood in the doorway and watched as Melanie pulled plates and glasses from the cupboard and placemats I didn't even know I had from the drawer beneath the microwave. Jasmine had placed the bags of food on the kitchen table and was rummaging through each, pulling out various sized white paperboard cartons and placing them at the appropriate place setting. Something about watching the mother-daughter team in action made me feel the warmth of domestic bliss; it was easy to imagine this as an everyday occurrence.

We caught up with each other over dinner. Jasmine had spent the day with a group of girls she had met in the neighborhood behind Melanie's apartment complex. They had listened to music and traded makeovers while discussing which boy band was the cutest—typical stuff for girls her age. Melanie and I were both relieved Jasmine had made new friends; she had been lonely since moving away from her old schoolmates in Lymont. Hopefully, these new acquaintances would act as a general boost to her flagging morale. Melanie only stiffened slightly when Jasmine mentioned she had spoken with Scott Nichols on the phone earlier in the afternoon.

"How's he doing?" I asked.

"Pretty well, I think," said Jaz, through a mouthful of almond boneless chicken. "He said you were supposed to pick him up sometime today."

Shit. I had forgotten all about it. Since he had no remaining family, I had extended an invitation for Scott to stay at my place if Franklin County Children's Services would allow it. He had spent the previous evening as a guest of Brady's son, Billy, at the insistence of Nola and Wendell Caudill, Billy's caretakers. They hoped it would help keep Billy's mind off his father while Brady recuperated in the hospital. I thought it might be a nice diversion for Scott, as well, and I had told them I would pick him up after I finished at Total Care Landscaping. It had completely slipped my mind. I suppose it wasn't a very good indicator as to my parental capability. I jumped up from the table and headed for the phone.

"Oh, hey, Dwayne," said Nola, sounding a little breathless. "Had to run for the phone. We're out back barbequing. Celebrating Brady's improved condition."

"Sorry to disturb," I said. "But I didn't want you to think I forgot about Scott. Melanie, Jaz and I are sitting down to dinner, but I'll be over right afterward to—"

"Actually," interrupted Nola. "I was going to call you and ask if you'd mind if Scott stayed with us for a few days."

I blinked. "Doesn't he want to come back here?"

"Oh, sure, it's nothing like that. He's just been such a big help with Billy, and they get along so well. Scott's been doing some work around the yard for Wendell, too, and he seems to be enjoying himself. I hate to disrupt things when they're running so smoothly."

I hesitated. I knew Nola Caudill was generous and kindly, but I hated the idea of taking advantage. "Are you absolutely certain?"

"I wouldn't offer otherwise," she said.

"If you need anything at all—"

"I'll call. Right now, I've got burgers burning in the backyard. I'll have Scott give you a call later if you'd like."

"Thanks. That'd be nice."

I listened to the dead air for a second before disconnecting. It was odd. I hadn't really known what to expect of my harboring Scott, but I had assumed at least my participation would have been required. I felt strangely abandoned and unnecessary.

"Everything all right?" called Melanie from the table.

"Yeah, sure," I said, replacing the receiver in its cradle before rejoining dinner.

······•••••⊖◯•••••·····

We watched back-to-back Disney flicks, *The Lion King* and *Pocahontas*, before moving Jasmine to one of the guest bedrooms. She had fallen asleep toward the tail end of *Pocahontas* and barely stirred when I transported her up the stairs. This was the first time she had spent the night in my house, so I put her in the room directly beside my own. I practically felt like a lech knowing I would be sharing a bed with her mother just next door, but Melanie insisted it would be fine.

"She asked me the other day if we'd 'done it' yet," said Melanie as we went back downstairs to watch another movie, an R-rated actioner starring Bruce Willis.

"What?" I was mortified. I would never be able to look Jasmine in the eye again. "What did you say?"

"I told her to mind her own business," said Melanie, settling onto the couch.

"Which was as good as a confession." I could feel my cheeks burning crimson.

Melanie grinned. "No, the look on your face is as good as a confession. I hope she doesn't decide to grill you on the matter."

"Well, that's it," I said, folding my arms across my chest. "You're not getting any more until after we're married."

Melanie raised an eyebrow. "Is that a proposal?"

I looked at her like a deer caught in headlights, and she couldn't help but laugh. I stammered like a fool, but nothing resembling words surfaced.

"Relax, Dwayne," she said. "I was only kidding. I hope you were, too."

I slid beside her on the couch as the movie began to play, wrapping an arm around her shoulders and pulling her close. We looked into each other's eyes for a moment before sharing a sweet, tender kiss that carried the promise of better things to come.

23

"What do you think?" I asked.

We abandoned the movie and headed for my room.

Melanie snored softly beside me as I watched the moonlight cast strange shadows across the walls and ceiling. Despite our rigorous workout, I couldn't find sleep to save my soul. It was almost eleven, and the phone hadn't rung all evening. While I knew Gina maintained a busy schedule, it simply wasn't like her to not call after saying she would. It would only take a minute to extend excuses and apologies, and I was beginning to worry. I had tried her cell phone earlier, between movies, but only reached her voicemail. I debated calling Mom to see if she'd heard anything, but that would only cause her to worry, too. Matt and Sheila were honeymooning in nearby Put-In-Bay, and there was no reason to think they might have heard from Gina.

There was nothing else to do but toss and turn, hoping sleep might find me sometime before sunrise.

I was only half-awake when I arrived at Total Care Landscaping, bypassing the donut Sue Slattery offered in favor of a large cup of black coffee.

"Are you all right this morning?" she asked. "Your eyes look like hell."

"I didn't sleep very well," I said, blowing it off. I knew my eyes looked like hell; I had slept in fits and starts a combined total of one hour. Melanie and I were supposed to go car shopping that evening, but I had a feeling I'd be begging off in favor of a nap. "I'll be fine after I get a little more coffee inside me."

"If you're sure," said Sue, leading me into her office. I stumbled along after her, my leather satchel knocking against my leg. "This is my own little fella." She patted the top of a mid-sized ivory tower that was completely covered with stickers. Some of them were happy faces, some hearts, a rainbow-colored peace sign, one of the Power Puff girls...I felt like I was staring into the locker of any one of the girls with whom I had attended high school. I stared open-mouthed at the atrocity; I believe that computer equipment should be crisp and sterile, and what I was seeing offended my sensibilities. "I can't wait 'til you're finished."

I mumbled something incoherent and squatted down on the floor next to the beast. I fought back the urge to begin peeling the stickers away and twisted the case around so that I could reach its various connections. I found it helped if I didn't look directly at it.

I began the upgrade process on Sue's machine, and then repeated the steps with the other two administrative computers. Alvin Bramblett was severely miffed that he was being interrupted, despite Sue's repeated reminders that he had known this was coming. Eventually, he moved his things to one of the desks in the outer office and grumpily began working at one of the machines I had already finished. I suspected he appreciated the difference in speed but would be damned if he would admit it.

I began installing the new components into the computer cases mechanically, my thoughts elsewhere. I had done procedures such as these so often I felt completely safe on autopilot. I fleetingly wondered if Doug had found a way to handle the Parsons case. I didn't want to admit it, but I felt guilty for potentially costing the firm some income. Doug may be a creepy little shit, but he was my best shot for getting my license. If I completed my current job at the end of the day, as I suspected I would, I would call him and see if we might still be able to pick up the case. He promised it was something more interesting, and while I shuddered at the thought of what his interpretation of 'more interesting' may *be*, it would certainly mean the end of my suspension.

I wondered how Brady was doing. I hadn't even spoken with him since he had regained consciousness after our latest adventure. Another reason to feel guilty. Great. I made a mental note to stop by the hospital after Melanie and I found a car for me—sleep was going to have to wait. He was probably going stir crazy in there—or else he had half of the nursing staff wrapped around his little finger. That was not only plausible, but entirely probable.

I wondered why Gina hadn't called.

Something about it niggled at me all morning. It just wasn't like her not to call, even if only to postpone our meeting until later. I worried intermittently throughout the morning, thoughts finally overpowered by hunger as the noon hour drew near. I was putting the screws back into Sue's case, thinking about a patty melt and onion rings from Frisch's, when I became aware I was being watched from the doorway.

Sue stood in the doorframe, an unsettling look on her face. Her eyes flitted over me quickly, and she looked down. "He's in here."

Every hair on my arms stood on end. I didn't know what was going on, but intuitively, I knew it wasn't good. I didn't want to know. I didn't want to know who was going to appear in the doorway. I didn't want one more minute to pass.

Melanie appeared beside Sue, her eyes swollen and puffy. She didn't say anything, just cocked her head to the side and looked at me so sadly, so very sadly...

I knew nothing would ever be the same again.

CHAPTER THREE

Those next few hours are even now still a blur.

I remember standing over Sue's computer, unsure whether I should finish putting the screws back into the case before leaving. Melanie guided me away, mumbling something to Sue about retrieving my work bag later, and I followed her out to the parking lot, numbly plopping myself into the passenger seat of her silver Mazda. We pulled out of the parking lot in silence, the radio playing softly in the background, Melanie apologizing in the foreground. None of it made sense. None of it.

There had been an automobile accident on SR 33, halfway between Columbus and Lancaster. My sister's rental Camry had crossed the median and struck a propane truck head-on, resulting in a fiery explosion that had gutted the interior of the compact car, incinerating its contents—as well as its driver. The driver of the tanker had emerged with third-degree burns over most of his body, but he was still desperately clinging to life at Mount Carmel East.

My sister was gone.

Realization had dawned like a thunderstorm breaking, and I sobbed convulsively while Melanie navigated the familiar path to my house. To know I would never see Gina again was more than I could bear. She was in my house two days ago; the recollection so vivid I could almost reach out and seize it, pull it near and never let time run its course. I should've never let her go that night, and I blamed myself. Life is a series of interconnected events. Preventing her from leaving would have altered her ultimate fate. She wouldn't have been behind the wheel at that particular place and time. I *knew* something was wrong!

Melanie was my anchor while I was unable to keep my shit together. She called my parents, who had already been informed by the Ohio State Highway Patrol. She contacted Sheila, and she and Matt were waiting to be ferried back to the mainland. Melanie didn't speak directly to Matt; much like me, he was unable to come to the phone. I went to my room as Melanie called Doug Boggs. I couldn't stand to hear the news repeated ad nauseam. I had wept until my throat hurt and my eyes were dry. I was astounded when I slipped fairly easily into a deep, dreamless sleep.

······•••●◐◑●•••······

The drive to Lymont seemed longer than usual, perhaps due to the lack of conversation. Jasmine remained warily alert in the backseat of the Mazda, unsure of what to say but ready to offer support in any way that she could. She spent most of the journey futilely attempting to settle my cat. Like most cats, Dexter abhors long car rides. His constant keening was in perfect synchronicity with my general disposition.

Melanie had been at my side since the moment she had picked me up at Total Care Landscaping. She had held me silently while I fell apart, shushed me and rocked me and made sure I knew she was there for me. I held onto her for all she was worth, knowing I couldn't face the coming days without her beside me. And still, there was really nothing she could do.

My mother met us at the door in hysterics. She was certain we had suffered a similar fate as Gina's because it had taken so long for us to arrive; in actuality, it had taken no longer than usual, but Mom's perception of time had gotten bent in her tumultuous mindset. I stood there while she yelled at us irrationally, either unable or unwilling to find my voice. My father tried valiantly to hide behind his normally stoic exterior, but the cracks began to show shortly after we arrived. He spent the majority of the evening by himself in his bedroom, dealing with the tragic event in his own particular way.

Mom put Melanie, Jasmine and me in mine and Matt's old room. Dexter stayed nearby but sensed the emotional temperature of the room, choosing to hide beneath various pieces of furniture and observe from a distance. Melanie and Jasmine were exhausted after our long day and were soon asleep on one of the twin beds. I sat in a daze on the other, my chin propped on interlocked fingers. The room was completely dark except for a small nightlight near the door, and it was easy for my mind to wander backward through time. It was easy to imagine myself at fifteen, listening to record albums through headphones while I pretended to sleep, Matt on the other bed snoring soundly while Gina was out on a date with Ricky or Paul or maybe even Victor. Dad was especially overprotective of his oldest child and only daughter. He set an unrealistic weekend curfew of ten o'clock for a girl who got into no more trouble than sneaking a smoke or occasionally losing track of time. Unfair as it was, the same rules never applied to Matt or me. Our curfew was somewhere between eleven and midnight. As long as we weren't escorted home by the police, all was good. Still, Gina and I had worked out a sort of "early warning system" to prevent the occasional late-night clash with the parents which was always worse if caught red-handed trying to sneak in post-curfew. I had stained a horse head desk lamp as my first project in ceramics class. It was really quite laughable—not unlike the leg lamp from *A Christmas Story*—but I was enormously proud of my accomplishment, and I kept it on my desk framed by the bedroom window. I would turn it on if the folks had gone to bed and the coast was clear. It gave Gina a little more time to decide which friend had run out of gas or had a flat tire and get her alibis in order, provided Dad even realized she had been late. You never knew when a late-night bathroom trip could be your undoing.

The memory brought a fresh wave of anguish, and I realized how easily Mom had worked herself into a state waiting for us to arrive. I was worried about Matt and Sheila's drive. I knew they were going to stop in Columbus before heading south, but I didn't know for how long or exactly when to expect them. I was beginning to envision his car being sideswiped by a semi or a drunk driver crossing his path. I closed my eyes and tried not to think at all.

· · • • • • • • • ⊖ ⊝ • • • • • • · · ·

"What do you mean, you don't know?" I demanded. Melanie lurked in the corner, watching me warily as I felt color creeping into my cheeks. My parents were with Matt and Sheila in the large family room at the rear of the house. I had phoned the State Highway Patrol unit that had investigated Gina's accident, demanding answers to questions I was making up as I went along. I had to do *something*. I had been connected to Lieutenant Horace Blanker, a weary-sounding man whose every sentence was delivered with tired patience. "It can't be *that* difficult to determine. How about the other guy?"

"Wally Porter worked for Tri-County Propane for over ten years. Not a single blot on his driving record—not even a speeding ticket, much less drinking and driving. As he is currently struggling for his life at Mount Carmel, I can't help but feel your question is inappropriate. Now, as far as your sister goes, it's too early to know. Her body was too—it will take the coroner a little time to determine whether she had been drinking or not. It's possible she had a stroke or heart attack, as well, but that's just supposition on my part. Hell, a bee could've flown in the open window and startled her."

"That's ridiculous," I said.

"Maybe so, but there are at least a half-dozen possibilities that spring to mind without even thinking about it. Can I give you some advice, Mr. Morrow?"

"What?" My voice was flat and hard.

"Stop trying to find a reason. It isn't going to help anything right now. Your family needs you, and you need them. It doesn't matter *why* it happened. It won't change the reality of the situation."

"But—"

"But what, Mr. Morrow? What possible good is going to come from sifting through the ugly details?"

I shook my head and pinched the bridge of my nose. "I don't know. Gina was always such a careful driver. It just doesn't make sense."

"Things like this rarely do," said Blanker. "Go be with your family."

I disconnected and sat down heavily. I didn't know what I had expected from the phone call, but I wasn't satisfied with the outcome. I realized how desperately I needed the accident to be someone else's fault, someone I could blame for taking my sister away from me. I wanted someone to be punished. I was so absorbed in my own thoughts of vengeance that I didn't even notice when Melanie stepped up behind me and began massaging the tight cords of my shoulders and neck.

"Do you want to get out of here for a while? Maybe grab some dinner, just the two of us?" she suggested.

I pivoted abruptly, pulling away from her soothing hands. "You want me to take you out to dinner?" I asked indignantly before slipping into outright sarcasm. "Sure. Would you prefer candlelight?"

"Hey, you know I didn't mean it like that. I just thought you might—"

"Maybe you should mind your own business and stop trying to get inside my head."

Melanie took a step backward and held her hands up in a gesture of surrender. "Look, if it makes you feel better, then take your best shot. I can take it."

I dropped my forehead into the palm of my hand and squeezed my eyes together. My head was pounding at the temples. "I'm sorry, honey. I feel so helpless. I—I just want to be alone for a while." I looked up at her, the anger and sarcasm gone as quickly as it had erupted. "Is that okay?"

She smiled and touched my face. "Of course, it is. Tell you what. I'll take Jasmine and go visit Sarah for a bit. We'll come back in a few hours. How would that be?"

I took her hand and kissed her knuckles before pressing them against my cheek. "I love you," I said, and my voice almost broke again.

She smoothed my hair and kissed my forehead. "I know."

A steady progression of relatives and friends descended over the next few days, many of whom I hadn't seen in years. Their faces and words blurred from the onset; identical sentiments offered in varying pitches.

How are you holding up?

Such a senseless thing.

You need to be strong for your mom and dad.

She's gone to a better place.

Who are we to question God's will?

That last one really got underneath my skin. What kind of God would allow this type of heart-wrenching anguish? What kind of God would intentionally do a thing like this to His own people? What had we done to inspire His wrath? *What?* No. Unacceptable. I carry no strong religious beliefs, just a righteous sense of good and evil. I suppose if pressed, I would lean toward reincarnation, but even the thought of my sister's spirit reborn only made me angrier.

Two of my dad's brothers went with him to select a casket, and when they returned, Dad fled immediately to his bedroom, his complexion ashen. The purchase had been another dose of cold reality for him, and he wasn't willing to accept comfort from anybody. My own misery was compounded with worry for his general health. I knew keeping everything bottled up was an unhealthy course to navigate, and yet I didn't know how to be there for him. As much as I wanted to try and ease his pain, I didn't want to discuss it any more than he did.

The only positive thing that happened during the course of those black days was the instantaneous healing that occurred between my brother and myself. There was no more talk of how my involvement in a serial killer case had nearly gotten Sheila and his unborn child killed. There wasn't even a residual trace of the anger he had carried for months. Instead, he was the big brother I needed, tending to family and friends when I couldn't, propping Mom up when she was at her lowest. I don't know how he found the strength. He wasn't any less close to Gina than I was, yet somehow, he was able to take charge and keep things moving forward.

It was Thursday night, close to midnight.

At my request, Melanie and Jasmine were spending the night with Jasmine's grandmother, Sarah. I sat in the dark on one of the twin beds in mine and Matt's old room, staring vacantly toward a wood-paneled wall I couldn't see. I thought I had wanted to be alone, but now that I had run everyone off, I regretted the decision. I thought a gentle reminder of childhood might soothe me, but nothing was the same. Mom and Dad had replaced the familiar beige shag carpeting with hardwood flooring. The creaky window unit that had air-conditioned my summers had been replaced with central air. The windows themselves were new. A ceiling fan replaced the tri-globe chandelier that had lit my evenings. Matt's bed, with its crisp covers and plumped pillow, was a not-so-gentle reminder that the days of brotherly cohabitation were long gone.

There was a gentle knock at the door.

"Come in."

Matt poked his head around the corner, his pillow-tousled hair standing on end. "You still awake?"

"No. I'm talking in my sleep."

I caught his grin in the half-light from the hallway. "Mind if I turn on a light?"

"Hit the one on the desk," I said, not wanting to be blinded by the overhead fixture. I lost track of his shape as he navigated the room with familiarity. A second later, a desk lamp featuring the ships of Christopher Columbus's fleet flicked on.

Matt crossed the room and perched on the edge of the bed. "Tomorrow's the funeral," he said. "Are you gonna be all right?"

I shrugged. "Don't see that I have any choice."

"Anything you want to talk about?"

I stood and began anxiously pacing the room. "What's there to talk about? We all just have to do our parts and get through this thing."

Matt nodded silently, reflecting. After a moment, he said, "I think Mom's gonna have it rough for a while, but Dad's the one I'm worried about. Beyond pleasantries, he hasn't said two words." His gaze shifted toward me. "I'm worried about you, too."

"Me?" I asked, genuinely surprised. "Don't worry about me. I'll be fine."

"You know, you and Dad are a lot alike. You pull things inside, try to deal with them on your own. It's okay to lean on someone now and then."

I turned around, bewildered. "Matt, really. I'm fine. Maybe you should practice your armchair psychology on Dad for a while."

"I don't know what to say to him," he said. "He knows that I'm here for him, but he isn't extending any invitations right now."

"And I am?"

He cocked his head. "I think I have a little more of an open dialog with you. I think I know you a little better."

"God, Matt," I said. "I just want to be alone. I just want to turn the light off and sit here in the dark and be alone."

"I know. That's what you've been doing ever since—ever since it happened. Tonight, I'm not going anywhere. I want to know how you are."

His words were simple, and I completely lost it. Fresh tears spilled over, and I was sobbing again. I hated myself for it, for the weakness. I wasn't any good to anybody like this. Words came, and I couldn't control them. "She was just *here*," I wailed, pointing at the new flooring but picturing my own living room. "She was coming back to-to-to take Mel and J-Jaz—and I could have *stopped* her from going. It-it-it was so late, and I shouldn't have let her *go*—"

"Hey, hey." Matt pulled me close, and I disgusted myself further by soaking his shoulder with salty tears and snot. He then held me at arm's length and gave a gentle shake, forcing me to look into his eyes. "Did you ever meet Gina? You couldn't have stopped her from doing anything. You need to let that go."

I concentrated on my breathing and tried to regain my composure. My cheeks were burning hot, and my hair was sweaty. I clumsily dabbed at my face, trying to wipe away the mess. "I don't know if I can," I stammered.

"You don't have a choice," said Matt. He threw an arm around my shoulders. "Come on, man. We'll get through this. I don't know exactly how, but we'll make it. Tomorrow's gonna be rough—"

I groaned.

35

"—but we can do it. We've got to hold it together for Mom and Dad."

I nodded mutely.

Matt held on a moment longer before heading to the door. "I'm gonna try and catch some sleep."

"I'm sorry to keep you up."

He shrugged and grinned. "Not entirely your fault. You try spending the night with a pregnant woman in her third trimester. She tosses and turns and kicks the covers all over the damn place. I haven't gotten a good night's sleep in months."

I found a laugh. "Good night."

"Night."

I listened as he padded down the hallway to the guest room he was sharing with his wife. I crossed the room and flicked off the desk lamp, but not before snagging my cell phone from its charger. I plopped down on my bed as I had done so many times as a teenager, rolling onto my back and placing a call.

She answered on the first ring.

"Hey, you. I've been thinking about you all night," said Melanie. "How are you doing?"

"Better now. I wish I hadn't asked you to go."

"I can be there in five minutes."

"Make it three."

She giggled. *"Five.* You're pretty good, but I don't think you warrant a speeding ticket."

"I love you."

"I love you, too."

The funeral was surreal.

We were a picture-perfect family, decked out in our finest black attire, standing shoulder to shoulder as we received endless condolences from family, friends and neighbors. The turnout was spectacular, a sea of faces both familiar and unfamiliar, paying their respects to Gina in the most final circumstance. After a while, the lines between factions began to blur, and I wasn't completely sure I knew the difference between family members and others. My father is one of thirteen children, and their various children have children of their own. I can't honestly say I've even met all of them. But their well-wishes were sincere, and we received them with numb graciousness.

Flowers sprung from every corner, elaborate arrangements in multi-colored hues, occupying every available surface and floor space. Due to the nature of the accident, Gina's casket, a handsome mahogany cylinder with gold-plated trim, was closed and sealed long before anyone had arrived. I was ambivalent about the closed casket. Part of me needed to see her resting in her final repose. Another possibly larger part wanted to remember her face without the aid of a funeral director's reconstructive capabilities. A framed picture that was almost five years old sat on top of the casket, surrounded by three candles and a handful of red roses. Her black hair was short and curly in the picture, and I remembered how much she had hated the style. Unfortunately, it was the most current head shot we had.

Traditional organ music haunted the background, and eventually, the pastor of our family church, Jacob Hunter, stepped up to the podium. The immediate family dutifully took their seats in the front row, and I clasped Melanie's hand in my own. It had been decades since I had attended Midland United Methodist, and he had been the preacher even then. I was surprised at how small he looked, as if he had lost height in the subsequent years. When he turned, I realized that the ever-increasing slump of his shoulders was responsible for the illusion. His rust-colored hair had turned to silver, but he still possessed a fiery glint in his eyes and a commanding presence in his voice. Despite the conviction in his words, I simply couldn't listen to them. They were more assertions about God's will and assurances of a better place. All I could think about was how much of life Gina was going to miss. A glance down the line at Sheila was a reminder she would never meet her niece or nephew, and I almost cracked again.

Eventually, the eulogy drew to a close, and we began milling out to our cars. Mom and Dad rode with Matt and Sheila while I followed in Melanie's old clunker. I caught Jasmine's eyes in the rearview mirror, and she smiled, patting me lightly on the shoulder. She was such a good kid. We crept along US 52 with our headlights on, second in a procession of purple-flagged cars headed toward Lymont Memorial Cemetery. When we arrived, we drove in deep, finally stopping as we reached the last hill that marked the edge of the grounds. Woods bordered the cemetery at this end, and ancient trees extended shade over the burial plot, which rested at the bottom of a gentle slope. I had the absurd notion that this would be a great place for a picnic. It was a cool day, with the sun ducking in and out of frequent cloud cover and providing sporadic warmth against my exposed skin.

We settled ourselves on folding metal chairs underneath a canvas canopy that straddled the grave. After the casket had been positioned above the yawning hole in the ground, Jacob Hunter resumed his duties at the head of the congregation. I wasn't listening to his words any longer; I had become oversaturated with clerical wisdom. I found myself scanning the crowd, absently noting people I hadn't recognized at the funeral home. It helped to see them standing with their families, and I was able to attach some names to faces merely by their grouping. Two women stood together in the periphery of the canopy, and I finally recognized them as high school friends of Gina's. A tall man with dark, curly hair stood just behind them, watching the proceedings with obvious angst. I didn't recognize him at all, but he reminded me of Brady Garrett, and I wondered what his connection to my sister was. A boyfriend, maybe? Three middle-aged businessman-types huddled in the other corner, and I suspected that these had been men with whom Gina had worked. There were a handful of others I couldn't identify, but the service was ending, and Melanie was pulling me up by my arm.

People straggled back to their cars in slow motion, frequently stopping to chat with each other. There was another long procession of well-wishers filing past us in a line, most of whom would be reconvening at Mom and Dad's house in just a few minutes laden with trays of cold cuts and casseroles in microwave-safe dishes. For the bereaved family, the day was far from over.

I scanned the departing crowd as we slowly made our way back to Melanie's car. Gina's schoolmates had already departed, and I had lost sight of the tall man with hair like Brady's. The businessmen were chatting with Dad, offering extended hands and somber condolences. As I shifted my attention to the path I was walking, I caught something out of the corner of my eye, something just beyond the line of trees at the edge of the cemetery. I inhaled sharply, and my breath caught in my lungs. I squeezed my eyes together tightly.

"Dwayne? *Dwayne?*" Melanie was tugging at my sleeve. "Are you all right?"

I slowly opened my eyes, and my breath hissed out between clenched teeth. I nodded and giggled, but the sound was shaky at best. I rubbed my eyes and smiled. "It's nothing. Really. I—no, it's nothing."

Melanie turned me around to face her, the concern evident on her face. "Why don't you let me decide?"

Again, with the warped giggle. Jasmine was several paces ahead of us, aware that we had slowed but trying to offer us a moment of privacy. "My eyes are playing tricks on me," I finally said in a hushed voice. "I could have sworn I saw Gina standing in the woods." My eyes trailed involuntarily to where I had seen her, and Melanie's eyes followed.

Darin Miller

There was nothing to see.

CHAPTER FOUR

We returned to Columbus on Sunday, exhausted from the entire grieving process. I had communicated shamefully little with my parents before leaving, still unable to face them without being instantly reminded of the tragedy at hand. Matt and Sheila planned to stay for a few days longer. It wasn't until we were on our way out of town that it occurred to me Melanie had taken quite an extended break from her new job without any explanation. Omelet Hut isn't known for its benefits.

"When do you have to be back to work?" I asked from the passenger seat as we veered into opposing traffic to pass a pickup truck from the wrong lane. I clenched the armrest and held my breath until Melanie swung the Mazda back into its proper channel. Jasmine was half-asleep in the backseat and missed the opportunity to see her life flashing before her eyes. Resting beside her in the seat was the goofy horse head lamp I had made all those years ago in ceramics. She had found it in my old room, and Mom had insisted she have it. I couldn't quite look directly at it.

"I don't. I quit."

"What?" I stopped myself before I said any more. Omelet Hut was a real dive. The floors were sticky, the food was greasy, and the customers were mostly horny old men who specialized in the game of grab-ass. Still, Melanie landed the job on her own and had accepted it immediately, relieved to no longer worry about how her rent was going to get paid. She was typically

responsible with a capital 'R.' "I hope it isn't my fault," I added as an afterthought.

She shrugged. "Bill didn't *want* to give me the time, but he would've." She glanced at me briefly, a smile playing on her lips. "I got another job."

"Really? That's great! Where?"

"Clerical work for a fertilizer company on West Broad. A-1 Fertilizers. Sounds kind of generic, huh? It's not too far from where you and Doug are. I told them I couldn't type for shit, but they said the typing was pretty light. It's mostly filing and processing accounts. The schedule's perfect. I work nine to four, Monday through Friday, so I'll have my weekends and evenings free with Jasmine. I couldn't believe how much they offered. I would have had to have busted my ass into overtime at Omelet Hut to make that kind of money."

"When did all of this happen? Why didn't you tell me?"

She glanced at me awkwardly. "I got the call right before—well, and then it didn't seem that important. I was able to tell them I would be away for several days, and they said it wasn't a problem."

I smiled and stared through the passenger window at fields of corn and soybeans as they whipped past. At least *something* was looking up.

Melanie started her new job the following morning. I hadn't reconnected with my own business yet, and I used the time to my advantage. I headed out in the rental Fiesta, praying to God that it would be the last day I'd have to deal with it. I drove from one used car lot to the next, looking for a replacement for my dearly departed Optima. I was considering a late model Hyundai SUV when my cell phone rang. It was Brady Garrett.

"You must be doing better," I noted, ignoring the fact that he sounded like hell.

"Supposed to get out in a day or two," he croaked.

"That's good," I said and paused. "I'm sorry I haven't been by to see you. Things have been—"

"I know. I heard. That's why I called. I'm just so sorry, man."

God, I didn't want to do this again. I pinched the bridge of my nose. "Thanks. Look, how about I stop by when you get settled in at your place? I'll catch you up on everything you missed while you were napping in that basement."

"Hey, yeah, sure, that'd be fine. My throat is killing me anyway. They only took the tubes out yesterday, and it still feels like sandpaper."

"Get better. I'll call you soon."

I disconnected as the salesman returned, all capped teeth and wavy hair. He clapped his hands and spread them wide like we were old pals. "So, what do you think, my man? At $9,500, she's a real steal."

"Make it $8,000, cash, and no more of this back-and-forth shit," I said. "I'm not entertaining any counteroffers."

The smile faltered in time with his step, but he recovered quickly. "I don't know if the manager will approve this—" he said dubiously. I could almost hear him mentally retabulating his commission.

"Why don't you go ask?" I suggested. "And I'm serious. $8,000—cash. You come back here with an offer that's one dollar more, and me and my cash are gone."

An hour and a half later, I drove away in my new used car.

I spent the latter part of the afternoon in my home office, catching up on phone messages and unopened mail. There were volumes. I started playback on the answering machine but stopped it after only a few messages. A string of taped condolences was the last thing I needed to hear.

Maybe I could get Melanie to sift through them next time she stopped by. My email wasn't much better; the only business-related note was from Total Care Landscaping, asking me to contact Sue Slattery at my earliest convenience to reschedule the completion of my job—no hurry, just whenever I could get around to it. I jotted out a quick response saying I would be in Tuesday morning to finish up. I figured I could use the distraction. After I sent the reply, I padded down the hallway to the kitchen and nicked a bottle of Canadian Mist out of the pantry and a Pepsi out of the refrigerator. I wanted to drown my sorrows for a while. I grabbed the current edition of *The Columbus Dispatch* and headed out to the swing on my front porch, where I spent the next half hour taking shots of whiskey and scanning the headlines but not really reading them. I found a follow-up piece on the case I had just finished and was pleased to see that it was credited to J. Pierce. Jacko's work on the original story must have been impressive enough to warrant more from the author. I didn't know Jacko very well, but he had once helped me dig up some information when I hadn't been able to reach Brady. I knew he had hoped to graduate from obituaries to headlines, and it was good to see that he may well be on his way. I was trying desperately to live vicariously through someone else's good fortune, since I seemed to be having none myself.

After a while, I wandered back into the house, bored with tranquility. I turned on the television and found myself channel surfing, a habit I usually detest, but I couldn't find anything that grabbed my interest. My thumb froze on the remote when I hit VH-1. They were playing a 70s retro special on the disco phenomenon that had crept in through the backdoor on a post-Vietnam society.

The group was ABBA, and the song was "Dancing Queen."

ABBA was Gina's all-time favorite band. I knew the lyrics and harmonies almost as well as she did, and my heart ached all over again. No matter how I tried, I couldn't seem to escape.

⊷••••••••••••⊷

"So how was your day?"

"Fantastic." Melanie was almost breathless with excitement. "I think I did almost everything right. The people are nice, and the office is clean. I think I could learn to love this job. How was your day?"

"Not bad," I lied. I was glad she couldn't see my face through the phone. "I bought a car."

"Oh, really? Good. I hated that damned rental you had. It was like riding around in a Jetson car. What else did you do?"

There was a little too much sunshine in her voice; she was subtly attempting to psychoanalyze my day. "Mostly hung out here," I said, not rising to the bait. "I had a lot of bullshit to catch up on." My day-drinking brought a slight slur to my 'bullshit.'

There was a pause. "Do you want me to come over?"

"I always want you to come over," I said. "But I think it's probably best if you spend the evening with your daughter. She could use an evening without having to walk on eggshells around me."

"Dwayne, you know she loves you. She's just young, and—"

"I know, I know. I really didn't mean anything by it. I just think I could use some time myself. It's just—"

"What?"

"There's a certain pressure that comes with company, you know? Pressure to put up a brave face. It's exhausting."

Another pause. "Are you sure?"

"Yeah," I said. "I told Sue Slattery I'd finish up at Total Care tomorrow morning, so I have to turn in early myself. In the meanwhile, I'll stay occupied with a little housework. Lord knows this place could use it."

• • • • • • •●── (─ ●• • • • • • •

Long ago, I came to terms with my general slovenliness. I've lived alone my entire adult life and was never much for company. When you only have yourself to please, it's amazing how standards tend to slide. I am prone to drop clothing on the floor, leave an occasional plate or glass on an end table, forget to wash the dishes for a day or so—there always seems to be something more important to do. That evening, I had nothing else. I started in the kitchen, pulling everything off the counters and piling it on the small Formica table in the center of the room. I scrubbed surface and grout before heading for the dishes, three days' worth that were stacked haphazardly in the left basin of the sink. I emptied the refrigerator of things spoiled—of which there were more than I care to admit. Having gone that far, I went ahead and sponged out the interior of the fridge before replacing the things I could salvage. Next on the agenda was mopping. I dragged my yellow plastic mop bucket along, swabbing the deck like I hadn't done in— well, ever. I found corners I didn't even know the kitchen had. Afterward, I set the mop on the back stoop to dry and dumped the gray-black mop water in the sink.

I glanced at the clock as I moved into the living room with a trash bag in tow. It was almost eleven, but I wasn't even remotely tired. The stereo was fixed to WNCI, and my mind remained occupied so long as my hands were. Dexter perched on the back of the sofa, visibly amused as I circled the room, tossing junk mail and other odd bits of refuse that had accumulated over time. It's amazing how much shit turns up during a thorough cleaning. I found countless fingernail clippers I long since had written off as lost. I found a set of keys I lost three years ago wedged in the bottom of the fireplace poker rack. It was when I moved the sofa to vacuum underneath that I found the most interesting item.

It was a small canister of film.

46

I knelt and scooped it into my palm, turning it over and looking at it curiously. Prior to working for Boggs Investigations, I didn't have much use for a camera, and when I did, I used a film-free digital one. Since then, I had become proficient with a Minolta 35mm, documenting various infidelities in progress. Although the roll I held in my hand was the same type of film I used, I didn't recall misplacing one. It was not only unlikely, but damn near impossible. I would have gotten three kinds of hell from Doug (and his mother) when he reviewed the file and saw that prints were indicated but omitted. I flashed briefly upon the evening of my sister's final visit and remembered she had put her handbag beside the couch at the same end where I found the film. Photojournalism was her trade, so odds were good it had belonged to her. It may well contain the last images Gina had ever snapped, and it would be a disservice to her memory for those images to remain unviewed. Ah, but it was late, and I needed to get my sorry ass to bed. I dropped the canister in my work bag and made a mental note to drop it off for developing either on my way to or from Total Care Landscaping.

······•••••◦◯◦•••••······

In what is definitely not my norm, I found myself up and about with time to spare the following morning, so I swung through One-Hour Photo in Hilliard on my way to Total Care and dropped off the canister of film. Despite my best efforts exhausting myself through housework, I had slept poorly, and was almost fully awake when the sun peeked over the horizon. I dreaded returning to Total Care, because I would forever associate Sue Slattery's office with notification of my sister's death. I just wanted to finish the project and hopefully never have to return—not my usual sentiment regarding well-paying clients.

47

I braced myself for the inevitable condolences of Sue and her staff members and plodded through them amicably. Squatted down over Sue's computer, I had a brief moment of déjà vu, half-expecting Melanie to appear in the doorway with that awful expression on her face. As I applied myself to my craft, the sensation drifted away, and soon enough, I was running on autopilot again. I took advantage of the lunch hour to horn my way into the remaining workstations needing attention, and within a few hours, I was applying the final updates from Microsoft's website.

"You didn't have to come back so soon, you know."

I jumped. Sue Slattery was behind me, leaning in the doorframe for God-only-knows how long. "I didn't see you," I mumbled self-consciously.

"I got that. I'm serious. Nobody expected you to run right back here and finish up, although I certainly do appreciate it."

I avoided her eyes and kept my attention on the PC, clicking 'OK' to restart when prompted. "Life goes on," I said with a shrug. I returned my full attention to the computer and wished Sue would go away, but she remained where she stood, watching me as I worked. I was quickly growing uncomfortable under her silent scrutiny and eventually turned to meet her gaze. "Was there something else?"

She took a few pensive steps across the room and perched on the corner of the desk. "I've been debating whether to share this with you, because I know right now, it's mostly meaningless. But sometimes when people say they know how you feel, they really do, and sometimes what they have to say might prove valuable. Do you know what I mean?"

I grimaced. Here we go again. Determined to get through it as quickly as possible, I nodded jerkily.

"I lost a sister once," said Sue absently, and my eyes automatically flicked to hers. She was gazing out somewhere beyond me, and I could see the pain fresh in her eyes.

"I'm sorry," I said. "How long ago?"

Her smile was bittersweet. "Almost fifteen years. I was about fourteen at the time. Janice was nineteen." Her smile tightened. "It seems like a million years ago, and yet it seems like only yesterday. There's no way you can be prepared for such a thing. No way."

"What happened?"

"She was traveling between here and Lexington," she said. "She attended the University of Kentucky but came home every few weekends to visit. This was just like any other weekend that Jan would be making the trip—except it wasn't. She apparently chose a bad time to stop at a rest area along the US 68." She paused and swallowed hard, and I desperately wished her story ended right there.

"His name was Marty Ferstein. He worked at a Firestone in Lexington, one that Jan had taken her car to a few weeks before for an oil change. The guy had done some time for petty theft, breaking and entering—nothing violent, though. He *did*, however, have a history of stalking." Her smile was back, but I recognized it for the brave front that it was. "He took her from there, leaving her car and purse behind. We didn't know what happened to her for months—seven months and five days, to be exact. Then one day, a policeman showed up at our door. Remains had been found in Carlsbad Cavern that fit Jan's description. Dental records confirmed it was my sister. Forensics confirmed things had been done to her, the details of which I'll spare you. Ferstein was no professional criminal. He left evidence all over the place." Her eyes locked on mine. "I *know* how you feel."

I sighed and sat back in the task chair, easing away from the desk. I wasn't thinking with my entire brain, and I was selfishly offended that Sue had chosen this exact moment to unburden herself upon me. "Okay. So, you know how I feel. What compelled you to share with me? I certainly hope you're not trying to comfort me, because—"

"Look, I'm sorry. I don't really know you, and I certainly have no right to intrude. It's just that—everybody tells you they're sorry, everybody tells you the pain will heal with time—nobody tells you about how abrupt the change in your family dynamic can be. Every time you go home, it will be a reminder your sister isn't there anymore, and you're all having to learn how to deal with that. It's important that you be there for each other. You have a new dynamic developing, and you have to participate in its evolution. Personally, I really blew it there. I kept everything to myself, bottled it all in. I avoided any reminders of Jan at all, which basically included my whole family. Our relationship has been strained ever since, and as lame as this sounds, I'm not strong enough to try and fix it. I think I could have been if I hadn't shut them all out so long ago. I don't know."

I didn't know what to say. I stared at her stupidly, still wishing she would go away.

"Don't fuck it up worse than it already is." She nodded once and headed for the door, relieved of her burden of duty.

"Hey," I called after her.

She stopped and turned around. "Yeah?"

I fought to keep my voice steady. "Will it always hurt like this?"

"The day-to-day gets a lot easier," she said. "But there will always be that little place, you know? That little place that hurts like hell if you stay there too long."

I nodded, and she retreated to her office.

Traffic was heavy as I headed home, finally finished with the Total Care Landscaping job. The day had been exhausting, and I just wanted to curl up with my cat and take a nap. There was an accident somewhere ahead and traffic was bottlenecked, with people squeezing left with no regard to their fellow motorists and the proximity of their bumpers. As I neared the Cemetery Road exit, I decided I would take the scenic route home. It may be more mileage, but at least I could keep moving. Normally, I might even enjoy such a detour, considering I was riding in my new SUV, but I found no pleasure in driving the vehicle, although it was no fault of the car's. I felt gloomy and was weighed down by Sue Slattery's commiseration. I didn't immediately recognize the relevance of her condolence and was slightly offended she had selected that particular moment to mount her soapbox. Even so, the less self-pitying part of me recognized she had shared something extremely personal and unpleasant, something she didn't do easily, and I should at least listen. I wasn't ready to commit to an opinion quite yet, so I turned the radio up as I eased onto the exit.

I turned left and headed onto Mill Run, determined to collect Gina's final photos before I went home. I didn't know if I'd look at them quite yet; I was still smarting from Sue's words. Yet I wanted to have them near me, know they were safe in my possession so I *could* view them whenever I felt capable. I was surprised as traffic continued to crawl. I attributed the slowdown to interstate runoff until I rounded the bend east of the interstate. I immediately spotted the police cars surrounding the freestanding structure at the foot of Giant Eagle's parking lot.

It was the One-Hour Photo that had been my destination.

CHAPTER FIVE

I circled the lot, unsure of what I should do. There were four Columbus City Police cruisers blocking the entrance to the photo shop, and a few nondescript white sedans I assumed belonged to the detectives working the scene. I wanted my pictures, but that wasn't gonna happen. A dumpy lady cop stood grim-faced at the entrance, prepared to direct incoming foot traffic elsewhere, should anyone miss the message sent by the police tape applied liberally to the entire scene. I pulled forward, sliding my Hyundai into a slot closer to Giant Eagle and shut down the engine. I sat behind the wheel, trying to decide upon the best approach that wouldn't get me automatically escorted off-premises when I spotted a familiar face in the sea of uniformed and plain clothed officials. I tooted my horn and got out of the car waving. Countless heads turned, but it was a moment before Nina Crockett spotted me, and yet another before recognition set in. She broke away from the two gentlemen with whom she was speaking and started across the lot toward me.

Nina Crockett is a special agent with the FBI, and it occurred to me her presence probably meant something more than a simple robbery, although I had no idea what. She strode toward me purposefully, her facial expression blank. She was an Amazon of Xena-like proportions, with chestnut hair that fell just over her broad shoulders, and I had no doubt whatsoever she could set several of her co-workers on their asses if she were so inclined. I had met her the previous winter when she was working to catch a serial killer who hacked his victims to pieces; she had told me then that I now had a contact inside the Bureau, and I decided it was time to see if the offer was sincere.

"Nina!" I called, hurrying to meet her halfway. "It's been a while."

She allowed herself a slight smile. "Well, if it isn't Dwayne Morrow. Do you plan on turning up at every one of my Columbus assignments?"

I returned the smile and shrugged. "Don't know what to tell you. What happened over there?" I pointed toward the photo shop as an ambulance arrived on the scene. I noticed there weren't any sirens. Apparently, there was no need to hurry.

Nina shook her head. "We're still piecing it together. The short version is this is the scene of a holdup. The clerk was a young lady who picked up hours here and there so she'd have some spending money while attending Capital University. I doubt she reckoned on this."

"Who in the hell would rob a photo shop?" I asked. "I can't imagine there would be much cash on premises."

"Hard to say."

"What are you doing here, anyway? I didn't realize it was usual protocol for the FBI to investigate every armed robbery."

"It isn't." She smiled at me and offered nothing more on the subject. "So, how's Brady?"

Ah, I thought. *I see.*

Brady and Nina had embarked on an ill-fated union during our earlier case, and her tone of voice implied she was still bitter. I also realized she must not know of Brady's current status, and I hated being the bearer of bad news.

"He's doing better now," I said cautiously. "I think he's supposed to be released from the hospital this weekend."

She raised an eyebrow. "Really? What happened?"

"He was, you know, sort of shot," I said, adding, "But he's much better now."

"Damn," she said. "When I imagine him being shot, it usually ends with him dying."

"Um, yeah, I'm sorry about all that. But you know, I'm not Brady. In fact, I don't even really like Brady. Ask him. He'll tell you."

She massaged her forehead and found another smile. "I know. I'm sorry." She looked up at me. "So, what brings you here today, Dwayne Morrow?"

"Actually, I was coming to pick up some film I had left for developing," I said, glancing at the activity surrounding the photo shop. "I'm as surprised to see you as you are to see me."

"I imagine it will be a while before anyone is allowed to collect anything from inside there," she said. "The lab boys will have to go over everything, bagging and tagging and recording contents. Right now, everything's evidence."

This didn't feel right. Sure, I was disappointed that I would be delayed in taking possession of Gina's final work, but the feeling ran deeper. I couldn't explain it, but alarms were sounding all through my head. I *needed* to see those pictures, and I needed to see them *now*.

"What's wrong?" asked Nina, noting the apparent change in my expression.

I shook my head. "I'm not sure. It's just—these pictures. They're important to me. I recently lost my sister, and she was a photojournalist. I found this roll of film after she—" I found myself swallowing excessively and paused to regroup. "I think it's her last work, and I can't imagine not having the opportunity to see it."

Nina studied me for a moment. "Look, everything's going to be a mess here for a little while. Why don't you leave me a phone number where I can reach you? After we have a chance to catalog the items in the shop, I can check to see if your prints are still there. Would that ease your mind?"

I pulled one of my business cards from my wallet and handed it to her. It was the one for my consulting business, which contained both my home and cell phone numbers. "Thank you," I said. "It really would."

She smiled and touched my hand briefly. "I'm sorry about your sister," she said softly before heading back to the crime scene. I nodded after her and returned to my vehicle empty-handed and uneasy.

I returned home and fed my cat, throwing a Totino's pizza into the oven for myself in the process. I went back to my office and booted my computer. Since the job with Total Care was finished, there was no sense in delaying the invoice, and I could frankly use the cash. I crossed back into the kitchen and snagged a Pepsi, pausing to stoop and scritch Dexter behind the ears. I pulled the pizza from the oven, grabbing a stack of napkins and was about to return to my office when there was a knock at the door. I glanced at the clock. Five-thirty. A little early for Melanie, but I wasn't complaining. I emptied my arms onto the counter and headed to the front door.

"Hey," I said, opening the door. My words froze in mid-trickle. It wasn't Melanie.

"Hi," said a man I recognized from my sister's funeral. He was the one with dark, curly hair, the one who had seemed so genuinely distraught. "I'm sorry to disturb you, but I was wondering if I might have a minute of your time." His smile was hesitant, and his eyes were heavy and dark.

"So long as you're not selling anything," I said. "I saw you at Gina's funeral. Were you a good friend?"

He looked at his feet. "You might say that," he said. He looked back up at me. "I'm so sorry about your sister. You have no idea."

"Come in," I said, stepping back and holding the door open. He could be a mass murderer for all I knew, but curiosity had the better of me. "I didn't catch your name."

"Michael," he said, offering a hand. "Michael Arthur."

He met my eyes as he shook my hand, and in a flash, I gathered much of what I needed to know. "You were seeing my sister," I said.

His smile turned sheepish, and he scratched his head. "I wanted to marry your sister," he finally said, and I raised my eyebrows. "She wasn't so keen on the idea."

"I'm sorry," I said, not sure if I was or not.

"Oh, don't be," he said. "It wasn't that she didn't love me. I'm pretty sure she did. It's just that she wasn't so hyped about the institution of marriage. She didn't much like conforming to the system."

I smiled and could certainly picture that. I pulled myself back into the moment before melancholy could take hold again. "You said you wanted a minute of my time. What's up?"

Michael took a seat on one of my overstuffed sofas, and I sat across from him. Dexter wandered into the room, spotted a stranger and made off, but not before imparting a fearsome hiss, loaded with free-flying spittle. "I work for *The Washington Post*," he said. "I met Gina while I was on assignment a few years ago. She was taking pictures of an industrial landfill, and I was trying to dig my way to the parties responsible for same landfill—no pun intended. We found we had a good bit in common, so we stayed in touch, seeing each other whenever we had the opportunity."

He paused, and I felt I should say something, but I didn't know what to say. It wasn't as if Gina had ever even *mentioned* this guy. Of course, upon reflection, I would have to admit she hadn't really discussed much of her personal life. Michael cleared his throat, and I was glad when he broke the silence.

"I was with her just before she came to Columbus," he said. "She was photographing some mining town in West Virginia, and I was working a piece on industrial waste being pumped into the Ohio River. We were only about thirty miles apart, so we were split the difference and shared a room at an old motel off Route 50. We did our respective bits through the day and met up at night."

I was more than a little uncomfortable hearing a postmortem account of my sister's sex life, and I hoped details wouldn't follow. I was relieved when he fell silent, but my relief was short-lived as the silence began to grow into infinity. "I'm sorry," I finally said, adjusting my position on the sofa. "I don't mean to be rude, but I'm not sure exactly what it is you want."

He smiled with teeth that were perfectly straight. "I'm not really sure either," he admitted, sitting back and closing his eyes. "Your sister said you were some kind of detective. Is that right?"

I blinked. "Well—yeah, in training, I suppose."

"This is going to sound completely paranoid," he said, shaking his head and struggling for words to follow.

"Go on."

His eyes met mine and locked on. "I'm wondering if what happened to Gina might not have been an accident at all."

I looked at him curiously. "What are you suggesting? Murder?" His expression didn't shift. *"Murder?"*

"Look, I have nothing more than a bad feeling, so I can't really prove anything one way or the other. But toward the end of our stay in West Virginia, she saw something that really disturbed her."

"Like what?"

He shook his head. "I have no idea. She didn't talk about it. But there was a sudden shift in her demeanor, a *definite* shift. I'd never seen her act

57

like that, so I didn't immediately know what to call it. If I had to say now, I think I'd say *fear*."

Like it or not, I was reliving the evening of my sister's visit, searching for behavior I simply hadn't recognized. "She seemed fine when she was here," I eventually said. "What could she possibly have been afraid of?"

"I don't know," he said, and I realized my questions were redundancies he had already been pondering. "I *do* know she was glad to get out of there. She couldn't pack quickly enough."

"Look, I'm not sure how I can help you here," I said, standing abruptly. I didn't want to go through all this right now. If Michael Arthur were suffering a delusional fantasy based on his grief for my sister, I couldn't afford to get caught up in it. The wounds were too fresh.

"I want you to come with me to Briarstaff, West Virginia," he said, standing and stepping toward me. His focus was so intense that I couldn't look away, and believe me, I tried. This was all too much—too soon. "I want to see what she was digging into, see what she might have stirred up. I want to know what happened."

"What if nothing happened? What if Gina came to visit me and had the bad fortune to die in a traffic accident while here? What do you do then?"

His smile was despondent. "If that's what happened, then that's what happened," he said. "I'm not a lunatic, Mr. Morrow, but I've seen a lot of bad things in this world. I have no delusions about the capabilities of our fellow man. He tends to eliminate things that are in his way. If Gina was one of those things, I need to know. I need to *know*."

His jaw was steely and set, and I suddenly understood the conviction of his words. He was looking for revenge, and for that, there was an undeniable appeal. If Gina had died through the deliberate actions of someone else, that person or persons would have to pay. If there was nothing to find, I was no worse off than I was today, but I couldn't let the possibility go ignored, could I? What harm could come from asking a few

58

questions in some piss-ant little mining town? I hated myself for being drawn so easily into this, but the seed had been planted, and it was already growing at an alarming rate. I hadn't accepted the assignment Boggs was begging me to take, and I had already completed my work at Total Care. I had nothing but free time in front of me.

"When do we leave?" I asked.

⸻ ● ● ● ● ● ◉ ◉ ● ● ● ● ● ⸻

"Are you sure you're okay to do this?"

I could hear the concern in Melanie's voice, and I smiled. "No. But I'll be worse if I don't go. Now that I've heard the beginning of the story, I have to know the ending."

"I'm sorry I didn't stop by. I would've liked to have met this guy." Melanie had phoned to beg off this evening. Jasmine was complaining of an upset stomach.

"Is Jasmine all right?"

"Oh, yeah. She's just got a bit of a tummy ache. No fever or anything. All she needs is a good night's rest, some Pepto-Bismol and an evening away from junk food. So, tell me about this Michael Arthur."

I frowned. "What's to tell? I only talked to him for a little bit. He seemed like a nice enough guy."

"Is he your sister's type?"

"I guess I didn't know my sister's type," I admitted. "Why?"

"I don't know. It's just got to be weird, that's all. You're interacting with a part of Gina's life that you never had access to before. I hope it's not too overwhelming."

"I hope not, either." I thought about how difficult the last several days had been, how difficult the mere mention of Gina's name had been, and yet I was preparing to embark on a journey that would undoubtedly immerse me in every detail of her life. I wasn't sure I was strong enough to do it, but now that the question had been asked, I simply had to know the answer.

"How long do you think you'll be gone?" asked Melanie.

"I'm not sure. Couple of days, probably. Can you stop by and feed Dexter?"

"I'm sure Jasmine would love to. For some reason, that cat despises me."

"He does not," I insisted. "He's just of the opinion that he belongs in my lap more than you do."

I could almost hear her grinning. "You call me every night, okay? And any other time you need someone to talk to—I don't care what time it is."

"Yes, ma'am. You want me to pick up any souvenirs?" I asked sarcastically, sensing that Briarstaff would be lucky to have a Dollar General.

"Just come home soon."

Almost as an afterthought, I placed a quick call to Jacko Pierce, the reporter for *The Columbus Dispatch* whom I had recently befriended when Brady had been unavailable.

"Great to hear from you, man," he enthused. He was still riding high on the accolades garnered from the story I had given him. "I've been so busy since the story hit—and it sure the hell ain't from writing obituaries." His tone became hopeful. "Something going on?"

"Maybe," I said. "It's really too early to say. But I was wondering if you might have access to some information about a little town in West Virginia called Briarstaff."

"What am I looking for?"

"I don't know exactly," I admitted. "I'm just curious if there's been anything newsworthy in the last decade or so."

"Jeez, Dwayne. That's not much in the way of direction."

"Honestly, Jacko, I don't have much now, but the town's so damn small I would think anything worth mentioning would leap right out. I'm going to search the internet myself, but I figure you have more resources than I do."

"Okay," he said dubiously. "I'll run the name through, but I wouldn't hold my breath."

"Thanks. I'm heading that way tomorrow with Michael Arthur from *The Washington Post* on what is most likely a fool's errand, so I'd better give you my cell number." I could hear his pen scratching paper as he jotted it down. "I know reception can be sort of spotty out there, so if I don't hear from you by tomorrow night, I'll call back."

It was too much to hope for a startling revelation using a Google keyword search. Briarstaff wasn't even a real word, although I did locate an amusing entry for 'briar staff' which could be used in a transmutation spell. The only information consistently returned confirmed Briarstaff was, in fact, in West Virginia and Google would be more than delighted to provide detailed directions on how to get there.

I pushed away from my desk and was startled to find Dexter nestled comfortably in my lap. I had no recollection of him arriving; cats are sneaky that way. I scratched behind his ears, evoking a deep rumbling from within. "Sorry, fella," I said as I boosted him from his perch. It was getting late, and I still had things to do.

I went upstairs and dragged my soft-sided bag from underneath my bed, reminded by its heft that I hadn't bothered to unpack after my lengthy stay in Lymont. Most of what was inside had already been worn, so I dumped the contents into a pile on my bed and began rooting around my closet for clean clothes. After a few fruitless moments, I realized that I was delaying the inevitable, so I scooped up the rumpled items from my bed and headed downstairs to the laundry room. It was already after ten, and Michael Arthur would be picking me up at six in the morning, so I set the machine for a short cycle and padded into the living room to wait it out. I had only just settled onto the sofa when the phone rang, which of course was charging in its cradle in the hallway. I groaned aloud as I extracted myself from the deep cushions and was embarrassed by how much I sounded like my grandfather.

"Hi, Dwayne. Sorry it took so long to get back to you. I hope it isn't too late to call." It was Nina.

"Not at all. I was just doing some laundry. What did you find out?"

"I'm afraid it's not good," she said, and somehow, I already suspected it wouldn't be. "Alan cataloged everything, but he didn't list any photos or negatives that had your name attached. I double-checked under your sister's name, too, just in case."

I rolled the information around in my head for a moment and began connecting mental dots. "Doesn't that strike you as odd? I mean, wouldn't that indicate there was something in her pictures worth killing for?"

"Slow down, Sherlock," she said. "Your sister's pictures weren't the only ones taken."

I blinked. "Really?"

"Yeah. As a matter of fact, the place had been emptied of almost *all* pictures. There were only a handful of negatives found in the entire place, and those were in the process of being developed, so our killer might not have even been aware of them."

"Still, doesn't that suggest that this wasn't a simple robbery?"

Nina was silent, and I suddenly remembered how evasive she had been when I had asked what the FBI was doing at the crime scene. Her mere presence had already suggested it wasn't a simple robbery, and she apparently wasn't at liberty to indulge my curiosity.

"Do you have any idea what might have been on that roll of film?" asked Nina, and I realized she had shifted into investigative mode.

"None whatsoever," I said. "I found it under the couch in my living room."

"Hmm."

"What?"

"Well, do you normally put film that's ready to be developed underneath your sofa?"

I paused. If the film had been some vacation shots of mine, it would not only be plausible but, in fact, highly probable that the canister might have been dropped or kicked under the couch. However, the film *wasn't* mine. Selling photographs was my sister's business. For her to casually lose her latest work out of the corner of her bag would be recklessly out-of-character. Had she intentionally left that film behind for me to find? What in the hell was on that roll? Was it the evidence Michael Arthur suspected Gina might have witnessed on that last day in Briarstaff? Was it the reason she might have been murdered?

CHAPTER SIX

Michael pulled into my driveway at quarter after six, looking a little disheveled and barely awake. Normally, I would have appreciated the extra time, but my imagination had been working overtime, and I had barely slept. By the time he arrived, I had convinced myself he wasn't coming at all. I was already certain his earlier visit had been a vicious prank. He grinned sheepishly as he emerged from his car—a bright yellow Ford Fiesta, no less—and was already offering apologies as he ascended my porch steps.

"I never sleep well in motels," he said. "I only drifted off a couple of hours ago, and I didn't hear my alarm."

I dragged my travel bag, which was essentially an oversized backpack, out to his car and tossed it beside his own into the tiny hatchback. Almost as an afterthought, I had brought my own camera, adding it to my backpack as well. "Don't worry about it," I said. "Have you eaten yet? I'm starving."

He drove through McDonald's, and we feasted on buttery biscuit sandwiches and piping hot coffee. I was thankful for the distraction; I was uncomfortable traveling several hours with someone I barely knew. The long night had given me time to reevaluate his suppositions, and they sounded more ridiculous by the minute. More than likely, we were wasting time and money on this little adventure, and it would be like salt in a fresh wound to simply confirm Gina's death had been the accident that police said it was.

"Sausage and egg biscuit, add cheese, huh?" Michael was looking at me with amusement.

I returned the gaze suspiciously as a shower of crumbs cascaded down my front. "Yeah. So?"

"It's the same thing your sister always ordered."

"You know, let's not do this," I said, irritated. "I really don't want to hear about how similar or dissimilar I am to my sister."

"I'm sorry. I didn't mean to—"

"I know. And I didn't mean to snap. It's just so soon after the funeral. It would probably be a good idea if we set a ground rule or two, the first one being that Gina isn't the only topic of conversation between us. I don't think I could handle it."

He nodded slowly. "Fair enough." We drove through downtown Columbus in silence, continuing east on I-70. Traffic was beginning to thicken with morning commuters. "How about those Reds?"

"What?"

"Don't you follow baseball?"

I wadded up the paper from my sandwich and tossed it into the empty McDonald's bag. "Not really."

"So, what *do* you like to do?"

"I like to track down bad guys and make them pay for what they've done." I sounded like a poor man's Dirty Harry, all catchphrases and attitude. I was being particularly insolent, and I didn't know why.

He sighed. "Okay, so *you* pick the topic."

"Fine," I said. "The topic is music." I reached out and punched the power button on the radio, tuning it to QFM 96.3, classic rock. I reclined my seat as far back as I could, closing my eyes and making it plain I wasn't feeling conversational.

Somewhere along the way, I actually fell asleep.

I was jolted back to consciousness as a rear tire found the bottom of a pothole. I rubbed crust from the corners of my eyes and adjusted my seat into an upright position. "Where are we?" I asked.

"About a half hour outside of Briarstaff," said Michael, glancing at me before returning his attention to the road.

I looked around, trying to reorient myself with the outside world. I couldn't believe I had slept so soundly; I'm usually unable to sleep while riding in a car. We were traveling on a rutted two-lane highway that didn't look as if it had been repaved in some time. The lanes were hazardously narrow, and I winced as a semi roared past us, our little car pulled toward the wind tunnel it created. The sky was overcast and gloomy, promising an eventual rainfall. Thick woods lined the right side of the road, and the Ohio River was a murky ribbon on the left. If it weren't for the pitted roadway and overhead power lines, there would be no suggestion of civilization whatsoever.

"I figured we'd stay at the same motel where Gina and I stayed. It's just a few miles ahead. If possible, I'm going to get the same room and the one next to it," said Michael.

I didn't ask why. If we were trying to trace Gina's actions while in Briarstaff, we needed to align ourselves as closely as possible with her previous actions. Acid churned inside my stomach as I realized how near the surface my emotions were. I wasn't looking forward to following in my deceased sister's footsteps. I lapsed into pensive silence as the miles rolled by, tugging at my bottom lip for lack of something better to do.

"What's our story?" I asked, suddenly realizing our presence here made no real sense. I couldn't imagine we would be well received if the locals knew we were on a fishing expedition to discover if one of them might just be a murderer. "I can't imagine we're leading with the truth."

"No," Michael, agreed, sliding into opposite lane, and slipping past a logging truck that was at best going twenty miles per hour. "I saw you brought your camera. I think we should operate under the premise that you're after more location shots to supplement the story Gina was working on."

"Gina would have taken tons of photos," I said with an uncertain chuckle. "I can't imagine her ever needing someone to supplement her work."

Michael shrugged. "I don't know. We could say some of the pictures didn't turn out very well—I don't really think we'll get grilled over that. I doubt any of these people know of Gina's reputation as a photographer much less anything at all about you. We just need a reason to be here. We could always say that she had moved on to another assignment and couldn't come back."

Moved on to another assignment.

Well, that was certainly one way of putting it. The suggestion that any of her pictures might not "turn out" seemed equally ridiculous until I remembered the missing roll of film from the One-Hour Photo in Hilliard. I could lean into that without feeling like I was fibbing outright—an important distinction for someone who has been told repeatedly he is perhaps the world's worst liar. I'm prone to inappropriate giggling and involuntary facial tics. On the upside, we wouldn't be rehashing the details of the accident over and over again, which I simply wouldn't be able to do.

"This is it," said Michael, slowing the car and signaling right.

When he had mentioned they stayed in an "old motel," he certainly wasn't kidding. Images of the Bates Motel sprang to mind, and the acid in my stomach began trickling through the rest of my digestive tract. Totally enshrouded by woods, the motel was arranged in an "L," with the office and five rooms on one arm and three more on the other. A narrow, covered porch ran the entire length of the motel, affording a place to cower if you found yourself caught in the elements as well as a place to congregate, if you were willing to trust the ancient and rusting metal outdoor furniture that was placed between each room. The groupings were an eclectic mix of card tables, folding chairs and gliders, all of which looked equally uncomfortable. The building itself was in desperate need of a facelift; what shutters remained hung haphazardly, framing grimy, paned windows. The once-white paint had peeled and flecked and eventually turned gray after untold years of exposure to the elements. The parking lot was an empty dustbowl, with just enough gravel to make noise against the undercarriage of the car as we slowed to a halt. The only other vehicle in the lot was a 1970-something Ford LTD that was more rust than sheet metal. I assumed it belonged to whomever operated the place. Emblazoned in faded yellow letters on the office window was "Fred's Beds," with a newer red-and-white placard hanging on a chain underneath that declared, "VACANCY!"

"I don't think we'll have any trouble getting the rooms," I commented as we got out of the car.

A slender and prim woman appeared in the doorframe of the office. She wore a faded gingham dress with deep pockets stitched into the front. She was somewhere between fifty and death, but I wouldn't dare hazard a guess after spotting the suspicion on her face. Her narrow eyes were nearly hidden behind granny glasses, her mousy brown hair too short for her angular features. As we approached, I could see a liberal dusting of gray scattered throughout.

"Hi, Mrs. Shepley," called Michael, with an easy grin and quick wave. "I enjoyed my stay here so much, I just had to come back."

Mrs. Shepley harrumphed and put her hands on her hips. "Likely," she said sarcastically. "I wasn't buyin' that Americana crap the last time you was here. Who's this?" She jerked her head toward me.

"Dwayne Morrow," I said, trying a smile on to little effect.

"He's Gina's brother," added Michael.

"I recognize the last name," said Mrs. Shepley, crossly. "You datin' the whole family?"

I glanced quickly at Michael and watched him flush and fumble, stammering, "Of course not, I—"

Mrs. Shepley rolled her eyes and harrumphed again. "Just a joke, Mr. Arthur. Don't get your knickers in a twist."

"Of course," said Michael, glancing toward the shorter arm of the structure. "Do you think we could get Rooms 7 and 8? Or 6 and 7?"

"What the hell difference does it make?" snapped Mrs. Shepley. "One room's the same as the other, and they're all empty."

Michael floundered again, so I interjected, "My sister said the view was something else." I tried another smile, but it faded quickly when I realized that all of the rooms looked directly into the thick woods.

"Horse shit," Mrs. Shepley uttered with a deep sigh, but turned around and went into the office, stepping behind the counter. "It don't make no never mind to me which rooms you take. They're all empty and they're all the same price." She slid a clipboard across the counter toward Michael, and I saw that the registration form consisted of a legal pad with handwritten column headers. My heart clenched when I saw my sister's handwriting midway down the page. There had only been two other customers since then.

"It's fifty bucks per night per room," said Mrs. Shepley as she took the clipboard back from Michael. "How long you stayin' this time?"

"Haven't really decided yet," said Michael while I fished for my wallet. I laid my debit card on the counter and Mrs. Shepley promptly slid it back to me.

"We don't take no credit," she sniffed.

"I've got it," Michael said to me as he counted out ten twenties from his wallet and handed them to Mrs. Shepley. "I'm sure we'll be here at least two nights."

In a move almost too quick to see, she snagged the bills and tucked them into one of her front pockets. "Hope so, because there's no refunds," she said as an afterthought. She turned and retrieved the keys to Rooms 7 and 8 from a pegboard on the wall behind her. She handed them to Michael, and said, "Better not be no funny bid-ness goin' on here. I don't want no drug traffic or any kinda horseshit like that. And these rooms are no smoking. That means *none*. People think I can't tell, but I promise you I can."

Michael shook his head and smiled easily while I looked on in astonishment. "No, ma'am." We returned to the car.

"Charming," I said as I got back into the passenger seat.

He pulled the car around, parking near our rooms and killing the engine. "Why don't you take Room 7?" Michael suggested. "That was the room we stayed in. Maybe fresh eyes will see something mine won't."

We lugged our bags out of the hatchback, and I fumbled with the key to Room 7 before finally managing to unlock the door. Michael left his bag on the wooden slatted porch and followed me inside.

The interior was as grimy as the exterior. Walls, carpeting, bedding—despite Mrs. Shepley's earlier warning, it had all been stained faintly yellow from years of nicotine-imbibing occupants. The air was musty, and I immediately crossed the room to try and open the only window, but it had been painted shut years before. I peeked into the bathroom and flinched at the rust-colored mold and mildew that adhered to the bases of all the fixtures. In Columbus, fifty dollars would buy a night in a relatively clean Super 8. This was no Super 8.

I tossed my backpack on top of one of the double beds and plopped down beside it. The moss-green bedspread smelled of mothballs and old age. "You *voluntarily* stayed here?" I asked. I had a hard time picturing my sister occupying this very room. It was depressing to think she had spent some of her final days in such a shithole.

Michael chuckled. "There isn't exactly a lot to choose from around here. There's a charming bed-and-breakfast in town if you don't mind monkeys and parakeets."

"Monkeys and parakeets?"

He shrugged. "Not much of a pet person myself, so who's to say why some people choose the pets they do? I think Erma Irvin just opened up her house because she was lonely after her husband passed away."

"You seem to know a lot about the people in this town," I observed.

"It's hard not to," he said. "You'll see. They don't trust strangers very much, but they sure can't help their curiosity."

I sighed. "So, what now?" I wasn't used to following someone else's lead, but I didn't know the paces that my sister and her boyfriend had run, and my own ideas weren't coalescing with any sort of promise.

"Let me drop my bags off next door. Then we can head into Briarstaff, and I'll give you the grand tour. That should take about five minutes. Afterward, we'll stop at the diner and grab a bite to eat. Maybe ask a few questions of the locals. If anybody around here knows anything, we'll find 'em at Ida's."

······●●●●●⊖⊙●●●●●●······

As we headed toward Briarstaff, I tried Melanie on my cell phone. All I received was a robotic voice saying my call could not be completed as dialed. I looked at the phone's display with frustration; even roaming was out of the question, apparently. I slid the phone back into my pocket

Michael cast a quick glance and shrugged his shoulders. "I hope you weren't relying too much on that thing," he said. "I'm not sure these people have moved on to pushbutton technology, much less cellular. I think there may be some payphones in town."

Payphones. How quaint.

I nodded curtly and watched as we rounded a bend, the road winding its way out of the woods and down into a grouping of two-story structures, some sided in ancient, warped wood, others faced in grimy brick. They huddled together around a quaint, community park where children played while parents socialized, and pets ran freely across the well-maintained lawn. Well-tended flowerbeds were scattered throughout with an assortment of outdoor seating, both benches and picnic tables. The layout was pure Americana; it was an authentic town square, with each of the outlying buildings facing the central plaza in which a small, covered pavilion had been erected. There were no more than thirty buildings total, and they housed Briarstaff's center of commerce in one convenient pit-stop. I spotted Brenner's Five-and-Dime wedged between Sally's Flowers and Harvey's Videos—so much for souvenirs from Dollar General. At least modern technology extended to DVDs and televisions.

Michael entered the square and coasted to the lone stop light, flipping his turn signal on as he braked. Local citizens openly gawked, curious about the strangers who had invaded their tightly woven circle. I noticed an inordinate need for dentures and realized that sometimes stereotypes exist for a reason. When the light changed, we continued straight through, passing a Ford pickup that was at least as old as I was. Its sweaty, sunburned driver stared with eyes that didn't look at us in unison. He spewed a nasty trail of tobacco juice as he slowly rolled through the intersection. Michael eased the Fiesta into a narrow alley on the left before backing up and executing a five-point turn to bring us back the way we had come. After waiting for the light to cycle again for traffic that didn't exist, we crossed back through the intersection and Michael eased to the curb in front of a maroon-sided building whose windows proclaimed it to be Ida's Town

Diner. Either vanity or lack of imagination was at work when naming one's business in Briarstaff.

The glass-paned door creaked in agony as Michael tugged on the door, and the restaurant's patrons literally froze in place as we entered, staring openly as we worked our way through. I could feel my skin burning as conversation slowly resumed and people refocused on their dinners. Booths lined the south wall and half of the north, with an L-shaped counter occupying the remaining space. Behind the counter was a swinging door that led to a kitchen I wouldn't want to inspect closely. Few of the cracked vinyl booths were empty, although several stools at the counter were, so we headed there and parked ourselves on the rusting pedestals. The air was musty and deep-fried, and the yellowed wallpaper looked shiny in the insufficient glow of overhead lighting. A rail-thin teenage girl with mousy hair pushed through the swinging door with bowls of soup balanced on each arm. Her face was a minefield of acne scars, and she seemed to be talking to herself as she kept trying to blow an errant strand of limp hair from her face. She plodded around the counter and approached a table near the entrance to unburden herself.

"Well, look who's back."

I returned my attention to the counter and found myself looking into the narrowed gaze of a beefy woman with steely hair and even steelier eyes. Her aged skin was like leather that had been seasoned in the sun, with freckles dotting every square inch of her sagging face. Her attention was fixed upon Michael, and I noticed that he was smiling.

"Ida," he said. "Don't you ever get a day off?"

Her lips barely moved as she harrumphed. "Not too often I see a stranger twice in just about as many weeks." The suspicion in her voice was tangible, and her eyes shifted over to me. "Who's this?"

"I thought I'd bring my girlfriend's brother by," said Michael, still cheery and conversational. "Show him what good cooking is all about."

Ida's expression remained flat, and I had the creepy sensation that I was caught in *Invasion of the Body Snatchers*. Nevertheless, I extended a hand. "I'm Dwayne Morrow, ma'am," I said, attempting what I hoped was a congenial smile. "Nice to meet you."

She looked from my hand to my face, almost sneering. She didn't even make an effort. "Penny will be around to get your order—when she's got a minute. I 'spect you can see she's pretty busy. I got things to tend to in the kitchen. I don't want no trouble in here." Without another glance, she turned and marched through the swinging door.

I slowly lowered my arm from where it hung and stared open-mouthed at Michael. "What the hell was *that?*"

He simply shrugged. "Small towns," he said, as if that perfectly summed everything up. "The people are naturally suspicious."

I snorted. "I don't think so. Lymont is pretty small. The people don't act like *that*."

"Compared to Briarstaff, Lymont is a metropolis, Dwayne. The population here is maybe in the hundreds. These folks have been victimized by every slimeball traveling insurance man, bought vacuums and encyclopedias from salesmen who had no intention of ever delivering the goods—you name the scam, and I'll bet it's been done here. After a while, it sends a message: Strangers equal trouble."

"It's pretty close-minded," I commented, scanning the room for Penny. I was beginning to grudgingly admit that the hovering scents were making my stomach growl. It had been long hours since my McBreakfast. "I guess that explains why there's no corporate presence here."

Michael arched an eyebrow. "What do you mean?"

I shrugged. "Everything here's a mom-and-pop," I said. "I haven't even seen name brand gasoline."

Penny appeared with two glasses of water and an impatient glare, her pen poised above a pad of tickets. "You boys know what you want?" On closer inspection, Penny looked like she was about twelve.

"Two specials," said Michael automatically, not bothering to confer with either the menu or me.

"Grits or potatoes?"

"Potatoes."

"Home fries or mashed?"

"Mashed."

"Gravy?"

"Oh, yeah. And a couple of Ale-8s, please," Michael smiled politely, and Penny was off.

"Thanks," I said dryly. "I haven't had my dinner ordered for me since I was five. What's the special?"

"Slow-cooked rabbit," said Michael, and I involuntarily grimaced. "Oh, come on," he said. "You can't tell me you've never had rabbit. Gina said your father used to hunt all the time."

"Then she must have told you we never actually *ate* it," I said. "I mean, Dad loves the stuff, but to me, it's like dark meat chicken. Yuck."

Michael laughed. "That's almost word-for-word what she said. But she agreed to keep an open mind, and she absolutely loved it. Ida may not be the friendliest old gal, but she knows her way around a kitchen. Wait until you taste the gravy. I've never had anything like it in my entire life. If I drowned in a vat of the stuff, I could almost say I'd died and gone to heaven."

I was irritated. I didn't like this stranger telling me things he shouldn't know about my family. "For future reference, I'm capable of choosing my own lunch," I warned.

"Hey, if you want, I'm sure you can change it." He started to flag Penny, but I caught his arm and pulled it down.

75

"I'll try it," I said. "Just don't do it again." I was aware of inquiring glares that continued to emanate from the diner floor and was growing uncomfortable under the scrutiny. I didn't want to turn my nose up at what was obviously popular with the locals, judging from the grisly heaps on their plates.

Michael returned to my earlier observation. "It's really not surprising that there's no corporate presence here," he said. "There aren't enough people here to make it worth their while."

"I suppose not." I was watching through the plate glass storefront as two men in coveralls scaled ladders across the street from one another, pulling a banner high into the air. *Apple Festival. Thursday through Sunday's Apple Bake-Off. BRING THE WHOLE FAMILY!*

Michael followed my gaze. "Must be some festival," he said with a grin as Penny placed our food in front of us.

"It sure is," she said with a thin smile. His sarcasm hadn't been lost on her. "Matter of fact, it's a hell of a good time. Everybody just sort of cuts loose and hangs out in the square. There's corn dogs and cotton candy and pony rides. I bet the kids 'round here would rank it about second after Christmas." She leaned across the counter toward Michael. "What do *you* do for fun?" she asked sweetly, and I wasn't sure if she was flirting or teasing. I caught a distinct trace of alcohol on her breath and wondered again how old she could possibly be. I was turning beet red on Michael's behalf, yet he seemed to take it all in stride.

"Might just have to give the festival a try. Sounds like fun," he said with a smile. "Are all the girls as pretty as you?"

My embarrassment shifted to downright outrage as I watched my sister's supposed boyfriend flirt outright in response to this pit-scarred skank's come-on. "I don't think Gina would appreciate that," I said, my words tight and clipped. Michael tried to communicate his intent with his eyes, and had I not only recently lost my sister, I would have probably realized he was trying to sweeten her up so he might ask some questions. I might also have heard the diner door slam. Instead, I added, "I mean she *is* your girlfriend, isn't she?"

"No, you bastard, she's *my* girlfriend!"

I swiveled my stool toward the booming exclamation just in time to see one of the behemoths who had been hanging the banner charge through the restaurant and knock Michael Arthur to the floor.

CHAPTER SEVEN

I jumped to my feet and took a couple of steps backward. The entire diner had fallen silent, and all eyes were locked on us.

To my astonishment, Michael laughed. He dabbed at the trickle of blood at the corner of his mouth and *laughed*. The behemoth was not amused. His hand, still clenched in a fist, drew back as Michael stood up.

"Carter!" barked Penny with more authority than I would have guessed her capable. "Leave this boy alone! He didn't do nothin'!"

The behemoth named Carter paused, then turned his hateful gaze to his girlfriend. She jutted out her jaw and stood her ground. The air was so tense, I don't recall breathing. "I don't remember asking your opinion," he flatly stated.

Ida burst through the swinging kitchen doors, flustered and in no mood for any of this. "Carter Jenkins, get your ass out of my restaurant! You know I don't put up with you boys roughnecking."

Carter turned his fury on Ida and ground his teeth.

"I mean it," she said with a firm nod. "Do you want me to call Bill? How would that look?"

I was lost, but I could feel the situation starting to deescalate. Michael stood and took a sip of water, looking far smugger than I would have dared in his position. Carter Jenkins's forearms were the size of fire hydrants.

With a final grunt and a slight spray of spittle, he turned around and stormed out.

I stood open-mouthed as conversations resumed and Ida and Penny returned to their duties. "What in the hell just happened there?"

Michael shrugged as Penny returned with our dinners. "He thought I was flirting with his girlfriend." A booth had opened along the southern wall, and we claimed it.

"You were," I reminded. Penny flashed a quick smile.

"I didn't *know* she was his girlfriend."

I turned to Penny. "Are you going to be in any trouble over this? I mean—"

"You mean, is he gonna smack me around when I get home?" she smiled again. "He wouldn't dare. He's just real jealous, you know?" She turned her smile to Michael before returning to the kitchen.

I shook my head as I took my seat. I tried not to look directly at the questionable pile of gelatinous glop in front of me. "So, this is just all in a day's work for you?" I asked. "That guy was *huge*. It had to have hurt like hell when he hit you."

Again, a shrug. "Yeah, sure it hurt. But it pissed me off more than it hurt. I don't back down."

"Back down? From what?"

He looked me squarely in the eyes and lowered his voice. "Anything. That's why I need to know what's really happened here. I need to know if there's any possibility that Gina's death was not an accident. If it wasn't, there are some people who are gonna have to pay."

I mulled that over and was glad Michael was on my side. "You know, about that—exactly how are we going to proceed from here? We really haven't put together any kind of game plan."

He looked at me expectantly. "You're the private detective," he said. "That's why I brought you along."

"I'm not *really* a private detective—"

He sighed and impatiently waved my words away. "You can't hide behind that forever," he said. "You've solved three pretty high-profile cases. I think it's okay to claim responsibility."

I supposed he was right. I wasn't exactly sure why I insisted on reminding everyone of my perceived limitations, but the words always seemed to be falling from my mouth. And it wasn't like anyone was paying me for my time here. I had the best incentive I'd ever had to work a case. My sister may have been murdered, and I had to know the truth.

"So, we're tracking her movements," I said.

"Bingo. You'll just carry that camera around your neck wherever you go and take an occasional picture for 'authenticity.'" He provided air quotes. "I don't know the full scope of her day any more than she knew mine. If she saw something that really shook her up, we need to find out where she's been."

"And you were going to accomplish this by flirting with that waitress?"

"Hey, you have no idea how much Penny sees. This is the only diner in town that serves the lunch crowd. Gina probably ate here every day. Penny might have seen her meet with someone or overheard her talking about something. That could apply to any one of the people in this place. But if we don't make a couple of inroads here and there, they're not going to say a thing to us."

I poked at the glop with a fork and dragged some through a pile of mashed potatoes. I had to admit, it *did* smell good, and I was starving. I decided one bite wouldn't kill me and lifted fork to mouth. My eyes may have rolled completely back in my head as the savory concoction found my tastebuds. "Okay," I said, after swallowing and suppressing the urge to moan inappropriate appreciation. "What do we actually know? How long were you and Gina here before?"

"I think she had been here since late-June," said Michael, wiping the corner of his mouth with a napkin.

"You didn't arrive at the same time?" I asked.

"Nope," said Michael. "I didn't get the lead on the story I was working until about a week later. I guess it was just chance that put us in such close proximity."

"So weird," I said, absently collecting another forkful from my plate. "I could have sworn Melanie said Gina was flying in from Italy for our brother's wedding."

"Who's Melanie?"

"She's *my* better half," I said, grinning. It hadn't even been a day, and I missed her already.

"Well, it's entirely possible Gina told people that. If she's working undercover, she might bend the truth a little. Not to mention it made your mom a lot happier to imagine her daughter against a European backdrop versus some of the places she's actually been."

"So, what was her cover story?"

Michael cleared his throat and took a drink from his Ale-8. "She told folks she was here to learn about life in a small mining town now that the mine has been closed for decades. She wondered what kept people here when the economy was drying up around them."

I surveyed the room. While we still drew the occasional side eye, most of the folks had returned to their own lunches and earnest conversations, and it was difficult to pick up any particular thread. Clinking and chewing were punctuated intermittently by laughter, and I had the strangest sensation I had traveled back in time. Country music wafted through unseen speakers at a barely detectible level, and I suddenly realized what seemed so out-of-place.

There wasn't a cell phone in sight.

I did a double take and checked again. Not a single one. I hadn't seen a gathering of people so firmly engaged in the moment—so *present*, in quite some time. Conversation flowed without text messages or news alerts to distract participants. No abrasive electronic ringtones intruded into the exclusively human soundtrack. It was downright eerie.

"What?" asked Michael, finishing the last of his rabbit.

"No phones," I said absently as Penny sidled up to our table.

"Did you boys save room for dessert?" she asked, poised to add to our lunch tab.

"No—" I began, but Michael interrupted.

"We'll each have a piece of Ida's heavenly pecan pie," he said. "Warm with vanilla ice cream on top."

I shot him a look as Penny headed back to the kitchen. "I thought I told—"

He lifted his hands in surrender. "I promise, it's the last time. But you haven't lived until you've had this pie."

I'm not sure we walked so much as waddled out the restaurant. Michael had to again foot the bill because I was completely cash poor. I was so accustomed to covering expenses with either a credit or debit card that cash had pretty much completely fallen out of favor with me. I'd rather cancel a lost or stolen card than say goodbye forever to lost or stolen currency.

"I'm going to need to find an ATM," I said, eyeing the businesses that fronted on the town square. "Otherwise, this trip is going to get very expensive for you. Is there a bank in this town?"

"There's a credit union for the local farmers just down the street," he said, pointing to a cinderblock facade on the opposite corner. *Briarstaff Farmers Savings & Loan* was engraved above the door with *Members Only* in smaller text just below. "Let's walk off some of this lunch. I can give you the lay of the land, or at least as much of it as I know."

"I left my camera in the back of your car. Maybe I should grab it. You know—authenticity."

He nodded. "Sure."

After I collected the Minolta and strapped it around my neck, we headed south on a broken and buckled sidewalk that would have been daunting to anyone who was even remotely balance challenged. It was difficult to ignore the eyes following us everywhere we went. I fought the urge to do a quick 360, waving hello to everyone just to get it over with.

We approached the southeast corner of the courtyard, technically the intersection of Summit and Main Streets. Straight ahead and across the street was the aforementioned Sally's Flowers, and if I wasn't mistaken, Sally herself was doing a pretty poor job of pretending to maintain the plants in the window display as she strained to get a better look at us. She had gradually drifted away from the flowering plant she was misting with her spray bottle and was currently dousing the front glass, all the while her mouth hanging slightly open. I *did* wave at her just to see the startled expression on her face as her mouth snapped shut, and she quickly pivoted away.

A large flatbed truck entered the square from the southwestern corner, diesel engine grumbling and pumping black exhaust into the air. On its bed was what appeared to be the makings of a Ferris wheel. It turned left and eased its way to the curb along an area that had been designated by orange cones. A smaller truck filled with migrant workers followed, and they swarmed like busy ants towards the carnival attraction just as soon as the truck had come to a complete stop. Just as they began unloading components, an officious looking woman in a tangerine pantsuit practically burst out of the entrance of Briarstaff Farmers Savings & Loan, hustling across the street while waving her hands above her head to get the workers' attention. She had fiery auburn hair piled high and was extraordinarily surefooted in heels that lent inches to her height. She was yelling and pointing directions that didn't carry all the way back to us, but she looked supremely irritated. A wave of confusion was followed by one of understanding, and the men shifted course and began carrying their payload about a hundred feet further north in the town square, the woman barking at them the whole while.

"I guess this Apple Festival is some big deal," I remarked, shielding my eyes, and watching more locals gather to watch the wonder before them. Children of all ages were drawn like magnets, on foot and running or legs pumping pedals of their bicycles for all they were worth. They didn't give two shits about us—*this* was the stuff of wonder. They collected in small groups and watched in awe as components began to be unloaded from the flatbed. It reminded me of when I was young and how much I looked forward to the Scioto County Fair every year.

"I would guess this is no small boon to the local economy," said Michael. We had reached the corner nearest the truck and found ourselves momentarily mesmerized. "I imagine the concession stands will arrive soon, but there isn't room for many more rides."

"Mr. Arthur!"

I looked up and saw the woman in tangerine hustling our way, waving like she was trying to hail a taxi.

"Caroline!" Michael said warmly, taking her hand while she struggled to catch her breath. "It's Michael…remember? Looks like a lot of excitement."

"Looks like a lot of *work*," she said, smiling as she neatly equated her spastic guidance with the labor-intensive efforts of the workers. "Where's your lady friend?"

"I'm actually doing her a favor," he said smoothly, and I was glad he was taking the lead. "Gina wasn't able to return this week but thought it might add to the piece she was working on if she had additional photos from the Apple Festival. This is her brother, Dwayne Morrow. He's no stranger to photography."

"Caroline Peterson," she said, shifting the back of her dainty hand to me. I felt like I should either kiss it or bow but settled on a light handshake instead. "I'm the president of Briarstaff Farmers."

"Nice to meet you," I said. "Michael was just saying how the Apple Festival must be wonderful for your local businesses. How is attendance?"

She blinked at me absently. "I think just about everybody comes at least once. Most participate in one way or another."

"I guess I meant attendance from your surrounding counties," I clarified. "It must be helpful to have additional money flowing in."

Her expression suggested I had just taken a shit on her foot. "Mr. Morrow, the Apple Festival is a celebration for the people of Briarstaff *by* the people of Briarstaff. We are quite fiscally sound. We don't require the assistance of outsiders." The temperature in our immediate vicinity had dropped by degrees as color crept into Caroline's cheeks.

"I'm sorry," I said, automatically backpedaling. "And please—call me Dwayne. It wasn't my intention to imply there was any sort of codependency necessary here, and I certainly didn't mean to offend." I glanced at Michael who looked equally lost.

Caroline pressed her lips together, and it was like watching a pressure relief valve in action as her color slowly returned to normal. "I'm sure you didn't," she finally said. "I'm just a little high-strung today. Among other things, I am the event organizer and am responsible for just about everything in our 'little event.'" The phonetic air-quotes let me know I wasn't *entirely* off the hook.

Michael chuckled uneasily before producing another warm smile. "I was just about to give Dwayne a ten-cent tour of the town square, but as a lifelong resident of Briarstaff and senior member of the Executive Council of the Chamber of Commerce, I'm sure you would do a much better job than I ever could—provided, of course, you have the time."

Turning toward Michael, she warmed considerably. "Well—oh, all right, Michael. Only for you." She cast a dubious glance toward the men who continued to unload the festival attraction. "It's probably helpful if they see me out here anyway. You wouldn't believe how things grind to a halt when they think they're not being watched. It's hard enough to make them understand the simplest of instructions."

She turned and headed the direction from which we'd come. Michael followed, and I fell in step beside him.

"I think it's appropriate if we start here," said Caroline, indicating the smattering of buildings that were east of the town square on Main Street. "Our town jail is that narrow little red building on the left side of the street. Built in 1923, most of its framework is original, which is why, you might notice, it leans just a bit. It also has a real tendency to flood when there's a heavy rain, but we consider it a landmark and have learned to live with its shortcomings. Sheriff Charley Daniel's office is inside, and *no*, before you ask, he is *not* the singer of that demon in Georgia song. There is exactly one jail cell, and it is almost always available, so my advice is to stay out of trouble." She directed this at me, followed by an affected arpeggio of laughter that was delivered in a staggering assortment of sharp notes before resuming her tour guide cadence.

"That's Emmitt's Family Restaurant. Emmitt Brown is perhaps Briarstaff's most distinguished councilmen as well as one of its oldest citizens. But don't let his age fool you. He's still very active in community affairs. He spends at least a portion of every single day in his restaurant, not just overseeing but rolling up his sleeves and preparing some of its finest dishes as well." I flashed on the rabbit we had just consumed for lunch, and it was as if Caroline had read my mind. "Don't even bother showing up dressed as you are now. Gentlemen are required to wear jackets and ladies their Sunday best. You'd be turned away."

"I'm surprised there's enough business to share with Ida's up the street," Michael noted.

"Completely different clientele. And besides, Ida is Emmitt's daughter. It all stays in the family." She indicated a vacant store front beside Harvey's Video. "Another story entirely with these folks. Guy from Ohio tried to make a run of a pizza shop with his son and his family. It was called the Pizza Depository, or something ridiculous like that. You can get personal pizzas at Tommy's Chevron about a half mile down Main. What in the world were they *thinking?*"

A-ha! Chevron! At last, a business name I recognized!

"Well, then, clearly Tommy must be Ida's son," I joked, and Caroline turned abruptly.

"How did you know? I certainly hope you gentlemen aren't wasting my time."

Michael was quick to cover. "Of course not! Dwayne's just being funny." He shot me a warning look, and we silently agreed it would be best for me to keep my big mouth shut.

"I should beg to differ," said Caroline, and this time, the side eye was all mine. "In any event, they barely lasted a year before realizing they just didn't belong here. The son was amusing, but all of the rest were just—" She trailed away and shuddered.

We rounded the corner and continued past Ida's Town Diner. Caroline's ability to navigate the uneven sidewalk in her heels was extraordinary. I feared she could take a tumble at any moment, and I, of course, would laugh which would likely be my final misstep.

"Here we have our 'his' and 'hers' grooming," she said, indicating twin one-story bungalows that sat side-by-side next to Ida's. Paul's Barber Shop was emblazoned on the front window of the nearest, with an old-timey barber's pole, rotating red, white and blue at a snail's pace. Next was Pauline's Dippity Do, its front window featuring what appeared to be the silhouette of a 1950s Barbie perched beneath a hooded hair dryer. "Paul and Pauline Dixon are our twins. He keeps our fellas presentable, and there isn't a thing Pauline can't do with a few bobby pins and a teasing comb."

We continued past, and Caroline paused at the next building, a two-story symmetrical Colonial with a wide, covered porch supported by ornate fluted columns. She turned with her hands on her hips, her cheeks flushed with pride. "And *this*," she said, indicating the house with a flourish, "is one of my very favorite Briarstaff institutions—"

The front door opened as if on cue, and a well-groomed gentleman straight from a high-end menswear catalog emerged, smiling and waving. "Caroline!" he called before trotting down the porch steps and joining us on the sidewalk. She put her arms around him and give him a quick peck on the lips.

"This is Briarstaff's most brilliant legal mind—"

"*Only* legal mind," he interrupted with a laugh, casually smoothing his all-too-perfect hair.

Caroline squeezed him again. "My husband, Troy. He handles any and all legal matters for the community and is a real force to be reckoned with. He's not so hard on the eyes, either."

I struggled not to roll my eyes. *Get a room!*

"Dwayne Morrow," I said, extending a hand.

He took it and shook the teeth right out of my head. "Morrow? Isn't that—"

"Yes. You met my sister, Gina. She was here taking photos of the old mine and the town it helped support. She asked me to follow-up with some shots from the Apple Festival. It's hard to imagine you would have much to do here," I mused aloud and instantly regretted it. Caroline and Troy turned in unison, their expressions competing to convey the most disdain.

I attempted to correct course. "What I meant to say is that everything seems so ideal here, it's hard to picture a lot of litigation amongst the residents."

The hard lines in Troy's face softened first. "Well, no. We *are* a peaceful little American town. Generations have grown up here. We wouldn't want to be anywhere else. Much of what I do is act as a liaison between local, state and federal governments, as well as dealing with any zoning issues that might arise."

Caroline crinkled her nose. "We wouldn't want to let any of the wrong people in."

I struggled to keep my mouth from dropping open and chanced a peek in Michael's direction. His expression remained remarkably neutral.

"I know it's not particularly 'politically correct' to admit this," Caroline continued, "but whenever we take a chance and let down our guard, we almost always regret it. Do you remember me telling you about those fellows from Ohio?"

"The ones with the pizza store," said Michael. "Sure."

"Son had a thing for alcohol and gambling," she said. "Now, technically, Briarstaff is dry—if you want beer or hard liquor, you'll have to go to Shawnee or Burkettsville to scratch that itch. Of course, you're welcome to imbibe on your own premises—far be it from *me* to dictate what goes on in the privacy of one's own home."

I had more than a little trouble believing that.

"But he was very charming," she continued. "Had several of the town's ladies under his spell and was always able to find common ground with the gentlemen. I say all of that to say this: most of the business owners on the square are members of the Fraternal Order of Eldermen. You can always find several of them any night of the week in the hall over there, playing cards and shooting the breeze." Caroline pointed toward a squat, grey structure facing the northwest corner of the square.

"Some friendly wagers, nothing more," added Troy. "And while we don't sell liquor here, it's pretty common for members to bring their own, maybe even share. I have been known to spend the occasional evening myself."

I couldn't tell from Caroline's expression whether she approved or not. "Anyway, as a representative of his little pizza parlor, he was determined to ingratiate himself to other businessmen in this town—"

"Especially, Emmitt Brown," added Troy.

"Yes," Caroline nodded. "Emmitt saw these outsiders as a direct threat to his own family businesses. He wasn't nearly so trusting as some of the other men, but they allowed him to apply for membership to the Order, and once he paid his dues, he was provisionally accepted, pending a vote by the entire group."

"Always puzzled me," Troy observed, frowning. "I know they were struggling to keep their little business afloat, but he always seemed to have cash when we came to the table, and it was at least two or three nights a week."

"Word around town was he was dipping into their nightly deposits," Caroline almost whispered. "But far be it from *me* to gossip."

Far be it, indeed. Sheer willpower kept my eyes from heading toward the heavens.

"One Saturday night, he didn't bring very much to the table. Beer? Yes. Money, not so much. Claimed he had left his wallet at home when he changed his clothes after work, and several of the members offered to spot him so they could just go on playing." Troy's expression conveyed he *wasn't* one of said members. "I've never seen such a losing streak. Kept thinking the next hand would be better, and it never was. By the end of the evening, he was down several thousand dollars."

"So, what happened?" Michael asked.

"He had bought himself enough goodwill among the members to hold them off until the following Monday. Neither his pizza shop nor the F.O.E. hall was open on Sundays—not much *is*."

"The Lord's Day," I added, and I really needed to get a handle on my tone. While I meant nothing whatsoever by it—I have a healthy respect for the religious views of others—it came out remarkably condescending even in my own ears.

Color crept back into Caroline's cheeks. Her eyes narrowed and her mouth opened, but her response was cut off by a bloodcurdling scream reverberating throughout the square.

It sounded like a child.

I immediately broke away from our group and headed toward the center of the square. Michael took the perimeter while Troy and Caroline froze like statues. I couldn't immediately detect the source. The sound was so piercing even the workers had paused, silencing their power tools and other equipment. I realized none of the children who had come to watch the Ferris wheel be erected were still in the square when the scream cut through again, louder and even more chilling. I ran toward the western side of the square, following my ears toward a narrow alley between the two central business fronts on that flank.

I rushed into the alley and skidded to a stop.

Here were all the children, gathered in a semi-circle with their bikes and skateboards tossed to one side of the alley or the other. They were throwing rocks and chanting obscenities at a small young boy whose stick-thin arms did little good in shielding himself from the onslaught. He was outnumbered ten to one, and only one obvious difference hit me immediately.

He was Black.

CHAPTER EIGHT

"*H*ey!" I dug deep and found my loudest voice, disrupting the chanting and inserting myself into the semi-circle. My sudden presence jolted the children from their tribal state, and they began to back away, lowering their arms and dropping projectiles. A few on the periphery made a break for it, but not before I uncapped my camera and began snapping pictures of the little monsters.

"What in the hell do you think you're *doing?*" I demanded of all of them, and they continued to sneak away until the last one practically ran headlong into Michael, who had just reached the mouth of the alley. I kneeled to help the little boy to his feet. His eyes were wide with terror and filled with tears, and he only accepted my help long enough to right his own bicycle. Once that was accomplished, he hopped aboard and tore away just as fast as his thin little legs could pump.

"What happened?" asked Michael looking from me back to the children scattering across the town square and off into the surrounding neighborhoods.

I was dumbfounded. "I'm not completely sure." I headed back toward the entrance of the alley. "I think I might have just stopped a lynching."

Troy and Caroline chose that moment to join us, and Caroline laughed dismissively. "Oh, now, Mr. *Morrow!* Don't be so melodramatic. I'm sure it was just boys being boys."

I couldn't believe my ears. *"Boys being boys?* 'Get your ass back up to Spook Ridge where it belongs'—is that *boys being boys?"*

"Calm down, Mr. Morrow," said Troy, his smile back in place. *"Spielman* Ridge—you must have misheard."

"I'm pretty sure I understood what they meant to do with all of those rocks," I said, indicating the cast aside ammunition.

"Who *knows* what happened?" Caroline said airily, shrugging her shoulders. "He must have done *something.* That many boys couldn't have been wrong."

I was thunderstruck. Disbelief widened my eyes as heat rushed into my face. My mouth opened on full autopilot when Michael took me by the shoulders and gave an almost imperceptible shake of his head. He guided me toward the mouth of the alley where the Petersons waited, but not before I caught another warning glance begging me to shut up. Acid was beginning to roil through my stomach, but I held my tongue. Focusing on the Petersons, Michael managed a smile and tried to pull us back on course. "You were telling us about the pizza guy losing his shirt."

Troy and Caroline exchanged a glance before continuing down the sidewalk toward the southwest corner, and we fell in step behind them. "Where was I?" he continued. "Oh, yes—he was going to repay his debt on Monday. But when Monday rolled around, he and his entire family had completely cleared town. They just dropped everything and ran. Left behind all sorts of equipment in his restaurant."

"And the houses they were renting?" Caroline gasped and patted her chest. "You wouldn't *believe* the state they left them in."

"And no one has heard from them since," said Troy. "And that is just one example of why we are slow to warm to strangers. Always seems to bite us in the end."

We had come full circle and once again stood in front of Briarstaff Farmers Credit Union.

"You'll have to excuse me, gentlemen," said Caroline. "I've given you as much of my day as I can. I can only imagine what's waiting for me back on my desk." She shifted her attention to her husband. "Can you pick up Audrey after practice? I'm sure I'll be running late tonight after all this." She gestured in our general direction as if there was any doubt we were the source of her inconvenience.

"Certainly, darling," he said, leaning in for a kiss. "Do you want me to pick something up for dinner?"

"I'm guessing it won't be pizza," I said, attempting a little humor once again. They stared at me like I was from Mars.

"That would be lovely," she said, patting his hand.

"One last thing," said Michael as Caroline started to break away. "Is your bank able to provide a cash advance for Mr. Morrow against his credit card? He didn't realize how few places accepted credit here."

She looked at me pityingly. "I'm so sorry. We only transact business with Briarstaff Farmers customers. But I'm sure you can find someone to help you in Shawnee. It's only about thirty miles west on Route 5. You all have a good day, now."

She turned and trotted up the stairs, disappearing through the double glass doors while her husband looked on appreciatively. "Well, if there isn't anything else, gentlemen, I should probably get back to my own office," he said. "With so little to do, I'm overdue for my afternoon nap." His sarcasm was duly noted as he winked at me and shot me with a finger pistol.

"Maybe just one more thing," I said, and Michael's expression pleaded with me to stop before I dug us any further into a hole. "My sister asked me to take some shots of the Apple Festival, but since it doesn't actually begin until tomorrow, I've got a little time to kill. I'm interested in seeing the mining site she was here to photograph. Could we get directions?"

"Well, I don't see why not," said Troy, shielding his eyes and scanning the square. He noticed Michael's bright yellow Fiesta parked across the way near Ida's Town Diner. "Is that your car? You'll never make it there in that. The main roads to the quarry have been closed for over twenty years and the only access is by rural routes, but I might just have a suggestion."

We followed him as he crossed the street to where an ancient, rusting Ford F-150 pickup was parked at an angle, its homemade wooden bed facing the workers who had resumed assembly of the Ferris wheel. A lanky, dark-haired boy wearing overalls and no shirt lounged against a bale of hay in the back, a baseball capped tipped down over his closed eyes, and a piece of straw jutting out from between his teeth. It was like walking into the world of Tom Sawyer.

"Hey, Shane," Troy called, startling the boy.

He sat upright and pushed the baseball cap back, squinting against the sun and focusing on us as we approached. A broad grin brought dimples to his freckled and slightly sunburned face, and he offered a loose, two-fingered salute. "Mr. Peterson! How are you doing this fine Wednesday afternoon?"

"Right as rain, Shane," said Troy, pleased with his own impromptu rhyme. "And you?"

"Just supervising," he said, gesturing toward the small army of workers. They had finished unloading the components from the first flatbed truck and were in the process of guiding it back out of the square and onto Route 5 in the direction from which it had come. I noticed another flatbed pulled to the side, waiting its turn to enter the square and unload cargo once the first one was gone. "They're doing fine work, now, aren't they?"

Troy nodded and laughed, while the pronouns hit me all wrong. I worked to suppress the sour expression that threatened to creep across my face. Troy took the boy's hand and pulled him toward the open gate of the truck from which he sprung to his feet onto the sidewalk. I am a little over six feet in height, and he was slightly taller than me, which I found a little disconcerting. I wasn't used to looking up for many. "This is Michael Arthur and Dwayne Morrow. I believe you may have met Mr. Morrow's sister a couple of weeks ago."

Shane's face lit up. "No *way! You're* Gina's brother? Well, how about that!" He grabbed my hand in both of his and jerked it up and down while Michael looked amused. "You don't look a thing alike. She's so nice and pretty, and—" His words caught up to him and he flushed.

"You left out smart," I said, finally able to extract my hand before all the blood had been separated by centrifugal force. "But yes, she's my sister. I've got pictures of us and the parents to prove it. And this is her boyfriend, Michael Arthur."

Michael was subjected to the same bone-rattling two-handed handshake.

"Shane Van Buren," the boy said, goofy grin still firmly in place. His face had the same effect as a smiley face emoticon, and it was impossible not to return his smile. "Most happy to make your acquaintance." He surrendered Michael's hand. "You, sir, are a very lucky fella."

"Well, thank you. I'd like to think so," said Michael, beaming. He was really quite good at keeping his emotions in check.

"I seem to recall you assisted Ms. Morrow with transportation around town," interjected Troy, and Shane nodded enthusiastically. Troy turned to us. "Well, there you go, fellas. I'm sure Shane would be happy to assist you with the locale, if he's available and you're willing to compensate him for his time and gasoline."

"Oh, don't you worry about my time," said Shane. "I'd be happy to do it. Haven't had a thing to do all day. But Opie *is* a thirsty beast." He patted the side of his truck.

"Of course," said Michael, pulling out his wallet and handing Shane a couple of twenties. "Will this do?"

He snatched the twenties and snapped to attention, attempting a more authentic salute. "Shane Van Buren, at your service!"

·······•••⊖⊙•••••·····

Michael had chosen the passenger side of the F-150's bench seat while I opted for the true hillbilly experience and had hoisted myself into the open truck bed. I nearly sat on an acoustic guitar before almost impaling my hand on a pitchfork, both of which were partially obscured by the liberal dusting of hay scattered within. The throaty rumble of the truck's powerful engine vibrated through my frame, and I sincerely doubted the presence of a muffler or, for that matter, any sort of emissions control. I hunkered down and hoped Shane's driving wouldn't bounce me straight out onto the pavement.

We stopped at the aforementioned Tommy's Chevron on Route 5 so Shane could top off his tank. Weatherworn signage advertised the current price of various grades of gasoline, but more importantly, the cheapest prices in the state for cigarettes and other tobacco products. The small cinderblock storefront was situated on a narrow strip of land with two antique fuel pumps in its side lot and a handful of parking spaces facing the building, most of which were occupied. Apparently, accessibility was of no concern—none of the parking was designated as handicapped. It was beginning to dawn on me that none of the vehicles in town had been manufactured in the past decade or so, and domestic automakers were the clear preference. While Shane waited for his turn at the pump behind another ancient and corroding truck, I hopped out of the truck bed and joined Michael at the side of the building.

"What in the hell kind of place *is* this?" I said, finally able to freely express myself. "Did you hear what those kids were *saying?* Did you see what they were *doing?*"

"I did not," said Michael, shaking his head.

"Well, *I* did. It was unbelievable. I can't believe in this day and age—"

"You need to calm down," said Michael, scanning the lot to make sure we weren't overheard. "Take a good look around. Our concept of 'this day and age' is considerably different than what we're experiencing here."

"Well, they won't get away with it," I said, indicating the camera that hung around my neck. "I got pictures of each and every one of those hellions—"

"And who are you going to show them to?"

"I can't believe the parents would—"

"You have no fucking *idea* what the parents may or may not think," he hissed, staring me into silence. "I am absolutely *not* condoning any of that, but you really need to refocus, here. They probably learned all that behavior right at home. Our priority is Gina, remember?"

I nodded grudgingly. "Yes. Of course."

"If we have any hope whatsoever of finding out if she stumbled into something that might have brought trouble her way, we can't begin by pissing off all of the natives. I lost count of how many times you almost single-handedly derailed us in less time than it took to walk around the fucking town square!" His eyes were hot and angry, and I immediately felt foolish.

"I'm sorry," I said. "It was just so unexpected—"

"Why should you expect *anything* at this point? Right now, we're just trying to follow in Gina's footsteps, gather some information—"

"Okay, okay—"

"Which we will not be able to do if you alienate every single person in this fucking town!"

"*Okay!*" I threw my hands up in surrender. "Fine. I get it."

Our volume had crept up several decibels, and we both noticed Shane watching us from the pump, where he was now dispensing gasoline into his still-idling truck. Ignoring everything my father had ever told me about this dangerous practice, I kept the safety advice to myself. I had said too much today already. I took a deep breath and massaged my forehead, trying to formulate a plan for how best to utilize Mr. Van Buren's time.

···•••••●◯●•••••···

"So, where to, fellas?" Shane asked once we had regrouped in the truck. I was still propped up in the truck bed on a bale of hay, but he had slid open a panel in the back glass so I could interact with him and Michael. "I can't say there's a whole lot to see, but I'd be happy to show you what there is."

"We'd like to see the mines," said Michael. "Gina said they were really something to see."

Shane beamed. "I think that's maybe me and my friends' favorite place."

"The abandoned mines? Aren't they dangerous?" I asked.

"We don't go *in* the mines. They've been barricaded forever. But there's a rock quarry across from the main entrance that's filled with the most beautiful water you ever did see. It's the best place in the whole county to swim, and if you're brave enough, there are a couple of awesome spots to dive. Also, the girls like to keep up their tans by sunning on the rocks, which ain't exactly hard on *our* eyes." He winked, his laugh good-natured and contagious.

Shane pulled onto Route 5 and headed back the way we had come, taking us past the town square, where the workers had almost finished assembling

99

the base of the Ferris wheel. We continued further east, past the jail and Emmitt's Family Restaurant. As the town faded into the distance, the two-lane road narrowed, and we were soon under cover of ancient maples, spruce and pines whose interlocking branches were like hands held high overhead. The road had been laid where geography allowed, and we soon were zigging and zagging through a series of hairpin curves, over hills and into stomach-dropping dips, all of it a little too quickly for my liking, but Shane navigated with the familiarity of a native. Occasionally, the dense foliage would abruptly drop away, affording magnificent views of a cloudless, deep blue sky with mountains in the distance as well as a sudden reminder of our current elevation by virtue of a steep drop-off immediately to our left.

We traveled maybe five miles or so before Shane slowed and eased right onto what could only loosely be called a road. It would be easy to miss entirely if you didn't know it was there. A narrow ribbon of rutted dirt peppered with coarse gravel ran up a steep, densely wooded hill only to disappear over its crest, leading to who knows where. With barely enough width for one vehicle, it was an invitation to the greatest game of chicken ever, and I wondered how many vehicles had fallen prey to poor timing.

Shane glanced back over his shoulder and said through the open sliding panel, "You might want to brace yourself, Mr. Morrow. I'll try and take it slow, but it gets a little bumpy through here." With that, he launched us up the dirt road, my teeth clacking together with a sudden jolt. I dug my hands into the bale of hay and held on for dear life as we sped forward, traversing terrain that had been pitted and scarred by years of exposure to the elements. There were moments I could have sworn we were airborne only to be reminded otherwise when the truck's suspension bottomed out, jarring every bone in my body. Never one prone to motion sickness, I was struggling mightily to keep my lunch down when we suddenly crested a final hill before grinding to a halt, gravel crunching underneath the truck's tires. Shane killed the engine, and after one backfire that sounded like a gunshot, the silence was immediate and deafening.

"Here we are," he said, dropping down from the driver's side.

I struggled to free myself from the bale of hay and into an upright position without losing any more of my dignity while Michael stepped down nimbly from the passenger side and surveyed our surroundings, whistling long and slow.

"Kinda takes your breath away, huh?" Shane beamed from ear-to-ear, clearly pleased.

"It sure does," agreed Michael.

I hooked my right leg over the side of the truck bed and nearly face planted when my left foot caught a shoelace on one of the tuning keys of Shane's acoustic guitar.

"Here, let me get that," said Shane, steadying me with one hand while extracting his guitar with the other.

"Yeah, sorry about that. I don't think I broke anything, but—" I fumbled.

"No worries at *all*, Mr. Morrow," he said, slinging it by its strap over his shoulder. "This old thing has more battle scars than you have teeth. No harm done. Are *you* okay?"

Other than complete and utter graceless humiliation, *sure!*

"I'm fine," I said, finally putting my feet on the ground. "I'm not usually so clumsy. I—"

I had been brushing errant strands of hay from my khakis, but when I finally looked up, my voice trailed away. We stood at the edge of a vast clearing of hard-packed sand, silt and clay that stretched in a long, narrow semi-circle downward to our left and upward toward jagged rock precipices to our right. Dense foliage bordered the woods behind and around us, and several hundred feet ahead, the earth dropped away abruptly while affording a spectacular view of the wooded mountainside miles ahead. My eyes followed the edge of the ridge to the left as its elevation dropped in fits and starts, and shimmering blue water was visible below in the distance. At the furthest end, roadblocks had been erected to dissuade adventurous souls from venturing further, but I doubted they had much impact on the truly curious.

I glanced back toward the right and was startled to see we weren't alone. A mid-80s yellow Camaro and was parked on the incline beside a decomposing and boxy Oldsmobile sedan. Its windows were rolled down, and I could vaguely hear the Eagles' smooth harmonies advising us to "Take It Easy." A pretty, dark-haired girl wearing a two-piece yellow swimsuit sprawled on an outcropping of rock beside a gangly, red-headed boy, shirtless in cut-off denims. They were oblivious to our arrival, blissfully soaking in the rays of the sun. A third teen was headed our way, bare feet accustomed to the craggy terrain. His blond hair was shaved close to his head, and his freckled and sunburnt skin made me wonder if they even knew about sunblock in these parts. Shane spotted his friend, shouting, "Yo!" before veering off to meet him halfway. They chest-bumped and fell into horseplay borne from years of friendship.

Michael and I exchanged a glance, shrugged and followed.

Shane dragged his friend back toward us with an arm thrown around his bare shoulders. "This here's my very best friend in the whole wide world, Nick Pollard. Nick, this is Mr. Dwayne Morrow and Mr. Michael—"

"Arthur," supplied Michael, extending a hand. Nick took it in both of his and pumped like he was priming a well. "And please, guys, it's just Michael and Dwayne."

"Nice to meet ya," he said, and then it was my turn. My knuckles throbbed when he finally released my hand. "What brings y'all to these parts? We don't get many strangers." There was no suspicion driving his question, only genuine curiosity.

"We're just getting some supplemental photos for my girlfriend, Gina, who spent a little time here recently," said Michael. "Maybe you met her?"

Both boys laughed. "Well, hell, yeah!" said Nick. "She spent a fair amount of time on this very spot. Seemed drawn to it. It really is something else." He openly admired our surroundings, and it would be impossible to argue his point. It was slightly surreal to know I was standing where my sister had stood only weeks before, and I couldn't afford to dwell. I was already having trouble keeping my grief in check.

Shane clamped an arm on my shoulder. "Mr. Dwayne, here, is Ms. Gina's brother," he said. "He's a photographer, too."

I smiled and nodded. "Nowhere *near* as good as Gina, but I get by," I said, surprised at the steadiness of my voice and the ease of my lie. I might someday get the hang of this. "She asked me to get some pictures of the Apple Festival to complement her article about Briarstaff and life after the mines."

"Oh, sure," said Nick. "The Apple Festival's loads of fun. Weather's supposed to be good, too."

By then, we had attracted the attention of the two sunbathing teens, and they had made their way over to join us. Shane handled introductions once more, and we learned the red-headed boy was appropriately named Rusty, and the dark-haired girl was Rose. All four were schoolmates at Briarstaff Senior High. I wondered to myself if they comprised the *entire* senior class—population couldn't have allowed for many more. Rusty had little to say beyond a single grunt, shifting awkwardly from foot to foot as the hot sand was clearly uncomfortable underneath, but Rose could barely contain her curiosity. Hands on hips, she stepped forward and squinted up at me. "You don't look much like your sister," she observed.

"I've heard that," I said. "She got the good genes."

She smiled crookedly. "I don't know I'd go *that* far," she said, and I felt my cheeks flush. Last thing I needed was a teenage Lolita fixating on me. "Where y'all from?"

"Grove City," I said, taking a step backward. "It's a suburb of Columbus in Ohio."

"And I've been based out of Washington, D.C. for the last few years," said Michael.

Rose's face soured. "Yuck. I can't imagine living there on purpose—no offense." Her apologetic grin was completely sincere, and Michael laughed.

"No harm done," he said. "I'm not crazy about it sometimes, either. Especially during the election cycles. But you go where your job takes you."

"Well, then, we've got nothing to worry about," said Rose, with Shane and Nick nodding in agreement. Rusty added nothing, just stared ahead with his mouth hanging slightly open. I was beginning to wonder if he might have special needs. Rose continued, "My daddy owns the IGA behind the town square. One day, it and all of its faithful customers will be mine, all mine."

Shane's thumb waggled between himself and his best friend. "Family farms," he said. "Mine does apples, and Nick's does corn. When we're in charge, we're going to combine them into one gigantic agricultural dynasty like nothing Briarstaff has ever seen." He and Nick sealed the deal with a quick high-five and more good-natured wrestling. Ah, the boundless exuberance and optimism of youth.

"How about you, Rusty?" asked Michael, and Rusty's face flushed while he began to stammer.

"Awwww, Rusty, don't you worry," said Rose, wrapping an arm around him and giving him a quick squeeze. "McCain's IGA can always use a good cart boy."

Rusty broke away as his complexion mottled to the point his freckles were practically green. "F-f-fuck you!" he said, and Rose laughed and clapped.

"Oh, come on, Rusty," said Nick, unable to keep a smile from playing across his lips. "Rose is just teasing you. You know how she is."

Shane was grinning too. "Yeah, don't get all bent out of shape. Besides, I don't think you could handle more than a few carts at a time, anyway." He grabbed Nick and they doubled over, their laughter loud and raucous.

Impossibly, Rusty's face burned an even deeper crimson. I watched uncertainly as his fingers coiled into fists, and he flexed them until his knuckles practically glowed white. Tension had gathered like storm clouds, and I felt rooted to the spot, waiting for the inevitable clap of thunder.

"FUCK...THE...BUNCH...OF...YOU!" he screamed abruptly. There was no stammering this time; each word was clear as a bell and punctuated with a jab of his forefinger. He turned on his heel and bolted to the edge of the nearest outcropping of rock where, without hesitation, he flung himself over the edge.

CHAPTER NINE

My heart leapt into my throat as I tried to coax my feet into action. They were surprisingly heavy, but I managed to break into a sort of stumble-run and scrambled forward with Michael right on my heel. I slowed as I neared the edge—not gonna lie, I'm no big fan of heights. I suffer from a sort of vertigo wherein the ground seems to rush up at me when I look down from a distance. It's very disorienting, and I had no intention of following Rusty over the edge. Nevertheless, my legs threatened to jellify when I peered over the edge and realized I was approximately sixty feet above the sparkling water below.

"Rusty!" I called, shielding my eyes against the sunlight glinting off the water's surface. *"Rusty!"*

"Do you see him?" Michael was just behind me, scanning left and right.

"No," I said, frustrated and helpless. I didn't see any easy way down the rock wall. It was either straight off the cliff or nothing at all. With no cell service, there was no way to call for help. In the time it would take Shane to drive us back to town to bring reinforcements, Rusty would be long gone. I was beginning to feel a swell of panic when I suddenly realized the others hadn't joined us in searching for their friend. In fact, it was the sound of muffled snickering that caught my attention.

I turned around to find them clutching each other and laughing, and I'm pretty sure they were laughing at *us*. I felt angry heat rush into my face. "What the literal *fuck*, guys?" I demanded.

Rose had laughed until her eyes were wet with tears. "Oh, my *gosh!*" She held her midsection and doubled over, dropping to her knees.

Shane held his hands up in surrender, trying to get his laughter under control. "I'm so sorry, man. Really. But you should *see* your faces!" And away they went, laughing their asses off again.

I looked at Michael, and he was equally perplexed. It just made my anger spike. "Would someone please just tell us what is going on?" I turned around and scanned the water again, and this time, I spotted someone slicing through the water, swimming toward an area where the quarry edge met the surface several hundred yards to our left. Rusty's red hair was unmistakable as it bobbed up and down.

"We dive from here all the time," said Shane, finally back in control of himself.

"It's no big," added Nick. "There's also a couple of other points at different heights, but we know the depth of the water below. It's safe if you know what you're doing."

"I am *so* sorry," said Rose, back on her feet and working to regain her breath. "That was so rude of me. Y'all were genuinely worried about Rusty. It just never occurred to us that you wouldn't realize. I really *am* sorry."

"Maybe you should be apologizing to Rusty," I suggested, still a little miffed. Like most people, I don't care for being laughed at, and I was acting as Rusty's advocate by proxy. "He didn't seem very amused by all that 'cart boy' shit."

"Oh, pooh," said Rose, waving it away. "That's how we all are with each other. Rusty knows we don't mean anything by it. Look, here he comes now."

I glanced over and saw Rusty shaking his head like a dog before working the water out of his ears with his fingers. He brushed past us and resumed his position stretched out on one of the rock outcroppings to finish drying in the warmth of the sun. He still didn't look very happy to me, and I wondered exactly how adept Rose was at reading her friend.

"You surely are different from your sister," observed Shane.

I turned my attention to him. "How so?"

"Nick tried to impress her by jumping in from that very spot, and she turned around and followed him right in. Ms. Gina wasn't afraid of nothing. Total badass. You looked like you were going to pass out," he said.

I couldn't fight the smile that played at the corners of my mouth. The image was easy to conjure, and he was completely correct. And I had suffered worse teasing by own sister than Rusty had from Rose. Time to trust they knew each other's boundaries and just let it go.

"So," said Michael, clapping his hands together. "Family farms and the local grocery. Anyone heading off to college after graduation?"

"What for?" asked Nick, as if it was the dumbest thing he'd ever heard. "There ain't nothing I can learn there that I can't learn from my old man." His friends nodded their agreement as a foregone conclusion.

"Aren't you interested in anything beyond your vocations?" asked Michael. "Social sciences or humanities?"

Vacant stares.

I didn't really feel qualified to have an opinion, as my own college experience was limited to a few electives I had crashed and burned straight out of high school and the online courses I would soon be taking to obtain my PI license. I opted for a different tactic. "How about travel? You know, get out there and see the world?"

"But what could be more beautiful than all of this?" Shane spread his hands out overhead and turned 360 degrees.

"How will you know if you don't ever leave?" I challenged.

"Exactly."

The female voice came from behind us, startling me. I turned to find a willowy teen with honey-blonde, shoulder-length hair approaching from the tree line. Trailing behind her and holding her hand was a sinewy boy with doe-like eyes and closely shorn black hair. His dark brown skin gleamed with perspiration under the relentless sun, and I was pleased to see that racism hadn't entirely permeated this strange little town.

"Audrey," she said by way of introduction, nodding curtly. "This is Trevor."

The young man extracted his hand from hers and shook hands firmly with me, then Michael. "You're not from around here," he stated the obvious in a deep baritone.

"No," I said. "We're following up on some work my sister was doing here a few weeks ago. I'm Dwayne Morrow."

Audrey's face brightened as she recognized the surname. "You're Gina's brother! Is she with you?" She looked around expectantly.

Michael stepped in as words stuck in my throat. "Not this time," he said. "Hi, I'm Michael. Michael Arthur. Gina is my girlfriend."

"So, what are your plans after graduation?" I asked, trying to pull the conversation back to when they had entered the scene. "Doesn't sound like you're content to just stick around."

"Hell, no," she said, and Trevor nodded. "Who knows how much time we even *have* on this planet? I want to see everything there is to see, go everywhere there is to go, taste things I've never tasted! Life's too short to settle for just *this*. I don't know what's wrong with these lunkheads. We're only *seventeen*, for Christ's sake!"

"Oh, right, Audrey," said Rose, laughing. "Like your mama will *ever* let you out of here. You've gotta be dreaming."

"A girl can dream," said Audrey defensively. "And I *will* get out of here."

"We," corrected Trevor, taking Audrey's hand once more.

"That's right, *we*." She leaned in and gave him a quick peck on the lips while the others squirmed at the overt display of affection.

Rose shrugged and sighed. "And we have Gina to thank for this."

"Not true," countered Audrey. "We were *always* going to leave. It's just that she kinda got me stoked. This coming senior year is going to be painful. All our textbooks are so *ancient*. I want to learn things from that global spider thingy, you know, the interweb—"

"The internet?" I asked, and I was sure I must have misunderstood. "You all don't have internet?"

"Not even one little bit of it," said Audrey.

I was dumbstruck. I glanced at Michael, and he simply shrugged. "How can you not have internet? How do you keep in touch with each other? I understand cell service is pretty much non-existent here so there's probably no texting, but surely you have email?"

I was in *The Twilight Zone*. The sea of blank expressions before me was all the assurance I needed. Granted, Information Technology was my line of business. I had been doing it for so long it was impossible to remember a time before we transacted so much of our daily lives with the assistance of a keyboard, mouse and monitor or touchscreen device. I maintain my household budget using bill pay and online banking—*Audrey!* A little slow to engage, my mental tumblers finally fell into place, and I snapped my fingers.

"You must be Audrey Peterson," I said, and she nodded. "I met your parents a little while ago in town."

"Then you know exactly what I mean," said Rose, firing a finger pistol at me. "Hell will freeze, thaw, and then freeze again before Caroline Peterson lets her out of this town. She's got Audrey earmarked for succession at the bank. It's practically preordained, just like the rest of our futures are."

"She doesn't control me," Audrey protested. It seemed probable to me she spent a lot of time in deadlock against her mother's agenda, whatever else that agenda may encompass. She tucked herself against Trevor, and I couldn't help but wonder if their relationship might be as much an act of rebellion as genuine attraction. I hoped not.

"So, wait a minute," I said, pivoting back to their apparent total lack of technology. "You're telling me no Facebook, no TikTok, no Netflix—do you have television?"

That brought a round of laughter.

"*Of course*, we have TV," said Shane. "And telephones. They may not be like those fancy cell phones you're talking about, but we can hear each other just fine."

I was having trouble reconciling this. If they had television, wouldn't they be exposed to all the things they seemed to find so completely foreign? Michael seemed to be riding my same brainwave when he asked, "What kind of shows do you like on TV?"

"*Andy Griffith* is my favorite," said Nick. "That Don Knotts just cracks me up."

"I'm partial to *Petticoat Junction*," added Rose. "*Green Acres* isn't bad, but it can be pretty hokey."

Shane grinned. "*Wonder Woman*, hands down. That Lynda Carter is one hot babe."

Michael and I exchanged glances. What in the hell—?

"How many channels do you get?" I asked.

"One," said Rose, as if I had asked the most ridiculous question ever. "Channel 3. Mr. Brown broadcasts from above his restaurant."

Well, of course he does!

"How about movies?" I asked.

"There's an old drive-in out on Route 5," said Nick. "But it's mostly just western marathons or Disney flicks." He squirreled his face and stuck his tongue out. "Bo-*ring.*"

"No *Fast and the Furious?* Marvel Cinematic Universe?" I ventured. I was met with universal perplexity. I was completely through the looking glass here. "How about music? I heard the Eagles when we first got here."

"Oh, man, they're *awesome!*" enthused Shane, grinning broadly. He indicated the guitar he still held at his side. "They're who inspired me to learn how to play this thing. Well, them and a little Skynyrd." He shifted the guitar into position and expertly plucked out the intro to "Sweet Home, Alabama."

Michael nodded his approval. "That's pretty good."

Shane's cheeks flushed with pride. "It's all right."

"All right, my ass," said Trevor, poking Shane in his side. "You are the *shit!*"

"Don't forget *my* favorite," Audrey chimed in, and Shane immediately lit into a blazing rendition of the opening to Heart's "Crazy on You." This kid was really *good.* He stopped short of the first verse, and everyone clapped enthusiastically except for Rusty, who was still stretched out in the sun and sulking. I doubted if Shane's ears could have burned any brighter, but he was humbly pleased by all the attention.

Audrey glanced at her watch and did a double take. "Oh, *shit!*"

"What, baby?" Trevor attempted to draw her close, but she pulled away.

"It's after three-thirty," she said. "My mom is supposed to pick me up at four. She thinks I've got track practice."

"It will be your dad," I said to her surprise, and she looked relieved. "We bit into a little too much of your mother's schedule this afternoon. I heard her ask your father if he could pick you up instead."

Audrey turned to her friends. "Can one of you take me? I'll never make it on time if I walk."

Ever the gentleman, Shane stepped forward. "Sure...I mean, if you fellas are finished here and don't mind both riding in the back of my truck." He looked at us expectantly.

I was really hoping to get a better look at the abandoned mine site, but frankly didn't want to do so with all the extra eyes and ears around. I made a mental note for a return engagement when I could focus without distraction. "I'm good," I said. "I need to find a bank in—what is it?—Shawnee?—before they roll up the streets for the night. I'm completely out of cash."

"Yeah, sure," added Michael. He glanced at Trevor. "Are you coming?"

Trevor smiled and shook his head. "No, thanks. I think I'll just hang out here for a while before heading home."

I didn't need to ask why.

• • • • • • ⊖⊖ • • • • • • •

Apparently, Shane prioritized Audrey's urgent need to be timely above ours for basic safety as we bumped and thudded back along the narrow, wooded path that led to civilization. Michael and I were nearly ejected from the truck bed as he rejoined Route 5 abruptly, cutting the wheel hard to the left and gunning the engine. Nauseating blue-black exhaust poured from underneath the truck, threatening to overwhelm us both with carbon monoxide before finally dissipating.

He slowed as we reached the town square, pulling off to the curb in front of the Briarstaff jail and shifting into park. "Is this okay, fellas?" he asked through the sliding pane in his rear glass.

"Sure thing," said Michael, extracting a twenty from his wallet and offering it to Shane. "Is this enough for your time this afternoon?"

113

Shane waved the money away. "You don't owe me anything," he said with a good-natured grin. "You already filled up my gas tank. If y'all need anything else while you're here, I'll be around."

"Thanks, Shane," I said. "It was nice to meet you and your friends."

"Nice to meet you, too, Mr. Dwayne! You make sure and tell that sister of yours that we all said hello, all right?"

I nodded numbly. The weight of sustaining our cover story was becoming unbearable, and I was quite ready to dispense with pretenses for at least a little while. A simple request borne of courtesy was yet another painful reminder of the fact that I would never again speak with my sister, and it was beyond my skill set to keep my emotions suppressed for much longer.

"Um, I don't mean to be rude, but—" Audrey tapped her wristwatch. She was partially slouched in the passenger seat, apparently afraid one of her parents might spot her in Shane's truck as they passed through the square.

"Oh, sure," I said, and Michael and I boosted ourselves over the wooden sides of the truck bed and down to the sidewalk below. "Thanks, again."

"You betcha," he said, shifting into drive and enshrouding us in another cloud of noxious fumes as his truck backfired and pulled away from the curb.

We made our way back to Michael's car but had to pause as waves of heat rolled out to meet us face-first once we opened the doors. With its bright yellow exterior and black plastic and fabric interior, the Fiesta was like an angry bumblebee. I indicated the town square where substantial progress had been made in the short time since we had left.

"Wow," I noted, and Michael nodded his head appreciatively as he scanned the scene. The entire base of the Ferris wheel was finished, and the men had begun assembling the wheel itself. A tri-pronged contraption with rotating teacups on each appendage was being assembled on the opposite corner. Vendor booths had begun popping up on the sidewalks along both sides of the main drag which ran parallel to the southern side of the square. The ones facing us bore signage and colorful artwork promising fried foods and assorted desserts while the other side seemed destined for carnival games and local crafts. There was even a makeshift fortune teller's booth at the far end, directly across from Sally's Flowers. Everything seemed to be on schedule for the Apple Festival to open as promised the following morning.

We climbed into the car, and Michael navigated slowly through the hubbub, exercising far more caution than the workers who labored to meet their deadline. Once we had passed the southwest corner of the square, Michael allowed his speed to reach the posted limit, and we were soon zipping down Route 5 toward Shawnee, air conditioning on full blast.

• • • • • • • ◦ ◦ • • • • • • •

"Oh, my God!" I stared at the face of my phone. "I've got service!"

My phone was a regular symphony of soundbites as emails, texts and notices of missed calls landed in quick succession for some time, and I was almost giddy with bliss! It was an unexpected tether to normalcy, and I hadn't fully realized how much I needed one until then.

"Hallelujah," agreed Michael, slowing and using his left turn signal before pulling into an oversized lot that serviced a small strip mall that still had ample room for growth. The shopping center was anchored on one end by a small grocery store called Foodland and on the other by Shoe World. Storefronts between included Bovine & Porcine Barbeque Palace, Little Italy's Secret Garden, Trixie's Big Hair and Nails, Jeb's Vapes and Smokes and the Tri-County Veterinary Hospital—of which three counties, I had no idea. Most importantly, an ATM was mounted in the cinderblock wall near the entrance to the grocery store.

"Is this Shawnee?" I asked absently, thumbing through my messages, most of which were from Melanie, as were most of the missed calls. Nothing urgent—she was checking progress and offering words of encouragement. I couldn't imagine a time before I had her in my corner.

"I guess?" Michael pulled into one of the many empty parking spots near Foodland. "I didn't see anything that indicated city limits, but where else could it be?"

I looked up and frowned. This was more of a rest stop than an actual town. Across the street and about a half-mile ahead was another strip mall similar in size to the one we were in. A marquee advertising beer and liquor prices was positioned near the entrance with an arrow in flashing lights pointing the way for those needing even more guidance. A free-standing building that looked as if it had once been a Kentucky Fried Chicken was just beyond, the Colonel's head removed from the signage but the chicken bucket still intact. A family meal, including two sides, was just $19.99!

"I need to touch base with work," said Michael, turning the engine off and releasing his seatbelt.

"Yeah, I want to call Melanie," I said, unfastening my own. "I'll stop at the ATM and pull cash when I'm done."

"Sounds good," he said, and we both unfurled our legs from the tiny car, pausing long enough to allow the blood to circulate back into our extremities before heading in separate directions to give each other some privacy while we tended to our individual affairs.

"I hope it's okay to call you," I said as Melanie answered on the second ring. "I don't want to get you in trouble at your new job."

"It's fine," she said, and her voice made me homesick in a way I can't describe. "My boss has been extremely understanding."

"Good," I said. "I'm glad you like it so far."

"Beats the hell out of Omelet Hut. I almost have the smell of grease and bacon out of my hair. I hope I wasn't pestering you with calls and texts earlier. I've just been so unsettled about all of this. I needed to hear your voice."

I smiled. "You could never pester me. I only just now got your calls and texts. This place is like no place I've ever been. There isn't any cell service here at all, and I mean *none*."

"You're kidding me. Even in Lymont, there is service near US 23 and 52."

"Lymont is a regular metropolis compared to Briarstaff."

"Are you making any progress following Gina's footsteps?"

"Maybe a little," I said. "Michael and I went out to the abandoned mine she was photographing and met a few of the local teens. They all knew Gina. Wanted me to pass along their greetings whenever I see her next." I tried valiantly and yet in vain to keep my voice from catching.

Melanie was silent for a beat. "I'm sorry. This must be incredibly difficult."

I pinched the bridge of my nose and nodded. "I knew it would be, but I'll get through it. I need to know if there's anything to Michael's suspicions. We're going to stay through the weekend and keep poking around. My story is that Gina asked if I could get some additional photos of town life to go along with what she's already collected about the mine. The town is hosting an Apple Festival from tomorrow through Sunday, so it's perfect cover, but I'll be out of touch, and I don't want you to worry."

"Too late for that," said Melanie. "I want you back home."

"I'll be back before you know it," I said. "How's Jasmine doing with Dexter?"

"Oh, just fine. They're fast friends. He sits on her lap and purrs and is just the best thing *ever!* I, however, am the enemy. He's sharpened his claws on my shin at least twice and has attempted to trip me on the stairs more times than I can count. That cat is homicidal."

I laughed. "It's his way of showing affection."

Melanie harrumphed. "Right."

"I'll make it up to you later," I promised.

"Make it soon," she said, and her concern was sweetly evident. "I don't like this one bit."

"I'll be home as soon as I can. I love you."

She sighed. "I love you, too."

We disconnected, and I glanced around until I spotted Michael, who was still engaged in an animated conversation on his phone further up the walkway. He was the type to talk with his hands, and from where I stood, he looked as though he was conducting an imaginary orchestra. I wandered down from the grocery to peer into Trixie's Big Hair and Nails, where a heavyset middle-aged woman sat underneath a hooded hair dryer staring up vacantly toward a television screen that featured Vanna White flipping letters. The beautician was nowhere to be seen, possibly on a restroom or smoke break.

Even though I was still full after our jumbo-sized lunch, the smoky aroma of barbequed meat was making me salivate, and I began to feel a compulsion to investigate the Barbeque Palace further. I took a few tentative steps in that direction, but before I made a decision I would undoubtedly regret, I turned around and headed for the wall-mounted ATM near the entrance to Foodland, mentally starting a tab of how much cash I should pull.

I already owed Michael $100 for the motel, and if we stayed through Sunday, I would owe another $100. I hadn't seen the bill for lunch, but I'm sure it had to be somewhere between $10 and $20 with tip. Gas—both for Michael's car and for what he had given Shane—was probably in the ballpark of $40. Meals for several days would be another $100-$150, and pocket money for unexpected expenses—maybe another $300? The numbers began to swirl and change in my mind—I never *could* do math in my head. All I knew for certain was I would need more than the daily limit for ATM withdrawals, which was $500 with my bank. I inserted my debit card and entered my PIN number, choosing the maximum amount before pressing the 'Enter' button. The machine whirred and clicked and immediately spat my card back to me.

TRANSACTION DECLINED.

CHAPTER TEN

"I'm sorry, Mr. Morrow, I don't know what to tell you," said the sunny-voiced representative from my bank's 24-hour customer service line. Her name was Tish, and I wanted to reach through the phone and strangle the sunshine right out of her. "I can order you another card—"

"That really isn't going to help me *now*," I said, kneading my forehead while pacing back and forth in front of the infernal ATM. Assuming I had misremembered the daily limit, I had dropped my request to $400 and tried again.

TRANSACTION DECLINED.

I had lowered the amount to $300.

TRANSACTION DECLINED.

At that point, I had become desperate. I was certain my bank account balance was fairly healthy. I had lowered the amount to $200 and tried again.

TRANSACTION DECLINED.

Only that time, the machine hadn't ejected my card. Instead, it was pulled deep into the bowels of the ATM to prevent any more potentially fraudulent activity. A concise message in green block letters appeared on the screen advising me to contact my bank as soon as possible, which I was currently doing.

"We don't show any attempts whatsoever to withdraw money from your account," Tish said.

"And you would see that even if the transactions were declined?" I asked.

"Absolutely. We would also see a code that would tell us why the transaction was declined, but there's simply nothing in the system. Some of these third-party ATMs are subjected to a lot of abuse, so my guess is that the machine is faulty. But since it ate your card—"

"All you can really do is ship me a replacement," I finished for her.

"Yes," she said, sunshine still firmly in place. "And I can reassure you that your funds are still safe and sound. Now, if I can just confirm your mailing address?"

I ran through the paces with her and disconnected, frustrated and embarrassed. I was also carrying two credit cards, but I never used them for cash withdrawals since the APR for cash advances was significantly higher than that for purchases. I didn't even know what their PIN numbers *were*. I barely knew Michael, but it appeared I would have to remain in his good graces for longer than I was comfortable. I hoped he was prepared to shoulder the entire financial burden until I could square up once we were back in Columbus.

Michael had finished his own call and was heading back, looking unamused. "We've got a little problem," he said, tucking his phone into his pocket.

"You're telling me," I said, and I told him about my altercation with the ATM.

"Awesome!" he said sarcastically.

"Hey, I'm not happy about it either," I said. "It's not like I won't pay you back—"

"No, it's not that," he said, waving my words away. "I'm going to have to head back to my office tomorrow. The file containing my story got corrupted somewhere along the way, and the deadline is right on top of me. I didn't bring my laptop, and my hotspot wouldn't work here anyway. There's also a mandatory staff meeting tomorrow afternoon that I completely forgot about."

"Your office? You mean in Washington?"

Michael nodded. "It's about a three-and-a-half-hour drive each way. If I leave early tomorrow morning, I can get everything all straightened out, and I'll be back by evening. I could drop you off in town before I go, so at least you wouldn't be wasting your day. I just don't like the idea of leaving you without any money. I'm running a little low myself, at this point."

"I'll make do," I said. Who needs food? Wasn't I just commiserating with myself over how full I still was from lunch? Michael was eyeing the ATM and pulled his wallet from his back pocket. "What are you doing?"

"You said it didn't eat your card until you used it a few times, right?" He extracted his debit card.

"Yeah, but—"

"I'll give it one shot. What's the harm?"

He inserted his card and punched in his PIN. Initially, he entered $300 but backed up to edit the amount to $400. He glanced to the heavens and crossed his fingers before pressing 'Enter.'

The machine whirred and clicked. Then a slot opened, and twenty crisp $20 bills emerged, followed by a ribbon of receipt tape and finally, Michael's ATM card. He looked at me victoriously before scooping it all up.

Neither of us wanted to be first to suggest it, but it soon became apparent we were both thinking the same thing. Michael turned the car left and traveled the short distance up the road to the other strip mall, drawn by the flashing marquee promising the lowest prices on beer and liquor in the state. He parked near the entrance and shifted the car into park. He counted out $100 for himself and offered me the rest.

"That's too much," I protested. You're only going to be gone for one day."

"Yeah, but I'll have access to more if I need it. You're going to be stuck here until I get back. Who knows what might happen?"

Well, *that* sent a shiver down my spine. I felt like a child about to be orphaned at a fire station.

"If you're sure—"

"I am," he said, putting the money into my open palm. "Besides food, you might need to hire transportation like we did with Shane this afternoon. You may be able to fill the day in town, but let's face it, town isn't really that big. You might also meet someone who has information but isn't willing to part with it without a little—" He rubbed his thumb and forefinger together, the universal sign for moolah.

I took the money and stuffed it into my wallet. "This is just so humiliating—"

"Stop it," he said. "We're good. I'm sure."

I made a mental note to begin carrying at least *some* cash with me. I had always felt it far less risky to carry cards than cash because the former offered fraud protection and could be replaced while the latter, well—didn't and couldn't. I never imagined myself in a situation like this.

"I know it's not even six, but I'm exhausted," said Michael, and I completely understood. The only sleep I had gotten in the past twenty-four hours was an impromptu nap in the car on the way here.

"So, what do you suggest?" I asked.

He indicated the liquor store. "I'm going to buy a little 'sleep aid.' I can't afford to toss and turn for a second night in a row. I'll never survive the drive back and forth tomorrow—there isn't enough coffee in the free world to make that happen. Maybe we could pick up some carryout from the barbeque place back there and take it back to the hotel. I'm not really hungry now, but it sure did smell good, and I doubt we'll want to go back out once we get situated."

"I'm guessing room service is *not* an option," I pondered rhetorically and was rewarded with the mental image of Mrs. Shepley assembling sandwiches of indeterminate meat from within the probable state of her kitchen. "Yeah, no thanks."

I got out of the passenger side and headed for the entrance to the liquor store.

·········●●○○●●········

When we arrived back at Fred's Beds, I noticed we had company. An ancient, wood-paneled station wagon was parked outside of Room 1, and the door to that room was partially open, although there was no sign of any guest or guests. Mrs. Shepley was visible behind the office's screen door, watching us like a hawk. This was probably more lodgers than she had accommodated in months, maybe years. I would have expected her to be happy, but she merely looked inconvenienced.

It took us a couple of trips to cart all our purchases back to our rooms. Not only had we stopped at Bovine & Porcine Barbeque Palace, but we had also dropped by Foodland to pick up soda, bottled water and a few other amenities. I didn't recall seeing any vending machines at the motel when we had checked in, a fact that was easily confirmed upon our arrival. We paused on the porch outside our rooms after the car had been emptied.

"I'm going to have a quick bite and call it a night," said Michael. "Are you good with that?"

I nodded. Don't get me wrong, Michael was pleasant enough, but I didn't need a constant companion. The single common thread we shared was my sister, and there was only so much small talk we could make without circling back to the topic of her untimely demise.

"I'm aiming to be on the road by eight, if that works for you," he added.

"It does," I said. "I think I'll have you drop me off at the road leading to the quarry, if you think you can find your way. I'd like to investigate the mine itself."

"I'm sure I can," he said. "How will you get back to town?"

I shrugged. "Maybe I'll run into Shane or one of the other kids out there and can catch a ride. Worst case scenario, I'll walk back. It's not like I'm on a schedule. I'll just hang out in town until you get back."

"Sounds good. Good night."

"Night," I said, retreating to my room. I attempted to engage the deadbolt, but the mechanism was completely frozen. I engaged the flimsy chain and hoped for the best.

The room was just short of sweltering. A window-unit air conditioner had been mounted into the wall at the back of the room, but I hadn't had the good sense to turn it on before we had gone into town. I twisted the knob to turn the unit on high and winced as its fan screeched in protest, slowly accelerating into a steady chirping rhythm while initially expelling tepid air that smelled like wet earth. I held my hand in front of the vent for a moment and was pleased to note the air continued to cool in temperature despite the cantankerous protestations of the air conditioner's inner workings. I said a quick prayer it would continue to do so for the duration of my stay. I don't tolerate heat well, and we were experiencing the hottest temperatures of the season.

I rummaged through my duffel bag and found gym shorts and a t-shirt. I briefly considered taking a shower, but after glancing at the rust stains and mildew multiplying exponentially in the bathtub, I decided to postpone for at least a little while. I stripped out of my khakis and polo shirt and slipped into more comfortable attire.

125

I had placed my dinner and groceries on the scarred wooden desk and wandered over to nose through the bags. I still wasn't hungry, so I folded the top down tightly on the takeout barbeque and set it aside. Out of the corner of my eye, I spotted the bottled water and 12-pack of Pepsi I had deposited on the floor beside the door and thought how nice an ice-cold beverage would be. I scanned the room for a mini fridge, completely customary in most hotels and motels, but apparently too much to expect for Fred's Beds. I was pretty sure there was no ice machine outside, either. *Shit.* Maybe I would check with Mrs. Shepley to see if there was any ice in the office, but not now. I just couldn't make myself do it. Fortunately, I hadn't purchased anything else that required refrigeration, so it could have been worse.

I proceeded to empty the next bag—three varieties of chips, an assortment of Little Debbies and a few containers of microwavable soup, a nutritional nightmare. I scanned the room again, confirming what I had already come to suspect—no microwave. I sighed and set the cans aside. Next was a traveler's assortment of miniaturized toiletries including toothpaste, toothbrush, mouthwash, soap and shampoo. I had forgotten to pack any of those things when Michael had proposed this impromptu trip. I carried the toiletries into the bathroom, thought better of placing them directly on the grimy countertop bordering the sink, and instead returned them to the plastic bag from which they came and placed the whole thing on the back of the toilet.

From the next bag, I pulled a small bottle of Canadian Mist whiskey— well, okay, I *intended* to buy a small bottle of Canadian Mist, but standing in the liquor store, turning the tiny plastic bottle around and around in my hand, it didn't seem like very much whiskey at all. So, I asked for the next bigger size. The cashier nearly scanned that one before I stopped him, reconsidering. I was going to be in this godforsaken hellhole for four nights, and there was no guarantee I would make it back to the liquor store. I opted for the jumbo size, reasoning with myself that it made the most sense, both practically and economically. I added a small pack of disposable shot glasses conveniently located with other impulse items near the register. When the cashier, an older gentleman with heavy-lidded eyes, no hair up top but plenty on his arms had gruffly asked if that was everything, I paused, my eyes shifting to the sea of cigarettes on display behind him. I could barely believe my own ears when I heard myself ask for a pack of Pall Mall Blue, king size, and plucked up a disposable Bic lighter from the display beside the register. I hadn't smoked in *years*. What was I *thinking?* Clearly, I wasn't, even after I saw the exorbitant price of the cigarettes flash across the cash register screen. My hands were in cahoots with my mouth, fumbling out three twenties and looking guiltily over my shoulder to see if Michael was watching me squander the money that he had just lent me. He wasn't. He was intently studying the selection of vodka on the other side of the store. I felt like a child pulling one over on his parents as I had tucked my purchases under my arm and rejoined him. Now, I picked up the cigarettes and shook my head, astounded at my poor choices. I should just throw them away. Instead, I put them down beside the whiskey and shot glasses and pushed them to the back of the desk.

I stepped back and took a long, slow look around the room, trying to see it as Gina might have. I couldn't imagine our impressions would have been that different. Exactly how many ways can you say, *"Ewww?"* It was both comforting and unsettling to know that she had been in this very room only a couple of weeks before. It made me feel both closer to her and farther away than I had ever been. I flopped backward onto the bed and laughed out loud when the mattress tried to swallow me whole, save for a couple of springs strategically placed to provide maximum discomfort. Had I really expected anything else?

I stared at the swirls in the plaster on the ceiling and tried to formulate a plan for the following day, but my mind kept jumping from one track to the next. I missed Melanie. I wondered how Jasmine was adjusting to their new apartment in the big city. I hoped Brady was back home with his son and recuperating from his injury. I never thought I'd miss his annoying face, but I kind of did. I wondered if Dexter was behaving himself, and I sincerely hoped he had kept his annoying penchant for upchuck to a minimum. I closed my eyes and realized just how exhausted I was. In no time, I was asleep.

········•••●◦◯●•••••···

I woke with a start in a darkened room.

A rhythmic, motorized squeaking shrilled from behind me, and I could see a faint square of light to my left, through gauzy curtains that weren't even remotely room-darkening. I smelled the musty undercurrent of the space and tried to shift into an upright position, but it was like trying to pull myself out of a bed of quicksand.

Fred's Beds. Of course.

I finally succeeded in freeing myself from the bed and groped my way to the desk, where I had left my keys and cell phone. It may not be good for much here, but it had an illuminated clock, and I could see it was almost ten. I used the ambient lighting to find the desk lamp and switch it on. My stomach gurgled loudly, and I realized it was way beyond dinnertime now, and I was starving. I grabbed the bag of barbeque takeout from the back of the desk and used the wrapper from the beef brisket sandwich as a placemat on the desktop, proceeding to lay out my spread. Other than the sandwich, I had a side order of potato salad, a paper tray of hush puppies and four covered plastic sauce cups containing what was guaranteed to be the best barbeque sauce in the whole wide world. I completed the feast with a warm Pepsi from the carton on the floor.

The food was, in fact, delicious, and I ate every bite, acclimating surprisingly quickly to the warm soda. I was pleased to note that the air conditioner was continuing to do its job, and the temperature inside the room was almost where I'd like it to be. I glanced around the room once more and noticed an ancient portable tube television on a small wire rolling cart in the corner by the door. I didn't see a remote, so I crossed the room and turned it on at the set. It came to life slowly, its soft picture growing sharper as it warmed up. Through its singular tinny speaker, I heard Laura Ingalls ask her sister if she told her something bad, would she tell their Pa?

Little House on the Prairie. Wow.

I turned the old-fashioned dial on the television all the way around, but that was the only station available, undoubtedly the same as the one the kids had mentioned at the quarry. *No thanks*, I thought, turning the television back off.

I looked around the room again, fully awake. *Shit.* I was never going to get back to sleep, and I needed to be up early. My eyes landed on the whiskey and cigarettes.

Next thing I knew, I was easing out onto the porch, arms full of contraband and another warm can of Pepsi. My room was one of the ones with a metal card table and folding chairs beside it, and I set up shop there, trying to make as little noise as possible. I didn't want to disturb Michael's slumber next door. I poured a shot and winced as I chased it down with a slug of warm soda. I played with the cellophane on the pack of cigarettes but opted for another shot instead. I sat back in the folding chair and breathed deeply, listening to the symphony of nocturnal insects all around me. I would have expected it to sound like what I am accustomed to on my own front porch, but the only real similarity was the absence of traffic noise. There was an entirely unique set of instruments at work here, emanating from creatures who resided in the thick woods behind the motel. Still, it was calming, and I closed my eyes, taking in a deep lungful of the sweet night air. The temperature and humidity had dropped considerably with the sun's descent, and stars were plentiful in the sky beyond the edge of the porch roof. I could almost forget why we were here.

"*Pssst!*"

My eyes popped open, and I scanned the lot. On my second pass, I spotted the tenant of Room 1 waving from the porch outside his room. He reminded me a great deal of Christopher Lloyd from *Back to the Future*, with wisps of silvery hair leaping from his head in all directions. He was smiling broadly and gestured for me to join him. I stood, stretched and gathered my things. Why not?

·····•••••◦⊙◯•••••·····

"Otis McElroy, at your service!" he said as I deposited my booze and smokes beside the open longneck bottle of Budweiser on his table. He seemed oblivious to the hour, and his voice carried in all directions. He shook my hand earnestly while I glanced around to make sure we weren't disturbing Michael, or perhaps more importantly, Mrs. Shepley. He glanced over his shoulder back toward the office, which was completely dark. "You're not worried about *her*, are you? She took off about an hour ago. She doesn't live on site. There's a phone number posted to the door in case of emergency."

I hadn't noticed until then that her Ford LTD sedan was gone.

"Dwayne Morrow," I said, and we both eased ourselves into folding chairs on opposite sides of the card table. "What brings you to these parts, Otis?"

"Insurance," he said. "Accident and health, mostly. I travel this great state from top to bottom, front to back, 365 days a year, helping poor folk find the best coverage available to them at the very best price. I have this terrific little accident policy that actually pays you *cash money* for every bump and bruise you—*hey!* Let me show you what I've got to offer." He pushed himself to his feet and headed for the door to his room.

I smiled and shook my head. "I really don't think so, Otis."

He waved off my objection. "Now, look, I wouldn't feel right if I didn't at least give you the opportunity to take advantage of this little piece of gold. I don't need any money down. Let me ask you this: do you have a checking account? It doesn't matter if you have anything in it, I promise. You can post-date a check for whenever works best for you. I can go as far out as thirty days—"

I threw my head back and laughed long and hard. The whiskey was kicking in, and it was surprisingly cathartic to let go just a bit. Otis, however, looked completely perplexed.

"I'm sorry," I said, urging him back to his seat. "I didn't mean to offend you. You just don't know the kind of day I've had. My bank card was eaten by an ATM earlier today, and I literally have no access to money until I get home, which is far, far away."

"Not from around here, then?"

I shook my head. "Nope. I live in Grove City, Ohio. It's a suburb of Columbus."

"Well, then, you wouldn't qualify for my product any-hoo." He took a long pull from his beer. "So, what brings you to these parts? It's not exactly a vacation destination."

I poured myself another shot and tossed it back. My face felt a little flushed, and for the first time in days, I felt myself beginning to relax. "No," I said. "Not a vacation."

I picked up the pack of cigarettes and again fumbled absently with the cellophane. When I looked down, I was surprised to see the pull-tab had come completely loose and the pack was open. I tamped the top of the box against my palm a few times, packing the tobacco tighter within the cigarettes. It was an old habit, and muscle memory was frighteningly like riding a bicycle. I set them aside long enough to take another shot of whiskey.

"So, where do you live?" I asked, belching abruptly, and adding, "Excuse me." My *s*'s were getting a little soft.

Otis pointed to the station wagon. "Cheap motel rooms all over the state, but mostly right there. I've got a few leads around Briarstaff I plan to follow up on tomorrow, then I'll be off to the next little town. I get most of my business from loggers and other folk who live up hollers and down backroads you wouldn't even notice unless you knew where to look. They don't even realize what insurance can do for them, so I have to spread my own gospel, so to speak." He smiled and leaned back in this chair. He took a pack of unfiltered cigarettes from a front pocket and lit up. My eyes automatically slid to my own pack, and I picked them up again, this time snagging the lighter, as well. He looked at me expectantly. "So, again, what brings you to these parts?"

Telling myself it would be the last, I took another shot, sighed and leaned back in the chair. The desire to unload on a stranger was growing stronger by the second, and I took a deep drag from the cigarette I was startled to discover I had lit. The soothing warmth filled my lungs, and I only coughed a tiny bit. "Did you see that fella down there?" I asked.

I pointed in the general direction of Michael's room, and Otis nodded.

"He and I are playing detective," I continued. I glanced at my watch, noted that it was almost eleven-thirty, and decided I could allow myself another shot. I sloshed a little of the whiskey over the side of the glass as I poured.

"Detective, huh?" I had Otis's attention now. He leaned forward and propped his elbows on the table, resting his chin on closed fists. "What's going on?"

"It's my sister."

"Is she in trouble?"

I laughed. "She's dead." I took another deep pull from the cigarette, this time like an old pro—no coughing whatsoever.

Otis raised his eyebrows. "What happened?"

I proceeded to fill him in on everything I knew, beginning with her attendance at our brother's wedding, followed by her abrupt departure from my house that same evening, and then the world-altering revelation that she had been killed in a horrific traffic accident. My words were getting very thick by then, partially because of the booze but also due to emotion. I explained that Michael had been seeing my sister, and he had approached me about the work she had been doing in Briarstaff with his suspicion that something might have happened here that tied into her death. Almost as an afterthought, I explained our cover story and asked if Otis could keep what I told him to himself. Once I finished, Otis sat back in his chair and popped the top off another beer. He whistled, then lifted the bottle to his lips. I used the opportunity to take another shot I most certainly didn't need.

"I'm very sorry," he said sincerely. "That's terrible. Of course, I'll keep it to myself. Don't really have anyone to share it with any-hoo."

I nodded. "Thank you."

I clumsily squashed my cigarette out in the ashtray on the table. I realized the butts of my smokes were white while Otis's were brown and was surprised to see two other white ones already extinguished in the tray. I didn't specifically remember lighting any of them.

"So, why are you operating as if nothing has happened to her?" he asked.

"I doubt the news of her accident would have traveled this far, and we don't want to alert anyone to why we're really here."

"But if someone here is responsible, they'll *know* you're lying."

"And it might draw them out. I don't know. We're kind of flying by the seats of our pants here. But Gina hid a roll of undeveloped film in my house before she left that evening. I didn't find it until after she—" I couldn't say the word, but Otis nodded and waved me on. "I dropped it off to have it

133

developed, and the store was robbed. The employees were killed, and all the film was taken. I think she may have captured something somebody doesn't want seen."

"So, have you discovered anything suspicious yet?" he asked.

"The whole damn town is suspicious," I replied, reaching for the whiskey bottle before thinking better of it. "Haven't you ever noticed?"

He shrugged. "Like I said before, most of my business is conducted in private residences, you know? In a living room or at a kitchen table, not at any of the businesses in town. I've passed through this way a time or two, but I can't say anything has ever struck me as out of sorts."

I indicated my cell phone lying on the table. "No cell service whatsoever. The kids in town act like they've never even heard of them. The only television they have is from decades ago, and they have exactly one channel to choose from. Their only exposure to movies is at some drive-in, and it's all old stuff, too. Now that I think about it, the only music they listened to was classic rock. It's like stepping back in time."

Otis finished his beer and popped the top off another. "Well, I can assure you, cell service is mighty spotty in pockets throughout the entire state. I can't speak to the rest."

"These kids seem content to step into their parents' shoes when they get out of high school, with very little exception. It's just *weird*."

We sat in silence for a moment longer. I glanced at my cell phone again and was surprised to see another hour had passed. Morning was going to come mighty early.

"Have you ever wondered if your sister might still be alive?" he asked, lighting another cigarette.

I looked at him in astonishment. "What do you mean? I'm pretty sure I attended her funeral. I'm pretty sure I watched my parents' lives—*all* of our lives—get ripped to shit. I'm pretty sure—"

He held a hand up. "I'm sorry. I probably shouldn't have said anything. It's just—"

"It's just *what?*" I asked, pouring another shot and tossing it back, feeling the slow burn all the way to my stomach.

He sighed. "You said she was burned beyond recognition. You said the funeral was closed casket. You said she had only been identified by dental records. No one actually *saw* her. I don't mean to give false hope here, but if she witnessed something and the stakes were high enough—" His voice trailed off, and he shrugged.

Impossible.

I shook my head. I couldn't imagine a scenario in which she would do this to all of us. But then I flashed back to the graveside service and recalled the instant when I thought I saw her, viewing her own interment from the cover of woods near the cemetery's edge. A glimmer of hope attempted to ignite, but I forcibly pushed it away. I couldn't allow myself to believe something so completely ridiculous.

Could I?

CHAPTER ELEVEN

I awoke to the sound of hammering on the door to my room. I squinted and lifted my pounding head from the pillow, trying to find my cell phone on the nightstand, only to succeed in knocking it to the floor. I nearly joined it as I reached over the edge of the mattress, and the world tilted precariously in front of my eyes.

"Dwayne! Are you in there?" More hammering.

I pulled my phone back up and rolled onto my back, forcing myself to focus on its screen. Eight-fifteen.

Shit!

"Hang on!" I yelled, rolling out of bed. My mouth was dry and tasted like an ashtray. My voice sounded strange in my own ears. I glanced at the bottle of whiskey on my desk and was shocked to see I had consumed almost half of it. The hammering at the door had mercifully stopped, and I hobbled across the room, unfastening the chain before opening the door a crack. The morning sun was blinding.

Concern was evident on Michael's face as he stepped past me into the room. "Are you all right? I've been knocking for five minutes."

I shielded my eyes and scanned the parking lot, realizing Otis's station wagon was already gone. I thought we had imbibed at a similar pace, but truthfully, I could barely remember staggering back to my room. I *had* been consuming whiskey compared to his beer. I wondered how thoroughly I had embarrassed myself before letting the man go back to his room.

"I'm so sorry, Michael," I said. "I forgot to set an alarm."

He was examining the partial bottle of whiskey. "Mm-hmm," he said. "Dammit, Dwayne, I *told* you I had to start early—"

"I know, I know," I said, and the room threatened to spin away again. "I really *am* sorry. I just need maybe fifteen minutes to race through the shower and get ready. I don't suppose you have any Excedrin?"

"Sorry, bud. You're shit out of luck," he said. "I'll be in the car. *Hurry.*"

I nodded and headed for the bathroom. He had barely pulled the door closed behind him when my stomach roiled and hitched, and I raced to the toilet, retching myself into dry heaves.

· · ·•••••◌◌••••• · · ·

It actually took closer to twenty minutes, but I managed to race through the shower, gargle with mouthwash, brush my teeth and slap some deodorant on, hopefully dispelling any trace of the prior evening's indulgence. I grabbed a fresh pair of khaki shorts and a lightweight t-shirt and slid them on. Since I anticipated spending much of my day on foot, I figured I might as well be comfortable. Since my travel bag doubled as a backpack, I loaded it with my camera bag, some snacks and several bottles of water before cracking one open and drinking it in two long swallows. Hopefully, in lieu of Excedrin, I could hydrate this headache away. It had already lessened somewhat from the hot water in the shower. I locked the flimsy door behind me as I stepped outside.

I tossed the backpack into the backseat of Michael's car and started to get in on the passenger side but stopped short. *"Shit."* I said. "Hang on a sec. I forgot something."

137

Michael groaned, so I quickened my pace, letting myself back into the room and snagging the bottle of whiskey from the desk. I hurried back to the car, checked its lid to make sure it was secure, then added it to my backpack.

Michael was studying me intently as I settled into the seat and fastened my seatbelt. "Do you have a little issue we need to discuss?" He rocked his hand with his thumb and pinky finger extended in a universal sign I knew meant *drinky-drinky.*

"No," I said, shaking my head. The world had *almost* stopped tilting with such movement, and I hoped that boded well for potential motion sickness once we were actually underway.

"Are you sure? I mean, all of this—" He outlined the space around me with both hands. "—is *not* the product of oversleeping."

"It is not," I agreed. "And again, I'm sorry. I fell asleep as soon as we got back yesterday, but I got a second wind around ten. I didn't think I could find sleep again without a little assistance. I didn't use very good judgment."

"Do you expect to need a little more assistance while I'm gone?" He glanced knowingly at my backpack. "I mean, hey, it's your own business, but if there's some sort of problem going on here—"

"No," I repeated. "There's no problem. I don't know exactly how long you're going to be gone. If you're not back by nightfall, I might try and talk my way into the card game with some of the councilmen. Do you remember what Caroline said? They bring their own alcohol to these things, and it might be worthwhile to hear what they have to say, especially if they are a little loosened up."

"If you say so," he said dubiously, putting the car into reverse and backing up.

"I'm not an alcoholic!" I insisted crossly.

He shifted into drive and pulled around Mrs. Shepley's old Ford which was back in its customary position outside the office. We bounced through a chuckhole in the hard-packed dirt on the way to the highway, causing my stomach to flip and clench unexpectedly. I fought back the bitter taste of bile as Mrs. Shepley watched our progress from behind her screen door.

"Slow down," I said, as we neared a bend in the road.

Michael eased off the gas. "What?"

I pointed through his window at a craggy, tar and gravel lane that lay off to the east. A county sign comprised more of rust than metal hung cockeyed at the entrance, identifying it as Spielman Ridge. A diamond-shaped yellow sign was mounted below it, advising, 'Dead End.' There were two houses on each side of the street, single-story and identical in construction—well *almost* identical. The house on the far left was merely a burnt husk, its walls blackened, its doors and windows boarded over. 'No Trespassing' signs were liberally posted and were visible even from this distance. The other three houses were weatherworn and tiny. I couldn't imagine there were more than three or four rooms in each one. I recognized the bicycle belonging to the boy from the alley yesterday leaning against the porch rail of the house that was next to the blackened husk, but there were no signs of life anywhere to be seen. It didn't prevent the sensation that we were being observed from behind dirty windows.

"Good," I mumbled, observing the scene. "It looks like that young man made it home all right."

"And it *is* Spielman Ridge, just like Caroline said," said Michael, as if confirming I had misunderstood those nasty, taunting children. There was nothing wrong with my hearing. I knew what I heard. Michael accelerated and we continued toward Briarstaff.

139

We passed a sequence of handmade signs posted along the way:

APPLE FESTIVAL IN PROGRESS!!!
EXPERIENCE THE BIG O!!!
RIDES FOR THE LITTLE ONES, TOO!!!
GAMES FOR ALL AGES!!!
SLOW DOWN!!!
FLAGGER AHEAD

COME ONE, COME ALL!!!
GET YOUR FACES FED AND YOUR PALMS READ!!!
APPLE FESTIVAL
THURSDAY – SUNDAY
SLOW DOWN!!!
FLAGGER AHEAD

DON'T MISS THE BIG BAKE-OFF!!!
SEE WHO TAKES THE BLUE RIBBON
FOR THE BEST APPLE CREATION IN THE LAND!!!
SUNDAY!!! SUNDAY!!! SUNDAY!!!
SLOW DOWN!!!
FLAGGER AHEAD

I was amused by the innuendo of the first one, unsure of whether it was intentional or not. The O in BIG O had been altered to resemble the Ferris wheel we had seen being erected the previous day. Each sign was decorated with artistic renderings of festival rides and fortune tellers, games of chance and food of all varieties. The recurrent theme, of course, was apples—

apples in their natural state as well as processed into apple butter, apple fritters, apple pie, applesauce, apple biscotti…the possibilities were apparently endless.

We reached a flagger at the edge of the town square and were directed left into a small neighborhood adjacent to the main drag. The entire town square had been closed off with sawhorses and yellow tape—only foot traffic was permitted within. Beyond, I could see that the workmen had completed their tasks and the Apple Festival was ready to begin. It was still very early, just a little after nine, and there weren't many attendees at this point, mostly just vendors tending to last minute details in their individual booths. The rides lay dormant, not yet eliciting the squeals of delight and screams of terror that would come later.

The road to which we had been directed ran parallel to the town square, just one block back. We continued to its end, where more handmade signs waited to guide us to our appropriate destination. We could turn right by the town jail and take an immediate left, where a side street led to McCain's IGA. A section of its lot had been designated for festival parking. We could also turn left with the promise of more parking, or we could continue out of town on Route 5, which was what we elected to do.

After several miles, Michael turned on his hazard lights and eased off the road, or at least as much as he could without dropping into a shallow ditch.

"Are you sure this is right?" I asked, squinting through my window and into the woods.

"Pretty sure," said Michael. "You can see where tire tracks have cut through here." He pointed, and I spotted them.

I got out of the car and reached into the backseat for my backpack.

"Are you sure you're gonna be okay? I really hate leaving you here by yourself."

I nodded. "Do what you have to do. I'll be fine." I closed the passenger door and stepped back from the car.

He looked unsure but began a series of maneuvers to get himself turned around on the narrow road and was soon headed back the way we had come. He gave a brief toot on the horn, and I waved. The sound of the Fiesta soon trailed away as the taillights disappeared around a bend.

I surveyed my surroundings and sighed. This was going to be one helluva long day.

•••••••�𝇈𝇈•••••••

It felt like I had been trudging along the uneven path through the woods for hours, up long stretches then down others. Yesterday's ride from Shane hadn't taken nearly this long, and after a while, I was beginning to wonder if Michael had dropped me off at the wrong location. I was about to alter course when I finally reached the point where the tree line ended, and the hard-packed dust began. I wasn't exactly on the same path Shane had traversed but emerged midway between the abandoned mine entrance and the elevated rocks on which the kids had been sunbathing. I had the entire run of the place to myself today, and I wasn't entirely surprised. As gorgeous as this place was, the Apple Festival was a limited time engagement, and I remembered how I used to feel about the Scioto County Fair in Southern Ohio when I was a teen. The objective had been to arrive early and stay until close each and every night. I suspected the sentiment was somewhat universal.

I walked forward until I reached the edge of the rock face, peering down into the shimmering water below. It reflected the brilliant blue of the cloudless sky above. I was only about ten feet over its surface from this point, and vertigo was unlikely to engage at this height. There were several options to descend to the water's edge, pathways formed along outcroppings in the quarry wall. A small beach area waited at the bottom, and I was impressed to see that the teens kept their area neat and tidy. A metal wastebasket was secured in the sand, and sunlight reflected off the contents within. I dared to glance up and to the right at the various elevations the kids used to drop into the quarry waters and immediately discovered that vertigo hadn't been all that far away, after all. I stepped away from the edge and took a deep breath of clean air.

I turned toward the mine and headed that way. I was relieved to realize my headache had lifted, and I was beginning to feel a lot more like myself. It had been stupid to drink so much the night before, and I would have to watch myself more closely in the future. Apparently, I was the cheapest drunk *ever*. With only the slightest buzz, I had spilled absolutely everything to a complete stranger. I couldn't afford to be so indiscreet dealing with the folks from Briarstaff. I flashed back to Otis's question from the previous evening.

"Have you ever wondered if you sister might still be alive?"

It was utterly ridiculous, and consciously, I understood this. But desperate hope is a difficult thing to suppress, and it was busily becoming an earworm trying to burrow the possibility into my subconscious.

I sidestepped the sawhorses blocking the main entrance to the mine, noticing the remnants of railroad tracks that had long since stopped leading anywhere. Weatherworn signs were scattered about, warning trespassers to stay away, but I suspected they were more about denying liability than offering any practical guidance.

Essentially, I was in a fairly shallow cave that housed three narrow openings into the face of the mountain. The one furthest from me had sealed itself off from outsiders; its internal collapse had spilled out through its entrance like a rocky trail of cat sick. The entrance near the cave's midpoint had been closed off by a massive piece of sheet metal bolted into the rock face surrounding it. The same had been attempted on the one closest to me, but it had been no match for vandalism inflicted by the curious and determined. A large section had been pried back from one corner, providing access to anyone who dared investigate further.

It was getting warmer as the sun rose in the sky, and I slipped my backpack off to rummage inside for a bottle of water. My shirt was already sticking to my back, and I could only imagine the state I would be in by the time I walked back to town. I looked around, trying to envision what Gina might have found photo worthy here and had to assume the thrust of her article *had* to have been on the townsfolk themselves. Not that a few shots of the quarry and the sparkling water within wouldn't have supplemented nicely—

It occurred to me I didn't even know what kind of mine this was. I had automatically assumed coal, but that didn't seem to track with what very little I knew about mining. I pulled my phone out of my pocket and started to Google it but was promptly rewarded by a rudimentary block outline of a dinosaur advising me, "No Internet." I sighed and pocketed my phone again.

I approached the entrance on the left and peered around the metal barricade that had been pried back. The dank, earthy smell immediately suggested graves amongst other unpleasant things, and I couldn't see anything that might lay beyond. Realizing my phone might serve another purpose, I brought it back out and turned on its flashlight, shining it into the dense gloom. Ancient, wooden support beams held the narrow passageway open, and I could see traces of more tracks, much narrower than the ones outside, leading off into the darkness. These most likely conveyed carts in and out, carrying what I could only guess. Iron? Quartz and other minerals? If we had ever covered it in school, I clearly hadn't paid enough attention.

I slid my backpack to the ground and carefully examined the floor on the other side of the barricade. No broken glass or snakes, no jagged rocks or unexpected pits. I carefully stepped around the barricade, holding the flashlight on my phone in front of me. I wandered several feet into the passageway and found that the deeper I went, the more my eyes acclimated, no longer torn between the brilliance of the sun, the artificial illumination provided by the phone's LED and the inky pitch black ahead. I followed the broken tracks deeper into the tunnel, discovering abandoned hand tools as well as some really witty limericks etched into the wooden supports. It wasn't long before I found collections of empty beer cans and bottles, scattered around scorched sections of railroad ties that had once been used for impromptu campfires. Apparently, neat and tidy only applied to areas that were visible.

Stupid teens, I thought, wondering if there had been any real possibility of accidentally igniting combustible gas in the mine shafts. I also realized that as a teen, I would have likely been the one to bring the matches.

I passed through several junctions where alternate paths led to my left and to my right, but I stuck to the main corridor, afraid I'd find myself hopelessly lost if I strayed. My own footfalls rebounded and echoed against the walls and throughout the chambers, a sensation that was slightly disorienting, conjuring the illusion I was no longer alone. I stopped more than once just to ensure the footsteps stopped with me. I could hear dripping water from somewhere ahead in the distance, and I wondered if there might be an underground lake somewhere within.

I continued forward, rounding a slight bend. A quick glance behind confirmed that I had left the entrance to the shaft far behind. The hard-packed dirt beneath my feet was damp in spots, and I jumped when a droplet of water splashed onto my face from overhead. It was difficult to imagine workers packed into these cramped quarters, digging for whatever it was they were after. I was practically claustrophobic all by myself.

I tried to imagine what, if anything, might have caught Gina's eye to capture with her camera. I doubted if anyone in any official capacity would have allowed or encouraged access to the mine, considering all the signage outside warning trespassers away, but I knew my sister. If she was properly determined, she would have gone wherever she felt she needed to. I wondered if Shane or any of the other teens might have acted as unofficial tour guides and decided I would ask when I inevitably ran into one of them later at the Apple Festival. I wasn't seeing anything even remotely remarkable, only remnants of a time past, where supply or demand—maybe a little of both—had ceased to exist.

The corridor began a gradual descent while the ceiling remained at a consistent height, and after rounding another bend, I could see a shimmer of flickering phosphorescent light far in the distance. I noticed the droplets falling from overhead were more frequent, and I wondered if the corridor had cut far enough back to run underneath the lake. I was catching a different scent now, foul and acrid. I wrinkled my nose and held my breath but pressed on. I was curious about the source of the eerie light ahead.

I took a few more steps and paused again, suddenly aware of a subtle shift to the acoustics. In addition to dripping water, I heard scratching and chittering noises coming from all directions, a soft yet persistent susurration. I pointed my phone's flashlight at the floor and scanned in all directions, expecting to be up to my ankles in rats, but there was nothing to see. As I leveled my gaze, my forehead was splattered with something slightly more substantial than the droplets of water I had experienced so far. I wiped the oozing muck away and as I brought my flashlight around to examine it, I realized it was the source of the malodorous scent I had begun to detect. It smelled strongly of ammonia.

Shit. And quite literally.

I slowly shifted the focus of my flashlight toward the cavern's ceiling and found myself completely surrounded by a large colony of bats, suspended from above with their leathery wings wrapped around themselves as they slept the day away. The scratching and chittering emanated from them, and subtle movements of individual creatures presented like a slow ripple across an inky black lake.

My breath caught in my throat.

Don't know if I've mentioned it, but I'm *terrified* of bats. Spiders, snakes, mice and rats—no problem. I'm not crazy about any of them, don't get me wrong, but they don't inspire the white-hot terror and suffocating panic I experience with bats. It borders on chiroptophobia, although mere pictures of bats will only make me flinch.

I blame my father.

When Gina, Matt and I were children, our father found it amusing to share that his mother—our grandmother—had been bitten by a bat while pregnant with his sister, Eunice. She had to endure a series of rabies shots directly into her pregnant abdomen to avoid the risk of rabies. The story gave me *weeks* of nightmares, and I honestly don't even know if it's true! My father has a twisted sense of humor, and I could easily picture him amusing himself while simultaneously riling his easily flappable sister and gullible children. But to this day, he has never fessed up, and I've been scarred for life. You *do not* want to be between me and the exit if there's a demonic bloodsucker in my airspace. I will knock you right out of your shoes.

The legion I now surveyed paralyzed me—well, all except for the arm which was attached to the hand holding my phone and its flashlight. Of its own volition, it continued its slow upward creep, illuminating more and more of the evil little creatures, all of whom were growing increasingly agitated as artificial LED light pierced their slumber.

Realization dawned as the first wave of screeching reverberated through the cavern. I jerked the phone downward and tried to pull my head and neck into my shoulders as I reversed course, heading for the exit. I had only managed a few steps in that direction when the flashlight on my phone abruptly winked out, and I was plunged into complete and utter darkness.

147

"You have got to be *kidding* me," I groaned, squeezing every conceivable button on the sides of my phone. The only response was the red outline of a battery flashing in the center of the screen, showing 0% charge. I smacked my forehead. Whether due to my prior state of intoxication or the fact that the phone was pretty much useless in a village with no cell service, it hadn't occurred to me to charge the damn thing overnight. A series of obscenities converged into a single strangled cry as I was flooded with outright terror.

The keening had turned into a cacophony, and I could imagine leathery wings extending and stretching in preparation for the assault that was inevitably coming my way from these fanged creatures of the night. I stumbled blindly down the corridor in the pitch black, keeping a hand on the wall to my right while also attempting to keep my profile as low as possible.

I shrieked when the first bat whipped past me, hitting a note that would have done Mariah Carey proud. I tried to pick up the pace and only succeeded in tripping over a remnant of old track that ran down the center of the corridor. Mercifully, I faceplanted onto the hard, wet ground instead of the metal track itself, but I felt my cell phone fly out of my hand as I fell, and I had no idea where it landed. Once down, I coiled up like a fetus and prayed like I've never prayed before. I could feel the disturbance of air above me as bats flooded down the corridor, angrily complaining about the disruption of their sleep.

I may have peed a little.

After what seemed an eternity, I realized the relentless sound in my ears was no longer that of the bats but instead the hammering of my own heart. The fluttering and screeching had receded down the corridor and was diminishing by the moment. I decided to give the bats ample opportunity to discover their new destination and laid still in the dark, working on getting my breathing under control while slowly unfurling from my fetal position. I crawled around on my hands and knees, feeling around for my cell phone. Frustration was morphing into a different sort of panic when I finally found it several feet away. I tucked the useless thing into my pocket, stood up and brushed myself off.

And froze.

I no longer heard bats nor the sounds of water dripping from the ceiling above.

I heard footsteps, and they were rapidly approaching.

CHAPTER TWELVE

Agradual lightening of the darkness at the far end of the corridor soon narrowed into a focused beam of light cast from a flashlight far more powerful than the LED unit in my cell phone. I shielded my eyes as the beam rounded the bend and shone directly into my face.

"Hello?" I called out.

"Why, hello there, Mr. Morrow!"

I was at a complete disadvantage. I didn't recognize the deep, male voice, and he was unrelenting with that damn flashlight, keeping it fixed to my face. Only its intensifying brightness and the sound of his footfalls gave me some idea of his proximity.

"Do you mind with that thing?" I asked, waving it away.

"Oh, sure, sorry about that," he said, shifting the beam to the side. "It's darker than batshit in here."

Batshit. Funny.

Through the phantom spotlight that had been burned into my retinas, all I could make out was his vague outline. He was approximately my own height and appeared to be wearing a cowboy hat. "Can I help you with something?" I asked.

"Charley Daniel. I'm sheriff of these parts. I might ask you the same." He stepped close enough that I could begin to see his individual features. He was lean and lanky with a big bushy mustache above what may have been the biggest, widest bucktoothed grin I'd ever seen. He wore jeans and a uniformed shirt with his badge firmly affixed to its breast pocket. The cowboy hat was no illusion—it sat on a mop of bushy salt-and-pepper hair. He didn't offer a hand to shake.

"Oh, hey, yeah…I didn't mean any harm. I was just curious. I hope I didn't break any laws—"

"Well, as a matter of fact, you *did*. There are 'No Trespassing' signs all over the place out there, but I'm guessing you must have missed those." He had a slow, steady cadence to his speech, and the grin never left his face.

"I, um, I—"

"Are you intoxicated, Mr. Morrow?" He cocked his head to the side and looked me over.

"What?" I was taken aback. "Of course not! Why would you ask that?"

"Well," he said, close enough now that I could smell cigarette smoke on his breath. "I found a half-empty bottle of whiskey in your backpack."

"You went through my *things?*" I was outraged. *Of course*, he'd gone through my things. He must have also rifled through my wallet. How else would he have known my name?

"I didn't think you'd mind," he said before the grin dropped and he stared me directly in the eyes. "Unless you've got something to hide. Do you have something to hide, Mr. Morrow?"

"Nothing whatsoever," I said, forcing aside the urge to blink or turn away. "As I said, I was just curious. If there's any sort of fine, I'll gladly pay it. I'm actually relieved to see you. I was using the flashlight on my phone, and it just died. I will happily follow straight out of here."

"You're the brother of that photographer girl," he noted, and I nodded. "She seemed to be unusually interested in these old caverns herself."

"Yeah, well—"

"I'm going to tell you the same thing I told her," he said, and there was no doubting his sincerity. "These old mine shafts are dangerous. Supports shift, rocks fall and there are cave-ins all the time. Over the years, we've lost a few of our own in these very corridors. I can talk myself blue in the face to the kids 'round here, and they're still gonna sneak in. They're hard-headed and think they're invincible. You're old enough to know better, Mr. Morrow. What's your excuse?"

I felt appropriately reprimanded and had no response. I looked at my feet.

"Now, let's get out of here before you get yourself hurt."

"How long have you lived in Briarstaff?" I asked, attempting small talk from the passenger side of his police cruiser. I considered myself lucky he hadn't made me ride in the caged backseat. I had collected my belongings from outside the mine entrance and followed him subserviently through the woods to where his car was parked at the side of the road. He had offered to give me a ride back into town, and despite the awkwardness, I wasn't about to turn away a free ride. To be completely honest, I'm not sure it was an offer so much as an order.

"All my life," he said, and the grin was back.

"Is *everyone* here native to the area?"

"Is there something wrong with that?" He shot me a look from the corner of his eye.

"No. It's just a little unusual—"

"Not at all," he said. "Folks are happy here. Content. Are you saying we're unusual?"

"*No!* It's just—" I sighed and fell silent. Conversation was futile.

After a moment, he asked, "You planning to stay long?"

"A few days," I answered, and couldn't resist adding, "Is there anything wrong with *that?*"

It was his turn to sigh, and we both fell silent for the remainder of the short ride.

······•••••◦◎◦•••••••·····

Sheriff Daniel pulled to the curb in front of the jail and shifted his cruiser into park. Ahead, I could see the Apple Festival was in full swing. Children of all ages ran from ride to ride, squealing and laughing, while mothers pushed infants in strollers around the midway square and couples walked hand-in-hand. The aroma of deep-fried wonder wafted through the air, and my stomach growled audibly in response. I had bypassed breakfast and was now ravenous.

"I'm gonna let this slide with just a warning, Mr. Morrow," said Sheriff Daniel, looking at me earnestly. "I guess there's no harm been done here. But I'd like to encourage you to keep yourself focused on the task at hand. I believe Caroline told me you were taking some additional pictures of the festival for your sister's article?"

I smiled tightly and nodded. "That's right." Apparently, Caroline wasted no time in spreading my agenda around town.

"Don't let me catch you sharing any of that hootch with them kids you and that other fella were with down at the quarry yesterday, you hear me?" He waggled a finger at me, and I recoiled.

"Of course not!"

"Good. As a matter of fact, you should probably just stay clear of those kids altogether. It don't exactly look right, men of your age running around with a bunch of innocent teenagers."

I was getting angry, and I could feel my cheeks burning red. He was making us sound like a couple of lecherous old men.

"And exactly where *is* your buddy?" he asked, almost as an afterthought.

"He had to tend to some business that required modern accommodations," I replied hotly, glad to know *something* that Caroline couldn't possibly have already relayed. "He'll be back tonight."

"Hmmm," he nodded, pushing his hat back a little on his head. "All right. You're free to go."

I got out of the car and extracted my camera from my backpack before slinging it the pack over my shoulder. I turned it on and took a series of pictures of Sheriff Daniel as he stepped out of his car and lit a cigarette. He wasn't amused.

"I better not see any of those pictures of me in any damned magazine," he said. His miles-wide grin had dropped entirely.

Yeah, right. Like he would *ever* peruse a magazine that would carry my sister's work.

"Yes, sir." I held my hands up in surrender and backed away, turning toward the bustling activity of the festival.

I crossed the street at the corner, investigating the southern side of the square first. All the roads leading into the plaza had been cordoned off with sawhorses, traffic rerouted into neighboring streets, just as Michael and I had been earlier that morning. Vendor booths lined both sides of the street, and the sumptuous smells from an assortment of delicacies practically had me drooling. I paused to snap pictures of both sides—food booths on the left, games and local vendors on the right. I was acutely aware of the side eye cast in my direction by various passersby, but I was determined to go about my business—well, at least my *alleged* business. I glanced at my watch and saw that it wasn't even quite noon yet.

It was going to be a very long day.

My stomach emitted another obscenely loud gurgle, and I followed my nose's lead to a booth erected in front of Harvey's Videos. I ordered a foot-long corn dog slathered in mustard, a sleeve of shoestring fries with a generous drizzle of ketchup, and an ice-cold Pepsi-Cola. I fumbled my way to an empty park bench in the square and spread my feast beside me. I sat in the footprint of the teacup ride, and its triple pronged tentacles spun and tilted perilously close to me. Whoops and squeals of delight washed across the square as centrifugal force held riders firmly in place. I glanced across to the Ferris wheel, which was less aggressive in rotation and only partially filled with riders. By my best guess, there were maybe around three hundred people in attendance—not bad for this hour, but I was sure the numbers would swell as day turned to night and workdays ended for many.

I took a bite of corndog and immediately dripped mustard on my shirt. *Shit!* I reached for a napkin and realized I hadn't grabbed any. *Double shit!* I licked my finger clean and tried to scoop the excess off with it, succeeding only in spreading the stain to the approximate size of a half-dollar. It looked like I'd been shot by a yellow paintball. *Triple shit!* I closed my eyes in frustration, throwing my head back and muttering a select stream of obscenities. I was startled when I opened them to find an older woman standing before me, smiling and offering a handful of dampened napkins. She carried a Tide pen in her other gnarled hand.

"You're making a mess of yourself, young man," she chided. She was dressed like a gypsy in multi-colored flowing robes, a scarf of complementary hues draped loosely around her head. A collection of beads and necklaces dangled around her throat, and oversized rhinestone rings helped disguise the deformities inflicted upon her fingers by rheumatoid arthritis.

"Thank you," I said, accepting the napkins and wiping away as much of the splotch as I could. Next, I accepted the Tide pen and applied a liberal amount to the soiled area. I capped the pen and handed it back, and she gave me several dry napkins in exchange. I smiled and added, "It's very kind of you."

She winked at me. "You're Mr. Morrow, aren't you?"

I sighed. "Yes. Caroline must have really made the rounds." I took another bite of corn dog, successfully avoiding any more spillage. It was quite delicious.

"Caroline?" she inquired impishly. "No, I haven't spoken to Caroline in days. I'm Madame Phalange." She extended a hand.

I took it delicately and grinned. "Are you pulling my leg? Madame *Phalange?*"

"Why, of course!" She stepped back and put her hands on her hips, striking a theatrical pose. "I see things no one else sees! I hear voices from across the Great Beyond! I have answers to questions heretofore unspoken! I heal wounds unseen and mend hearts profoundly broken!"

"Yeah?" I took another bite of corn dog and a sip of Pepsi. "What am I thinking now?"

She scowled at me. "I'm not the Amazing Kreskin!" Her expression eased. "I was given my gift at birth, and I have chosen to share it with the world."

"Really?" I opted for fries this time, my hunger interfering with my manners. "And just how do you share your gift?"

"You must stop by my booth and see for yourself." She gestured to a makeshift shed I had passed when crossing the street earlier. It faced the opposite direction, but I could see a young woman in its rear entrance, shielding her eyes and watching us.

"And just what would all of this cost me?" I asked.

She shrugged. "Five dollars for a simple reading. Ten if you wish for a longer session. It's not very much but an old woman needs to make a living."

I smiled and slowly nodded. "Fair enough. I'll stop by in just a little bit, I promise." I gestured to the camera hanging around my neck. "Would you mind if I took a few pictures?"

She clapped her hands and bounced on the balls of her feet, nodding enthusiastically. "Yes! Yes!"

"My sister was here a few weeks ago, and I'm getting some shots of the Apple Festival to supplement her article," I said, peddling the lie that was our cover story. I set my food aside and stood, lifting the camera and fiddling with its controls. Unable to help myself, I added, "But I suppose you already knew that."

She touched the tip of her nose with one finger and winked again before striking one frightening pose after another. I could barely keep up with her as I snapped a dozen or so pictures and then gave her a thumbs-up to let her know I was finished. People were beginning to stare.

"Are you sure you don't want more?" she asked with a hint of disappointment. "We could go down to my booth and take a few at my table. I'm very effective with a crystal ball, card readings and Ouija boards. I could pose with any of them, or—"

"Mama!"

We both turned, and the young woman who had been watching us from the rear of Madame Phalange's booth was approaching. She was fresh-faced and smiling apologetically, her cheeks dimpled. Her shoulder-length light brown hair was pulled into bouncy pigtails. She wore cutoff jeans and a sleeveless, pale orange top. She was slightly winded by the time she reached us. She took her mother by the elbow, but her contrite gaze never left me.

"I'm so sorry," she said, as Madame Phalange attempted to wrest her elbow away. "Mama gets a little excited around new people."

I nodded, smiling. "Dwayne Morrow," I said, offering my hand.

"Joy Beth Perkins," she replied, taking my hand lightly before dipping into a slight curtsy. "How do?"

"Would you let me *go*, child?" Madame Phalange adjusted her robes, recovering her dignity.

"You've got customers, Mama," Joy Beth said, pointing toward the booth.

"Oh!" And she was off, a multi-colored swath of free-flowing silk gliding down the hill to meet her marks.

"I'm so sorry about that," Joy Beth apologized again. "She also gets a little excited about the festival. It's her one time of year to 'shine.'" She floated air quotes before hugging herself timidly.

"No need to apologize," I said. "She was just in the nick of time for me when I spilled—" I glanced at my shirt and winced. The Tide pen had not only removed the mustard stain but had also neutralized the light blue of my t-shirt, leaving a large white spot in its wake.

Joy Beth giggled, and I couldn't help but join in. Her laugh was infectious.

"So, you take pictures, huh?" she asked before tapping her forehead with the heel of her hand. "Well, duh—of course, you take pictures. I mean, I *saw* you taking pictures—" Her freckled cheeks flushed red.

"Yes, I'm following up on some work my sister, Gina, did here a few weeks ago." I glanced to the corner where Briarstaff Farmers Savings & Loan was largely obscured by a vendor selling bourbon chicken. "I'm guessing Caroline Peterson has kept you informed."

Joy Beth blinked. "Why would Caroline Peterson keep me informed about anything?"

I shook my head and sighed. "Never mind. So, tell me about yourself, Joy Beth. Have you always lived in Briarstaff?"

She tucked her hands into the pockets of her shorts and shrugged. "All my life."

Of course.

"Do you go to school with Shane and the other kids I met yesterday?"

She snorted. "Not hardly. I mean, *yes*, we all went to Briarstaff High, but I graduated a couple years ago. Worked for a little while at Staker's Drugs, but then me and Jimmy—" She stopped short and looked away, the rosy hue in her cheeks deepening and spreading to the very tips of her ears. "Well, we got married, and I stopped working."

"How old is your baby?" I asked, reading between lines that were about ten feet tall.

"We just celebrated James Jr.'s second birthday last Tuesday," she said proudly.

"How nice," I said. "Do you all live with—Madame Phalange?"

Joy Beth laughed. "Her name is Delphine Bartlett. She only uses the other when she's working. And heavens, no. Jimmy and I have our own little place just a little ways down Route 5 at the trailer park. I *do* check up on Mama a good bit, though. You might have noticed she's a little eccentric. She runs her business year-round up on the corner." She pointed to a narrow, weatherworn shotgun house across the corner from the F.O.E. hall. "She lives there with my older sister, Hattie, but Hattie's not really all there either." She drew a circle in the air beside her temple.

"I guess they're lucky to have you," I said, and she beamed. "What does Jimmy do for a living?"

"He's a custodian at the Academy."

"The Academy?"

"Sure," she nodded. She pointed in the general direction of the mines. "It's out that way on Route 5. It's just a small, private school for certain kids who are recruited. Kind of like a talented and gifted program."

"And you didn't go?"

It was so easy to make her blush it was almost a game at this point. "Heck, *no*. There's nothing special about me."

"I find that hard to believe," I said, collecting the remainder of my food from the bench and depositing it in a nearby trash receptacle.

"Well," she said, taking a step backward. "I really should get back. Sometimes I have to sort of keep Mama on track. She's been very distracted lately."

"Why's that?" I asked.

"She's convinced Sue Grafton came to her in a vision, summoning her to complete the final book in her alphabet series. She's been taking longhand dictation for months via the Ouija board."

I was surprised. "Your mother's a writer?"

"No," she said, with a quick shake of her head. "She never really learned to read past maybe the sixth grade. But she's sure filling up the legal pads."

"What's it called?"

"*Z is for Xenophobe*," she said with a grin.

I raised an eyebrow. "Xenophobe doesn't start with a *Z*."

"She ain't the best at spelling, either." She waved and turned, heading back toward her mother's booth. She stopped short and turned back. "You should really come and let her give you a reading. I would wait until after dark, though. My opinion, the whole thing works better after dark."

I laughed and waved. "I will."

As the sun reached its full height in the sky, it brought with it sweltering humidity. There was still no cloud cover as the temperature rose into the nineties. My backpack continued to weigh me down, and I took frequent breaks, sipping from the water bottles I had brought, trying to reserve some for later. Loudspeakers played Journey, REO Speedwagon and more as the handful of carnival rides kept delighted patrons engaged. More folks had arrived, and foot traffic intensified along the midway. The customer demographic was just as white as white could be, and I wasn't surprised.

I wandered around the square for hours, snapping occasional pictures to keep up appearances. I was aware of eyes following me as most locals kept a wary distance. I felt a bit like a turd floating in a pool, folks scattering if I even remotely entered their personal space. The sole distinction was the vendors, who had no problem taking my money. I tried to exercise self-control, but the delicious aroma of cotton candy, popcorn and fried Oreos was impossible to resist completely. I had just purchased a candy apple and was carefully wrapping its stick in a napkin when I literally bumped into Shane.

"Well now, hey, Mr. Dwayne!" he said. "Excuse me—I didn't see you there."

"My fault entirely, Shane," I said, indicating the candy apple. "I was completely focused on this. Once you get your fingers sticky, next thing you know, it's everywhere. I can't seem to stop eating. Are you enjoying the festival?"

"Oh, sure," he said. "Although I've mostly been running errands for the folks working the booths. I pick up a little extra moolah through the day, so I'll have some spending money at night. Where's your friend?"

"Michael had some business he had to tend to," I said. "He should be back later on."

"Awesome, awesome. Here's hoping he's not *too* late."

"Oh, yeah?"

Shane grinned and pointed toward the pavilion that stood in the center of the busy square. "It's kinda our 'big night' tonight. Me, Nick and Trevor are set to perform at eight. They're giving us forty-five whole minutes—they're shutting rides down and everything. I'm just about as nervous as shit—pardon my French—but I'm super excited."

"Well, that's just tremendous, Shane! Congratulations!" I shook his hand and patted him on the shoulder. "Did you say that Trevor is performing with you?" I was more than a little surprised, considering the racist behavior I had witnessed yesterday.

"Yeah, sure. He plays bass and has one hell of a voice. Why do you ask?"

I scanned the crowd, and it was still just as white as ever. If Shane didn't recognize the disconnect, far be it from me to bring it up. Michael had warned me against poking at the issue, and I was determined to stay out of trouble—if at all possible. I shrugged. "What does Nick do?"

"Pounds the *shee-at*—pardon my French—out of ze drums. Not as strong with the vocals 'cause he gets nervous, so we just turn his mic down a little." He put a finger to his lips. "But don't tell him I said that."

"No, no—of course not," I nodded. "Very exciting for you guys. I'll be there cheering you all on."

"Thank you, sir! Now, if you'll excuse me, I was just on my way to grab a couple bags of ice from the IGA for the burrito stand. Their icemaker bit the dust."

"Sure thing," I said. "I'll catch you later."

Shane waved and trotted off toward the grocery while I opted for the opposite direction, which took me past Briarstaff Farmers. Caroline Peterson was nowhere in sight, and I was glad for that. I only seemed to speak the language of self-sabotage with her, and I didn't think I could withstand much of her condescension without my mouth going on autopilot. I turned left at the corner, stepping away from the bustle of the festival. I glanced at my watch and was surprised to see it was nearly five o'clock. While I didn't expect Michael anytime soon, I thought the odds were fair he might be back in time to see the guys perform.

I took a bite of candy apple and discovered it had remained distressingly sticky in the heat of the sun. I was out of napkins and reluctantly decided it had been a bad idea. Before I made any more of a mess of myself, I started looking for a trash can to toss it away, and that was when I saw Rusty round the far corner, looking at his feet and heading in my direction.

"Rusty, isn't it?" I asked as he passed.

He cast a sideways glance and grunted.

"Wasn't very cool how your friends were teasing you yesterday," I said.

He shrugged. "I'm used to it."

"I don't think they realize how much it bothers you."

He paused, still focused on his feet. "Doesn't *bother* me."

"Could've fooled me."

The look he shot me was pure disgust. "What in the hell difference does it make to you?"

"Hey, I didn't mean to offend. I just thought they might have embarrassed you, and I—"

He snorted. "They're just pissed because *I* got chosen and not *them*."

I blinked. "Chosen?"

He nodded. "They're all headed for Briarstaff High in the fall, but *I* start at the Academy. Pushing carts *my ass*." He shoved his fists into his pockets and pressed on, anger radiating out of every pore as he slipped into the growing crowd of festival attendees beyond the corner.

"Wow," I said aloud, shaking my head and making a mental note to find out more about this Academy.

I turned back just in time to glimpse a slender woman disappearing into an alley on my left about twenty feet ahead of me, her long, jet-black hair shimmering in the sun.

I froze, dropping my candy apple on the ground.

It couldn't be…

Gina?

CHAPTER THIRTEEN

A hard lump rose in my throat as I forced my feet to action, hurrying down the sidewalk to the mouth of the alley. I skidded to a stop just in time to see the young woman vault over the edge of a commercial waste dumpster parked by the rear door of a business midway down the lane. She dropped inside of it noisily—from the sound of it, the dumpster wasn't empty.

My heart pounded as I let my backpack slip from my shoulder and laid it on the ground. It seemed suddenly heavier than I could carry, and I focused on getting the lens cap off my camera to capture whoever might eventually emerge from the dumpster.

I took a few steps closer and barely whispered, "Gina?"

No response, save for rustling which continued unabated inside the dumpster.

I inched closer.

"Gina?" I was louder this time, but my voice sounded far away in my own ears. It couldn't possibly *be*, but I had to know. I took a few more steps, drawing within feet of the waste receptacle.

"Gina!" I practically barked, and the rustling abruptly stopped.

A slow, mournful keening began from deep within the dumpster, growing louder and raising the hackles on my neck. I bridged the remaining distance and wrenched the side access panel open with a screech, raising my camera and snapping a series of quick shots.

The woman erupted from the top of the dumpster, and I pulled back, not expecting her escape to be so fluid. As soon as her feet met pavement, she scuttled away from me sideways, clutching something fiercely in one hand and shielding it with her body. She paused a few feet away, looking back over her shoulder while continuing to rhythmically wail.

I let the camera fall back against my chest.

It wasn't Gina—of course, it wasn't. Her body shape and hair color were close, but the similarities ended there. Her nose was long and crooked, and her lips pulled back to expose an overbite built with yellowing and crooked teeth.

"They're *mine*," she hissed, spittle spraying from the corner of her mouth. "You can't *have* them!"

I took a few steps back and held my hands up to show I meant no harm. "I'm not trying to take anything away from you, Miss. I was just making sure you were all right."

The guttural grunts slowed and stopped, and she shifted to look at what she clutched in her hands. It was an old pair of canvas tennis shoes, nearly worn through on the bottoms. The woman kicked off the bright pink flip-flops she wore and worked her feet into the tennis shoes, focusing intently as she tied each one's laces into a tight knot. She stretched her legs out and admired her find one foot a time.

"Very nice," I called out, and she turned to me, smiling proudly. I braved a step in her direction. "I'm Dwayne Morrow. What's your name?"

"Hattie," she said, rising to her feet and brushing herself off. She stooped to collect her pink flip-flops and tucked them under her arm. "Hattie Bartlett."

"I met your mother and your sister just a little while ago," I said, recognition dawning. "Madame Phalange and Joy Beth."

165

Hattie snorted and laughed. "Madame *Phalange—hee hee—*"

I couldn't help but laugh, too, and I felt foolish for ever thinking this young lady might have been my sister. I was dismayed to discover exactly how much Otis had gotten into my head with his preposterous supposition, but I'd be lying if I didn't admit I was more than a little disappointed.

"So, what are you doing back here?" I asked.

She shrugged. "People throw things out all the time, and there's nothing *wrong* with them. I take old things and make them new. Do you see my pretty dress?" She wore a sleeveless, pale pink seersucker sundress with deep pockets on each side. She tucked a flip-flop into each pocket and then twirled around, causing the dress to billow in the wind.

I nodded appreciatively.

"Found it and a bunch of other neat stuff just *tossed away* behind the IGA," she said, shaking her head before breaking into a giggle. *"Tossed AWAY behind the IG-A-A-A-A!"* She sang, her voice echoing down the alleyway. "I mean, *shoot*—all they needed was a good washing." *Washing* came out *worshing.*

"So, you do this a lot?"

"Oh, sure. Garbage is picked up on Fridays, so I make my rounds all week. Never know what I might find. I'm not real picky at first. Some folk don't like me rummaging through their garbage, so I fill my cart and sort it all out at home later."

She pointed to a rusting IGA cart she had parked beside the dumpster. I hadn't even noticed it before. It was almost half full of Hattie's assorted finds. Housewares, clothes, small kitchen appliances and shoes—none of which I would have touched with a ten-foot pole, much less dragged back to my house.

She brightened, adding, "Hey, if you want to stop by later, I could show you my collection. You might even see something you might wanna buy—"

"Hattie!" Joy Beth appeared at the far end of the alley, hands on her hips. "Would you leave Mr. Morrow alone and get back here? Mama's getting real busy, and I need you to keep an eye on the baby while I run over and get Jimmy his dinner." She briskly headed our way.

Hattie sighed and pouted, kicking at the ground with her "new" shoe. "Why do *I* always have to be the one to watch the baby?" she whined. "I got things to do, *too*, you know."

Joy Beth retrieved the cart from beside the dumpster and wheeled it over to her sister, who snatched it away with a little more force than seemed necessary. "I know you do, honey. But you know how Jimmy likes his food on the table when he gets home from work, and I really don't have any other choice. I can't just leave Junior in with Mama. Her readings scare him. And his crying scares the customers. We don't want to scare a bunch of people who're just looking to see what their futures hold, now do we?"

Hattie's eyebrows furrowed. Clearly, she was still unhappy. *"Fine."* She cast a parting glance at me over her shoulder and waved her fingers. "Maybe I can show you later."

I returned the wave, and said, "Sure. It was very nice to meet you, Hattie."

She giggled again, and I have never seen such a ferocious blush. She bumped her cart to the end of the alley and turned left, pausing to wave again before disappearing around the corner.

Joy Beth watched after her sister, shaking her head. "Well, I'll be. I think someone's got a little crush on you, Mr. Morrow."

It was my turn to blush. "Oh, I don't know about that—"

"I do," she said, smiling. "Hattie doesn't take to folks very easy. Matter of fact, she's been known to bite if she thinks folks are mean and she takes a notion to. But I have never seen *that* before. Now, if you'll excuse me, I really *do* have to get going." She stepped past me and headed in the direction from which I had come.

"Dinner for Jimmy?"

She turned, smiled and nodded. "Dinner for Jimmy. See ya later, alligator."

If I had known then what I know now, I would have never let her go.

I spent the next few hours wandering around the town. I could only take so much of the continuous assault on my senses from deep-fried delicacies and a pounding 80s soundtrack. I briefly considered riding one of the attractions, but there were only five to choose from, and four of those were geared toward younger children. That only left the Ferris Wheel, and all I had to do was look to its peak to feel a wave of vertigo wash over me—no thanks.

Flanking the northern and eastern sides of the town square, blocks ran three deep—four on the western side. Behind the businesses along the southern edge was the alley in which I had met Hattie, and just beyond that a single row of two-story brick industrial buildings that had once been warehouses or factories, all of which appeared vacant. A checkerboard collection of tall windows faced a narrow gravel road that ran parallel to the town square and marked the end of the city limits. The windows were so grimy daylight could only seek admission where multiple panes had been broken out. Just beyond lay abandoned railroad tracks, stretching off toward the mine in the east and to who-knows-where in the west. Across the tracks in the southeast corner was McCain's IGA. With little to see here, I ventured into the neighborhoods beyond the eastern side of the town square.

Sidewalks in various states of disrepair ran along both sides of each street. Weathered, compact houses with postage stamp lawns sat side by side, built mostly from one of four blueprints. Dogs barked from behind windows and fences, but I didn't see any trace of the residents at all. Perhaps they were all at the festival, but occasionally, I had the sensation I was being watched from behind drawn curtains.

As I wandered the northeast sector, I briefly considered hiking up the main road to Spielman Ridge, but I had no idea what I'd do once I got there. I couldn't imagine anyone would be willing to talk to me if they lived in the repressed state that I suspected was the case. I still marveled that Shane and his friends seemed to openly accept Trevor, and I wondered if this caused friction for any of them at home. After witnessing what I had seen the previous day with the younger children in the alley, I recognized this acceptance wasn't universal among the town's youth. Still, I had no brilliant insight on how to cleanly resolve an issue that had clearly festered and become deeply ingrained in this community. I continued on to the next block.

Sheriff Daniel cruised by twice, slowing to make sure I knew he was keeping an eye on me. I waved exaggeratedly on the second pass. He wasn't amused.

I had to take more frequent breaks as the day wore on, easing the backpack off of my shoulder and resting it on the ground. While I had the good sense to carry the thing over my left shoulder, at times my right one still throbbed from a gunshot wound I had suffered a few weeks back. I fished my last bottle of water out of the backpack and downed half of it, wincing at the realization the contents had grown tepid from being stored all day in a bag made of material that absorbed the heat of the sun. I glanced at my arms and groaned. I hadn't worn sunscreen—hadn't even *considered* it—and the bright pink of my forearms promised an uncomfortable evening. I imagined my face hadn't fared much better. I collected my things and moved on, adjusting my route to angle south toward the IGA. Hopefully, I could collect some aloe for tonight and sunscreen for the remainder of the time we would be in this strange little town.

I glanced at my watch and saw it was nearly seven-thirty. Based on Michael's estimation, he should be pulling into town any time now, if he wasn't wandering the midway already. Without the benefit of cell phones, I needed to be somewhere he might actually find me. I also intended to take in the teens' showcase. Previously witnessing a brief sample of Shane's talent on the guitar, I was genuinely interested in hearing tonight's performance.

The parking lot of McCain's IGA was filled to capacity, but I soon discovered most of the cars belonged to festivalgoers. Most businesses would prohibit use of their lot for such an event and would promptly tow anyone foolish enough to park illegally, but like everything else in this crazy town, normal convention did not apply.

Foot traffic inside the store was minimal and only one cashier manned the front. There were no self-checkouts whatsoever, and the town's technological blackout extended here, as well. I had only seen cash registers so old in movies. There was no familiar beep as barcodes were scanned—everything was entered manually with a series of rapid keystrokes on a complicated-looking keyboard.

I grabbed a cart simply to have a place to store my backpack and give my aching shoulders some relief. What few patrons roamed the aisles cut me a wide path or avoided me altogether, curiosity and hostility present in almost equal measure. At this point, I had grown quite used to it and didn't let it phase me as I scanned the aisle markers for "Health & Beauty." I found sunscreen and aloe vera lotion priced *way* above cost, but what choice did I have? I put a bottle of each in my cart and headed to the front of the store, adding a few bottles of equally overpriced water from the coolers near the registers. I got in line behind an elderly gentleman who wore the day's work on his denim overalls. I sighed as he paid for his purchases from a wad of rumpled ones before reaching for a small change purse deep inside his pocket and counting out coins one at a time. At this rate, I was going to miss the entire performance.

Once he finally collected his plastic bags and shuffled toward the door, I stepped forward and was met by the open palm of the cashier's hand, warning me to stop. She was a tiny little thing with a steel-wool beehive pinned to the top of her head and narrow, suspicious eyes peering out at me from behind horn-rimmed glasses. The tag affixed to her apron identified her as *Ruby*, and she looked like she meant business.

"We don't take no credit cards here," she said in a voice borne from years of smoking unfiltered cigarettes. "Cash or *local* check only." She looked at me as if she expected me to simply walk away.

I nodded and placed my items on the belt. She slowly rang me up and took my money, never offering to bag my items, only stepping away to light a cigarette as soon as she had dropped my change—from a distance—into my palm. There was no one in line behind me—I guess it was break time. I bagged my own items and headed for the door.

·····•••••○••••••·····

The sun was well on its way to the western horizon by the time I made it back to the town square. A quick glance at my watch showed me it was seven-fifty. All the rides had temporarily ceased operation, and the glaring lack of arena rock blasting from all loudspeakers was like an acoustic vacuum. A nervous energy had settled over the square as residents began to assemble, laying out sheets and blankets on the ground around the central pavilion, which was now home to a drum kit, a couple of big box speakers, several microphone stands and a pair of guitars resting upright on stands of their own. The boys were nowhere in sight but were probably getting ready in the small tent that had been erected behind the pavilion.

I scanned the growing crowd for any sign of Michael but didn't see him anywhere. I hoped he hadn't had any issues with traffic or anything else for that matter. I didn't relish the thought of walking back to the motel in the pitch dark. I saw Rose McCain clutching the arm of a young fellow near the stage, eyes locked on his face and laughing at every little thing he said. Ah, to be young and in love. Other teens gathered in small cliques near the stage, presumably to support their fellow classmates while parents and grandparents opted for positions farther away from the stage. After a moment, I spotted Audrey Peterson lurking in the shadows behind the pavilion, trying not to draw attention to herself.

I nearly jumped out of my skin when I felt fingernails skittering at my elbow, and I turned to find myself face-to-face with Caroline Peterson.

"Mr. Morrow," she said, and I couldn't help but feel like she spent considerable time practicing in the mirror, perfecting every nuance of appearance and inflection to achieve exactly the desired effect. Tonight, she wore a white sleeveless sundress cut a smidge above her knees and cinched at the waist with a wide black belt to emphasize her ample cleavage. Open toe slingback wedges accentuated her calves and lent her artificial height, as did her light auburn hair, which had been teased into a decidedly egg-shaped bouffant that cascaded around her shoulders.

"Please," I said, forcing a smile. "It's Dwayne."

"Yes," she nodded, and her smile was no less forced than my own. "Dwayne. When I saw you standing over here, I thought I really *must* take the opportunity to apologize for yesterday. I feel that we may have gotten off on the wrong foot."

I blinked. Was she *shitting* me? In my recollection, she had set the entire uncomfortable tone. Still, with great effort, I managed to hold my tongue.

As if the thought had only just occurred to her, Caroline suddenly looked from side to side, a cat in search of a mouse. "Where's your friend?" she mused.

"Michael got called back to his office to tie up a few loose ends," I said. "Since the internet is apparently a matter of science fiction here, he didn't have much choice." *Shit.* So much for holding my tongue.

She smiled crookedly, deciding not to take the bait. "That's too bad. I really enjoy Michael. He is such a gentleman." Clearly, the polar opposite of me. Fine. I get it.

"Actually, I'm expecting him back any time now. I'm hoping he'll be here in time to see the show," I said. "I'm sure he would enjoy hearing Shane and the boys. We had a little sample yesterday of Shane's guitarwork out by the quarry, and he's pretty impressive."

"That's *right*," Caroline nodded. "You and Michael were out at the quarry yesterday. But why on earth would you want to go out *there*? I thought you just needed some supplemental pictures of the festival for your sister's article?" She squirreled her face up as if it was the most ridiculous idea ever conceived.

"Well," I said slowly, deliberating carefully. I had the feeling I was taking a test and failing miserably. "The festival hadn't started yesterday, and we had time to kill. Gina said I should really check out the quarry if I had the chance. She said it was really breathtaking."

"Oh, yes, it is," Caroline agreed. "Some of the clearest water I've ever seen."

I nodded and opted not to wade in any deeper.

"I just have to wonder—" she paused, tapping her chin with the pale pink artificial tip of a fingernail.

"Yes?"

"What is your interest in the mine?" she said, and there it was. "Sheriff Daniel told me he found you creeping about in the dark, possibly *drunk*—"

I shook my head and held up a finger—and not the one I wanted to. "I was *not* drunk. Yes, I was in the mine, but I was just curious. I've never seen anything like it. Gina told me—"

Caroline's eyebrows arched impossibly high. "And just what did Gina tell you?"

I took a deep breath and exhaled slowly. Conversation with this woman was exhausting. It was walking on eggshells, and I had no idea why. "It's nothing, really. Obviously, she learned the mine's history as context for her story, but she never went in there. It's clearly marked as hazardous."

"And yet you did," she said, watching me carefully.

"Yeah, well, apparently I'm every bit as stupid as I look," I said. "I thought I might be able to give her a little more than a few pictures of the Apple Festival."

Caroline threw her head back and laughed. "Oh, that's sweet."

I shrugged, leaning into the moment. "I hoped she would be impressed."

"I'm sure she *will* be," she said, and her fingernails were skittering across my sunburnt elbow again. "Listen, as I said before, I feel like we got off on the wrong foot yesterday. I'd like to make amends, if I could."

I shook my head. "Really, I can't imagine what you're talking about. There's nothing to—"

"Nonsense," she said, cutting me off. "I was rude. Troy is always telling me I must be a little more understanding with folks who aren't from around here, but I'm telling you, it's hard. It seems like every time we've let down our guard, it hasn't gone well. I'd like to offer you an opportunity to make your sister's story even better."

"How so?"

"The members of the F.O.E. are playing cards tonight at the hall. Troy will be there. He told me to invite you and Michael, but since you are the only one here, I'm inviting you." She clasped her hands together and smiled. "Obviously, if Michael shows, you can bring him, too."

While I had hoped the opportunity might present itself, I never imagined it would come in the form of an invitation from Caroline Peterson.

"But why?" I asked, nonplussed.

Caroline sighed. "I guarantee you Gina was never invited to the table. No woman ever has been—not even me! But Troy thinks that an evening with the town's elders will provide a clearer understanding of how this town operates. Now, don't get me wrong—you'll need to keep your camera turned off. But I'm sure it could help shape the narrative in a way that is mutually beneficial to us all. Gina will be so proud of you! You'll provide a perspective she never would have *dreamt* of!"

Every time she uttered my sister's name, I wanted to smack her face. Todd Morrow may have raised his sons to never *ever* strike a woman, but I suspected he had never met someone quite like Caroline Peterson. Every single thing about this screamed of cold, hard calculation, yet it was leading me in the direction I'd hoped to go. Who was I to argue?

"Sure," I said. "What time?"

"They meet around ten," she said. "But you won't be judged on punctuality! It's just that the festival winds down around then, but believe me, the fellows will come and go as they're able."

I nodded. "Thanks. Sounds like fun. I appreciate it."

"And don't forget to invite Michael!" she stepped back, ready to be done with me.

"Of course," I said. "Whenever I see him."

A brief guitar riff sounded from the stage, and I turned my attention in that direction as murmuring from the crowd respectfully petered away. The boys had taken their places on stage in darkened silhouette, adjusting their instruments and waiting for the crowd to focus its attention fully on them. With near silence achieved, Shane lit into the intro for "Sweet Home Alabama," impossibly better than what we had heard yesterday. As Shane muttered, "Turn it up—," spotlights sprang to life, illuminating the pavilion from strategic vantage points, and the three young men within were entirely in the moment, hitting every mark and keeping every beat. When they began singing, it was nearly ethereal, and I couldn't help myself. I applauded and howled, and I wasn't alone—the entire crowd was drawn in. It was difficult to see these guys as the same ones Michael and I had met yesterday. I couldn't imagine the amount of practice required to get them to where they now stood, and looking at their faces, completely confident and self-assured, I had never felt like a bigger failure in my life by comparison, but that was my own problem. They had earned this moment completely, and I felt privileged to witness it, even if it was only by stupid circumstance. I readied my camera and began taking stills of the performance.

They finished to thunderous applause and barely took a pause before sliding into "Take It to the Limit." I was astonished at how smoothly their voices melded into sweet harmony, and if Nick's microphone was turned down, I would've never guessed.

When Shane launched into the intro from "Crazy on You," I was the first to scream out loud. I *knew* he could play it, but could they carry the *whole* song? Trevor took the lead vocal on this one, and his interpretation was nothing short of genius, carrying the verses in a direction Ann Wilson would have never seen but would have surely appreciated.

Next came "Free Bird," and as the song proceeded, the town square lit up with handheld lighters, waving from side to side. I have been to a concert or two in my time, but I have never felt so immersed as I did here. There was never a misstep nor false note. Whether I was welcome here or not, I was swept up in the collective appreciation of the raw talent of these young men, and I was well on my way to screaming myself hoarse.

Eventually, the boys bowed to the crowd, and their spotlights dimmed, signaling the end of the show. And as with other concerts, the crowd refused to dissipate, with thunderous applause and repeated calls for an encore.

After a few long moments designed to heighten anticipation, Shane stepped back on stage to his microphone, and one of the spotlights focused on his smiling sweaty face.

"Thank you," he said, smiling broadly and bowing. Trevor appeared behind him, retrieving his bass, and Nick stepped behind the drums. "We can't tell you all how much this means to us—*truly!*"

The crowd responded with a roar.

Shane flashed a thumbs-up and smiled. "We'd like to try something a little different tonight." He turned to his bandmates and nodded. The spotlight dimmed, and the crowd fell silent, lighters flickering out in anticipation.

A shadowy figure stepped onto the stage as Shane counted down quietly into his microphone.

The opening notes of Fleetwood Mac's "Rhiannon" fell from Shane's guitar, and when the backbeat engaged, the spots centered on the young woman who had taken the stage, holding tightly to Trevor's arm as they swayed to the hypnotic rhythm.

Swathed in scarves and bangles and holding onto a tambourine like a lifeline, Audrey Peterson launched into the opening verse with sultry intensity.

CHAPTER FOURTEEN

My mouth fell open as the crowd went wild. Although I couldn't be certain, I suspected this was Audrey's debut with the band. It was clear from the onset that she was focusing every bit of herself on Trevor as she smoothly transitioned into the chorus, and it occurred to me this was more than a mere performance; it was a coming out of sorts. Audrey was announcing her relationship with Trevor in the most public way possible.

I turned to scan the crowd, attempting to locate Caroline, but the lights had begun pulsing in time with the song, and it was difficult to focus on anything but the stage. I eventually spotted her to my far right, mouth hanging open in horror with those pink-tipped fingers pressed to each cheek. Troy stood behind her, one hand on her shoulder to steady her while he scowled intently at the stage.

As the song drew to a close, Audrey sealed the deal by tracing a finger along Trevor's jawline and kissing him lightly before stepping back into the shadows at the rear of the stage. Thunderous applause erupted as the lights abruptly extinguished, but in the firefly-like glow emitted from the crowd's handheld lighters, I could see Caroline pulling free from Troy's grasp, pushing her way through the crowd and toward the stage. Troy followed closely behind.

The lights sprang back to life just as abruptly, focusing on the star trio who stood at the front of the stage, Shane in the middle with Trevor on his left and Nick on his right. Their sweat-soaked faces were literally beaming as they drank in the crowd's approval. They bowed to the audience with their arms thrown around each other, smiling and laughing before ending in a series of high fives and horseplay before exiting at the rear of the stage. Audrey was nowhere to be seen.

As the festival lighting returned to its normal state, the crowd began to dissipate in all directions. Canned arena rock resumed over the loudspeakers against the jangly backdrop of rides being brought back to life. Caroline and Troy had reached the stage, and Caroline was frantically seeking her daughter. She caught Shane by the arm, and I saw him shrug and shake his head. Nick looked completely terrified when Caroline finally reached him, grabbing him by the shoulders and shaking him roughly. Wisely, Trevor had chosen to make himself scarce. Exasperated, Caroline moved on while Troy hovered nearby.

I checked my watch and saw it was nearly nine. I frowned, scanning the crowd again. I had really expected Michael to be back by now. I was beginning to understand how my mother felt when, as teenagers, we had missed curfew. I hoped he hadn't run into any problems.

From the corner of my eye, a sea of swirling robes came rolling in like the tide as finger cymbals punctuated Madame Phalange's progress. "Mr. Morrow," she said, extending an arm.

I smiled and took her hand, kissing her knuckles lightly. "Madame Phalange," I said. "What a pleasure to see you again. And please—it's Dwayne."

She blushed and batted her eyes, before frowning slightly and cocking her head. "You haven't come to see me," she said, jutting her bottom lip out in exaggerated disappointment while clinging to my hand. I suspected most everything about Madame Phalange was somewhat exaggerated.

"Oh, well—yes, I guess I haven't. I—"

"Pssh, pssh, pssh!" She finally let go of my hand only to waggle a finger at me. "No need to apologize. It has been a good day for Madame Phalange. But the day is winding down. You'll come now, yes?"

And before I knew it, she had seized my hand again, dragging me toward her tent. "But Madame Phalange," I protested. "I really need to stay visible until my friend arrives. I'm afraid he—"

She *psshed* again. "You will not miss him."

"How can you be sure?"

She stopped abruptly and turned, smiling broadly at me before tapping her temple. "Because Madame Phalange knows *all!*"

I allowed her to pull me the remaining distance, and I ducked underneath the velvet flap that comprised the entrance to her tiny domain. She flipped a card that hung outside the flap stating, *"Reading in Progress! Do NOT disturb!"* A window unit air conditioner hummed from the back wall, and glorious refrigerated air washed over me as I entered the space. The room was lit by an assortment of carefully placed candles, most of which had devolved into lopsided globs of wax as the evening had progressed. A small, circular table was in the center of the booth, covered by a deep purple velvet tablecloth, gold symbols of the zodiac and stars scattered around its circumference. A crystal ball glowed ethereally in the middle, soft light shifting through the colors of the spectrum and emanating from somewhere within. She waved me toward one of the two chairs that sat in front of the table before taking her own seat behind the crystal ball. I slid my backpack off my shoulder and placed it in one chair before taking the other. Over her shoulder, I spotted a Ouija board leaning against the wall beside a stack of yellow notepads as well as copies of Sue Grafton's *"A" is for Alibi, "L" is for Lawless, "S" is for Silence,* and *"O" is for Outlaw.* I covered my grin with one hand. I guessed the entire collection wasn't necessary for reference or inspiration.

"Where are your daughters?" I asked as she retrieved a deck of Tarot cards and began shuffling them.

"They have gone home for the evening. Joy Beth has her own little family to tend to, and Hattie is afraid of the dark. She likes to be in before sunset. We made the mistake of letting her watch that *Salem's Lot* mini-series, and well—" She smiled and shrugged, her finger cymbals jangling. She looked at them in surprise, as if she had forgotten they were there and promptly removed them, scooting them to the far side of the table. "But enough about me and mine, let's talk about *you*."

She sorted her cards into five stacks, placing them face down in a semi-circle around the crystal ball on her side of the table. She squared each stack neatly, before fixing her crystal-blue eyes on my face.

"You've never had a reading before, no?"

I smiled and shook my head.

"Tell Madame Phalange—are you a believer?"

I blinked. "I'm not sure what you're asking me."

She pursed her lips and cocked her head. "Come now, Mr. Morrow—"

"Dwayne. Please," I interjected. "If you're asking me if I believe in Heaven and Hell, God and the Devil—all that stuff—well, yeah, I guess I probably do. I haven't really given it a lot of thought—"

"*Dwayne*," she shook her head, making a *tsking* sound. "I don't think that's true at *all*. But do not be afraid. Madame Phalange is only here to help you and would never cause you any pain or grief. My goal is to illuminate and heal." Her script was practiced, its delivery smooth and soothing. The sounds of the festival seemed to be fading into the distance, and I was feeling a little uneasy.

I attempted to laugh, but it fell flat. "I can't imagine what you think—"

"*Shhhhh!*" she commanded, closing her eyes tightly and resting her fingertips on the crystal ball in front of her. She began humming softly, and I felt an almost irresistible urge to bolt, just grab my things and go. A thrum of electricity filled the air, crawling across my sunburnt skin and causing all the little hairs on my neck and arms to rise. This garish cartoon facsimile of a gypsy fortune teller couldn't *possibly* be the real deal, could she? Was there even such a thing?

Her eyes snapped open, and I gasped, startled.

"You've suffered a tremendous loss recently," she said. It wasn't a question, but a statement of fact.

I stared at her stupidly, my mouth hanging open.

"Not just you, but your entire family," she continued, her eyes welling with tears. I felt a hard lump rising in my throat. "Such a terrible thing, *terrible* thing…"

I averted my eyes, staring at my own hands resting on the tabletop and focused on my breathing. I felt like I was being probed, and my eyes had been the point of entry. I really needed to get out of there as soon as possible before I blew my own cover.

Madame Phalange flipped a tarot card from the stack furthest to her left and laid it on the table in front of me. It presented upside-down and was marked *XI – Justice*. She steepled her forefingers beneath her nose and paused for effect.

"This is not surprising," she mused.

"What does it mean?" My voice sounded distant in my own ears.

"You have suffered a great injustice," she said, and my eyes were drawn back to hers. "But you already knew that, didn't you?" I felt tears welling in my eyes, and I struggled to blink them away. This was ridiculous! I had kept my emotions in check the entire day, but she was like a magnet, pulling everything to the surface. She took a card from the stack furthest to her right, and placed it in front of me, also upside-down. It was marked *0 – The Fool*.

"Let me guess," I said, trying to nonchalantly wipe away the dampness of my eyes without causing any noticeable leakage. "That's me."

Madame Phalange smiled broadly. *"Yes!* Yes, it *is!* I think you're getting the hang of this."

I managed a chuckle. "Great. I'm the idiot."

She shook her head vehemently, sending her beads chattering. "No, no, *no!* You do not understand. *Many* do not understand this card. They think it is some sort of insult when, in actuality, it refers to the central character in our reading. In this case, that would be you. However, the card has presented itself in a state of inversion."

"Inversion?"

"It's upside-down. It indicates you have a propensity to be reckless and is cautioning you against this instinct."

I nodded absently. I really couldn't argue the point. Fumbling through and making shit up along the way has sort of always been my go-to life plan.

Madame Phalange cracked her knuckles and pulled the top card from the deck second from her left. She placed it in front of me, once again reversed. It read *X – Wheel of Fortune.* Her tongue ticked against the roof of her mouth as she slowly shook her head.

"Well, that doesn't look good," I muttered, and my voice still seemed far away. I wondered if the tent's acoustics had been manipulated in some way as to cause this odd auditory experience. It was beginning to make me feel like my ears had been packed in cotton.

"It's not exactly *bad*—"

"But not exactly good, either," I finished for her.

Her eyes conveyed a knowing sympathy that felt invasive. I tried to make myself hold her gaze, but just couldn't do it. "You are currently experiencing frequent setbacks, and this is very unfortunate. What makes it all the more so is that you can do very little about it until you reach the end of this particular journey."

"This particular journey? What does that mean?"

She sighed. "Every reading is a journey. It encompasses a specific period in your life and provides insight to help guide you toward the resolution you desire. It helps you focus on the light and diminish the dark."

"But it sounds to me like with this card," I jabbed at the *Wheel of Fortune*. "I'm just kind of screwed?"

She laughed. "No. Not screwed. It's just that there are external forces at work here, and these are things that are beyond your control. Perseverance and tenacity are key—you mustn't allow yourself to become disenchanted or downtrodden if you wish to attain the best possible resolution."

I nodded, and it suddenly occurred to me how very different her inflection and vocabulary were while in the midst of divination. Joy Beth had said her reading level was on par with that of a third grader, but it wasn't what I was hearing. I glanced at the legal pads stacked behind her beside the Grafton novels and was suddenly very curious to read what she had written.

The next card came from the pile second from the right. Again, it presented ass over teakettle, and I was beginning to think the overarching theme of this reading was a not-so-subtle jab that my life as a whole was completely upside down. It read *XVIII – The Moon*.

This time, Madame Phalange's face lit up, and she clapped. *"Yes! Yes!* This is good!"

"Finally," I mumbled.

"Indeed," she agreed. "This indicates great vindication, overcoming obstacles to gain clarity and find the truth that you so desperately seek. This is *very* promising."

I felt a weird sense of pride, as if I had finally done something right. It lasted for all of two seconds as I watched her reach for a card from the center pile, and I caught myself holding my breath. I just *knew* it would be *Death*. Of course, it would be *Death*. I would have bet a substantial amount of money it would be *Death*.

She flipped the card over. It landed upright, *XVII – The Star.*

I let out a whoop and threw my fists into the air, pumping my arms in victory. *"Yes!"* I exclaimed while Madame Phalange sat back and observed me from a safe distance.

"This makes you happy?" she asked.

"Hell, yeah!" I grinned, whooping once more before settling back into my seat. *"Phew!"*

"Do you even know what it means?"

"I just know it's not *Death,* and that's good enough for me."

She cupped her head in her hands. "Aye-yi-yi, sweet Mother Gaia—you know nothing. *Death* should not be interpreted *literally.* Oh, my goodness. It signifies transition, one season ends as another begins—even in its transverse, it simply signifies resistance to change or repeating bad decisions or behavior. It certainly doesn't mean the Grim Reaper is upon you." She shook her head.

I looked back at the card she had placed before me. "Well, then," I said, victory slipping away as the wheels in my mind ground through alternative options. "Exactly what does this *Star* shit mean?"

Madame Phalange threw her head back and laughed. "You are a very funny man, Mr. Mor—er, Dwayne. It is a sign of hope. It signifies renewal and healing, and you are very much in need of that. I hope this provides you with some comfort."

She looked at me expectantly, waiting for confirmation, and I'm sure my expression likely conveyed I thought she was from Mars. I nodded slowly, which seemed to satisfy her, and I sensed an opportunity to make my retreat.

"Well, this has certainly been an interesting experience," I said, pushing away from the table and reaching for my backpack.

"Wait! Wait! Wait!" she said, waving me back into the chair. "We are not quite finished yet."

185

"Oh! Of course," I said, reaching into my pocket for my wallet. I remembered her quoting five dollars for a simple reading and ten for a longer session. I was prepared to give her twenty just to get the hell out of there.

Her head dropped into her hands again, and she chuckled. "No, no, no. I mean—*yes*, we'll get to that part of our business soon enough, but that's not what I meant. We haven't given audience to the spirits."

"If that's part of the longer reading, I'm actually quite fine with the shorter version. Very—illuminating. But I'm sure you have other customers waiting, and as I told you before, I'm supposed to meet a friend who is surely out there wandering around looking for me—"

"*Shhhhh!*" she again commanded, and I fell silent. She laid her fingertips on the crystal ball, and the light dimmed by degrees, as if she were pulling oxygen out of the room. "I feel in some cases, this is the most important portion of a reading, and this is most certainly true in your case."

I blinked.

"From the first time I laid eyes on you, I've felt a tremendous energy in the spirit world unlike anything I've ever experienced. I am certain there is a message of great importance waiting to be shared with you."

I laughed nervously, a sense of dread washing over me. This *had* to be part of the Madame Phalange Experience. I'm sure she ran through versions of this same script with every single customer who had ever sat at this table. Was I truly going to believe that this glowing crystal ball— probably available for two-day shipping to anyone with fifty bucks and Amazon Prime—was the necessary oracle to communicate with the deceased?

Maybe.

I held my breath as Madame Phalange's eyes fluttered. She caressed the top of the crystal gently while its internal hues continued to pulsate through the colors of the rainbow. Tension had twisted the cords in my shoulders and neck into knots, and the urge to make my escape was steadily rising. If I were to run screaming out of the tent, would that technically be a divine-and-dash?

"Sit still," Madame Phalange chastised softly but firmly. "I'm trying to concentrate."

I realized my leg had been ticking at the speed of light with nervous energy. It took extreme concentration to slow it down before stopping altogether. "Should I be asking a question?"

"*Shhhhh!*" Her eyes remained closed as she muttered, "This isn't a Magic 8 Ball."

"It's just that I—"

"*Shhhhh!*" she was more insistent this time, and her eyelids parted just long enough to shoot me a withering look that said she meant business. Once they had closed again, she reminded in a whisper, "Concentration is key."

I didn't like this at all. My entire backstory with Michael was predicated on the fact that Gina had asked us to visit this little corner of *The Outer Limits* to get additional photos for the story she was working on. If I were to suddenly receive a message from her from beyond the grave, it would be somewhat difficult to explain. Of course, there was the possibility that Madame Phalange was part of a much greater conspiracy, one that had known all along my sister was deceased because they had been the ones to orchestrate her murder. One that wanted to probe me to the breaking point to find out why Michael and I were really here and how much we really knew.

My mouth felt like sandpaper. I tried to clear my throat and nearly choked.

Okay, I thought to myself. *Let's be reasonable about this. This is nothing more than schtick. A practice used for centuries to entertain, enchant and yes, sometimes deceive, but let's be real! This is the same woman who pranced around the town square, hiking up her robes to show a little leg in her pictures. She thinks she has a line on* Sue Grafton, *for God's Sake! The only thing sinister about her was the lighting in the room! She couldn't possibly—*

I was suddenly aware that Madame Phalange had begun humming again, and as before, the air crackled with electricity. She continued to stroke the crystal ball with the tips of her fingers, and her humming grew louder, more insistent. I wondered if when she finally spoke, it would be like it was in the movies, in the voice of whomever was sending the message. I also wondered if she would sense me grabbing my backpack and slipping through the exit since her eyes were still tightly shut. I had just hooked a finger through the backpack's handle when her humming abruptly stopped and her eyes flew open, and she looked completely startled.

I shrank into my chair and waited to see what came next.

She smiled slowly, her eyes focusing on something that was beyond me. "Yes," she said, nodding. "I can see you clearly."

I looked over my shoulder to make sure we were still the only two occupants of the booth and quickly confirmed we were.

She nodded and blushed. "Thank you. You are very kind." She giggled like a schoolgirl, and I was seized by a full-on case of the willies. It was apparent Madame Phalange was talking to the open air, but I *felt* someone else in the tent—*something* else. Everything I had eaten that entire day was rapidly devolving into acid in the pit of my stomach.

"Of course," she continued. "It would be my greatest pleasure."

Her eyes shifted into focus on me, and I emitted an involuntary squeak. "I really need to see if my friend—"

"*Shhhhh,*" she hushed me softly this time, placing a finger against her lips. "We must remain calm and quiet to maintain our divine connection. Just *breathe* and let me do the rest. Can you do that, Dwayne?"

A chorus of voices in my head screamed no, but I nodded stupidly while everything else in the room seemed to fade away.

"Good." She sat back in her chair and took a deep breath, focusing again over my shoulder. "I see someone who was lost to you recently. Someone very dear but possibly estranged or separated by a great distance. Does this have meaning for you?"

Again, I nodded, not trusting myself to speak.

"This loss was the greatest of shocks. You can never prepare for such an event. You always think you will have another tomorrow."

Once more, my eyes welled with tears, and there was no blinking them away this time. I felt the first spill over and roll down my left cheek. I sat motionless and waited for Madame Phalange to continue.

"So many things left unsaid," she said, shaking her head woefully. "This unsettled spirit has seized the opportunity to share something with you, something very important."

I felt light-headed and wondered if I might pass out. The moment to flee had come and gone, and I was rooted to the spot, unable to do anything but receive whatever mysterious message was headed my way.

"Such a kind face," continued Madame Phalange, still focused over my shoulder. "Misunderstood for so much of his life."

I straightened in my chair. "I'm sorry," I quietly interrupted. "Did you say *his?*"

She nodded and smiled. "And so handsome, too, with hair the color of the setting sun. I'm sensing the name—Bryan?"

She may as well have driven a sledgehammer into my stomach. All the wind rushed out of me, and I had to grab the arms of the chair to steady myself. "Ryan," I managed to whisper.

"Yes! That's it—Ryan. Ryan McNamer, McGuyver, Mc—"

"McGregor." My voice was barely there, and little black spots floated before me, threatening to overtake my entire field of vision.

Ryan McGregor had been my best friend in high school, murdered just before our fifteen-year high school reunion. It had been the first time I had ever played detective, and not only had I nearly gotten myself killed solving the case, I had met the love of my life, Melanie, who also happened to be Ryan's estranged widow and the mother of their young daughter, Jasmine. There was no *way* this woman could possibly know all of this.

Madame Phalange continued to stare over my shoulder, nodding as she listened to a voice I could only hear in my memory. Finally, she turned back to me. "Ryan wants you to know what a great comfort it is to know you are taking care of his family. He was never the right fit for—I think he's saying Melody—but he sees that you are, *you are!* And it's his greatest comfort that you will help guide his little girl through childhood and into adulthood. I'm sorry, I can't make out her name—it's an odd one. He knows you worry because you were never around children, but he said to trust your instincts. You'll do just fine. He wants you to know you were always the brother he never had and how very much he loves you. He wishes he could tell you these things himself."

She was focused on me again, and I was just *gone*, tears flooding down my cheeks, gasping for air around great gulping sobs. By the time I got myself under some semblance of control, I realized the room had brightened, and the sensation of electricity in the air had dissipated. My hearing no longer seemed muffled. Whatever presence had been in the room was gone, and Madame Phalange was once more herself, standing behind her table, smiling crookedly while she clasped her hands together and rocked from side to side.

"I told you my goal was to heal and illuminate, and here we are. You feel better, yes?" she asked.

I nodded numbly and mopped at my face.

"So whaddaya think?" She hiked her robe up to show one varicose-lined leg and propped her foot beside the crystal ball. "Want some more pictures from inside the booth for your story?"

I peeled two twenties out of my wallet and laid them on the table, muttering, "Some other time. Thank you."

I grabbed my backpack and nothing short of physical restraint could have kept me inside that tent for one more second.

CHAPTER FIFTEEN

I stumbled out onto the sidewalk and into the heat and humidity of the summer evening. It was like walking into a sauna after spending so long inside Madame Phalange's refrigerated haven. I glanced at my watch, noting it was almost ten o'clock. Only a handful of people remained in the town square, most of whom were performing cleanup duty. Loudspeakers had quieted and only the oddly out-of-tune jangle from the Ferris wheel continued, with a handful of riders rotating on the final journey of the evening. The other rides had already gone dark, and their lack of illumination cast eerie shadows throughout the square. Vendor booths had either closed up shop or were in the process of doing so, and when I looked back at Madame Phalange's tent, she had already swapped out her sign for one that read, *"CLOSED – I Predict I Will See You Tomorrow!"*

I was shaken to my very core. When it came to the supernatural—clairvoyance, ghosts and such—I honestly hadn't given it much consideration. I enjoyed a good ghost story as much as the next guy, and I had certainly heard my fair share of paranormal tales in which inexplicable things happened to normal people—but I had never delved any deeper than that. I had certainly never experienced anything firsthand. I suppose in the back of my mind, I always assumed there was some logical explanation, but the kid in me never wanted to shatter the illusion. I had no explanation for what had just happened in that tent. Nothing. It truly felt like Ryan had been *right there*—and the biggest surprise of all was I never realized how much I needed to hear the words that came out of Madame Phalange's mouth. As much as I believed Melanie and I belonged together, a teeny-tiny part of me felt a little skeevy—like I was inserting myself into a position I had no right to hold. If Ryan were still alive and he and Melanie had divorced, I most certainly would have asked his permission before pursuing the relationship. Even though we hadn't seen each other in some time, we were once best friends, and some things were just sacrosanct. Whether my conscious mind believed in what had just happened, there was no doubt that my heart did. I felt like a weight had been lifted off my shoulders that I hadn't even realized I was carrying. Best of all, I felt like I had gotten another few moments with my buddy. It was both bittersweet and cathartic.

I scanned the dwindling crowd, but there was still no sign of Michael. He should have definitely been back by now, and I was beginning to imagine the unpleasant. If someone had orchestrated my sister's murder, who's to say the same fate couldn't have befallen Michael? Without my cell phone and access to the internet, I would never know. I was completely stuck here with limited resources and no transportation. For all I knew, I could be in the crosshairs next, with someone watching my every move from any number of shadowy positions. I shivered despite the heat and humidity. I spooked myself into thinking I heard footsteps behind me and when I glanced over my shoulder, I ran headlong into Troy Peterson.

"*Ooof!*" The breath went out of him in a rush.

"I am so sorry," I said, steadying him by his shoulders. "I didn't see you there."

He waved my words away and nodded, straightening his shirt. "Apparently. Are you all right? You look like you've seen a ghost."

"Only Madame Phalange, and that's close enough for me."

He laughed. "I can certainly understand that. She's our town soothsayer. She turns in quite the performance. Always popular at the festival."

I nodded. "I'm sure. I don't suppose by any chance you've seen Michael, have you? He was supposed to be back hours ago, at least by my best estimation."

Troy shrugged. "I can't say I have, but I'm not sure that means much. I've been in and out of my office, taking refuge from this heat whenever I could."

"I really enjoyed the kids' performance tonight. Audrey was really good in the encore." The thought had barely formed in my head before it found its way out of my mouth.

Troy stiffened perceptibly. "Yes, well—it certainly came as a surprise."

"Did Caroline ever find her? She looked very eager." I couldn't seem to stop myself—my mouth had seized control of the wheel.

His smile was more of a sneer. "I'm not sure. I had other things to attend to, but I'm sure Caroline will catch up with her eventually—she always does. As a matter of fact, Caroline is the reason I'm here. She told me she had extended an invitation to our card game this evening up at the hall." He pointed, as if I might have forgotten which building that might be.

"Oh, yes," I said. I *knew* I should take the opportunity to meet the other members of the F.O.E. and see if they might shed any light onto what Gina had stumbled into, but it had been a very long day, and it was looking increasingly likely that I might have to walk back to the motel. My legs were already aching from my day's travels. "I don't know. I'm really beginning to worry about Michael. He's my transportation back to the motel, and if he doesn't show soon, I'll need to start walking. It's every bit of five miles."

"Think nothing of it," Troy said, taking me by the arm and guiding me up the sidewalk. "When Charley—Sheriff Daniel—stops by during his hourly foot patrol, and he *always* does, if you know what I mean—" He winked and tossed back an imaginary drink. "—I'll let him know that you're expecting your friend. If he sees him, he'll send him our way. And if, for some reason, he doesn't make it back tonight, I'll take you to the motel myself. How's that?"

"If you're sure it's not an inconvenience—"

"Not at all! The guys are eager to meet you. They're interested in everything you have to say. I'm sure they won't mind prying a little cash out of you, as well." He winked at me knowingly.

I laughed uncertainly. I felt like a lamb being led to slaughter.

The hall was ancient and oddly constructed. Ten wide concrete steps led up to a small, covered porch from which dark-stained, heavy double doors provided entrance. The building's siding was in desperate need of replacement, flecks of white paint chipping away everywhere I looked. Troy held the door and ushered me into a narrow hallway housing a small restroom on the left and coat room on the right. The acrid stench of cigars hit me like a wall.

Directly beyond, the hallway opened out onto the main chamber, where a large, circular conference table filled the room almost to capacity. A vintage chandelier was suspended by a short chain from an oddly low ceiling, centered over the scarred, dark wooden tabletop, casting a pallid glow that seemed to only reach the faces of the gentlemen already seated at the table. They were already in the middle of a hand, cards fanned out before them, and a small pile of poker chips pushed to the center of the table. Bottles of alcohol and beer rested near their owners beside glasses that were anywhere from almost full to completely empty. They took no notice of our arrival, continuing to chatter and laugh amongst themselves as we approached. Four empty chairs remained of the twelve that had been positioned around the table, and they were directly in front of us.

Troy cleared his throat loudly. "Gentlemen, I'd like to introduce Mr. Dwayne Morrow. I'm sure you will all recall his lovely sister, Gina, who visited our fair town just a few short weeks ago."

Conversations stopped, and everyone turned simultaneously, staring at me. They certainly didn't *look* eager to hear anything I had to say. In fact, they looked at me as if I had just wandered in trailing dog shit behind me. I smiled and lifted a hand half-heartedly. "Hello."

"As you may have heard," continued Troy, "And let's face it, Caroline was doing the talking, so I'm sure you *all* have heard—"

The men laughed knowingly.

"Dwayne and Gina's beau, Michael, came back here at her request. You remember Michael, don't you? He accompanied Gina for a portion of her earlier visit. She felt like her story would be a little more complete if she had some pictures of our Apple Festival. I guess Dwayne's pretty handy with a camera, too, although I'm not entirely clear on why she wasn't able to return herself…"

He trailed away, and everyone looked expectantly at me.

"She had another assignment," I said, then added, "In Istanbul."

Istanbul?!? Where in the hell did *that* come from?

"That's in Turkey, which as I'm sure you know, is—overseas." I needed to stop talking, because I was at the limit of my knowledge on the subject I had just introduced.

"Well, all right then," Troy continued. "I thought it might be neighborly of me to invite Dwayne and Michael to sit in on our game, although I guess Michael has since been waylaid."

"Yes," I interjected, still feeling like a deer in headlights. The expressions on the members' faces hadn't shifted one iota. "Apparently, he had to make some finishing touches to his own story, and he couldn't do it from here since there's no—"

Now there was shifting. Eyes narrowed in expectation of what shortcoming I was about to accuse Briarstaff of having. The eldest gentleman, who sat directly across from me, looked particularly sour.

I shook my head. "Doesn't matter. He had to go back to his office in Washington. The nation's capital, not the state." Oh, good Lord. "He should really be back anytime."

As if on cue, Charley Daniel walked into the room, holding his Stetson by its brim. "Good evening, friends," he said, grinning with all his teeth. "Right nice start to the festival today, eh?"

The F.O.E. members murmured and nodded in agreement as he proceeded counterclockwise behind those who sat around the table until he reached a breakfront against the right wall. Behind glass-fronted doors was a collection of glasses and liquor bottles. He grabbed one of each and poured himself a healthy amount of SKYY vodka. As he turned, he spotted me, and his grin faltered.

"I believe you've met Dwayne," said Troy, and the sheriff nodded. "He's a little concerned about his friend, Michael. Says he should be back in town by now."

Sheriff Daniel shrugged. "Can't say that I've seen him." He downed his vodka in one gulp and refilled his glass, while I managed to keep my mouth shut about the impropriety of drinking while on duty. It certainly didn't seem to bother the gentlemen who ran the town.

"If you do, send him this way, please," said Troy. "We're holding a seat for him."

"Of course," said the sheriff, sipping his drink more slowly this time while his eyes continued to bore holes through me.

Troy began introductions, starting on our left. First was Tommy Pruitt, proprietor of the local Chevron and grandson of Head Elderman, Emmitt Brown, who sat two seats over, stone-faced and scowling. Between them was Harvey Phillips, owner of the local video store, followed by Alvin

Knopf, husband to Sally of Sally's Flowers. To Emmitt's left was Daniel McCain, owner of the IGA and Rose's father. To his left was Dr. Jebediah Morris, who ran the town's only family medical practice. Reverend Theodore Baxter was next, and finally Major Thompson, principal of Briarstaff High. Their expressions were guarded, and greetings were less than enthusiastic, as if they were being forced to play with the weird cousin who no one ever really wants to see. I rested my backpack beside one of the empty chairs and took a seat. Troy crossed to the breakfront and returned with a bottle of Jim Beam and a couple of glasses. He handed me one of the glasses and placed the rest on the table beside me, dropping into the chair next to mine. Sheriff Daniel continued to hover in the distance, watching the men play and privy to the content of several of their hands. I pulled the Canadian Mist from my backpack and placed it on the table as well.

"We'll deal you fellas in next hand," said Reverend Baxter, as he slid a couple of chips to the middle of the table. "I'll call." The expression on Sheriff Daniel's face suggested it wasn't a good move, and Major Thompson slid his cards to the center.

"I'm out," he said gruffly.

Tommy, Harvey and Alvin also folded, and it was down to Emmitt and Reverend Baxter.

"Full house, aces high," said the reverend triumphantly.

Emmitt's craggy face was emotionless. He flipped his cards over to reveal a four-of-a-kind, all queens. His gnarled hands reached forward in slow motion to rake the chips from the center of the table into his pile, while Reverend Baxter looked completely flustered.

Sheriff Daniel tutted and shook his head, moving toward the door. "Making the rounds, gents. I'll check back in a bit." He looked at me. "And if I see your friend, I'll direct him this way."

"Thank you," I said, pouring myself a shot and wincing as I tossed it back without a chaser. The heavy door closed with a thud as Sheriff Daniel stepped outside.

I'm not the greatest at card games. I never have been. Solitaire is probably my game of choice. I have trouble remembering rules and was bound to make a fool of myself before the evening was over, but seeing as I had nothing better to do, I dove in. "What's the buy in?"

"Fifty," croaked Emmitt, and his leathery voice matched his face.

I retrieved my wallet and was startled to find that I had just under $200 left from the money Michael had lent me. I knew I had spent some money at the IGA and with Madame Phalange, but apparently, I had eaten more than I realized over the course of the day. I pulled out three twenties, expecting change but only receiving chips of equal value. Well, okay then.

We began playing.

"So, what's your first name, Major?" I asked, finally loosened up after a few shots of whiskey and taking a stab at small talk. The others had warmed by degrees, but that really wasn't saying much.

"Major," he said gruffly, tossing a couple of cards to the middle of the table and drawing from the deck. "It's not a title. It's my damn name."

"Oh, sure, I see," I said, nodding. "I thought maybe the high school was under military direction. Never occurred to me it was actually your name."

I looked at my own hand and discarded three cards. After drawing three new ones, I held three queens. I upped the ante a little, and the turn passed to Troy. Unbelievably, I had won a couple of hands already, and I was up by around thirty dollars. Maybe my luck was improving after all.

"The high school's just a regular old high school," he said. "Nothing like the Academy."

"Yeah, some of the kids mentioned it yesterday," I said, pouring myself another shot from my bottle. I aimed to make it my last. I had no intention of repeating my transgression of the previous evening. "What exactly *is* this Academy?"

"It's a privately run institution for students of a certain caliber. Attendance is by invitation only," said Troy as he discarded and drew cards, only to fold immediately afterward.

"What's the criteria?" I asked. "I mean, I've met a few of the teens around town, and they all seem pretty bright. They mostly go to Briarcliff High, and yet I heard Rusty will be attending the Academy in the fall. What makes him different?"

The frown lines in Emmitt Brown's face deepened as he folded and tossed his cards to the center of the table. I had won another hand. I raked the chips toward me and began sorting them by denomination.

"A committee from area high schools makes recommendations based on student performance and profile, but the admissions panel at the Academy makes the ultimate decision," said Major Thompson.

"That really doesn't say much about the selection process, does it?"

"Why are you so interested?" Major was annoyed, but I couldn't tell if it was because of my questions or because I had just won again. It was his turn to deal, and he was shuffling the cards with a vengeance.

I shrugged, tugging at the collar of my shirt. It seemed to be getting warmer in the room. "I don't know. It just seems odd that a town of this size would have enough of a population to support two separate schools."

Emmitt Brown snorted. "You have no idea what you're talking about."

"The Academy is home to recruits from all around the tri-state area," said Reverend Baxter, picking up cards as Major continued to deal.

"Shut up, Teddy," barked Emmitt.

Reverend Baxter flushed, embarrassed. "I can't see the harm. The Academy is a point of pride for Briarstaff, as it should be. Its graduates have—"

"For heaven's sake, Teddy!" Emmitt slammed his hands down on the table, and I jumped.

The reverend's mouth snapped shut. Appropriately chastised, the flush in his cheeks deepened. He collected the rest of his cards and focused on sorting his hand.

"I didn't mean to offend," I said. "I was just curious."

Emmitt made another distasteful sound in the back of his throat, and we began playing the next hand in silence. This time, my cards were shit, and I folded early. I was uncomfortably aware of perspiration trickling down my neck and seeping into the fabric of my shirt. I was surprised to find a shot still standing in my glass. I could have sworn I had already drunk it. I brought the glass to my lips and tossed it back, bracing myself for the liquid fire that raced down my esophagus.

Reverend Baxter was mollified when he won the hand with a straight flush, regaining some of his composure while Emmitt Brown's mood continued to sour.

"So, what is it that you do for a living, Dwayne?" asked the reverend. "I understand that you're here to help your sister, but photography isn't your mainstay, is it?"

It was my turn to deal, and shuffling the cards took more concentration than it should. My fingers felt weirdly thick as I continued to manipulate the deck. Impatience was spreading around the table when I finally felt the cards had been sufficiently rearranged and began to distribute them.

"I'm a computer guy," I said. "Hardware and software upgrades. Network configuration issues. Things like that. Could never make a living here, right?" I was the only one to laugh, and it came out louder than intended.

"Don't suppose so," said Daniel McCain. "Damn things are more trouble than they're worth. Viruses, ransomware…*porn*."

Reverend Baxter nodded. "Opens the door to perversion, especially for children. Playing with fire, I say."

The others at the table murmured and nodded in consensus.

"I suppose it depends on how they're used," I said, and my glass was full again. I nudged it away with the tips of my fingers and looked at the cards I had dealt myself. I nearly had a royal flush in spades. All I needed was the jack.

Emmitt cleared his throat loudly, his narrowing eyes focused on me beneath bushy caterpillar eyebrows. "I heard you were some sort of minor league Sam Spade. Is that so?"

The room fell silent, and I was acutely aware that everyone was awaiting my response. My brain was churning sluggishly, and my mouth felt like cotton. I blinked and found myself looking up through the bottom of the empty glass of whiskey, another ribbon of fire racing from the back of my throat to my stomach. I set the glass on the table and pushed it out of reach.

Without access to the internet, how could anyone in this town know anything about me? Michael and I had arrived without notice. Was this information gleaned because Emmitt Brown had ordered some sort of deeper dive on Gina, learning about me incidentally?

"I've worked on a couple of cases for Boggs Investigations," I said vaguely, my voice sounding far away. An ocular migraine had manifested in my left eye as a field of floating stars that slowly gobbled my line of vision. I was starting to feel a bit nauseous.

"Is that why you took such an interest in exploring our mine this afternoon? Your sister couldn't seem to keep away from there, either. I'm starting to think this all a bunch of bullshit. What exactly are you people after?"

"Now, Emmitt," said Troy. "There's no need to be—"

"No, it's okay," I said, struggling to focus as the visual disturbance began to disrupt my equilibrium. My speech pattern was off, as well. Words came in fits and starts. "I've pretty much gotten used to the outright hostility by now. Actually, I have a question of my own. How in the world did you know about my history with investigation? I can't imagine any of those cases would have made the news down here. For that matter, is news even broadcast here? From what the kids told me, all you seem to have on TV are reruns of shows that are decades old."

Emmitt smirked. "Just because we're not online doesn't mean we aren't plugged in. I have my sources. And I make it my business to protect this town from the likes of you and your sister."

I felt my cheeks flush. "Don't bad mouth my sister," I warned. "I won't stand for it." Truthfully, I wasn't sure I could stand for anything at that point. I felt oddly detached from my limbs.

"*Fellas, fellas!*" Troy held up his hands. "Let's get control of ourselves, here. C'mon. This is just a friendly game of cards. No need for such aggression. And Emmitt—really? Gina was completely open about why she was here and was nothing short of gracious the entire time. Her article was about life in a former mining town, so to me, anyway, it seems quite natural that she would have an interest in the mine itself."

Emmitt's mouth snapped shut, but his face continued to speak volumes. The likes of me and my sister? What on earth did he imagine we were doing?

The room fell into uncomfortable silence, and we continued with the hand I'd dealt. Emmitt discarded two cards and came as close to smiling as I'd seen that evening when he drew two more. "I'll raise $100."

"Emmitt!" protested Troy. "You know we don't normally—"

"Then fold and cut your losses," Emmitt barked sharply, muttering, "Bunch of pussies." He had a mad twinkle in his eye and was firmly focused on me.

"I'm out," said Dr. Morris, sliding his cards to the center of the table.

"Me, too," said Reverend Baxter.

Major Thompson, sighed and flung his cards down, looking thoroughly disgusted with the lot of us.

I discarded a two of hearts and reached for the deck. I closed my eyes and said a quick prayer for luck. I wanted to wipe the smarmy smile from that old bastard's face so badly I could taste it and relieving him of some cash certainly wouldn't hurt my feelings, either. I held my breath and opened my eyes.

It was the jack of spades.

Summoning every bit of resolve I could muster, I attempted to remain expressionless—to what degree of success I could only imagine. There was no higher poker hand than what I held. I took a deep breath and let it out slowly, afraid I might giggle.

"I'll see your bet," I said, wrapping my palms around my entire stack of chips and scooting them to the center of the table. "And I'm all in." I couldn't help but grin as the old coot's expression shifted to one of delight.

"Shit," said Troy, tossing his cards in. "I'm out."

Tommy, Harvey and Alvin were out as well, cutting their losses and leaving just me and the old man to duke it out. It felt like we were on the cusp of a duel, and I couldn't wait to see the look on Emmitt's sour old face when I showed my hand.

He slid his chips to the middle of the table, knocking my stack over before turning his cards face up victoriously. He had a royal flush of hearts. "Take that, you smug little asshole."

He began to reach for the chips, and I cleared my throat, which was suddenly very thick. "You might want to hold up there, grandpa," I said, and I was slurring badly. What in the hell was wrong with me? I slapped my cards down clumsily. "I'm pretty sure spades trump hearts."

Oh, how I wish I had my camera ready for the look on his face. I watched the color drain from the top of his head to well below his collar, and then he started quivering with rage, his bony old hands clutched into fists. Color flooded back in as his blood pressure soared. "Son of a bitch—"

"Wait a minute," said Tommy. It was the first time he had spoken aloud the entire evening. "This can't be right."

He reached toward the cards he had just discarded and pulled them back, thumbing through them. He laid a queen of spades down, and all eyes shifted to me.

"You dirty little bastard," spat Emmitt, leaping to his feet. "You've been cheating this whole goddamned time."

"What?" I was utterly shocked and watched as expressions turned to universal disgust around the table. "I've never cheated at cards in my life. I—"

"Then what in the hell are these?" asked Troy. He had snagged my backpack and rooted through it, pulling out two decks of Bicycle playing cards, one red and one blue.

I tried to get up, but my legs weren't obeying my brain. "That's absurd! How could I have known what kind of cards you all used?" My words were mushy and disjointed.

"Well, I think *I've* had quite enough for the evening," said Reverend Baxter, pushing away from the table as others followed. "I think it would be appropriate for your ill-gotten wins to be redistributed to those you stole them from."

A general murmur of agreement passed between the others, and I was outraged. Somehow, I had been set up. Summoning all of the determination I could muster, I pushed myself to my feet, and immediately, the room began to wobble and spin. My stomach felt unusually full, and I was queasy. I steadied myself by clutching the edge of the table with both hands.

"I don't feel so well," I managed before leaning forward and vomiting explosively on the table, spattering a few of the horrified F.O.E. members in the process. My vision tunneled and narrowed, and the last thing I remember was the surface of the table approaching my face at high velocity as I descended into darkness.

CHAPTER SIXTEEN

I woke smelling of stale whiskey and with the taste of puke in my mouth. I urgently needed to take a whiz, but my limbs weren't cooperating. Moonlight shone in through a single window in the wall behind me, and as I tried to get my bearings, I realized there were bars in the window. My head pounded with a vengeance, and I struggled to lift it, but the world spun away from me again, bringing a wave of dry heaves that ended in gut wrenching cramps. In the process, I lost the fight with my bladder and felt a warm wetness spreading within my shorts and beyond.

Defeated and humiliated, I lay my head back down and closed my eyes, drifting away almost immediately.

········•••••◦◦•••••·····

Aromatic coffee brought me around the next time, its scent somehow penetrating the bounty of my own stench. Daylight now spilled through the barred window and into the cell, but I had no sense of time. I glanced at my arm, but my wristwatch was gone. I became aware of someone else in the far corner of the room, shuffling papers and conversing quietly on the telephone.

My head still throbbed in time with my heartbeat, but the intensity had lessened, and I was able to prop myself on an elbow without my stomach turning inside out. A quick scan confirmed that I was in Briarstaff's lone jail cell, and a double take confirmed I was not alone. A lanky man sprawled on a cot across from me, his back turned toward me while a steady, rhythmic whistle escaped his nostrils.

I sat up, sticky and unclean. My khaki shorts were still damp with urine which had also soaked into the flimsy mattress of the prison cot. I couldn't remember ever feeling such shame. How had I gotten myself into this mess?

"Mr. Morrow," boomed Sheriff Daniel from across the room. Was there ever a time he *wasn't* on duty? "I see you're awake. Feeling better, hopefully?"

I nodded. "I don't understand what happened. Why am I here?"

Sheriff Daniel crossed the room and stood at the entrance to the cage. "You should consider yourself lucky that no one is pressing charges. They really had a time talking Emmitt down, but they really just wanted to be done with you. I guess you really showed your ass last night."

"I don't understand," I repeated, struggling to pull the pieces of the previous evening together. "I only had a few drinks—"

The sheriff burst out laughing, causing the man on the other cot to squirm. "I'd say you had more than *a few drinks*. It took three of us to get you down here from the lodge. You were blotto."

Suddenly, the rest of the evening came rushing back—Emmitt Brown's aggressive unpleasantness, allegations of cheating, Troy Peterson rifling through my backpack—my backpack! I looked around the small cell and found no trace, not even underneath my cot.

"Where are my things?" I demanded.

"Relax, Mr. Morrow. Your belongings are locked up in a storage bin behind my desk. They will be returned to you once you are released, which I am about to do," said the sheriff before bellowing. *"Hey, Jimmy! Time to rise and shine!"*

The man on the other cot rolled over, rubbing his eyes deeply before mumbling, "Five more minutes, Ma."

"This ain't your ding-dang *Ma*, Jimmy. C'mon, son, let's *move it, move it, move it!*" He gripped a pair of handcuffs by one end and sent it clanking across the bars, much to Jimmy's dismay. "It's check out time. C'mon fellas. I've got better things to do."

Jimmy was quicker to stand than me, as I was still acutely aware of the telltale stain on my shorts. He loped to the front of the cell and waited patiently while Sheriff Daniel unlocked the door.

"You really need to slow your drinking down, Jimmy," said the sheriff. "I'm tired of doing this. What's this, the third time this month?"

Jimmy looked at his feet and mumbled something unintelligible.

"Yeah, well, you're going to end up losing your job if you're not careful. Get on outta here, and don't let this happen again anytime soon. You've got your family to be thinking of."

Jimmy mumbled something else before exiting the cell and crossing to the jail's door. I could hear the distant jangle of the Apple Festival stirring to life when he opened the door and stepped through.

"Michael Arthur never showed last night?" I asked.

Sheriff Daniel shook his head. "Nope. At least, I didn't see him."

Something was very wrong. Michael should have *definitely* been back by now.

"I don't suppose you have a shower somewhere in here," I said, looking around hopefully.

He laughed. "No, and what a shame. You're a mess! But you'll have to clean yourself up elsewhere."

"Am I at least entitled to a phone call?"

"You're entitled to as many phone calls as you'd like, you just need to make them somewhere else. You're a free man, Mr. Morrow. Once Dr.

Morris assured me you weren't in danger of asphyxiating in your sleep, we put you in there for your own good."

I peeled the blanket away and tossed it into the corner of the cell. I had a change of clothes back at the motel—the motel! Shit!

"What time is it?" I asked frantically, suddenly sure I was already past check-out time, and the rest of my belongings had probably already been seized or tossed by Mrs. Shepley. I exited the cell before Sheriff Daniel changed his mind.

"It's barely nine," said the sheriff, striding back to his desk and retrieving my backpack from the storage locker where he had placed it. I still had ample time before check-out.

"Do you think I could get a ride back to the motel?" I asked, taking my backpack and rummaging through its contents. I found my watch and slipped it on. My whiskey was gone, but no surprise there. My camera rested at the bottom beside my useless cell phone, and my wallet was there, too. I thumbed through its contents and saw they left me with $148, which was exactly the amount I had after buying into the poker game. The extra decks of Bicycle cards were gone as well.

"Sorry, Mr. Morrow, but I'm not a taxi service. Besides, it looks like you've got a little something on your pants, there. I don't want any part of that in my vehicle." He waggled a finger toward me and wrinkled his nose distastefully, and I could feel my cheeks grow warm.

"Fine, I can walk, then."

He caught me by arm as I started to leave.

"I don't know what you were trying to pull last night, but those are some of the most respected men in Briarstaff," he said, inserting himself into my personal space about two inches too close. "To think that you would actually *steal* from the very gentlemen who were only trying to welcome you—well, it's just appalling."

"I didn't *do* anything," I insisted, the warmth in my cheeks spreading to the tips of my ears.

Sheriff Daniel shook his head. "Caught red-handed, and you *still* insist you knew nothing about it." He stepped a little closer, and I could smell the coffee on his breath. "Let me give you a piece of advice you had better seriously consider. It's time for you to collect your things and get on back to wherever you came from."

"Believe me, I'd like nothing more," I said. "I just need to find my friend so I can—"

"Just stop," he interrupted. "I don't give a good goddamn what you think you need to do. But I assure you, if we have a repeat of anything even *close* to what happened last night, you'll be calling that jail cell your new home for quite some time, do you hear me?"

My jaw clenched painfully as we locked eyes.

"Well, *do you?*" He barked, and I flinched, nodding.

I stepped out into the bright daylight before my mouth could get me into any more trouble.

•••••••●⌒◯●•••••••

I hurried around the corner and up the sidewalk, passing Ida's Town Diner and Paul and Pauline's dual grooming establishments with my eyes glued firmly to my feet. It seemed like conversations faded away as soon as I entered the town square, but I don't know how much of that was my shame-riddled imagination. I felt like a leper scuttling out of town just as quickly as possible. I didn't relish running into any of the fellows from the poker game.

Once I exited the town square on the north end, following in reverse the path Michael and I had taken into town the previous morning, the sounds of the Apple Festival began to fade behind me. The sun was already warm, and my ruined shorts were chafing my inner thighs. Tall weeds lined both sides of the road, and there was very little shoulder for me to safely traverse. I slowed my pace, taking deep breaths to clear my head. I didn't have any bottles of water left in my backpack, and my throat was like sand.

What exactly had happened?

I am not a heavy drinker, but I am no lightweight, either. I'm not prone to blackouts, although I had come pretty close the previous evening with Otis. The way I felt in that room—it was entirely different than a good whiskey buzz.

Was it possible I had been drugged?

The more I considered it, the more likely it seemed. The entire evening had been nothing more than a setup, calculated to reduce me to my lowest point. It was certainly hard to argue its success as I hobbled along the two-lane blacktop with my shorts sticking to my skin and remnants of sick trapped in my hair. The only thing I'd had to drink was from my own bottle. Who would have had the opportunity to slip something into it? Sheriff Daniel had been through my things while I was inside the cave, but he would have been taking quite a risk slipping those additional decks of cards into my bag. I could have discovered them at any point throughout the day, and I certainly hadn't cheated at cards. Hell, it took everything I had just to remember the basic rules much less circumvent them. As quickly as my brain had turned to fog, sleight of hand would have been out of the question. The next most likely culprit was Troy Peterson, and it didn't take much imagination to picture Caroline's delicate hand wedged firmly up to the elbow in his ass, controlling his every action.

I was lost in deliberation when a rickety Chevy pick-up roared past, honking its horn and scaring the living shit out of me, cutting it far closer than necessary. I couldn't see the occupants, but a well-muscled arm sporting a Confederate flag tattoo flew a single-digit salute from the passenger window, and I heard rowdy laughter spilling out, undoubtedly at my expense.

I couldn't imagine what had happened to Michael. Had they done something to him as well, or was I just being overly paranoid? It was entirely feasible Michael had been delayed for any number of reasons, and it didn't necessarily equate to a death sentence. I might get back to the motel to find his stupid bright yellow rental sitting in the parking lot while he caught up on his Zs in the comfort of his room. I had to smile. If you had asked just the previous day if there was *anything* comfortable about the rooms in that motel, I would have laughed. Now, I wanted nothing more than to be in my own, stripped of these disgusting clothes and testing the limits of hot water in its grimy little shower stall.

The weeds to my right abruptly fell away, and I looked up to see I was at the entrance to Spielman Ridge. Just as I recognized Shane's truck parked in front of the first house on the northern side of the street, Shane and Trevor stepped out onto the porch, laughing at a joke I hoped wasn't about me. I didn't think that was the case because they didn't appear to have noticed me yet. In my current condition, I wanted to hide, but there was nowhere to go. As they rounded the back side of Shane's truck, Trevor noticed me and raised a hand, a smile faltering as he took in the sight of me. Shane was only a second behind him, his face falling almost comically.

"Hey, there, Mr. Dwayne," he called, inching closer. "Pardon my French, but you look like shit."

I grinned and nodded. "More like piss, but yeah—long story. You boys should probably stay back."

"We got time," said Trevor, as he and Shane paused in the middle of the tar and gravel street, shielding their eyes from the bright sun overhead.

"Maybe later," I said, relieved to see nothing but concern in these boys' eyes. It gave me hope that not everyone in this town was embroiled in whatever was going on here. "Hey, I really enjoyed your concert last night. You all kicked some serious ass!"

Both of their faces lit up.

"I don't know about *that*," Shane said modestly, kicking at the ground. "We sure did have fun, though."

"I'm thinking we should listen to the man," said Trevor, nowhere near as modestly. "We killed it."

"You most certainly did," I agreed. "You should be very proud of yourselves. So, what are your plans for the band? Have you thought about playing outside of this area? You know, take the show on the road? You certainly have the talent."

"Aw, shucks, no," said Shane, shaking his head. His smile was practically from ear to ear. "It's just something we do for grins. I certainly do appreciate your kind words, though. Means a lot coming from someone who isn't a parent, cousin or Sunday school teacher."

"Don't sell yourselves short," I said. "You guys could be the next big thing. And when you brought Audrey out for the encore—I mean, *wow!* You all were on fire!"

Shane and Trevor looked at each other, their smiles faltering. At that precise moment, I saw Audrey step out onto Trevor's front porch, curious about with whom her friends were speaking. Recognition dawned, and she tossed me a cautious wave, which I returned.

"Yeah, well, that probably was just one-time occurrence," said Shane.

I nodded. "Caroline Peterson didn't look too happy."

"It's such a load of *shit*, man!" Trevor said, angrily pacing back and forth. I noticed a wide-eyed woman had appeared behind the screen door, her arm draped protectively around the young boy I recognized from the alley a couple days' prior.

"You need me to call your father, Trevor?" she called, and I realized she thought I might be a threat.

"No, Ma," called Trevor. "This is just Mr. Dwayne. We're fine."

She didn't look too certain, but after a moment, she stepped back into the house, pulling the curious boy with her.

"Was that your brother?" I asked.

Trevor nodded. "Tyrese."

"I stopped a bunch of kids in town from pelting him with rocks the other day," I said. "I'm glad to see he's okay."

"Thank you for that," said Trevor. "Can't get that boy to understand he can't just go anyplace he wants to go. It ain't safe."

Audrey made her way from the porch to Trevor's side and put an arm around his waist. "It's okay, baby. Just gotta get through one more year, and we're leaving this place in the rearview."

"What did your mom say about the concert?" I had to know.

She shrugged. "Haven't seen her, and I really don't give a damn."

"Does your father feel the same way?"

"My father feels exactly how my mother wants him to feel," she said. "She's like a pint-sized steamroller in heels. She just rolls right over anyone in her path to get exactly what she wants. She doesn't listen to reason or facts. Her mind is made up before any discussion is ever entertained. She keeps handwritten notes on absolutely anyone she ever has met—including me—so she can use their words against them whenever necessary. My *very* favorite thing is when she tells me what I mean by what I say, like I don't have any idea of what is coming from my own mouth and mind."

She rolled her eyes and shook her head, exasperated. Despite her tough exterior, it was apparent she was very upset. Trevor kissed the top of her head and pulled her closer.

I thought of my own mother and how very lucky I was. Jo Morrow could manipulate with guilt or nag you into submission, but her motives were never selfish, much less insulting. She encouraged her children to dream big and take chances, live our own lives to the fullest. Even as she currently grieved the loss of her eldest daughter, I doubted she would alter course now. She might be a bit more of a worrywart, but I could live with that. We weren't raised with the expectation that free will was off the table.

"So, when are you going home?" I asked. "You *are* eventually going home, aren't you?"

She nodded jerkily. "I thought I'd hang out up here for a while until Her Majesty cools down. Mr. and Mrs. Anderson are really cool about things."

"But things could get ugly real fast if anyone caught wind that Audrey is up here," said Shane. "Can you—you know, please not say anything to anyone?"

"Please, Mr. Morrow," implored Trevor, and as I scanned the faces of the three teens, it was palpable fear I saw looking back at me.

"Of course not," I said, indicating my own sorrow state. "I'm not exactly on speaking terms with anyone back there, anyway."

"So, what happened?" Shane asked as the wind shifted and he caught a trace of my scent. His face squirreled up comically and he stepped back, fanning the air in front of his nose.

"I warned you to stay back," I laughed. "Let's just say I was the guest of honor at a card game held by the town elders last night. I'm pretty sure it was their primary objective to run me out of town by any means necessary. Ain't gonna lie, kids, this is me at my *very* lowest."

The sound of another vehicle approaching prompted Audrey to duck behind Shane's truck while the rest of us waited, staring as a maroon Pontiac station wagon rolled past. The driver was a tidy little white-haired lady who didn't so much as glance in our direction.

"I don't suppose any of you have seen my friend, Michael?" I asked, as Audrey rejoined the group.

They all shook their heads in the negative, and I wasn't surprised. They had their own drama to contain. I looked at my watch again and saw it was nearing ten-thirty. I was running out of time to get back to the motel before checkout was due.

I pointed to Audrey. "You should get back inside before somebody spots you. I hope you're able to come to some sort of understanding with your parents. I mean, this isn't the 1950s—"

Trevor laughed hopelessly. "You can't put an expiration date on hatred, Mr. Dwayne. It's as strong today as it's ever been. It just finds new ways to hide beneath the surface."

I couldn't argue his point. I nodded. "I wish I could be of more help to you all, but I'm pretty sure associating with me will only bring more shit your way. I really did enjoy the show last night. You all were amazing. Make sure and tell Nick I said so, too, all right? I'm not sure if I'll see you guys again."

They lit up with my compliment, and they had every right to. Public speaking gives me stage fright, much less attempting to navigate the intricacies of playing an instrument or staying on key for the full duration of a song. I had been totally blown away.

I started to walk away, determined to reach the motel before Mrs. Shepley locked me out, when Shane called out, "Is there anything we can do for you?"

I stopped, considering my options. "Would you be open to giving me a lift back to the motel?" I asked, adding, "I can ride in the back like before, so I don't get all this inside your truck. I'd give you gas money, too, of course." I slipped my backpack off my shoulder and started to unzip it.

He waved it away and opened the driver's door to his truck, boosting himself behind the steering wheel. "You fellas gave me more than you should have last time. I still owe you a ride or two. But I *do* agree you should keep your distance," he said with a wry grin. "Hop on in back there."

····•••●◦◎◦●•••····

I found myself almost holding my breath as we twisted and turned along the two-lane road, hoping with everything I had in me that Michael's car would be in the parking lot, and I wouldn't be flying solo anymore. I was completely out of ideas on how to proceed from here. I couldn't imagine returning to Briarstaff on my own. I would be about as welcome as the plague. My hopes were dashed as we pulled into the dusty parking lot, and the only vehicle there was Mrs. Shepley's old Ford.

"Shit," I muttered, climbing out of the truck bed and dismayed with the amount of hay that clung to my shorts and legs. I brushed it away and retrieved my backpack from where it lay in the back.

"Mr. Michael's not here, huh?" Shane shielded his eyes and looked around. "I don't feel right just *leaving* you here."

"It's all right, Shane," I said. "I really appreciate the ride. I'm going to see about staying another night before I get penalized for checking out late. I've only got so much cash left. Hopefully, Michael will show up before too long."

I really didn't believe that anymore, but no sense dragging Shane in any further than I already had. I looked up and saw Mrs. Shepley standing behind the screen door to the office, watching us with narrowed eyes.

"You better get out of here before she calls your folks," I said, nodding in her direction.

Shane laughed. "We're good. My mama passed away when I was just little, and my dad ain't batshit crazy like Audrey's folks. I'm really sorry you've had such a bad go. You seem every bit as nice as your sister, and I, for one, am happy to have made your acquaintance."

He held out a hand, but I reminded him of my current condition by holding my palms out and scanning myself from top to grimy bottom. He laughed and fired a forefinger at me before climbing back into the driver's seat, putting his truck in gear. I watched as clouds of dust dissipated and the tail end of his truck disappeared.

I turned back toward Mrs. Shepley, who looked less than pleased to see me. I sighed. I was getting used to this.

······•◐◑•······

"Your friend is gone," said Mrs. Shepley, obviously aware of the malodorous aroma wafting off every pore of my being. She positioned herself behind the front desk to assure some safe distance. I would have much rather showered before having this conversation, but since she had been hovering in the door, there was no putting it off.

"Are you *sure?*" I was speechless.

"He paid for two nights, he stayed for two nights."

"Did you actually see him get back last night?"

"Well, no, but that's not unusual. I head for home just as soon as the sun starts to set. Don't see well enough to drive after dark."

"Then how about this morning?" I persisted. "Did he return his key before he left?"

"No, but that's not unusual, either. Folks leave their keys in the rooms all the time before driving off, and that's exactly how he and your sister did last time. I was just getting ready to inspect the room when you arrived." She was getting annoyed with me. "Now, if *you* are ready to check out, you have approximately seven minutes to do so, or you're gonna owe me for another full night."

I pulled my backpack off my shoulder and retrieved my wallet, pulling out three twenties. "I'd like to stay one more night, please."

I slid them across the desk to her, and she looked at them as if they carried malaria.

219

"Seriously?" she said, reluctant yet unable to keep herself from retrieving the bills with greedy fingertips. From a cash drawer out of sight behind the counter, she pulled a ten and tossed it in front of me.

"Yes," I nodded. "And I'd like to see Michael's room, please."

"For heaven's sake, Mr. Morrow, why on earth would you want to do *that?* I'd suggest you take advantage of the opportunity to get yourself cleaned up. I can't believe I have to tell you this, but you *stink*—"

"Yes," I agreed. "Just as soon as we've checked Michael's room. You said you were going down to inspect it anyway. I'm very concerned about his whereabouts. He was supposed to be back in town yesterday evening, but I never saw him. He was my transportation to and from here, and I certainly can't imagine him leaving without me. I can't imagine any situation where he would do so." I swallowed hard before leaning into a lie. "After all, he's dating my sister. We're practically family."

She studied me long and hard before sighing and grabbing her set of keys to the room. I followed her down the plank porch past five rooms along the longer arm of the motel and continued right, proceeding toward the end. I deposited my backpack outside Room 7 as we approached Room 8.

Mrs. Shepley fumbled with her key but finally managed to unlock the door. She pushed it open, granting me a wide path, and I anxiously went inside, looking from side to side. The bed was made. There was no luggage or personal belongings anywhere in sight.

Michael Arthur was gone.

CHAPTER SEVENTEEN

"Are you satisfied?" asked Mrs. Shepley, hands on her hips.

"Not even close," I muttered, wandering around the room looking for any trace suggesting Michael had ever been here at all. There was nothing. My sense of dread was growing by leaps and bounds, and my imagination was venturing into very dark territory. What if the phone call Michael received had been a ruse, designed with the sole purpose of separating us before we could investigate Briarstaff any further? What was this town trying so desperately to hide? Had Michael been lured away only to meet a similar fate as that which had befallen Gina?

Two down and one to go?

I closed my eyes tightly and tried to focus on breathing to calm my runaway pulse. With no plan and no transportation, I felt completely caged.

"Mr. Morrow?"

I opened my eyes and turned to where Mrs. Shepley waited by the door. "Hmm?"

"If there's nothing else, I have things to do."

"Sure, sure," I muttered distractedly, taking in one last scan of the room as I headed toward the door. My eyes locked onto the bedside telephone, and I paused, pointing at it. "How do I get an outside line?"

"Dial 9, then the number you are trying to reach," she said, turning around and stepping out onto the porch. Over her shoulder, she added, "Local calls are a dollar apiece, payable at checkout."

"What about long-distance?"

She laughed. "We don't *do* long-distance."

My mouth fell open. "What do you mean, you don't do long-distance?" I joined her on the porch and closed the door to Room 8 behind me.

She sighed and turned around. "I don't see what is so hard to understand about that. We. Don't. Do. Long. Distance. Last thing I need is for someone to run up a huge phone bill and run out on me. I mean, take a look around! Do we *look* like we see many guests out here? That kind of horseshit could put me out of business. Everyone *I* know lives in town, so *I* got no need for long-distance. Truth be told, local calls don't cost me a thing, but I charge a dollar for each because I can, so there you are. Now, why don't you get yourself cleaned up? You're drawing flies!"

As she marched back toward the office, I looked down and discovered that, in fact, I was.

· · • • • • ● ⊝ ⊝ ● • • • • · ·

I washed my hair three times and scrubbed every inch of myself as if I were preparing for surgery. Afterward, I stood beneath the warm water until it ran cool, suddenly aware of exactly how much I ached all over. I had spent most of the previous day walking around the festival before spending the night curled up on a cot no thicker than a paperback book. My back ached, my feet were tender, and my skin burned from too much sunlight. Still, as I stepped out of the small shower stall, I felt a million times better than I had stepping in. I grabbed a towel and began drying myself.

I was beyond fucked.

222

I had plugged my cell phone in before entering the bathroom, but a fat lot of good it would do me, even once it was charged. I wondered how far I would have to walk to reach cell service. Would I have to go all the way back to Shawnee? It had taken a little more than a half-hour in the car to get there, so I imagined it would take most of the day to walk. I wished I hadn't slept on the way into town. I had no sense of how far removed we were from civilization. It felt like years since I had been in my own home. I missed Melanie so much it ached, and because I had forewarned her of the lack of modern amenities here, she wouldn't begin to *really* worry about me for days. It was only Friday, and I was slated to be here through Sunday.

Shit.

It was decision time.

If I was going to attempt to walk to cell service, I should probably go ahead and pay for another night's stay. I couldn't carry all of my things with me, and even if I walked nonstop, it would take most of the day to make the round trip, and that just wasn't realistic. I certainly didn't relish the thought of making the trip, but I was reluctant to ask Shane for a ride that far. I had a pretty good idea of how the adults in town felt about me, and I didn't want to ask him for a favor that might land him in a whole heap of trouble. These kids had been nothing but kind to me, Michael and, from what I could tell, Gina. Well—everyone had been kind except Rusty. I could easily imagine his probable evolution into future town elder—he certainly had the nasty disposition for it. I guess the ranks had to be replenished somehow.

I gargled with Listerine multiple times to drive the sour taste from my mouth and began industriously brushing my teeth.

A tiny voice in the back of my head wondered if leaving was the right thing to do. Our mere presence had clearly kicked the hornet's nest, and if I left town, I would be doing exactly what they wanted. They were clearly hiding something, but I couldn't begin to imagine what it was. These were a people who refused to acknowledge much less embrace change. The internet was to be feared. Television content must be approved by some unknown authority before being funneled through a single outlet controlled by the senior-most town councilman, Emmitt Brown. Cell phones were dangerous and long-distance landlines unnecessary. Most deplorably, they clung to a time when segregating a minority to a neighborhood casually referred to as 'Spook Ridge' was perfectly acceptable.

I didn't believe *all* of the townsfolk were co-conspirators. Likely, most were simply cattle, bending to the iron will of the those in charge. It was much easier to follow than to lead. As long as no outside influences penetrated their happy little bubble, life like this could go on forever. Appalling as that seemed to me, I wasn't sure how much of it would be considered an actual crime. There had to be something more, something that was worth killing my sister for discovering, and I hadn't figured it out yet. If I left now, I never would. Of course, if I stayed, I would be tempting the very same fate.

I heard the door to my room open and close, and I froze, toothpaste dribbling down my chin. I quietly spat the rest into the sink and straightened, straining to listen.

Someone was in my room.

I heard soft footfalls, and then crinkling from the plastic bags I had gotten at the Shawnee Foodland and left strewn about on the desk. A soft female voice came and went, a mixture of speech and song, but I couldn't make out any words. It was much too high to be Mrs. Shepley. Frankly, at this point, I didn't really care who it was. I was weary of being victimized, and this just seemed like one indignity too many. I wrapped and secured a towel around my waist, and finding nothing more fearsome, armed myself with a toilet plunger. I eased the bathroom door open a crack.

Hattie Bartlett whirled in a lazy circle at the foot of my bed, staring at the ceiling while helping herself to a handful of my Honey BBQ Fritos.

Between chomps, I could hear her singing an old Olivia Newton-John song, although I was at a loss for which one. I was so surprised, I let the door fall open, and as soon as Hattie heard it bang against the wall, she spun around and froze, her eyes wide, chips spilling from her mouth. She covered her eyes and screamed, a blood-curdling shriek I was sure could be heard for miles. She tried to flee, but with her eyes covered only succeeded in running into the dresser. She stumbled backward and fell over the corner of the bed. She curled into a fetal position and continued to wail, rocking and hugging herself tightly. She had squeezed her eyes shut, and tears flowed from the corners.

"Hattie," I called out, desperate to quiet her before Mrs. Shepley dragged Sheriff Daniel into this. That would just be perfect. *"Hattie, please!"*

Nothing.

I held my towel together tightly with one hand and crossed the room, kneeling beside the girl and placing my hand gently on her shoulder.

"It's okay, Hattie, *shhh*," I forced myself to speak calmly despite the hammering of my heart in my chest. "You're okay. I'm not going to hurt you. Please, just calm down. Everything is fine."

After a few iterations, my words began to penetrate, and Hattie's keening slowly tapered off as did the speed with which she rocked. I could see the tension in her body begin to release as the death grip she had around her knees loosened.

After a moment, I asked, "Are you okay?"

She snuffled and nodded, dabbing at her eyes, which remained firmly shut.

"Okay, good," I said. "Give me a minute to get dressed and then we'll talk, is that all right?"

She nodded again, and I stood up. I peered out the window to make sure I wasn't about to be raided by the authorities, but the coast was completely clear. No sign of Mrs. Shepley either, which was a great relief. I grabbed the

225

duffel with my clean clothes and retreated to the bathroom to make myself presentable.

‧‧‧‧‧‧●●●●●◉◯●●●●●‧‧‧‧‧

"Are you all right, Hattie? Why are you so upset? Did somebody do something to you?" I asked, sitting in the wooden chair beside the room's tiny desk.

After I had insisted several times that I was, in fact, now fully dressed, she had finally opened her eyes, and her tears were beginning to dry. She perched like a timid bird on the edge of the windowsill, remaining close to the door. I felt like she would flee at any moment. She wore a spaghetti-strap cotton top and cutoff blue jeans and was staring at her feet, which were wearing the same canvas shoes I had seen her "discover" the day before. They had been washed and bleached a brilliant shade of white.

Her face flushed red as she chanced a glimpse in my direction. "No. I just wanted to—never mind, I'm so embarrassed. *Stupid! Stupid!*" She smacked her own forehead twice, hard.

"Hey, hey—please don't do that," I implored, keeping my tone even and calm. I certainly didn't want to trigger her wailing again. "You're not stupid."

"I'm sorry. I didn't mean to almost see you naked. I knocked but no one answered. The door was unlocked. I didn't think you would mind."

I sighed and took a moment to reason before responding. Normally, I would have been outraged if someone had simply assumed permission and entered my space without invitation, even if I *had* been careless enough to forget to lock the door. But Hattie's brain didn't process things like others did, and she was one of the few friendly faces I had met in this town.

"It's all right," I said. "I'm happy to see you again. It was my fault that I didn't lock the door. So, what brings you by?"

226

"We-e-ll," she said, still having trouble meeting my eyes. "You was just so nice yesterday, and I told you I'd show you my collection, but then Joy Beth ran her big mouth, and I had to go. I thought maybe if I caught you before you got busy—" Her voice trailed away, and she stole another glance at me from beneath dark, bushy eyebrows. I remembered Joy Beth's words clearly from the day before: *I think someone's got a little crush on you, Mr. Morrow.* I believed she was correct.

I smiled. "How did you know where to find me?"

If her face had been flushed before, it was absolutely crimson now. "I followed you," she whispered, and I saw every muscle in her legs tense, ready to bolt.

"It's all right, Hattie," I said soothingly. I didn't know if it was all right or not. By strict definition, it was stalking. From my personal experience, stalking was rarely a good thing, but it was impossible to see malevolence in Hattie. She looked like a child who got caught doing something awful and was bracing herself for punishment. "I appreciate you following up. I would truly love to see your collection, but I'm not sure if I'm going to be in town very much longer. My friend is gone, and so is my ride. I may have to walk all the way to Shawnee. Do you know where that is?"

She nodded her head, relaxing a bit.

"It's a long way off. I may have to get started right away."

She sighed, looking defeated. "All right, then. I should go. If you change your mind—"

"You will be the absolute first to know," I said. "I promise."

She nodded, and I felt like shit. Her chin quivered slightly, and she looked like she was on the verge of tears. I felt completely responsible, but I couldn't imagine going back into that town. I felt like I had only just escaped!

She stood and pulled a small leather organizer from her back pocket and unzipped it from the side. There was a small, rainbow-colored pen fastened inside, and my breath caught in my throat.

"Where did you get that?" I asked, a little too firmly.

She instantly tensed back up, turning and guarding the item protectively. "It's *mine*," she said defensively. "I keep my private thoughts in here. It's my most favorite notebook I ever had."

I sighed, massaging my brow, willing my disposition forcefully back to calm. "I'm sorry. Of course, it is. It's very pretty. I just wanted to see it, and I'll give it right back. I promise I won't read what's inside."

She was clearly torn. It kind of broke my heart to watch her deliberate. I had the sense she had been deceived many times by the cruelty of others, betrayed by her own willingness to trust, the probable unwitting victim of countless games of keep-away. Finally, she sighed and thrust the organizer in my direction.

"Here," she said. "But you better give it back, and I will scream if you try to read it."

Well, we certainly didn't want *that*.

"Thank you," I said, turning the organizer over in my hands, confirming what I already knew as I spotted initials in the lower corner of its back, calligraphy in indelible blue ink with a swirl of butterflies drawn around them. I had seen this organizer countless times. My mother had bought it for Gina's birthday when she was twelve, and she used it for the very same purpose as Hattie. I had only tried once to peek inside, and Gina had responded by promptly beating the shit out of me and hiding all of my record albums. She swore she had dropped them into the burn barrel Dad kept in the corner of our backyard and only returned them after she had reduced me to tears. I learned my lesson well. My eyes were damp as the memory swelled larger than life in my mind.

"Are you all right?" Hattie looked at me fearfully, like she had done something wrong.

I nodded and regained my composure. "Sure. Where did you find this?"

"Miss Gina gave it to me," she said proudly. "She said I should have my own personal journal, something that's mine and only mine. Something Mama can't touch, and Joy Beth can't neither! I love Miss Gina. She's so sweet. I hope she comes back soon. She's the only one I know who doesn't think I'm crazy. She doesn't try to avoid me. She cares what I think and invites me to come along instead of just leaving me behind like everyone else does. She told me she used to keep her thoughts in here, too, but she didn't anymore. She bought me a fresh notebook from the IGA to put inside and a refill for the pen."

By now, she was beaming, and I handed the organizer back to her absently, processing everything she had just said. One thing in particular had caught my attention.

"Where did you go with my sister?" I asked, keeping the eagerness out of my voice. I didn't want to spook her again.

She shrugged. "She took me in to Ida's for an ice cream sundae once. And she gave me a pair of pretty green earrings—I'm not wearing 'em right now. They don't go with my outfit. She told me she'd take me to get a tattoo, but I think she was just joking. Either that, or my mom put the kibosh on it." She giggled. "Doesn't really matter. I'd pass out if someone came at me with a needle. They have to hold me down at the doctor when it's time for a booster! I'd just as soon bite 'em than let 'em jab me!"

I was disappointed. I had hoped for something revelatory, but this was just everyday stuff.

"Course, her favorite place to go was the mines, and I know them mines like nobody else. We went a few times."

Suddenly, she had my full attention again. "Really? I poked around in there yesterday and only saw some weird lights—and a whole lot of bats." I shuddered visibly. I simply can't help it.

"Did you go in the main entrance?" she asked, shooting me a look that she suspected I was an amateur. Of course, I nodded. "Heck, no! That's not where you want to go in! I mean, you can *get* to the cool stuff from there, but it's the absolute longest way! There's other ways in that are more direct, but if you don't know about 'em, you'd never see 'em. I can show you if you want."

She was pleased with herself, hopeful to maybe be of more use, and I was certainly intrigued. My phone had fully charged, so I would have a dependable source of light. Yes, there were bats, but I could face that obstacle when and if I encountered it again. Another violent shudder passed through me, and I waited for it to pass. I was really curious what would have drawn Gina into the mines so frequently. The need to know was rapidly overtaking my desire to flee, although either course was going to require a lot of walking.

"Yeah, I think I'd like that very much," I said. "That is, if you've got time. I don't want to be a burden."

And there was that blush I had come to recognize. She giggle-laugh-snorted and covered her face with one hand. "Course not. I ain't got a single thing to do today. Mama and Joy Beth will be tied up at the Apple Festival most of the day. And it's not like I got to ask permission. I'm twenty-three years old. I can vote and drink the beer if I want."

"All right, then," I said, standing and unplugging my phone from the charger. "Let's do this thing. It's a bit of a walk."

"I rode my bike. I go everywhere on it. It's just outside," she said, beaming. She stood and crossed to the door, flinging it open. Laying across the walkway was an ancient child's bicycle, bright yellow and spangled with little daisies all over it. "I can't double, but maybe you can?"

I smiled, suppressing a laugh—I certainly didn't want to insult her. I had difficulty picturing Hattie on the thing, much less both of us. "I don't think your bike is big enough. Tell you what, how about I walk, and you can ride alongside me?"

"Are you sure?"

"Oh, yes," I said. "Very."

I would definitely want to take my backpack. My camera could very well come in handy. Of course, I had the one in my phone, but it wasn't nearly as useful in areas where lighting wasn't optimal, such as inside the mine. I tossed four bottles of water into the bag, determined not to cross into town unless it was absolutely necessary, and following that train of thought, added a couple of the bags of chips. I slipped it back onto my shoulder, my cell phone into my pocket and grabbed my room keys, heading to the open door where Hattie waited patiently, a mile-wide grin on her face.

We walked the first couple of miles mostly in companionable silence. Amazingly, Mrs. Shepley hadn't seemed to notice our departure, and I was glad for that. All I needed was deceitful conjecture spreading like wildfire through the town about what I might be doing with Hattie. She rode along in lazy loops, never wandering too far ahead before changing direction and circling back to me. I worried about her getting creamed by an oncoming car, but she seemed in tune with her environment and even steered clear of me whenever one occasionally passed. Soon, she was back into Olivia Newton-John's catalog, this time it was "Have You Never Been Mellow?"—although I'm pretty sure she was singing, "Have You Ever Eaten Marshmallows?"

"Hey, Hattie," I called out.

She spun around and pulled up beside me, putting her feet down. "Yeah?"

"Do you think we could get around to the mines without actually passing through town and the festival? After the day I had yesterday, I'm not real keen to go back through there."

Anyone else would have probably asked me what I meant by that, but Hattie didn't miss a beat. "Sure. I know *lots* of ways around." She was proud to know the lay of the land and couldn't be more pleased than to share it with me.

"Awesome," I said. "I figured if anyone would know, it would be you."

She was delighted. She raced ahead and popped an awkward wheelie before returning. "You're going to be awful tired after all this walking. Hey, I've got an idea! We could *share* my bike! I don't have to ride *all* the time. We could take turns! Here—"

She dismounted and offered me the handlebars, but I shook my head and waved her back on. "Thank you, Hattie—I appreciate your offer, but no. I'm a wee bit big for your bike. You go ahead and ride."

She deflated, throwing a leg over the banana seat. "Are you *sure?* I really don't mind."

I smiled. "I'm sure."

"It's too bad we don't *both* have bikes. We'd be out there in no time— *oh!*" She hopped back off of her bike so quickly I thought she might have run into the wrong end of a bee. But then she started thumping her forehead again. *"Stupid! Stupid!"*

"Hey, *hey.*" I reached out and grabbed her arm. "Please stop. You shouldn't hit yourself like that. What's the matter?"

"I never think," she said, and she looked as though she was seconds away from tears. "Joy Beth has a bike at the house. She never uses it. I'm sure she wouldn't mind if you borrowed it. It's bigger than mine, but—"

"What?" I was thinking it was a pretty great idea. It had been *years* since I'd ridden one, but it sure beat walking everywhere.

She flushed bright red. "It's a *girl's* bike."

I laughed out loud and before long, Hattie was laughing right along with me.

"I can certainly live with that," I said, but then another thought occurred to me. "I don't suppose you know how we can get to your house without going through town and the festival, do you? I mean, isn't your house right there facing the square?" Just one corner removed from the F.O.E. hall.

Hattie nodded. "But we can cut in through the alleys. Ain't nobody gonna be back there with the rides going and everything. I use them all the time. Then we can just cut back and around through those same alleys to get to the mines."

"All right," I said. "It sounds like we have ourselves a plan."

Hattie had recovered her pride and once again seemed pleased with herself. She swung a leg back over the seat and resumed her lazy sway back and forth on her bike, never getting too far ahead nor too far behind me as I pressed forward. She was off Olivia and had moved onto ABBA—of course, it was ABBA. It was an earlier, lesser-known track, and the lyrics were *almost* right.

"Gina, pretty ballerina, now she is the queen of the dancing floo-o-o-o-r!"

I smiled. I believed my sister would very much approve.

CHAPTER EIGHTEEN

We made a game of avoiding cars by ducking off of the road after the first few had passed; paranoia had grown exponentially for me with each one, and I was absolutely certain the next would belong to the sheriff or one of the Petersons. Nearly an hour-and-a-half later, we departed the pavement for good, cutting west through the woods bordering Briarstaff. I could hear the festival jangling away in the distance, and I prayed we wouldn't be spotted. It felt ludicrous slipping back into this nest of vipers, but I was going to have to find my big boy pants and persevere if I wanted to get to the bottom of things. Otherwise, why had I even come in the first place?

We exited the woods onto a gravel lane that appeared to loop around the entire town. We were only a block removed from the town square, and I urged Hattie to pick up the pace. I felt incredibly vulnerable out in the open. Immediately before us was a narrow alley separating backyards that faced each other. Mercifully, all were empty. Some were open while others were enclosed by wooden or chain link fencing. The Bartletts' was the second to the left, open yet crowded with an eclectic collection of castoff oddities, many of which had likely been accumulated by Hattie herself. Hattie hopped off her bike and let it fall on its side near a rickety set of wooden stairs that led to the back door. I worried she might want to show off some of her handiwork, but she seemed to understand the need for discretion and proceeded to open the door, stepping inside. She turned, waiting for me to catch up.

"Are you sure nobody's home?" I asked, casting one more glance at the empty neighborhood before stepping through.

"Uh-huh," she nodded. "Mama and Joy Beth are down at the tent. They'll be there all day."

We were in a very tight mud room. A mismatched washer and dryer churned noisily at the far end and a collection of shoes surrounded us. I heard a cat chirp from somewhere inside the house, and soon, he (or she) poked its black and white face through the inner doorway leading to the kitchen.

"That's Kinsey," said Hattie, kicking off her shoes and passing through to the kitchen. "She don't bite."

I flashed on Madame Phalange's Sue Grafton collection and smiled. Kinsey. Of course! I scritched the top of her head as I passed, and she chirped again, a loud rumbling originating in her throat and spilling out into the room.

"You want something to eat?" Hattie called out, already collecting items from the pantry. "I'm *starved*."

I thought about the paltry collection of chips in my backpack and my stomach growled. "Um, sure. What did you have in mind?"

"Do you like peanut butter and jelly? It's my favorite. I could make us both a couple of sandwiches."

She had already twisted the top off of a jar of peanut butter and was spreading it about an inch thick onto a slice of white bread.

"Yeah, sure, sounds good," I said, and my stomach grumbled again. I hadn't realized how hungry I was. "But go lighter on the peanut butter for me, okay?"

"Okey dokey, Smokey!"

She set about her task industriously, humming nameless tunes as she progressed. I looked around the small, rectangular kitchen, guessing it had last been updated fifty years prior based on the age of its appliances and general design. There was no denying it was well-kept; every surface was spotless, if perhaps a little yellowed from age. The prevailing color scheme was avocado green. A small Formica-topped table with three chairs rested against the short wall nearest me, and I took a seat, staying out of Hattie's way. Kinsey promptly jumped into my lap, pushing her face into my open hand and purring. Although I was absolutely homesick and would have preferred tending to my own feline, she was a very sweet substitute.

"Water, milk or 7-Up?" Hattie asked from the fridge.

"7-Up, please," I said, rooting around my backpack for those chips, after all. They seemed an appropriate side dish.

Hattie placed a paper plate with two sandwiches in front of me as well as a can of 7-Up. She had poured herself a glass of white milk and a bowl for Kinsey. After placing Kinsey's bowl on the floor, she joined me at the table with her own meal.

"Thank you for this food, dear God in Heaven, amen!" she said, pointing at the ceiling. She took an enormous bite that sent jelly squishing out the back of her sandwich and onto her paper plate.

"And thank *you*, Hattie, for all of this," I said, taking a little more care with my own sandwich. I scooted the chips toward her so she would know they were up for grabs. "I didn't realize how hungry I was."

She beamed, licking a glob of peanut butter from the edge of her hand before plunging it into the nearest bag and scooping chips out onto her plate.

We ate in companionable silence for a while, and just as I was beginning to feel comfortable, I heard a door open at the front of the house.

Shit!

I stood and grabbed my backpack, ducking back into the mud room. I nearly tripped over the pile of shoes but managed to keep my balance as I continued toward the washer and dryer, trying to get as far away from the open doorway as possible.

"Hey, Hattie, whatcha into, girl?"

It was Joy Beth's voice, and I heard the refrigerator door open.

"Nothing," replied Hattie, a bit forcefully. "Why are you here? Shouldn't you be down helping Mama?"

"I am, but I needed to get a little ice." I could hear her scooping ice from the freezer. "Did you fix yourself some lunch?"

"Uh-huh," said Hattie, her mouth partially full. "Peanut butter and jelly."

"That's good." Joy Beth sounded odd, definitely less spunky than the afternoon before. I took a step closer so I could hear more clearly over the clatter of the laundry machines. "Now, why did you set two place settings?"

Uh-oh.

"Didn't Mama tell you not to use real food when you're hosting your pretend lunches with Kinsey?" Joy Beth sounded tired. It was as if she were chastising on autopilot.

"Kinsey eats food, too," protested Hattie.

"Not peanut butter sandwiches," said Joy Beth. "Wait a minute—there's *bites* taken out of this—"

The jig was up.

I returned to the kitchen, approaching Joy Beth from behind. There was no way to keep from startling her, so I mildly cleared my throat and said, "Hi, Joy Beth."

She whirled around, and suddenly I was the one who was startled.

"My God, what *happened* to you?" I stared with my mouth hanging open.

Joy Beth's left eye was an ugly shade of deep purple, impossibly swollen and completely sealed shut. The bag of ice she had just retrieved from the freezer was undoubtedly prepared to help ease the swelling. Her bottom lip

237

was also distended with a painful-looking split in its center. Her left arm dangled in a sling, forearm wrapped in an Ace bandage with fingers like sausages protruding from the end.

She tried to turn away when she saw me, but she was on the wrong side of the table to make a clean break. Trapped, she sighed and lowered her head, defeated and humiliated. Tears began to spill from her eyes. I looked to Hattie for some guidance, but she remained nearly frozen in her seat, chewing slowly and staring as her younger sister quietly fell apart.

"Joy Beth," I said, stepping closer to get a better look. "Please. Tell me what happened."

She snuffled and dabbed at her leaky eyes and nose with her good hand, forcing herself to find the closest thing she could to composure. When she finally looked up at me, the piteous laugh that issued from her broken lips was nothing short of frightening.

"Well, hi there, Mr. Morrow," she said, attempting a smile that ended as a wince. "I didn't expect to see you here."

"Joy Beth," I persisted. "No more small talk."

She pressed past me and wandered toward the doorway leading toward the front of the house. She paused behind Hattie's chair. "It's really no big deal," she said. "I'm just terrible clumsy, that's all. Had myself a little whoopsy. Happens to me all the time, doesn't it, Hattie?"

"Uh-huh." Hattie's response was wooden, an unreadable expression fixed on her face.

"So, you're telling me that you did all this—" I waved my hand in her general direction. "—to yourself?"

She nodded quickly, and the pain of the movement flickered across her face like lightning. "I ran home to fix dinner for Jimmy last night, just like I told you I was going to do. Missed the bottom step on my way up into the trailer. Ran face first into the door. Jimmy's always sayin' to me, 'Joy Beth, you need to slow yourself down, girl. Life ain't a race!'"

238

I stared at her. "What about your arm?"

"I tried to catch myself when I went down and landed on it funny. I'm hopin' it's just a sprain, but I think I mighta heard something sort of—pop."

I continued to stare, watching as her face ran a whole gamut of emotions in seconds. She was testing for holes in her story, grasping at the desperate hope it was just plausible enough for me to swallow whole, but of course, it wasn't. Nothing could mask the fear that clouded her eyes.

I sighed. "This isn't the first time, is it?"

"Heavens, no," she said, mistakenly believing she had convinced me. "I might be the clumsiest girl you ever did meet—"

"*Joy Beth.*" I was firm, and her breath caught in her throat. "How many times?"

"I don't know what you're talking about—"

"How many times has Jimmy done this to you?"

"I *told* you what happened, I—"

"What you told me was *bullshit!*" Joy Beth flinched as my words reverberated through the house, and I realized I was scaring her. I took a deep breath to calm myself. All she needed was one more big man to fear. "Do you need to go to a hospital? Maybe you could go see Dr. Morris—"

"*No!*" she shouted. She had begun fidgeting behind Hattie's chair and looked as though she could bolt at any moment. I had seen this posture before; it was identical to the one Hattie had assumed back at the motel. "I need you to just—leave it alone, okay?" She looked at me, her eyes pleading.

I massaged the bridge of my nose. "This isn't *okay*, you know? There are places that help women in your position. Maybe not in this town, but I'm sure we could find somewhere that would—"

"*No!*" she shouted again, loud enough to make Hattie flinch. Joy Beth's face dissolved into anguished tears, and Hattie reached up to give her sister a gentle hug as she sobbed uncontrollably. After a moment, she collected

239

herself, and I could see the wheels working in her mind as she started building a defense. "It's not like this happens *all* the time. Jimmy's a good man. He's a good provider. He doesn't ask too much from me, just a clean home and that I care for little Jimmy, Jr. I don't think that's too much to ask, do you?"

I shook my head in stunned disbelief.

"In fact, I *enjoy* it," she continued. "—mostly. If Jimmy works first shift, I have the early part of my day free to do what I want, and when he works second, I have evenings all to myself."

"Sounds to me like you're only happy when he isn't around," I noted.

"That's not true!" she said defensively. "I can be plenty happy when he's around. He just gets a little mean when he's drinkin'."

"Is that what happened last night?"

She looked at her hand which was clutched tightly to the back of Hattie's chair. "I was late getting home. I had to chase Hattie all over hell's half acre to get her back to Mama before I could go. By the time I got there, he had already poured himself a few."

"This isn't Hattie's fault, and it isn't yours, either," I said.

"A man's entitled to a nice hot dinner after a long day at work, isn't he?" She continued to grapple to justify this abuse, and I was completely at a loss, struggling to find a way to make her see the truth in my words.

"He's not entitled to beat the living shit out of you," I said quietly. *"Ever."*

Her eyes darted around the room, seeking to land anywhere but on mine.

"Does your mother know?" I asked. She was a fucking fortune teller; how could she *not* know?

Joy Beth shook her head. "I don't think so. I don't want to worry her with—"

"She knows," Hattie said quietly. "We all know."

Joy Beth hugged herself and groaned, growing increasingly agitated. She paced the kitchen, staring at the ceiling while hot tears streamed down her face. I felt a rage building inside me as I watched her struggle with shame, fear and embarrassment, none of which she deserved.

"I think it's about time someone had a word with Jimmy," I said, grabbing my backpack and heading for the door.

"*No!*" This time it was a plea. Joy Beth grabbed my hand with her right one—the only one she could use—and pulled me back into the kitchen. "I'm beggin' you—don't. I've already talked to him today, and everything's *fine*. He promised me he'd stick to beer, and he's never like this with beer. He said he was sorry, and I believe him. I mean, who are *you* to tell me all this anyway? You don't even *know* Jimmy."

I wanted to shake some sense into her, but that would only hurt and scare her more. "I don't *have* to know, Jimmy. I know his type. Tell me, how many times has he said he was sorry, and how many times has it happened all over again?"

"He's *always* sorry," muttered Hattie, picking at her sandwich and refusing to look at either one of us.

"*You shut up!*" Joy Beth screamed at her sister, and Hattie began to wail in that same high-pitched tone that signified her extreme emotional distress. Joy Beth immediately looked mortified, and wrapped her good arm around her sister, shushing and kissing the top of her head. "I'm sorry, Hattie, really, I am. Please don't cry. I didn't mean to upset you." Hattie leaned into her sister and her cries subsided as they rocked together.

I felt completely helpless as I watched them soothe each other. I couldn't comprehend how someone could tolerate such horrific abuse without simply picking up and leaving. It seemed so easy, and yet I recognized I was no psychologist. Who knew what else was at play inside Joy Beth's head, keeping her tethered to this disgusting creep?

Joy Beth reached for a napkin and dabbed gently at her eyes. Her complexion was less mottled, and her breathing had nearly returned to normal. Finally, she was able to meet my eyes again. "Please, Mr. Morrow. While I certainly appreciate your good intentions, this is my business, not yours. I promise you, I can handle this."

My lips pressed tightly together. I couldn't *force* her to accept my help. "If you're sure—"

"I am."

"Well, all right, then," I said. "Hattie was just about to give me a tour of the mines like she did for Gina when she was here."

Joy Beth nodded, clearly relieved the subject was changing. "Good. That should keep you both occupied for a bit."

"We stopped by so I could borrow your bike," I added. "If that's all right with you, of course. I've been walking so much my legs could really use a break."

"Of course," said Joy Beth, picking up the bag of ice from the table and easing through the doorway toward the front of the house. "I really need to get back to Mama. I've been gone far too long. She can't do readings when she's watching Jimmy, Jr. Hattie, girl, you be careful out there. I'll let Mama know what you're up to."

"*Just* your Mama," I interjected. "I can't say I made the best impression on Sheriff Daniel and a few of the others yesterday, so I'd rather they didn't know I was back out there poking around."

"Deal," she said, disappearing into the darkened front room. A moment later, I heard the front door open and close.

I looked from Hattie to my half-eaten lunch. "How about we dig out that other bike?" I asked. "Are you ready?" Hattie nodded eagerly, grabbing both plates and taking them to the trash can.

I had completely lost my appetite.

···•••••◦◦•••••···

I waited in the mud room while Hattie rummaged around the back yard, digging through pile after pile before eventually pulling a pale pink ten-speed from behind a shed at the rear of the yard. It had a white Easter basket strapped to the handlebars, its own handle roughly shorn off, and a step-through frame that was once indeed considered the appropriate model for young ladies. Its tires appeared sound, and I wasn't about to be picky at this point. Hattie found a wrench somewhere in the house, and I adjusted its wide, padded seat to a height more suitable for me. I climbed aboard and tested my balance. It had been years since I had last ridden a bike, and it took a moment before my wobble straightened and I found my rhythm.

I followed Hattie's lead as we pedaled out into the alley and back onto the gravel lane, turning away from the town square and heading west. Neighboring blocks passed on our left and woods on our right, and luck remained with us—no neighbors in sight. We rode side-by-side for a moment in silence.

"How do *you* feel about Jimmy?" I asked casually.

Hattie made a noise in the back of her throat. "He's a butthole."

"Not a fan, huh?"

She spat on the ground in response.

"So, how does a nice girl like Joy Beth end up with an asshole like Jimmy?" I asked. "I can't help but feel she could have had a better choice."

Hattie shrugged. "They always went together, all through school. Dances, proms—all that gross stuff."

I realized then that Hattie had likely never attended any of that 'gross stuff' herself.

"I always thought he looked like a turd," she added, and we both laughed. "'Course, junior year, she *had* to be with him, what with little Jimmy on the way and all."

A-ha. I was beginning to get the picture now.

She rode a lazy circle around me. "She *shoulda* gone out with Shane. I woulda."

I hooked a thumb back toward town, surprised. "Shane Van Buren?"

"Uh-huh." She popped an awkward wheelie and had to place feet on the ground to keep from capsizing. "He was always crazy 'bout her. And he's super cute. But she said he's too young, and that's *dumb*. He's only two years younger than Joy Beth. Jimmy is two years older. Same, same."

We continued on for a bit in silence.

"I hope you don't mind me asking, but you never talk about your father. I don't recall Joy Beth or Madame—er, your mother talking about him either. I'm guessing he's not around anymore?" I asked.

"Nope," she said matter-of-factly. "He took off right after Joy Beth was borned. I barely remember him. I think Mama is happier this way. Don't know if you noticed, but she's kind of a *lot*."

I laughed. "I suppose she is. So, how does your mother feel about Jimmy?"

"She don't like him, neither, but she tries to stay out of Joy Beth's business. Mama has enough to worry about."

"How so?"

"Caroline Peterson and her pack of cronies. Bunch of mean bitches." She gasped and slapped a hand over her mouth, surprising herself with her own frank assessment with which I entirely agreed. "They think she's crazy, and her readings are just a bunch of bull."

I thought back to the previous evening and my own reading. While I wasn't quite ready to declare myself a believer, I knew *something* had happened in that tent, and it was something for which I had no explanation. Another thought occurred to me, one so dark I had to pause and put my feet on the ground. I couldn't believe it hadn't occurred to me before.

"Hattie," I called, and she stopped, too, cutting her wheel to the left and looking back at me expectantly. "Has Jimmy ever hurt Jimmy, Jr.?"

She looked at her feet and shuffled them in the gravel, and it was all the answer I needed.

"*Son of a bitch!*" I swore, kicking at the ground. "How bad?"

Again, Hattie shrugged. "Don't know."

"What do you mean, you don't know?" My tone hardened as my temper soared, and I saw unease creep into Hattie's eyes. I took it down a notch. "I'm sorry, Hattie. I'm mad at Jimmy, not you."

She nodded. "I'm mad, too! Sweetest little baby. I mean, he's gross with all the diap-ees and slobber and stuff, but he can't help none of that."

I took a deep breath and tried again. "What happened?"

"The baby was sick, and he wouldn't stop cryin.' Joy Beth tried everything she knew to quiet him down—Jimmy was tryin' to sleep on the couch, but he couldn't 'cause the baby wouldn't stop. He just shook him so hard—we didn't know if he was gonna pull through. Still don't know if his brains is okay. Guess time'll tell."

I was outraged. "Didn't he go to the hospital?"

Hattie shook her head. "Huh-unh. Jimmy wouldn't let her take him. Folks tend to their own 'round here."

Of course, they did, especially in this instance. If Joy Beth had taken Jimmy Jr. to an actual hospital, the incident would have been reported to authorities a lot higher up than Sheriff Daniel and matters would have been taken out of their hands. As much as I empathized with Joy Beth, I was beginning to get upset with her, as well. She was the only thing standing between the safety of her defenseless baby and this monster.

"How far is this trailer park?" I asked.

Hattie pointed west. "About a mile out Route 5. Why?"

"Is Jimmy there now?"

245

"He works nights on Fridays, so yeah, he's probably gettin' ready right about now. *Why?*"

"I think it's time someone paid him a visit."

Hattie led the way, and as we entered the lot in a cloud of dust, I realized it was the first I'd seen of any residents since leaving the city limit. Barebacked children played in the sun as their mothers performed yard work or hung laundry from clotheslines to dry. These folks didn't have the time or money to spend the day at the Apple Festival, and suspicious eyes followed our progress until Hattie stopped short of a narrow little trailer nestled beneath a large oak, its shadow undoubtedly providing merciful relief from the heat of the summer sun. An ancient Chevy truck was parked nearby, its bed filled with assorted janitorial supplies. I wasn't concerned that any of these folk would raise an alarm, as long as I wasn't bothering any of them. I was no one to them.

"Is this it?" I asked, and Hattie nodded. I stepped off my bike and laid my backpack on the ground. "I want you to go back to the entrance of the trailer park and wait for me. I don't want him to know you brought me here, okay? No need to drag you into this."

She nodded, and her eyes were like saucers. She remained frozen in place.

"I just need a few minutes, and then we'll go on to the caves, all right?"

She nodded again, and slowly began pedaling back the way we'd come. I watched until she disappeared around the corner before turning back to the trailer. There was a decorative sign hanging beside the door that read, 'The Perkins – Home Sweet Home.'

Home sweet home, indeed.

I stepped up onto the stoop and rapped my knuckles sharply on the aluminum door. For a long moment, I heard nothing at all, but then I finally heard the sound of footfalls approaching the door from the other side.

"Hold yer fucking horses," was the reply muttered as the deadbolt turned and the door flew open. I was face-to-face with the scrawny asshole who had been my cellmate in Sheriff Daniel's jail. He looked me up and down with no recognition whatsoever, bleary-eyed and still reeking of alcohol. "What the fuck do *you*, want?"

I punched him hard, knocking the smirk right off his face as I drove him back into the trailer. I stepped inside and closed the door behind me, locking it.

CHAPTER NINETEEN

Jimmy stumbled back, fumbling for his nose, as blood gushed from both nostrils. I followed with an uppercut to the chin, snapping his head back and knocking him down. I had never done anything like this before and was running completely on rage and adrenaline.

"Who the fuck *are* you?" he cried out as he crawled backwards on his elbows.

"I'll tell you who I'm *not*," I said, following him and hovering menacingly. "I'm not some asshole who beats up defenseless women and shakes his own goddamn *baby!*" I drove my point home with a kick to his ribs, knocking the air out of him. He rolled with the momentum onto gold shag carpeting in the tiny living room, clutching his ribs and gasping for breath. Before my eyes fully registered his intent, he snagged a pistol from a nearby end table and leveled it in my direction, squeezing off a shot that was far closer than I care to admit. In my white-hot rage, I hadn't stopped to consider the bastard might be armed. But in that moment, it only threw gasoline on my fire. I grabbed his wrist with both hands and pushed the gun up toward the ceiling where it discharged again, showering us in remnants of ceiling tile. I twisted his wrist with all my might until Jimmy screamed, and I felt something give. The gun fell to the carpeted floor, and I grabbed it, pointing it directly at Jimmy's weaselly little face.

"What do you *want*, man? I'll give you anything—I swear!"

I took great satisfaction in watching Jimmy's life flash before his eyes, even if I knew I could never pull the trigger. My rage was beginning to dissipate along with the ringing of the gunshots that had just been fired. For all I knew, Sheriff Daniel could be racing here this very moment, alerted by the same neighbors who had allowed this abuse to go unabated for God only knows how long, and I needed to wrap things up. Looking at the whimpering mess before me, I thought I had made my point pretty well.

"If you ever so much as *touch* Joy Beth or that baby again, I will be back," I promised. "And next time, I won't stop." I surprised myself when the gun went off a third time, whizzing past Jimmy's head and landing with a *whump* in the back of the couch behind him. I felt a certain karmic justice when he lost control of his bladder, wetness blossoming across the front of his jeans.

I turned and headed for the door, unlocking it. I almost laid the gun down but had second thoughts when I realized how differently any one of those horrible acts of violence might have ended had Jimmy employed the use of his gun. People like Jimmy Perkins had no business with a firearm, and I was more than happy to rectify that. I clicked the safety on and carried it with me as I left Jimmy sniveling on the floor, nursing his wounded wrist and what I hoped were cracked ribs, soaking in his own urine.

···•••●○⊙●●•••···

Hattie paced furiously at the entrance to the trailer park. As soon as she saw me approaching, she hopped on her bike and bridged the distance.

"Is he dead?" she asked eagerly, her eyes practically shining. "Did you kill him?"

I blinked. "Of course not. Why would you even think that?"

Her expression crumpled. "I just thought—never mind." Her disappointment was startling. It was like I had just canceled Christmas.

249

"Look, I don't know what you expected me to do, but I'm not a murderer," I said. "There's only so much I can do. I strongly impressed upon him that he was done hurting your sister and little Jimmy. I'm pretty sure he got the point."

Hattie pressed her lips together and shook her head, looking to the sky. "He won't stop," she said, and I heard the wail of a siren approaching in the distance.

"Okay, listen, Hattie," I said. "I may not have done what you expected me to do, but I did rough him up pretty good. I'm pretty sure that siren means Sheriff Daniel is heading this way, and we shouldn't be here when he arrives. Can we get to the mines without going back out on Route 5?"

Hattie nodded and pointed toward the back end of the trailer park. "There's bike trails back there that lead to the railroad tracks. We can follow them all the way out."

"Then let's go."

As we turned our bikes in that direction, Hattie muttered, "I would have killed him."

And I believed she would have.

I had the weirdest sensation we were trapped in the movie, *Stand by Me*, as we followed the broken tracks east, heading toward a town I wished I never had to see again. Hattie was sullen for quite some time, unusually quiet as she led the way. There were no loose interpretations of once-popular music nor colorful observations about the passing scenery. She had decided I was Joy Beth's savior, and I had failed her. I almost felt like I should apologize.

As we neared the town, the sounds of the festival swelled, and we paused before reaching the back end of the square.

"We can cut back behind the IGA," said Hattie, hopping off of her bike. "But we'll have to walk. These trails ain't so good."

I followed suit, surprisingly aware of the added heft Jimmy's gun gave to my backpack. I sifted through my backpack and retrieved a couple bottles of water, handing one to Hattie. The sun was high in a cloudless sky, and I was dripping sweat in the sweltering humidity. The thought of taking cover on trails through the woods was an appealing tradeoff, although it would take us longer to reach our eventual destination.

I glanced at my watch, noting it was almost three o'clock. It suddenly struck me that I was officially on the lam. Regardless of what Jimmy told Sheriff Daniel, the truth wouldn't matter. I was the outsider, and Jimmy would play the victim. Joy Beth was too scared to speak out, and I began to understand the hopelessness that dogged Hattie. My actions had likely made everything worse because I wouldn't be here *forever*.

Would I?

If Michael suddenly showed, he would have no way of finding me, and without him, I wasn't sure how I would ever get back home. A panicky claustrophobia threatened to descend, but I forcefully reminded myself I only needed to get as far as Shawnee to use my cell phone. Sure, it was a full day's walk, but I might be able to cut that in half. Joy Beth wouldn't mind if I borrowed her bike a little bit longer. Would she? Or would she be furious with what I had just done? The more I considered the rashness of my actions, I was leaning toward the latter. Madame Phalange had told me in my reading I would have to overcome obstacles, but who knew so many of them would be self-inflicted?

We continued in uncomfortable silence, Hattie surefootedly leading the way while I ambled along behind, wondering how much time I'd be sentenced to for assault with a deadly weapon and possession of a stolen firearm.

251

⋯•••••●━◯◯━●•••••⋯

"It's right up here," said Hattie, laying her bike on its side off the narrow trail.

I placed mine beside hers and looked ahead. "I don't see anything."

She pointed to where the woods met an outcropping of rock that rose about three feet above the ground, and I strained to see. Still nothing. I shrugged.

"Just come on," she said, stepping off the trail and pushing through weeds I hoped weren't poison oak, ivy or sumac. As we got closer, I saw a narrow depression cutting deep into the rocky hillside, a tapered passageway like an extra-large rabbit hole leading deep into the darkness below.

"You're kidding me, right?" I eyeballed the circumference of the adit and could easily picture my ass getting permanently wedged in there, bats nibbling away at my lower half. Hattie was a tiny little slip of a girl. She'd slide right through like butter. I'm sure Gina had no issues, either. I, however, was built entirely differently. I had a little too much gluteus in my maximus.

"Aw, you can make it. It opens up pretty big just a little ways in. I seen boys bigger'n you do it."

Well, that was comforting.

I watched Hattie insert her feet into the opening and then boost herself forward, as if launching down a water slide. She disappeared completely.

I sighed and rummaged through my backpack, retrieving my cell phone and powering it up. It was still fully charged, so I wouldn't be without a flashlight this time around. I slipped it into my pocket and found a discreet place to hide my backpack behind a nearby rock, covering it with some detritus from the woodsy floor. It would have to do. I reluctantly placed my feet into the darkened entrance and scooted myself forward. I was fully immersed to my hips when I felt the rock walls close in on both sides, and I was certain I could never make it through. Suddenly, I felt hands around my ankles, and I yelped as they tightened and pulled, lodging me even more firmly into the opening.

"Hattie!" I yelled. *"Stop! Stop! Stop!"*

But she didn't. She tightened her grip and pulled even harder, and I worried I might never sing in the same key again. I put my hands flat against the rock face around the opening and pushed in the opposite direction, wriggling my hips and trying to free them. I felt Hattie's hands slide down my ankles, taking every last bit of hair with them. She adjusted her grip, and I barely had time to slide my cell phone out of my pocket before she pulled with even more determination. My hips jammed again, but I only had time to consider screaming before they suddenly popped through, and I went sliding into the darkness.

"Geez, Louise, you're fatter than you look!" exclaimed Hattie from somewhere below me.

"Thanks," I replied sarcastically, trying to get my eyes to adjust to the darkness. I felt like every bit of skin had been raked from my ankles while my midsection had been contorted into a painful new configuration that gave little regard to internal organs. Thankfully, I had managed to hang on to my cell phone as I slid through, and I turned on its flashlight to examine our surroundings.

We were on a narrow rock ledge that dropped down into a wider chamber similar to those I had seen when I was exploring the mine before. I had no sense of where we were in relation to the main entrance. I held my breath and sent a quick beam of light toward the ceiling, allowing myself to exhale only after confirming there were no bats directly overhead, suspended by pointy little toes.

"How did you find this entrance?" I asked as Hattie climbed down from the ledge and dropped to the hard-packed clay floor below. "I mean, is it common knowledge?"

"Don't think so. I been playing in these woods forever. There's a couple others, too, but this one got Gina real excited," she said, brushing off her shorts and examining her feet. *"Awww, shoot!* I'm gonna have to wash my new shoes again. Just look at 'em!"

I awkwardly fumbled off the ledge and landed beside her. I wasn't worried about any portion of my attire. I was just thankful to be physically intact. I looked back from where we came and couldn't imagine exiting that way, but what did I know? Hattie placed her hands on her hips, looking at the wall before her with great satisfaction.

"You see it?" she whispered.

She seemed undeterred by the darkness, but my eyes were still focused on the beam cast by my cell phone on her dirty shoes. I shifted direction, and a metal grate coalesced before my eyes, bolted to the wall in front of us, covering an opening that resembled a giant, yawning mouth.

"What is that?" I asked, pointing.

"Shhh!"

"What?" I whispered. "Do you hear somebody?" I quickly turned the flashlight off and pocketed it, afraid I was betraying our presence with its brilliant luminescence.

She shook her head but put a finger to her lips to shush me.

I strained to listen, but all I could hear was dripping water in the distance. The ground beneath us was bone dry. Hattie crept toward the grate in front of us, and I watched as she picked at the bolts holding the grate in place. It was soon apparent they had previously been loosened.

Hattie stopped just short of releasing the last bolt and hunkered down, pulling me with her. I felt like someone or some *thing* was going to suddenly hammer at the grate from within the dark recesses behind it. I couldn't really read Hattie's expression, but it was almost like she was enjoying the mounting tension. I wanted to ask her what we were trying to avoid, but I knew she'd only shush me again. The short hairs on the back of my neck were beginning to prickle.

She raised to a crouch and slowly released the final bolt, easing the grate to the ground. She waved for me to join her, and I stood, peering into the murky crawlspace before suddenly swatting at my own face, overwhelmed by the sensation I had just walked face first into a field of spiderwebs. It took a moment to recognize the feeling as fan-forced cool air spilling out from somewhere deep within.

"What in the hell—?" I said, completely perplexed, but keeping my volume down. "What is this place?"

"The Academy," Hattie whispered.

The Academy? Why on earth would there be a subterranean entrance to the Academy? What could justify the expense? Although I had never actually seen the Academy, I presumed it had normal entrances and exits just like any another academic institution. This was something straight out of science-fiction. And if memory served, the Academy campus was at least a mile down the ridge.

"Are you sure?" I asked, and Hattie nodded.

"Gina was."

That was good enough for me.

Hattie continued, "There's ducts back there that open out into it."

I blinked. "You've been through there? Didn't you worry about getting stuck? Or caught?"

She looked at me with such disappointment. "Are you scared of *everything?*" she whispered, shaking her head before looking at me earnestly. "This is how you *learn* things. If you wait to be invited everywhere you go, you're gonna miss out on an awful lot."

I blinked again. She had a point there.

255

"How many times did you bring Gina here?"

"Twice. The first time we couldn't get in. Didn't have a wrench for them bolts, but she sure was ready the second."

"Why are we still whispering?"

"'Cause we're playing spies, just like me and Gina did!" Her eyes twinkled with childlike delight, and I realized that to her, this was just a game. She looked at me expectantly. "C'mon! It's fun!"

Hattie boosted herself into the crawlspace and inched forward, disappearing in a matter of seconds. I followed close behind, afraid of losing her in the darkness ahead. The tunnel was approximately three feet by three feet, tight but not quite claustrophobic. We dragged ourselves along, elbow over elbow and crawling on our knees for several hundred yards until I noticed a brightening of the space ahead. We soon stopped outside of another opening that peered out unobstructed into an artificially illuminated space beyond.

"C'mon," whispered Hattie, rolling over onto her stomach and sliding her feet through the opening. I watched as she slid through, hanging suspended by her fingertips for a brief second before dropping out of sight. *"C'mon!"* I heard her urge again from below.

I sighed, flipping over onto my own stomach and working my way backwards through the opening. My fingers weren't nearly as nimble as Hattie's, and I lost my grip at the end, pinwheeling off balance before landing on my ass on a solid, cool floor. Near my hand lay another metal grate, bowed and bent as if it had been kicked out from above with some force, and leaning against the wall was a three-foot stepstool, likely left in place as Hattie and Gina would have needed a boost to get back up into the tunnel after their previous probe of the area.

I stood, turning around slowly, and the juxtaposition was so jolting, I couldn't find words. I had seen documentaries about underground architecture that was absolutely breathtaking in its beauty. While it was

256

certainly something to behold, this was not *that*. It was strictly 1950s utilitarian. We stood inside a dimly lit high-ceilinged hallway. The walls were cornsilk brick from floor to midpoint before giving way to textured plaster of the same color from midpoint to ceiling. A thick layer of dust and grime covered the floors and clung to the walls. Fluorescent lights were tucked behind yellowing plastic covers, and only a single row in each fixture was lit. The whole thing reminded me very much of Lymont Elementary School, where I had attended third through sixth grades. The only things missing were lockers to line each side of the hall. Behind us the hall terminated in a windowless wall displaying a large county map of West Virginia courtesy of the Beckley-Cardy Company of Chicago. The hallway extended about a hundred feet in the opposite direction before dead-ending into another dimly lit corridor that ran along a perpendicular track. About halfway down, there was a door on each side of the hall. I scanned the area for any sort of surveillance but didn't see anything. Still, it was unnerving standing out in the open as we were; I felt someone could enter the hallway from the far end at any moment. I looked to Hattie expectantly, and she was tiptoeing toward the door on the left. I followed suit.

"Aren't you afraid we'll get caught?" I whispered.

"Huh-unh," she whispered back, shaking her head. "There's no one in here."

"How can you be sure?"

"The hall down there is bricked off both ways. Can't get in from there."

"Bricked off?" My voice rose in surprise. "That doesn't make any sense."

"Would you *shhh*? You don't play spies right. Spies whisper."

"That's because I'm not playing, Hattie," I said a little too sharply and instantly regretted it. Her face began to crumple, and I certainly didn't want to test the limits of our solitude by virtue of her keening. I scrambled to correct course. "But that's okay, Hattie. This is much better than playing, and I absolutely need your help. Will you help me?"

For a long moment, I was unsure if I could keep her tears from spilling, but eventually her expression softened, and she nodded. I took a deep breath to clear my head and mentally prioritized my agenda. Unlike Hattie, I was not at *all* sure we were safe from discovery, so I started there.

"Why don't you show me how the halls are bricked off," I suggested, and Hattie sighed, nodding again. She stepped away from the door she was about to open and led me down the corridor to where it dead-ended into a 'T.' Once there, I could see exactly what she meant. Each direction led approximately ten feet back before ending abruptly in floor-to-ceiling cinderblock walls. This section had been intentionally cordoned off from hallways that apparently led back to the Academy. We turned and walked back to the midpoint of the hall, stopping between the doors on either side.

Hattie stood sullenly, her arms wrapped around her midsection. She pointed to the door that had been her original destination and said, "Here's where Gina went. Ain't nothing in that other room, but you can look for yourself if you don't believe me."

"Hattie," I said, striving for the correct tone of contrition. "Of course, I believe you. I wouldn't have found this place at all if it weren't for you. You know that, don't you?"

A little color crept into her face, and I took that as a good sign. I needed to remember patience with her. She didn't know the real reason we were here, and I didn't dare tell her. If she found out my sister, someone she admired greatly, had died—had likely been killed—I could only imagine her reaction. For the first time, it struck me I no longer considered her death a 'possible' homicide. Too much was out of kilter here. Gina had stumbled across something nefarious, and the cost had been her life. I was more determined than ever to find out exactly what that was and to bring whoever was responsible to justice.

Hattie turned the knob and pushed the door open, stepping into the dark space beyond. I followed with the flashlight in my cell phone guiding the way.

The windowless space was completely cluttered from one side to the other with castoff office furniture and equipment from the mid-1900s. Sturdy metal desks were pushed end to end, filling one side while matching two- and four-drawer file cabinets filled a portion of the other. A graveyard of cast iron typewriters and handle-cranked adding machines were piled in between. A cart loaded with folding chairs was just inside the door and loose papers were scattered amongst the dust covering the floor. The uncirculated air was cool but stale. I randomly tested one of the file cabinet drawers to find it unlocked and empty.

Hattie stood near the middle of the room, pointing casually at the ceiling over the corner filled with filing cabinets. My eyes followed, and I noticed a panel of the drop ceiling nearest the far wall had been disturbed.

I handed Hattie my cell phone and then used one of the nearest two-drawer file cabinets to boost myself on top of a four-drawer file cabinet, ducking slightly to keep from hitting my head on the ceiling. I reached down to retrieve my phone, then used the other four-drawer cabinets like steppingstones, crossing a creek of abandoned space until I reached the far corner that was my destination. I reached for the panel that was slightly askew.

"Um, I wouldn't do that if I—"

Hattie's words barely registered as I pushed the panel up and over, rising to my full height, my shoulders and head in the space above the drop ceiling. The contrast was abrupt; just above the drop ceiling were the unfinished walls and ceiling of the cave, extending to its full height overhead. Immediately, I heard a series of startled squeaks, and it only took a second to confirm with my flashlight what I already knew.

Bats.

Not nearly as many as I had seen before, but let's face it—one was more than enough for me. I fumbled with the ceiling tile and dropped to my knees, pulling it firmly into place behind me. I rested my back against the cool plaster wall and waited for the hammering of my heart to subside, praying the whole time the creepy flying rodents couldn't squeeze around the edges of the ceiling tiles. I don't know if it was my imagination or not, but I would have sworn I heard leathery wings scraping against the other side of the tiles near my head.

Hattie observed from below, doubled over and with hands clasped to her mouth to try and keep from laughing out loud. It was a losing battle, and soon she was slapping her thigh and roaring, wiping at tears that collected in the corners of her eyes. *"You should see your face!"*

I smirked. "I thought spies were supposed to whisper."

That only made her laugh louder, and soon enough, I was laughing, too. It felt good to release the last of the tension hanging between us.

"I *tried* to tell you," said Hattie, after she finally caught her breath. "Gina did the same thing. You want *that*."

She pointed at another intake grille near the ceiling behind me. It looked to be about two feet by three feet, and the screws that secured it to its frame had also been loosened. I worked at them one by one with my fingers, backing them out until the frame finally came loose and fell with a clatter to the top of the filing cabinet I stood on. I shone my flashlight inside and watched the beam extend into nothingness.

"She went in there?" I asked, pointing inside the vent and dreading the answer.

Hattie nodded eagerly. "That's where she found whatever it was she found."

"Did she say what she found?"

"Something about a barn? Didn't make no sense to me. She wouldn't let me go. She was afraid I'd get stuck, but I'm as small as she is. *You*, on the other hand—"

I looked at the opening and then at myself. It would certainly be tight. And once I went in, I'd have to work my way backwards to get out. It sounded very claustrophobic, and while that wasn't my favorite feeling, it wasn't one of my weaknesses. I looked back at Hattie, and while I knew she could crawl through much more easily than me, she wouldn't know what she was looking for and might not even recognize something significant if she saw it.

"I think I can do this," I said, reluctantly turning my flashlight off and slipping my phone into my pocket. There was no way I could both guide my path and work my way back and forth. "Stay put. I'll be back as soon as I can."

I boosted myself through the opening and soon was immersed in total darkness, elbowing and shimmying my way forward. My motion caused the metal ductwork to ping and pop in protest, and I hoped it would be accepted as the normal sounds of expansion and contraction if I crossed into an area that was populated. I had no sense of how far I had traveled. I hadn't come across any more grilles looking out into rooms abandoned or otherwise.

After what seemed an eternity, I sensed a lightening in the darkness ahead, a spectral green ambiance that solidified into a square along the left side of the ductwork ahead. I could hear a steady hum as well, and the air felt a little less stagnant than before. I forced myself to slow my movements, hoping to minimize the noise I made as I pulled even with this first intake grille I encountered.

I suddenly understood what Gina had been trying to tell Hattie, and I couldn't believe my eyes.

Through the grille and across the way was an entire wall lined with cabinets housing countless server racks. I couldn't tell where the room began or ended. A ganglia of network cables sprouted from the top of each cabinet, secured by plastic ties and running up the wall where they disappeared into the opposite ceiling. Overhead vents issued a steady stream of cool air into the space. They were interspersed with light fixtures casting the hazy green glow I had noticed.

Completely incongruous in this technology verboten town, this was a high-tech server farm.

CHAPTER TWENTY

It took at least twice as long to work my way back through the venting, a reverse crabwalk using my forearms and knees for leverage against the sides of the sheet metal. The noise I made in the process seemed incredibly louder than that of my entry, but I couldn't tell if that was truly the case or just an auditory illusion triggered by what I had just discovered. At any point, someone might wander through that particular section of computer hardware to provide some sort of maintenance, and there was no way they wouldn't hear the din I was creating. As I felt my feet strike nothingness, I knew I had finally reached the juncture that dropped down into the abandoned room where I had entered, and I hesitated for just a moment. I felt sure I would drop down into a room full of armed guards from the Academy, waiting to arrest me and haul me away.

With a hollow thud, my feet made contact with the top of the metal file cabinet, and I quickly ducked in and faced the room, prepared to jump right back in there if security or anyone other than Hattie was waiting. I would crabwalk my way all the way to the other end—wherever that may be—if necessary.

It wasn't. Hattie sat cross-legged on the floor, humming softly to herself and drawing stick figures in the dust with her fingertip. She looked up and said, "It's about time. You was gone forever!"

"I'm sorry, Hattie," I said, loosely reattaching the cover of the vent. "It was a little rough moving around in there."

I finger tightened each of the screws and paused to scroll through the pictures I had taken on my phone while in the vent. They were crystal clear, and the servers were cutting edge, but why so many? It made absolutely no sense. I had also thought to check my cell reception while hiding behind the intake grille, but nothing had changed there. I was still completely cut off from the rest of the world. I stair-stepped back down to the two-drawer file cabinet before hopping to the floor.

"Whatcha got there?" asked Hattie, getting to her feet and reaching for my phone.

"It's just my phone," I said, handing it over without fully considering she had likely never seen anything like it.

"Gina had one, too," said Hattie, turning it over and over. "She said hers was a camera, too, and it *was!* She took my picture. I never seen anything like it. She just tapped the screen and *bam!* She could show me right here on the screen. I have a camera, and sometimes Mama lets me take pictures, but I don't see any of 'em 'til I take 'em to Staker's to develop. And they're never as good. Almost always get my thumb in there." She snorted.

"Mine has a camera, too," I said, and I unlocked the screen and pulled up the pictures I had taken of the server room. "Is this what Gina saw?"

"Maybe," said Hattie, studying the screen with fierce determination. "She didn't use her camera phone. She used her fancy one, and she couldn't see the pictures yet. But it might be what she was describing. She was real excited about it. She said she had to show someone and left town real soon after. I don't really see a barn, but—" She shrugged her shoulders.

"We should get out of here," I said. Paranoia was creeping in, and I didn't want to try and explain to anyone why we were here. I needed a quiet moment to think, to process what little I knew and to formulate some sort of a plan. Hattie's help had been invaluable, but I couldn't imagine what more she could contribute. All of her information had been limited, and for her, everything was a game—well, except with Jimmy. I believe she meant business there. I needed to find someone who knew more than just a little bit about the Academy. What was their mission beyond the higher education of a select set of candidates? What was their criteria for selecting these students? Why were they so much more technologically advanced than their neighbors in Briarstaff? Ideally, I'd like to find a way in, maybe lob a couple of questions to the principal, dean or superintendent.

We exited the room and hurried back down the hall, using the stepladder to reenter the overhead passage. We began our backwards trek through the darkened corridor to our point of entry.

......•••••⊖⊙•••••......

"Told you it's easier getting out than in," said Hattie as she helped pull me through the narrow adit and back into daylight.

My eyes had acclimated to the darkness of the mine, and I was thankful for the shade provided by the trees as my eyes readjusted to the outside world. I collected my backpack from where I had stashed it and slung it over my shoulder. I stood my bike upright.

Hattie shielded her eyes and looked toward the sun. *"Shoot,"* she said. "Do you know the time? I'm supposed to be back with Mama no later'n five-thirty."

I looked at my watch. "It's quarter to six."

She let out a high-pitched squeak and clapped a hand over her mouth, her eyes widening. *"Oooooh!* I'm late! Joy Beth is gonna be so *mad!"*

Judging from the previous day, I figured she was correct. It seemed that Hattie relieved Joy Beth of whatever duties she had with their mother at the festival so she could go home and suffer the abuse of the scumbag she had married. As much as I dreaded returning to town, I was bound to accompany Hattie, not only to make sure she wasn't in trouble with her mother but also to do anything and everything I could to prevent Joy Beth from going home alone. I remembered Jimmy was supposed to be working the evening shift, but for all I knew, he could be lying in wait for her to return. As good as my intentions were, I had undoubtedly made her situation so much worse.

Hattie turned back and forth, agitated and not sure what to do. "I gotta go!"

"It's okay, Hattie," I said soothingly. "I'm going with you. I certainly can't find my way without you, and I'll explain to your mother why you're late. I'll let her know it's all my fault."

"But Joy Beth—"

"I'll talk to Joy Beth, too," I said. "Don't you worry."

She nodded, still nervous, but relieved by degrees. I positioned myself on the bike seat, suddenly aware of how sore I would be in the morning. I hadn't spent this much time on a bicycle since I was an early teen and frankly, my butt hurt like hell. Hattie turned her back to me, stooping to lift her bike from the thatch of leaves where she had laid it on its side. A sharp crack sounded far in the distance, echoing across the hills and valleys, and Hattie jumped at the sound.

"*Awww*," she said, disappointed and looking at her feet. "Now I *really* gotta wash these shoes."

She let her bike fall to the ground and turned slowly toward me, her eyes wide and her mouth slightly open.

Time shifted into slow motion as my mind struggled to process what I saw.

What registered first was Hattie's prized discovery from the previous afternoon, a white shoe that was no longer white, a dark red spatter soaking into its fabric. I looked up but couldn't make sense of the scarlet rose blossoming on the lower left side of her pale-yellow cotton top.

"Hattie?" My voice sounded sluggish and stupid in my own ears.

"Mmm?" Her eyes fluttered, and she was suddenly falling forward.

I snapped out of my trance, throwing my bike down and grabbing her arm just before she hit the ground. "Oh, *no, no, no, no, no, no, no—*"

Another sharp report sounded, and I felt the bullet sear the air beside my head before slamming into the rock wall behind us. I hunkered down protectively over Hattie, trying to keep our profile as small as possible while I desperately searched for a way out of this mess. I scanned every direction but could not see the gunman, nor could I get any sense of his location, thanks to the reverberation of sound that was geographically inherent. I was aware of a thin stream of respiration whistling from Hattie's nose, and I was thankful for that. I had no idea how badly she was hurt but knew I needed to get her medical attention immediately.

There was no way I could carry her to safety. As petite as she was, we were at least five miles from town, and it would take far too long, not to mention what a sizable and slow-moving target we would make for our hunter. Staying low to the ground, I wriggled my backpack off my shoulders and unzipped it, rummaging through the contents until my fingertips found the cold steel barrel of the gun I had taken from Jimmy. I didn't even have a target, but I'd rather have the gun handy if I needed it. I laid it on the ground beside me, looking from side to side for any sign of the shooter. While I saw no one or nothing out of the ordinary, my ears worked against me, casting sinister potential to every element of nature's soundtrack. Leaves fluttered in the breeze and twigs snapped while woodland creatures scampered in the underbrush, all of which had me on a razor's edge. I nearly yelped aloud as a flock of blackbirds burst into flight from a nearby treetop.

Trying to balance caution with a growing sense of urgency, I took another look at our surroundings, and there was really only one direction to consider: up and over the low rock ridge which housed the narrow entrance to the mine from which we had only just emerged. I had no idea what was on the other side—hopefully, it wasn't a steep drop off—but it was the only feasible option. Every other direction either sloped gradually down to where the shooter waited or would keep us completely exposed, easy targets for additional attempts. I had the slimmest glimmer of an idea about how to transport Hattie out, but it would be awkward and would require more muscle memory from me than I was convinced I had. How long had it been since I'd "doubled" someone on a bike? And exactly how difficult would it be to navigate with a rider who could contribute absolutely nothing to our equilibrium and might, in fact, work against it?

Questions that would soon be answered. Valuable time was slipping away in more ways than one, and I needed to act. Remaining low, I dragged the bicycle to the crest of the ridge and peered over the top. I hadn't realized I was holding my breath until it came out in a rush as I thankfully discovered solid ground on the other side. It sloped down gently in the opposite direction with a fair amount of space between trees and a fairly level forest floor, giving me a modicum of hope that I might be able to get us away from here. On the downside, I had no idea where we were in proximity to the highway, and that's where we needed to be, and just as soon as possible. From there, I might be able to flag for help from some good Samaritan passing by. I tried to remember the various twists and turns we had taken, but it was all jumbled inside my head.

One step at a time.

I pushed the bike up and over the ridge, then crawled back to where Hattie lay. I picked up the gun and double-checked to make sure the safety was still engaged before shoving its barrel into my waistband. Next, I grabbed the backpack and worked at its straps, expanding them to their greatest capacity. I turned Hattie on her side, carefully avoiding the area that was now drenched in blood, and slid the straps over her narrow shoulders, pulling the pack against her back. I laid on the ground with my back against Hattie's front, working the straps up and over my shoulders and tightening them, effectively binding her to myself. I hoped they would hold. I could feel the warm sticky wetness of her wound soaking into the back of my shirt, and I hoped I wasn't hurting her any worse, but I didn't have a better plan.

"Hang on, Hattie. Here we go."

I rolled onto my stomach and said a prayer before scuttling toward the crest of the ridge as quickly as I could manage. Although Hattie was sandwiched between the backpack and me, she seemed impossibly exposed, and it would only get worse before it got better. I was running on pure adrenaline at this point, and Hattie felt no heavier than a sheet of paper. I worked my way over the ridge and crawled to the bike, pushing it a little bit farther down the slope so we wouldn't be so exposed when I attempted to pull us upright.

My first attempt didn't go well. I lifted the bike and almost managed to get to my feet when Hattie abruptly coughed, a thick, wet sound that startled me so badly I let the bike drift away as I dropped back to my stomach. She grunted when we hit the ground, and I was equal parts delighted to hear her issue sound and yet worried I was inadvertently hurting her, but I needed to take advantage of this temporary cover and put some distance between us and the shooter before he made his way up the ridge.

I crab walked to where the bike now lay and tried again, pulling the bike upright and approaching it from behind. I had considered how awkward it would be to try and get Hattie's leg over the crossbar, even considering its step-through frame. I guided us up over the back tire and positioned Hattie on the wide seat behind me, giving myself just the very tip to perch. I checked the straps of the backpack once more to make sure they were just as snug as possible before pushing off.

There was absolutely no way I could peddle. It was taking everything I had to keep Hattie from slipping from the seat. I used my feet to move us forward and keep us balanced while guiding us toward a narrow path that sloped gently downward before leveling off. With a merciful assist from gravity, we were finally moving forward, albeit slowly.

It was very short-lived—once the path reached the bottom of the valley, I was back to essentially walking us along, straddling a bicycle that was more hindrance than help. As the path began to slowly rise toward another ridge, I knew this wouldn't work—it was simply too awkward. I put both feet on the ground and stopped, taking a moment to think. I glanced behind us to check our progress and was surprised to see our starting point far in the distance, maybe a few hundred yards back and partially obscured by trees.

It suddenly occurred to me to check the position of the sun in the sky. It was at least six o'clock. The sun should have begun its descent into the western horizon, and although I had gotten completely disoriented following Hattie's lead, I knew we had to travel west to reach town. We were heading in the right direction.

The incline before us wasn't too steep or too long, and after we crested its ridge, we would no longer be nearly as visible. Still, it was too steep for me to manage dragging both Hattie and the bike along, so something had to go. I lifted us up and backed us off the seat, walking backwards until I could let the bike fall to the ground. I reached behind myself and grabbed Hattie's legs, pulling them around me, boosting her up into a piggyback position on my back. I began the ascent, surprised again at how light Hattie felt. It gave me hope that I just might be able to do this, but I wondered how long this panic-fueled adrenaline would last.

As I neared the crest, I paused, straining to listen. There were sounds ahead—music, voices, animated laughter. It was all the motivation I needed to pick up the pace. I gave Hattie a quick boost higher on my back and plodded forward, cresting the ridge and finding myself suddenly at the woods' edge.

Before us was the hard-packed clay dustbowl that skirted the edge of the quarry, the main mine entrance to our immediate left and to our right, the glorious sight of a rusting old pickup with a handcrafted truck bed parked at an angle farther ahead. Music spilled from its rolled-down windows, and Shane sat on one of the rock outcroppings with his back to us, talking to Rose, who was perched on bare knees, laughing hysterically at whatever he had just said. Nick lay shirtless, flat on his back on another rock farther up the quarry's side, soaking up sun.

"Hey!" I shouted, emerging from the woods and moving as quickly as I could toward them. *"I need some help here!"*

Rose was the first to spot us, and her smile faltered as she tried to process what she was seeing. She tugged at Shane's arm and pointed in our direction, and he turned, assessing the situation much more quickly. In an instant, he was on his feet, running toward us while Rose hung back, unsure of what to do.

"What *happened?*" Shane asked just as my knees buckled, and I fell forward. Hattie let out another grunt when we hit the ground. So much for adrenaline.

"She's been shot," I said, pushing myself up. "Can you take her to—"

"Of course! Of course!"

Shane helped me loosen the straps of the backpack and untangle myself from Hattie. He laid her down gently on the ground, and I was startled to see how much blood she had lost along the way. It ran down her left leg, soaking into her sock. I looked over my shoulder and down at my own legs and saw how much had transferred to me during our short trek through the woods.

It wasn't lost on Shane, either, and when he spotted the grip of Jimmy's gun jutting out from the waistband of my khaki shorts, he hesitated only a second before tackling me and rolling us away from Hattie. Rose shrieked, finally attracting Nick's attention, and he was on his feet like a rocket, racing toward us.

"*Shane, wait—*" I managed before he reared back and busted me a good one in the mouth. My head slammed against the hard clay earth, triggering a field of stars across the periphery of my vision. His next blow was a solid shot to my abdomen, forcing what little breath I had out of me. "*Ooooof!*"

He snagged the gun, and pushed away from me, getting to his feet as Nick skidded to a stop beside him. He released the safety and leveled the gun in my direction.

"What the fuck, man?" demanded Nick, looking from where Hattie lay to where I lay, and then to Nick. "What the fuck is going on?" Rose stayed far in the background, hands clapped over her mouth as tears streamed down her face.

"Shane," I managed, pushing myself up on one elbow. "I didn't *do* this. There's someone out in the woods with a rifle. For all I know, they could be here any moment."

Indecision clouded Shane's expression, and I was exasperated at the turn this was taking.

"*Shane,*" I pleaded. "Why in the world would I shoot Hattie and then ask you to help me get her into town? It doesn't even make *sense.*"

Another flicker of uncertainty crossed his face, but he held the gun steady, pointing at my midsection. Nick shifted nervously from one foot to the other, ready to pounce if needed to assist his friend while also keeping an eye out for the gunman I had warned them about.

"*Shane!*" I snapped. "*You are wasting valuable time! Keep* the fucking gun! I don't give *two shits* about the gun! It's Jimmy Perkins's, and I'll tell you all about it *later!* We need to get Hattie some help *right fucking NOW!*"

That seemed to do the trick all the way around. Rose was suddenly by Hattie's side, patting her cheeks and whispering softly to her. Shane reengaged the safety on the gun and slid it into his own waistband—

apparently, he wasn't quite ready to trust me completely, but he offered a hand and helped me to my feet. Nick remained on alert, ready to roll with whatever was needed from him.

Shane kneeled beside Rose and took Hattie's small hand. "Hattie Mae?" His voice shook as he assessed her sorry state. "Hattie Mae? I'm gonna get you into town right away, but you gotta hang on for me, now. You gotta hang on for Joy Beth and for your sweet mama…can you do that?"

Hattie's eyes fluttered and she nodded weakly, prompting a fresh wave of tears from Rose. I stood back and watched as Shane effortlessly lifted Hattie into his arms and began the short trek to where his truck was parked. We trailed along, but I fell behind a little as a new consideration dawned on me. Why would anyone want to shoot Hattie? Hattie was as harmless as anyone could be. It was much more likely that I was the intended target, and Hattie had just been in the wrong place at the wrong time. I shouldn't have allowed her to tag along with me in the first place. It was completely irresponsible to rely on Hattie's knowledge of the surroundings just because it was *convenient*. So, what if Gina had done the same thing? She would have had no forewarning. But now, Gina was dead, and Michael Arthur was missing—probably dead as well. Something was drastically wrong here, and I should have known better. I felt nauseous.

At the truck bed, Rose and I worked to make as comfortable a space for Hattie as we could by pulling bunches of the hay together from the bales stacked in back, making what looked like an enormous bird's nest. Shane carefully lay Hattie down, and we bunched some extra hay behind her head. A thin trickle of blood had begun to seep from the corner of her mouth, and she looked horribly pale. I started to climb in the back with her, but Shane reached out and grabbed my arm.

"I don't know about this," he said. "Maybe you should hang back."

"Please, Shane," I implored, and I wasn't even thinking about the gunman who was likely still lurking in the woods. "I just want to help. I'll ride back here to make sure she doesn't jostle around. Once we get her into town, someone's got to talk to the sheriff, let him know what happened. It should be me. And the sooner I talk to him, the sooner he can get out here and search the area, maybe find the fucker who did this."

He thought for a moment before nodding, and I climbed into the back, sitting cross legged beside Hattie to keep her from shifting around. Shane got behind the wheel while Rose scooted to the middle of the bench seat and Nick sat on the passenger side. The engine roared to life and Shane turned us around, heading back along the rutted path that led to the highway. He did it with infinitely more finesse than he had when me and Michael were his passengers.

Without conscious thought, I had taken hold of Hattie's hand somewhere along the way and found myself quietly chanting, "Please, please, please—" With my other hand, I applied pressure to the wound, trying to staunch a flow that simply wouldn't stop.

The shift to pavement as we reached the highway was a rough one—no way around it. The old truck's suspension creaked and groaned in protest, and Hattie and I lifted a little from the truck bed before settling back with a thud. Hattie grunted and coughed, more blood trickling from the corner of her mouth.

Once we reached Briarstaff, Shane slammed his hands on the steering wheel. "Shit!"

"What's wrong?" I yelled through the open panel of his back glass.

"The goddamn Festival! All of the streets are blocked. I'll have to go around." He turned right into the neighborhoods east of the town square and begun circumventing the congested area.

"Where are we going? A hospital? Urgent Care?" I asked.

"Dr. Morris's," Shane yelled back. "He has a clinic behind his house. He lives out by the high school on the other side of town. He can get a life flight if we need one."

Looking down at Hattie, I was pretty sure we were going to need one.

Once Shane had finally rejoined Route 5 heading west, he pushed the accelerator to the floor, rocketing us the remaining distance to Dr. Morris's house. As we approached, Shane laid on his horn, announcing our eminent arrival by audible assault. We shot past the doctor's private drive, slowing to catch the next entrance which led to a small, paved lot behind the physician's large brownstone residence. The clinic had been attached as an afterthought, its pale-yellow siding and black shutters in sharp contrast to those of the main building. Shane skidded to a stop beneath an overhang that had been erected over a commercial sliding door, honking his horn persistently until Dr. Morris shuffled through, his dinner napkin still tucked underneath his chin.

The teens climbed out of the cab, rushing to the doctor to pull him toward the truck bed. Rose was crying again, and Nick and Shane's words collided into an unintelligible cacophony that had Dr. Morris's caterpillar eyebrows twisting in befuddlement.

"Slow down," he urged. "What's going on here?" He looked toward the back of the truck, and his mouth fell open when he saw me. I had risen to my feet, covered in Hattie's blood.

"It's not mine. It's Hattie's," I said, my voice a million miles away in my own ears. I looked down into Hattie's ice blue eyes, her lips slightly parted, a rivulet of drying blood stark against the pale white skin of her youthful face. A hard lump formed in my throat as I kept willing her to blink.

Blink, goddamn it, blink!

But Hattie Mae Bartlett was gone.

275

CHAPTER TWENTY-ONE

We watched in stunned disbelief as Dr. Morris climbed up into the truck bed and began administering CPR with surprising vigor. After a few moments, he signaled for Shane and Nick to help him get Hattie inside, which they did without hesitation, carrying her through the automatic doors while Rose and I trailed behind like zombies. They went into an examination room where they could lay Hattie flat on an industrial steel table, and as he did, his elderly wife appeared beside us, drying her hands on a dishtowel. As soon as she saw her husband hard at work, she tossed the towel aside and nudged her way to his side to assist. I would learn later that her name was Patricia, and she had been his medical assistant for the entirety of their marriage.

At that point, we were banished to the small lobby, where Rose cried onto Nick's shoulder and Shane paced furiously back and forth, seething. I stood with my back to the corner, reluctant to sit down for fear of getting blood all over everything. As bad as my day had started, I could have never imagined it getting so much worse. I tried to cling to some tiny shred of hope that maybe the good doctor could bring her back, but I had seen the stillness of her face, her eyes open but seeing nothing.

After what seemed an eternity, Dr. Morris stepped out into the lobby and confirmed the worst. Hattie had lost too much blood, and he simply wasn't equipped for this kind of trauma. He asked what happened, and I gave him the shortest version possible without lying. I suppose *technically* I was lying by omission, but I didn't see any point in trying to explain what we had seen inside the mine. It seemed awfully coincidental the shooting happened just after we had found the server farm. Maybe there was some sort of security or surveillance in place I hadn't seen, something that alerted someone to our presence. I still didn't know how all of this might link back to any of the individuals in town, and if I blabbed to the wrong person, I might well be further endangering myself. All I wanted to do was take a long hot shower and get the hell out of Briarstaff. I needed to regroup and return with outside reinforcements, and I was prepared to walk, if necessary.

Right about then, Sheriff Daniel strode purposefully through the door, looking for the doctor and giving us a quick glance as he passed. Mrs. Morris must have been making phone calls while her husband was quizzing us. The sheriff did a double take and stopped when he saw me, drenched in blood and standing in the corner. He marched over, inserting himself well into my personal space.

"What in the hell have you done?" he demanded.

"I didn't do anything. I—"

"Do you honestly expect me to believe that? I'm hearing we've got a dead girl here, and whaddaya know? Here you are."

"Hattie was—" I paused, realizing how awful what I was about to say would sound. I couldn't say she had been showing me the woods. I was more than ten years older than her, and why would a man of my age lure a simple girl like Hattie Bartlett out into the woods? Without context I couldn't provide, it was lurid even in my own mind. I decided it was best to just cut to the chase. "Someone in those woods shot Hattie, and he might still be out there. You need to get your men together and search those woods while there's still time."

He looked at me incredulously. "My *men?* It's just me, my friend, and don't you dare tell me my business. Why should I spend valuable time wandering around those woods when it's pretty clear who's responsible for this? And by the way, I been lookin' for you all fucking afternoon! Got a call out to the trailer park earlier. Jimmy Perkins got the shit stomped outta him by a fellow he'd never seen before and could only describe, and what do you know? He sounds an awful lot like you. I suppose you don't know anything about that either?"

I stammered, having completely forgotten about Jimmy Perkins. It seemed so insignificant at this point. Apparently, Jimmy hadn't recognized me as his cellmate from that morning, or he most certainly would have said so, and the sheriff would have had me dead to rights.

A quick word passed between the kids, and Shane stepped forward, clearing his throat. "Um, sir? I'm sorry to interrupt, and I don't know nothing about this business with Jimmy, but as far as Hattie goes, it couldn't have been Mr. Dwayne. I was out in those woods myself when I heard the shot. I ran into Mr. Dwayne carrying Hattie just a minute or so later, and the shot came from too far away."

I tried not to let the surprise register on my face. Why was Shane lying for me?

"That's right, sir," said Nick, stepping up behind Shane. "I was there, too."

"And me," added Rose, with a quick nod of her head.

Sheriff Daniel looked from one teen to the other, eyes narrowed in disbelief, but these kids had better poker faces than I could ever produce. I stared at my feet and tried to fade into the background, unsure of exactly what was happening here.

"So, let me get this straight," he said, pacing slowly back and forth in front of them. "You're telling me that you're willing to swear on God's

Holy Bible that there is no way that Mr. Morrow could have perpetrated this crime?"

"Yes, sir," said Shane unflinchingly. "It might have been someone hunting coyotes or opossums—and I've been hearin' about folks comin' across from Ohio and poachin' deer."

Sheriff Daniel pressed his lips together tightly, examining each earnest face for any sign of duress but coming up completely empty.

"*Sh-i-i-i-t!*" he finally exclaimed, turning toward the small reception desk where Dr. Morris waited with his wife. "Jeb, I'm gonna have to have a look around out there. I'll be back in a little bit. Patricia can reach me on the short-wave if anything else comes up."

He turned back to me.

"Do not leave this town, Mr. Morrow," he said, pointing a forefinger at me. "We have a whole lot more to discuss."

I fought the urge to give a smartass response. I mean, where could I go? I had no transportation, and I couldn't call anyone. I settled for a curt nod. He shot us a final disgusted look before striding through the automated door, returning to his cruiser and speeding out of the clinic's lot, his siren blaring while a single strobe on the dashboard flared blue, red and back again.

His siren was only just receding when a cream-colored Cadillac pulled into the lot, screeching to a halt directly in front of Shane's truck. I could see Caroline Peterson behind the wheel, her auburn hair piled high on top of her head. She slammed the car into park and killed the ignition, looking super pissed.

Shane spotted her almost as I did, and muttered, "*Shit.*"

"What?" I asked, following him outside. Rose and Nick stayed within the relative safety of the clinic's waiting room, looking far more afraid of Mrs. Peterson than they ever had of Sheriff Daniel.

Caroline's gaze swept over us, and she was out of the driver's side in an instant, mouth working and finger wagging while she tick-tocked across the pavement in another pair of expensive-looking slingback wedges. "Shane Van Buren! You come here this very *instant!*"

Shane nodded. "Hey there, Mrs. Peterson, I don't know—"

"Where is my daughter?" she demanded, hysterically shrill. Her carefully constructed public persona was showing visible cracks, especially in the lines around her eyes and mouth. It aged her about ten years. "I know you know where she is. I can't *believe* you let her take the stage with that— that—"

"That *what*, Mrs. Peterson?" I asked.

Her eyes shifted to me, and the look of revulsion was immediate. "What are *you* doing here? And my God—is that *blood* all over you? What exactly is going on? Oh, my God—it's Audrey, isn't it? What have you done to my poor sweet girl?" And she was suddenly on me, hammering me with a series of blows to my chest and face. I was more startled than hurt, although I certainly felt the few she landed with her formidable engagement ring.

Shane gently pulled her off me, keeping his voice calm. "It's not Audrey, Mrs. Peterson."

She looked from him to me and back again, unsure she had heard correctly. "It's not my baby girl?"

"No, ma'am," said Shane. "It's Hattie Bartlett. There's been an accident. She's—she's—" His words choked off as he covered his face with his hands.

Caroline's hand fluttered to her mouth as the fight went out of her. "Wh-what happened?"

"She was shot," I said. "We don't know exactly. Sheriff Daniel is on his way out to the woods right now. Someone needs to notify her mother and Joy Beth—"

"I'm on my way," said Patricia Morris, stepping up behind us. I hadn't even heard her exit the clinic. "I hate this more than you know, but Delphine deserves to get the news from a friend, not through the grapevine."

It took me a second to remember that Madame Phalange was only a stage name. We watched as Mrs. Morris got into a dark blue station wagon parked beside the clinic and steered out of the parking lot, heading toward town.

Seizing the advantage while Caroline's momentum had been derailed, Shane said, "I haven't seen Audrey today, Mrs. Peterson, but I'll be sure and let her know you're looking for her."

Caroline's eyes shifted back to Shane, and I could almost see the wheels turning behind her eyes. It was taking every bit of restraint she had to keep from shifting gears and resuming her interrogation, but even Caroline recognized how poorly that would be perceived under the present circumstances. She cleared her throat and patted Shane's arm. "You do that, young man."

She returned to her car and started the engine, casting one last scornful look at us before squealing her tires as she turned left on Route 5 and headed for town.

···•••••⊝⊙•••••···

I was nearly accustomed to traveling in Shane's truck bed by this point, although the bits of hay sticking to the blood on my clothes was distressing. Shane had dropped Rose and Nick at their respective houses and offered to take me back to Fred's Beds. I wasn't about to turn him down. It was nearly dark, and I felt completely run through. I leaned against the open back glass, feeling every bump and jolt as Shane navigated back roads first, then neighborhood streets that surrounded the festival, still in full swing, oblivious to the tragedy that had just unfolded. Laughter and music floated through the air as we passed, and it all seemed so obscene.

"Why did you all lie for me?" I asked through the glass, staring straight ahead and watching the festival fade into the distance. "What changed your minds?"

"Jimmy Perkins," said Shane.

"Yeah?"

"Uh-huh." Shane slowed and eased left onto the two-lane highway which would take me back to my motel. "While we were waiting for an update from Dr. Morris, I called my dad from the reception desk. I shoulda been home for dinner and didn't want him to worry. I'm glad I did. He was fit to be tied. He'd heard about Jimmy getting his ass kicked, and he thought I might have had something to do with it—not directly, but maybe I put someone up to it."

I glanced over my shoulder at his silhouette, firmly focused on the road ahead. "Why would he think that?"

"He saw Joy Beth at the festival this afternoon and how banged up she was. I had no idea. I was there earlier, but she must have been avoiding me." He angrily clapped his hands against the steering wheel. "That sumbitch has been beatin' on her for just as long as I can remember. I don't know why she stays. I would—" His voice broke, and he smacked his steering wheel again.

"Hattie told me you've always been crazy about Joy Beth."

He nodded, wiping his eyes. "I would never treat her that way. When you told me that gun you had was Jimmy's, I put two and two together. You done for me what I was never able to do. Nick and Rose and me, we think you're some kind of goddamn superhero. I don't even know how to thank you."

I let out a short sardonic laugh. "Don't thank me yet. I probably just made things worse for Joy Beth and her son. As long as she keeps going back to Jimmy, he's never gonna change. And speaking of the gun, what did you do with it?"

"It's under my seat. You want it back?"

"No," I said. "Last thing I need is for Sheriff Daniel to catch me with a gun on me. You should just get rid of it. Empty the chamber and throw it in the quarry. One thing's for sure, Jimmy Perkins has no business with a gun."

We rode in silence for a few minutes. I closed my eyes and tried to force the image of Hattie's vacant, open eyes out of my mind, but I couldn't. I should have sent her away just as soon as I discovered her in my motel room that morning. She would be safe at the festival right now with her mother if I had practiced just a little common sense.

"I don't suppose you've seen Michael Arthur," I asked, trying to get my mind off the subject.

"Huh-unh," Shane replied, slowing the truck and signaling left. We were approaching the motel. "He never made it back to town?"

"Nope," I said. "Shoulda been here sometime last night. I don't know what's happened to him."

"That's weird."

"Everything about the last couple of days has been weird. What's up with Audrey and Trevor? Do you know where they are?"

We turned into the dusty parking lot of the motel, and I was relieved to see that Mrs. Shepley had gone for the day. I wouldn't want her to see me looking like Carrie post-prom, returning to my room. Shane stopped in front of my room and shifted into park, killing the engine. He shifted sideways in his seat and looked back at me.

"They took off. They're planning on laying low until Audrey's eighteenth birthday. It's next Saturday. Then they don't have to put up with all the shit Mrs. Peterson is trying pull," he said.

"Yeah, Caroline seems like a real piece of work," I agreed. "Do Trevor's parents know what's going on?"

"Yeah, they know," Shane replied. "They don't like it, but they know. Trevor's already eighteen. Ain't much they can say."

"They don't like it the same way Caroline Peterson doesn't like it?"

"Naw, nothin' like that. They both think the world of Audrey," said Shane. He added with a half-laugh, "They just worry, is all. Mrs. Anderson still thinks what happened to her husband was no accident. She thinks Mr. Peterson meant to do it."

"Back up," I said. "What happened to Mr. Anderson?"

"Mr. Peterson hit him with his car a few years back. Happened in the IGA parking lot. Mr. Anderson broke his pelvis, and it severed his spinal cord. Been in a wheelchair and on disability ever since."

"So, what do *you* think?"

Shane shrugged and sighed. "I ain't give it much thought. I mean, sure the Petersons are kind of a lot, but I've always stayed on their good side—well, at least up until last night. And I couldn't help it. Trevor's been playing with us for over a year, and the first time I heard Audrey grab the mic when we were practicing—well, I knew it was something special."

I nodded. "That it was. I'm glad I was there. Thanks for the ride, Shane. I'm gonna get inside and get cleaned up."

"Is there anything else I can do for you?" asked Shane. "I could come back later if you need a ride."

I glanced at my watch. It was just after nine. I couldn't see myself doing anything more today. "I'm good for now, but if you have any free time tomorrow, how would you feel about giving me a lift to Shawnee? I need to make a few calls and see if I can arrange for some transportation."

Shane nodded. "Yeah, I can do that. I'm not supposed to start running errands for folk at the festival 'til after noon or so. What time?"

"Nine-thirty?"

"Nine-thirty it is," said Shane, firing his engine back up. I brushed off as much hay as I could and collected my backpack before jumping over the wood-railed side of his truck bed. My legs protested as they hit the ground, and I could hardly blame them. This had been one shit-sucker of a day. A long, hot shower and then straight to bed. I waved to Shane as he backed up, digging the room key from my pocket and letting myself inside.

······●●●●●◑◉●●●●●···

I showered until the water ran cold and still felt sticky from Hattie's blood, although I'm pretty sure it was just my imagination. I tossed my bloody clothes into the same reeking pile from this morning and figured I would burn it all at the first opportunity. I chose a pair of athletic shorts and a t-shirt and perched at the foot of my mattress, looping through the events of the day whether I wanted to or not.

I was surprised to discover I was hungry. I hadn't eaten since Hattie and I had shared peanut butter and jelly sandwiches for lunch. I rifled through my backpack and found the chips I had stashed earlier and one of the bottles of water. Not exactly gourmet, but it was all I had. I wished I still had some of the whiskey. I didn't know how I was ever going to fall asleep with dark thoughts racing through my head and guilt weighing on me like an albatross.

I was just eating the last of the chips when I heard a light knock on my door. I looked at the display on my phone and saw it was almost ten-thirty. Who could it possibly be at this hour? My mind was more than ready to supply several possibilities, none of which were good, most of which were deadly. I stood and quietly tip-toed to the picture window beside the door. Peering around the edge of the curtain, I spotted a frail woman standing at my door, but I didn't immediately recognize her. She rapped again, just as timid as before.

I weighed my options. My bedside light was on, so she probably already knew I was inside. I hadn't exactly been quiet digging through the bag of chips, either. She didn't look threatening, and from what I could tell, she wasn't carrying a weapon. I retracted the chain and unlocked the deadbolt, opening the door just a crack.

"Yes, can I help you?" I asked.

Her lined face was familiar, but she was wearing a worn t-shirt and jeans, and her hair was damp and pulled back in a ponytail. It took me a long beat before I realized Madame Phalange stood before me, minus all of her rigamarole. Her angular face was lengthened by grief, and I froze, not sure what I should say.

"May I come in?" she asked.

"Certainly, certainly," I said, opening the door and stepping aside. I offered her the chair closest to us, then scanned the parking lot but didn't see any cars. I wondered how she had gotten here. Surely, she hadn't walked—? She stepped inside and took the seat as I closed the door. "I, uh—I can't tell you how very sorry I am. I wish I—"

She waved my words away and stared at her lap where she folded her hands. She looked impossibly frail. I took the only other seat in the room, the office chair by the desk, and waited patiently for her to find words.

I was beginning to think that was never going to happen when she finally said, "First, I want to thank you for putting the whomp on that asshole who married my Joy Beth. It's been a long time coming."

"I don't know, Madame—er, Mrs. Bartlett—"

Her smile was tired. "Just call me Del."

I nodded. "I'm afraid I may have made things worse, Del. Jimmy's liable to just take it out on Joy Beth and God forbid, little Jimmy."

"I don't think so," she said. "I spent the whole day talking Joy Beth into taking the baby and moving back in with me. It wasn't easy, but the final straw was this whole business with Hattie—"

Her voice broke, and she began to sob, clutching herself tightly and rocking in the chair. I scanned the room for tissues, but apparently that was an amenity beyond the means of Fred's Beds. I made a quick jaunt to the bathroom and returned with a roll of toilet paper which I offered to Del. She took it, pulled off a few sheets and dabbed at her nose and eyes.

"It reminded Joy Beth of just how fragile—and how *brief* life is," she continued, and I felt my throat constricting. I was flashing back to the blanket of grief that had nearly smothered my own family as we prepared for Gina's funeral, and I was seriously about to lose it. Del abruptly looked up, staring directly into my tear-filled eyes. "I want you to know I don't blame you for any of this."

I was startled. Score another one for Madame Phalange. I was currently suffocating with guilt.

"But I—"

"But nothing," she said. "You were very good with both of my daughters, and even *I* couldn't see this coming. It's this town. I never wanted to come here in the first place." She shuddered.

"Then why did you?" I asked. I offered her a bottle of water from the case on the floor as I reached for one for myself, and she took it gratefully.

"I was pregnant with Hattie when Harlan got a job at the Academy. It wasn't anything fancy, just janitor work, but it was more money than we were used to, and he was taking the job regardless of what I thought. I didn't want to leave my mama behind. She was sick with lung cancer back in Barboursville. She was the only family I had left, but what could I do? I didn't know I was allowed to have an opinion back then." She paused to take a drink from the bottle.

"Anyway," she continued. "Mama passed before Hattie was even born, so I guess it didn't really matter in the long run. I suppose everything was fine for a while—I mean, I kept mostly to myself with my baby. Never did care for the way that Caroline Peterson and her snooty friends looked at us.

Pretty clear they thought we were far, far beneath them, and I'm just not one to suck up to folk.

"A couple of years later—I was pregnant with Joy Beth then—a family moved here from Ohio to open up a pizza shop. Frank and Pammie Conley, along with their son, Preston and his young family. They were just as nice as could be, and the pizza was *wonderful*," she said. "Preston's wife, Denise, made a point of checking in on me and Hattie. She had a little girl about the same age, and she and Hattie were fast friends. So were me and Denise. It was Denise who showed me how to read tarot cards and listen to my inner voice." Her smile was wistful, and *my* inner voice was whispering this story wouldn't end well.

"I remember Caroline mentioning them to me and Michael," I said. "She didn't care for them much. Said there was some sort of trouble over money?"

Del snorted. "That's what they say, but I don't know. I didn't know Preston all that well, but all the townsfolk seemed to like him. But one day, they were just up and gone, the uppity-ups at the F.O.E. saying he owed them a small fortune from a poker game. There was all sorts of talk. I found it hard to believe—I mean, they didn't take a single thing with them. Who does that? That's where I got my crystal ball and robes and—well, some things for my baby, too. Caroline was just going to throw it all out. At first, I told myself I was just holding on to it for them, but it wasn't too long before I knew they weren't ever coming back."

"How so?"

"It was just a few months after I had Joy Beth," she said, taking another sip from the bottle. "Harlan went out to fish in the quarry one Saturday morning. Hardly ever caught anything, but he liked to fish. Relaxed him, he said. Anyways, he came home all in a fluster, and that was *not* my Harlan. He didn't fluster. He was exactly the kind of anchor you hold onto in a storm. Told me he saw Troy Peterson and some of the other fellas from town pushing a car into the quarry. A car that looked an awful lot like one of the Conley's."

I sat forward in my chair, transfixed. "You're kidding me."

She shook her head slowly. "And it looked like there were people inside."

CHAPTER TWENTY-TWO

"So, was it them?" I asked, practically on the edge of my seat now. "My heart and head tell me yes, but I really have no way of knowing for sure. Harlan tried to sneak out of there just as careful as he could, but he was afraid one of the fellas might have spotted him. That was why he was so flustered. He made me promise to keep it to myself and not say a word to anyone while he figured out what to do. Of course, I agreed! I was scared to death—barely twenty years old and with two little babies to care for—I wasn't about to stir up any trouble." She took another drink of water and blew her nose on a few sheets from the roll of toilet paper. Her expression darkened. "And then I lost Harlan."

"Hattie said your husband left shortly after Joy Beth was born," I said.

Del nodded her head, dabbing at her eyes. "That's what I told them. It wasn't fair to Harlan's memory, but I had to stick to what they told me if I wanted them to believe I was buying into it."

"They? Who's *they?"*

"The people in this godforsaken town," she spat as angry color flared along her cheekbones. "Harlan didn't hear a thing from anyone for the rest of the weekend. Went to work like normal on Monday. I packed him a tuna fish sandwich, an apple and a handful of potato chips, just like any other day. Long about eleven o'clock, I get a knock on my front door. It's Caroline Peterson, looking just like the cat who ate the canary. Wants to know if I'd care to have lunch with her over at Ida's Diner—her treat, of course. I tried to tell her it would be too much work loading up the babies and taking them across the way, but she insisted. Said she'd help me. What a joke! She was afraid to touch my girls for fear they'd slobber on her or worse. She hadn't had Audrey yet and didn't have a clue how to care for children. She was absolutely *zero* help. But she wasn't taking no for an answer, so I let her drag us over to Ida's.

"She made small talk until we ordered, and the food arrived, and by small talk, I mean she talked about herself and every little thing she was planning for the credit union, and then she moved on to her husband, and all of his accomplishments." Del snorted, and in a frightfully accurate impression of Caroline's voice added, *"My Troy graduated at the head of his class faster than anyone ever has and ever will. He passed the bar on his first try with a perfect score!"*

She wrinkled her nose distastefully and made a retching sound. I couldn't help but laugh a little.

"Once the food came, she shifted gears," continued Del. "Wondered how Harlan was liking his job at the Academy, if he'd taken up any hobbies since we'd settled in. She asked if I had heard anything from the Conleys since they'd left town. It was all just so—*phony*. We'd been in Briarstaff for a little over two years, and this woman hasn't given me the time of day, much less offered to treat me to lunch. But here she was, acting like she was hanging on my every word, and I think I knew even then what she was up to. Troy or one of his friends had seen Harlan that Saturday morning out on the quarry, and they wanted to know how much he'd seen, and if he had said anything to me. She was mentally filing away everything I said, looking for any sign of trouble whatsoever. Her husband may be the highfalutin lawyer, but I've never been grilled like that in my entire life. By the end of lunch, I felt like I told her everything but the size of my underwear. But I remembered my promise and kept my answers simple, staying away from the topic almost entirely. I only mentioned that Harlan liked to fish at the quarry because everyone knew that.

"She seemed disappointed, and I was getting worried about Harlan. If they had gone to all the trouble of doing this to me, what were they doing to him?" Her laugh was bittersweet. "Harlan was a sweet man, had just the biggest heart. But—and I truly do hate to say this—he wasn't the smartest guy you'll ever meet, and he wasn't the best at holding his tongue. I had a sick feeling that something had already happened."

I remained rapt as she cleared her throat, took another drink and dabbed at the corners of her eyes again.

"She kept me there for the better part of an hour-and-a-half," she said. "When I finally got home, I could tell something was off, but I really couldn't look into it until I put my girls down for their naps. Once I did, I found the note on our bed." Her smile was tight. "It said he found someone else and had left us. Utter *bullshit!*"

She was so mad she was shaking, the wad of toilet tissue shredding in her clenched fist. I waited for her to regain her composure.

She took a deep breath and shrugged. "All his clothes were gone. All his personal effects, too. His wedding band was on the dresser. I never saw him again. I imagine he's down there somewhere in the quarry."

"Why didn't you leave?" I asked.

She shook her head. "Where would I have gone? I don't drive, I don't have any special skills—hell, I didn't even finish high school! I dropped out my senior year when I found out I was pregnant with Hattie. Was never any good at it anyway."

I've never been good with mental math, but the solution to this equation was startlingly clear: Delphine Bartlett was only a few years older than me. I had always assumed she was much older from the lines on her hands to her weatherworn face.

"So, you stayed," I said, stating the obvious.

She nodded. "Started waiting tables at Ida's after I found some teenage girls in the neighborhood who could help out with babysitting. It isn't how I wanted to raise my girls, but sometimes you don't get a choice. In the evenings, after the girls were asleep, I read all of the books Denise had left behind on fortune telling and tarot and such. Once I felt confident enough, Madame Phalange was born." She waved her arms above her head theatrically and smiled. "People thought I was crazy—hell, they *still* think I'm crazy, but they're curious. Everyone wants to know what the future holds, and I don't think I need to tell you, but I've tapped into something over the years." She tapped her temple with a forefinger.

I thought back to my own unsettlingly accurate reading and simply nodded.

"I still work part time at Ida's but doing readings has let me be home more and between the two, I squeak by."

She asked if she could use the facilities, and I directed her to the tiny bathroom, reminding her to take the roll of toilet tissue with her. While she was away, I processed all she had told me. I had zero qualms about accepting her version of events as gospel. It all rang true.

Del came back from the restroom and headed for the door. "Thank you for your time, Mr. Morrow."

"Dwayne—please," I said. I glanced at my watch and was surprised to see it was almost midnight. "I wish I could offer you a ride back to town, but I don't have any transportation."

She smiled. "That's quite all right. I'm used to getting around on my bike. And I could use the time to clear my head."

"Is there anything at all I can do for you?" I asked, trotting out that old grief chestnut that drops from so many lips in times of loss.

She shook her head and reached for the doorknob.

"Del?"

She stopped and turned around.

"Why did you tell me all of this?" I asked.

She took my hands into hers. "Two reasons. First, I don't want you to carry a burden that isn't yours to carry. You are not responsible for what happened to my Hattie."

"But—" That damn lump had worked its way back up into my throat, and I felt tears pooling in my eyes.

"*Shhh*," she ordered, giving my hands a gentle squeeze. "You have got to get that out of your head. You didn't pull that trigger. Anyone can be a victim of circumstance at any given time."

I wasn't entirely sure I agreed, but I snuffled and nodded.

"Second," she continued. "I've never told that story to anyone before for fear of what would happen to me and my girls, but I felt I needed to tell you now."

"Why is that?"

"People in town are talking about you ever since that card game last night," she said. "And ain't none of it good. These folks are dangerous, and it feels like they're up to something. You need to get out of here while you still can."

She gave my hands a final squeeze and stepped out into the night.

I stared at the darkened ceiling for what seemed like an eternity, completely exhausted but unable to sleep. My mind was racing with the events of the last few days. I felt like I should be able to rewind—just a little bit—long enough to prevent Hattie from tagging along with me that morning. Delphine Bartlett might have been willing to assign blame elsewhere, but I wasn't about to let myself off the hook so easily.

My need to see Melanie was nearly a physical ache. A fresh set of eyes and ears to help navigate this lunacy and provide a new perspective. A warm set of arms to hold me while I struggled with my own culpability in this fucked up mess. My greatest ally.

This fucking town!

From the first moment we arrived, there had been a sense of hostility. Okay, not from *everybody*, but almost. Mrs. Shepley was about as welcoming as a pit bull, and Caroline Peterson? What a piece of work she was! She had clearly played some part in orchestrating my humiliation during the poker game with the F.O.E. the previous evening. I wondered how many of the gentlemen around the table had been involved. I would have originally assumed they all were, but I didn't get that sense from Dr. Morris when we had brought Hattie to his clinic. He treated me no differently than any of the town's kids, and there was no sign he blamed me for what had happened. The eldest elder, Emmitt Brown, was probably complicit, but his grandson, Tommy, didn't seem bright enough to trust with a written grocery list. Reverend Baxter also seemed unlikely. But Troy Peterson? He had to have been the one to plant those decks of cards in my backpack and spike my drinks with something. Clearly, he was the yin to Caroline's yang. They had wasted no time at all in making sure the entire town would be abuzz with the scurrilous activities of its latest guest, namely me.

I didn't have a solitary shred of proof, but I was now absolutely certain Gina had found something here that had resulted in her death. Something related to the server farm embedded in the cave, but what? Had she been able to access the data? It didn't seem probable. Gina's specialty was photojournalism. *I* was the family IT geek. And Briarstaff didn't seem to have a single computer within its limits. What possible use could there be for a server farm?

I worried about Michael Arthur. Too much had happened in such a short period of time for his disappearance to be accidental. I had barely gotten to know Gina's—what, *boyfriend?* That word seemed very 'high school,' but I didn't know what else to call him. I had the sinking sensation I would never see him again.

Not alive, anyway.

And now I worried about Shane Van Buren. I probably shouldn't have asked him for a ride to Shawnee in the morning. Yes, I was desperate to get out of this town, but I couldn't bear it if something happened to another one of these kids because of their proximity to me. As much as I dreaded the walk, I made up my mind then and there to send Shane on his way when he arrived in the morning. It was only after I had made up my mind that my eyes began to feel heavy. One last glance at my watch showed me it was well after one.

Nothing ever goes as planned.

I awoke to a pounding on my motel door.

I was disoriented and groggy. Had I overslept? A quick glance at the window told me, no, I hadn't. Darkness still waited on the other side of the curtain. I turned to my watch next, and saw it wasn't even four o'clock.

More pounding on the door, and my heart was racing.

"Mr. Dwayne!"

It took a second to recognize the voice. *"Shane?!?"*

I pushed myself out of bed and unlocked the door. Shane shuffled in the doorway, wild-eyed with his hair all askew. He grabbed my arm. "You've gotta come with me. I don't know what to do!"

I pulled my arm back. "Wait a minute—what's going on?"

"It's the Andersons. They need help! *C'mon!*"

He grabbed for my arm again, but I raised a forefinger. "Okay, okay," I said. "Give me just a second. I need some pants and shoes."

"Hurry!"

He turned and raced away while I pulled on my shorts and slid into my shoes. What in the hell was this all about? I grabbed my keys, phone and wallet, slipping them into various pockets before pulling the door closed and locking it behind me. Shane was already behind the wheel of his truck, urging me with a flailing arm to hurry. I ran across the parking lot and hopped up into the passenger seat.

"So, what's going—*oof!*" I lost the last part of my question as Shane abruptly shifted into reverse and slammed on the gas pedal, throwing me toward the dash. Just as abruptly, he shifted into drive and floored it, kicking up an enormous cloud of dust and whipping me around the compartment like a rag doll as he maneuvered out of the lot and back onto the pavement headed toward town. "Can you give me a sec to get my seatbelt on, please?"

"I'm sorry, Mr. Dwayne," said Shane, strung tight with anxiety. "I just didn't know who else to turn to."

"It's okay, Shane," I said, finally finding the buckle for the seatbelt and securing myself as best I could. "But I need a little more. What's happening with the Andersons?"

"They're burning a cross on the front lawn. Setting fire to the bushes and trees in the yard. I just couldn't believe my *eyes!*"

"'They?' Who are 'they?'"

"I don't rightly know. They're all wearing hoods or masks." The engine roared as Shane pushed the accelerator even harder.

"*Masks?*" I repeated. My mind was swirling. "How many people are we talking about here?"

"Four, maybe five," said Shane, abruptly cutting his headlights and slowing down. "I brought Trevor back to pick up a few things he needed while he and Audrey lay low. Those bastards had just lit the cross when we passed the Ridge."

He cut across the oncoming lane and bumped into an abandoned and overgrown drive that I would have missed entirely. Once there, he killed his engine. I knew we were close to Spielman Ridge, but I didn't quite have my bearings. I could see a column of thick black smoke ahead, rising lazily into the cloudless night sky.

Out of nowhere, Audrey Peterson was suddenly pounding on the hood of the truck, tears streaming down her face, completely hysterical. *"Shane! You've got to *stop* him! He's gonna get himself *killed!"*

Shane was out of the truck in an instant, and I was right behind him. He grabbed Audrey's shoulders. "I told you all to wait until I got back. I—"

"I *tried* to make him wait, but they started burning the house. His family is in there!"

"Aw, *fu-u-u-ck!"* Shane kicked at the ground and grasped at his tousled hair, wild-eyed and desperate for a plan—*any* plan.

"Where's Jimmy's gun?" I asked. I certainly didn't want to use it, but we couldn't take much of a stand if we were completely unarmed.

"Under my seat," said Shane. "I completely forgot about it."

I ran around to the driver's side and fished underneath the bench seat until I found it. Pulling it out, I made sure that at least for now, the safety was on.

"Let's go," I said, grabbing Shane by the elbow. "Audrey, you stay here."

"No!" Her response was automatic. "Y'all are *not* leaving me behind!"

"Audrey," I pleaded. "We don't have *time* to argue about this. We need to get folks out of there, and you tagging along is just an unnecessary risk. You stay with the truck. Be ready to get us the hell out of here when we get back, 'cause we're liable to have to leave in a hurry."

"He's right, Audrey," said Shane.

She looked from one of us to the other and threw her clenched hands into the air. *"Fine!* Just go!" She headed for the driver's side of the truck while I did my best to follow Shane's lead as he plunged into the dark woods ahead.

•••••••⊖⊖•••••••

We reached the edge of the woods bordering the Andersons' backyard just as one of the hooded intruders in the backyard slammed the butt of a rifle into the side of Trevor's head. He went down hard, and I had to grab Shane with both hands to keep him from breaking cover to assist his friend. There was no point in running headlong into the thick of things. We should count ourselves damn lucky the assailant had used the end of the rifle that he did—no guarantee we should be so lucky if we went charging in. He left Trevor lying on the ground and went back to the corner of the house where a can of gasoline waited. He tossed his gun down and reached for the can.

I took a second to assess the scene. Trevor's assailant was busily sloshing gas onto the back of the house while a second hooded figure stood guard at the opposite corner of the yard, unarmed and shuffling in place nervously. There was a can of gasoline at his feet, but he seemed reluctant to use it. He looked like he was ready to bolt, and I could practically sense his fear from where we stood. His frame was much smaller than that of the first man, and I wondered if he was even a man at all. If there were more hooded goons, and Shane said there were, they must be working at the front of the house, where smoke was thickening, and a flickering orange glow began to lift the dark curtain of night.

I really didn't have time to process the full implications of what I was seeing. Was this the work of the Ku Klux Klan? They wore the saddest homemade hoods imaginable to disguise their identities—just white pillowcases with holes cut out at eye level—but their actions left no doubt about their intentions. They were eliminating all avenues of escape for the folks inside. This was a hit squad.

299

"Are Trevor's parents armed?" I asked. I didn't particularly want to face friendly fire, either.

"I don't know," Shane replied.

"Dammit!"

I needed to make a decision before the gasoline was lit. Judging from the amount of smoke and light spilling over the roof of the house, odds were better than good the front door was already impassable.

"We've got to *do* something! Just *shoot* them!" Shane was wringing his hands, and I couldn't hold him back forever.

"Let's see if we can't get this done without anyone else dying tonight, okay?" I took the gun out of my waistband and released the safety. "I want you to get ready. I'm going to fire a shot close to the guy with the gasoline—try and scare him away. You knock the shit out of the other one but keep hold of him. We'll use him as leverage while I get the Andersons out of the house. I'm hoping the others won't be willing to sacrifice one of their own. Hell, we'll use him as a shield if we have to—take him along as a hostage. Just wait for my shot."

Shane nodded curtly and moved left, staying under cover of the trees but drawing closer to his intended target. I took a deep breath to try and calm the hammering of my heart.

We are all blessed with certain skills, and while I wouldn't say my skill set is particularly bountiful, I needed to call on one of mine now. Since high school, I have had quite a reputation for unerring aim. My friends back home dubbed me 'Dead-Eye Dwayne.' I can't tell you the last time I lost a game of darts. As I've practiced shooting with my own handgun at Vince's Lodge, I always draw high praise from both Vince Holland and his son, Jack, for how tight the grouping is on my silhouette targets. They've made a game of it, telling me specifically which portion of the target to hit, and I've yet to fail. As I watched the man continue to swing the five-gallon container of gas, spewing its contents onto the siding of the house, I took sight and prayed my aim would be true.

I held my breath and pulled the trigger.

It was my intention to part the air close to him and hit the cinderblock foundation of the house, but at the very last second, he swung the plastic gas can into the path. The bullet pierced the container near its bottom, and the momentum pulled the man's arm out and up, sloshing gasoline all over himself in the process. He threw the container aside and screamed when it soaked into his cloth hood and reached his eyes. His immediate reaction was to rub them with his gasoline saturated hands which only made his situation worse. He plucked the hood from his head and ran around the corner of the house before I had a chance to recognize him.

Shane already had the other one in a stranglehold and jerked the pillowcase away in one fluid motion. It was Tommy Pruitt, proprietor of the local Chevron and grandson to perhaps the oldest and most respected man in town, Emmitt Brown. I can't say I was surprised.

As I ran toward the stoop at the back door, I wondered if the Andersons even knew what was going on, or were they sleeping away, snug in bed, blissfully unaware? I got my answer as I reached for the doorknob, and the door was pulled open by Mrs. Anderson, wide-eyed with a cast-iron skillet raised in her hands.

"*Whoa!*" I yelled, raising my arms in defense. "We're here to help. We've got to get you all out of here."

I saw recognition flash across Mrs. Anderson's eyes, and in an instant, she shepherded her youngest son, Tyrese, out the door. I directed him to the edge of the woods and told him to wait for us there.

"How are we gonna get Noah out of here?" she asked desperately. "He's right here beside me in his chair, but he can't walk and he's a big man! I can't carry him. And I don't even know where Trevor *is*."

Trevor. *Shit!*

The obstacles were piling up faster than I could think. I would need Shane's assistance getting Mr. Anderson to safety, but even then, how could we also manage Trevor if he were still out cold? I looked at the gun in my hand and realized I might have to start shooting people after all. I wondered how many bullets were even left.

I saw Mrs. Anderson's eyes widen and turned to follow their focus. One of the other hooded invaders had rounded the corner and grabbed the shotgun that was left lying on the ground. He had the business end trained on Trevor, who was beginning to stir.

CHAPTER TWENTY-THREE

'*H*EY!!!*"* Shane shouted from across the yard. He still had Tommy Pruitt in a stranglehold and lifted him roughly off the ground by his neck. *"I will snap this motherfucker's neck if you don't BACK OFF!"*

Right about then, Tyrese spotted his brother struggling and came running toward us from the cover of the woods.

"TYRESE! NO!" Mrs. Anderson shrieked, pushing past me and launching herself toward the hooded gunman who suddenly had three moving targets to choose from. He first lifted his gun toward Tyrese but quickly recognized the real danger was from Mrs. Anderson, an adrenalized mother hellbent on protecting her sons. As he pivoted toward her, I lifted the pistol in my hand, loath to use it but given no other choice.

Suddenly, the rifle jerked upward and discharged, hitting nothing but air as the gunman fell forward. Audrey Peterson was behind him, firmly gripping the handle of a pitchfork that protruded from between his shoulder blades. She had buried the tines deep into his upper back, and blood pooled on his cotton t-shirt at each point of penetration. She let go of the handle and ran to Trevor, helping him to his feet. Mrs. Anderson and I reached them just as Tyrese did.

"You didn't stay with the truck," I said, stating the obvious. Audrey shot me a look, and I added, "Thank God!"

"I found that in the back of the truck," Audrey said breathlessly, pointing to the pitchfork and wiping her hands on her backside. "I thought it might come in handy."

I tucked Jimmy's pistol back into my waistband and leaned down to grab the rifle. I looked to Trevor. "Are you okay?"

He nodded, and I handed him the rifle.

"Get everybody back to the truck and pull it around right up there." I pointed to the back corner of the lot where the woods had been parted to make way for the two-lane blacktop. "We'll get Mr. Anderson and meet you there. But *hurry.*"

Mrs. Anderson grabbed my arm, still panic stricken, with tears streaming down her face. *"You* hurry," she pleaded. "Get my husband out of there!"

I nodded with more conviction than I felt and looked back toward the house as they hustled away into the woods. Hungry flames were visible now, lapping at the edges of the roof and generating clouds of noxious black smoke which had also begun to seep through the open back door. I could hear Mr. Anderson calling for his wife from inside.

"Keaira! Keaira!"

I called over to Shane, "Let that little shit go and come give me a hand."

"Sure," said Shane. "Just one last thing."

He whirled Tommy around before rearing back and clocking him under the jaw with a devastating uppercut. Tommy dropped like a rag doll to the ground, and Shane tossed the homemade hood back at him. He then sprinted my way, and we headed into the house.

The smoke was much thicker inside, and I covered my mouth and nose with the inside of my elbow as I followed the sound of Noah Anderson's coughing to the right and into the kitchen. I stopped in my tracks when I spotted him, and Shane ran right into me.

"Whoa," I said.

When Keaira Anderson had casually mentioned her husband was 'a big man,' I had no idea she meant *this* big. It was hard to determine his height as he was seated in a wheelchair, but that chair was a double-wide, and he filled every square inch of it. If I had to guess his weight, I would say around 400 lbs. He coughed while holding a nasal cannula in place, pulling concentrated oxygen through a thin rubber tube that wrapped around to the rear of his chair where a pair of tanks were attached.

This wasn't good.

While science was never really my thing, even *I* realized that concentrated oxygen plus fire equaled *KABOOM!* And where there was one oxygen tank, I guessed there were probably more. Overhead, we heard ominous crackling and popping as rafters became engulfed unseen. They could come crashing down at any moment, and we needed to get the hell out of there.

I dragged Shane with me, and together, we pushed the chair toward the open back door. It was getting harder to see much less breathe as the smoke thickened in the air and heat built around us. I could see open flames swallowing the living room whole.

Once we reached the door, it was immediately apparent that the chair was never going to fit through, and even if it could, the rear entrance had never been made handicapped accessible, so we would run the risk of dropping Mr. Anderson face-first down three cinderblock steps.

A great splintering preceded a loud crash behind us as the kitchen ceiling abruptly gave way, spewing flames from above into the room we had just exited. Heat washed over us in waves as I tried to determine the best method of getting Mr. Anderson and his oxygen tanks away from this inferno. I noticed Tommy Pruitt had either run away or been carried off as there was no sign of him in the backyard, although the asshole with the rake in his back was still facedown. I fleetingly wondered if Audrey had killed the man and whether that would frighten off or enrage the other assailants.

I tried not to focus on how ironic it would be to finally get Mr. Anderson out of the house only to be gunned down by the assassins who remained.

"Okay, here's what we're going to do," I yelled to Shane, stepping around the wheelchair and out onto the top step. "Follow me out here and pull the wheelchair as close as you can get to the door. We're going to lower Mr. Anderson to the ground, then we should be able to collapse his chair and get it through the door with the oxygen tanks attached."

Shane shot me a quick thumbs up before squeezing through the door and pulling Mr. Anderson's chair to the edge. We took position on each side of the door, and Mr. Anderson leaned forward, freeing himself from the nasal cannula and hooking an arm around each of our shoulders. We braced ourselves and lifted, somehow managing to execute the awkward maneuver without sending him to the ground in a heap. We carefully lowered Mr. Anderson into a seated position on the ground where he propped himself up on his elbows. As we were retrieving the wheelchair, I heard an explosion somewhere deep in the house, and glass from the windows of the kitchen blew out like particulate from a strong sneeze.

I looked up to find Shane's truck idling at the edge of the yard, and I had never seen a sweeter sight. I flailed my arms, urging them to come for us— it would be infinitely faster. The truck bumped across the backyard, narrowly avoiding the pitchfork-impaled man still prone in its path. Trevor hopped down from the back of the truck and helped me and Shane hoist his father in. I detached the oxygen tank Mr. Anderson had been using from the back of the wheelchair and passed it and its rubber tubing to Trevor before collapsing the chair and lifting it up into the truck bed as well. Shane and I jumped in, perching on the wheel wells. Audrey was driving, with Tyrese between her and Trevor's mother in the cab. She glanced back, and as soon as Shane flashed a thumbs up, she stomped on the accelerator, kicking up clods of earth and propelling us back to the road and away from the burning remains of what had once been the Andersons' happy home.

········•–○○–•········

I slapped my hand against the back glass of the truck cab as we drew near Fred's Beds. "Pull in here," I directed. "I need to grab my things. Room 7. I'll be quick."

Audrey hooked a hard left into the empty parking lot, skidding to a stop outside of my room. It suddenly occurred to me that I was on the verge of escaping this place. I didn't have any of the answers I had come for, only more questions, but I was beaten down and nearly out of resources. I needed to fortify and regroup, and once my possessions were on board, we would be off into the night. The thought of seeing my own house, my new used car, *Melanie*—it was all so close and yet painfully far away.

I hopped out of the truck bed and let myself into my motel room. A quick scan showed I had little to collect. Most of my belongings were already in my backpack, and what clothes I wasn't wearing were soiled beyond use. I collected them in one of the bath towels and carried them out to the porch, tossing them into one of the rusting metal trash barrels positioned between every two rooms. I shook the towel out and brought it back to the bathroom, hanging it over a towel bar. After double-checking that the safety remained on, I shifted Jimmy's pistol from where it was tucked into my waistband and placed it into the pack. Last but not least, I grabbed my cell phone and its charger from my nightstand, slipping the phone into my pocket and the charger into my backpack, which I then zipped up. I took one last look around the room before pulling the door shut behind me and locking it. I sprinted across the lot to the office and dropped the room key through a slot beside the door. The thought of never seeing Mrs. Shepley again was an added bonus.

As I trotted back to the truck, I could see the occupants had rearranged the seating. The Andersons had all moved back to the truck bed to be near their patriarch, and for all the reasons that mattered, Audrey was one of them now. She sat beside Trevor with an arm protectively around his waist, her head resting on his shoulder. Shane had resumed control of his vehicle, which left the passenger seat for me. I still had the smell of smoke in my nose, and it was very telling that the only sound we heard was the steady rumble of the truck's engine. There were no sirens announcing the approach of fire trucks. This was a fire that was meant to burn.

"Do we have a destination?" I asked over my shoulder as I lay my backpack at my feet and fastened my seatbelt.

Mrs. Anderson nodded. "We got family in Claymore. It's about sixty mile out."

"I'm thinking my gas will hold," added Shane, holding up crossed fingers. "I ain't got no more money to fill up, though."

"And we barely got out with the clothes on our backs," said Mrs. Anderson. "But we'll be okay if we can just get there."

I pulled my backpack from the floorboard and unzipped it, rummaging around for my wallet. I still had $148 tucked away next to a picture of Melanie and Jasmine. I ran my finger across their faces, and my heart ached.

"I've still got some money," I said. "Long as we run into a gas station before we run out of gas, we're good."

Shane put the truck in gear, and we pulled back onto the blacktop, turning left and accelerating with a rumble, away from a town I'd be happy to never see again.

"Won't your father be worried about you?" I asked Shane, breaking the exhausted silence we had all fallen into. He had slid the panel in the rear glass shut to give Audrey and the Anderson family some privacy.

"Nah. He thinks I'm over at Nick's."

I smiled. Teens still relied on that tried-and-true method of parental deception, apparently. I had employed it on several occasions myself when my buddies and I had been up to no good.

We rode in silence for a bit longer.

"I'm hopin' you got the pictures you needed for your sister. I'm guessin' you ain't comin' back to see if Mrs. Peterson wins the big bake-off again on Sunday."

I laughed. The thought of Caroline Peterson baking *anything* was amusing. *"Again?"*

"Six years running, although truth be told, I don't know why. She always makes these dried out apple biscotti that get stuck in your throat if you don't soak 'em down with coffee or hot chocolate. Pauline Dixon's Dutch apple pie is *way* better."

"Yeah, well, I don't think I'll be here to see it."

"Ain't you worried about what the sheriff said? Didn't he tell you to stay in town?"

I rubbed the bridge of my nose. "He did," I said. "And I'm sure I'll be back. But not without transportation and not without my attorney." Lately, it seemed I was keeping my attorney, Sally Sheaffer, very occupied.

"I still can't believe what happened to Hattie," he went on, shaking his head. "Hey, I'm really sorry about—well, you know—thinkin' you mighta done it. I shoulda known better."

"I don't blame you one bit, Shane," I said, still feeling very much responsible, if only indirectly. "I don't know what I would have thought if our roles had been reversed."

"So, what do you think happened?" asked Shane before answering himself. "I'm guessing it was a hunting accident, like I told the sheriff before. Ain't been one in a while, but it's been known to happen. My heart's just breakin' for Joy Beth and Mrs. Bartlett."

I nodded, understanding completely. "You've really got a thing for Joy Beth, haven't you?"

Shane's ears burned bright in the reflection of his dash light. "Maybe a little. Goddamn Jimmy Perkins—pardon my French. He sure don't deserve her."

"Delphine stopped by to see me last night," I said. "Joy Beth took the baby and moved back in with her. Maybe it will stick."

"Yeah?" Shane brightened, and I could picture him imagining himself with Joy Beth and the life they could have together. It was a nice picture. "It's just not right, though. I can't believe the amount of trouble you've seen in just a couple of days. Nothing *ever* happens in Briarstaff. I mean, you're leavin' here thinking this place is maybe one level up from hell. Gina was here a whole week, and it really seemed like she was enjoying her stay. Said she'd stop back any time she's in the area."

My throat seized up a little, and I let out a short, sharp bark of a laugh.

Shane looked at me sideways. "That's funny?"

I couldn't look directly at him, so I studied my hands in my lap. "She won't be coming back, Shane."

"I don't understand. I thought she liked us."

I nodded, biting my lip. "I'm sure she did."

A long moment passed as Shane processed what I had just said. "What do you mean, *'did?'*"

"She's gone, Shane."

And just like that, I was done perpetuating this ridiculous story. When Michael had first proposed the idea of pretending Gina was still alive, it was with the thought that anyone bearing responsibility for her death would immediately be on to us, knowing full well that she wasn't. Their efforts to silence us would reveal them—or at least that was our hope. But at this point, I only trusted most of these kids and a couple of the adults. The rest of the town seemed complicit, especially after Michael had disappeared. It was too easy to picture the tail end of his bright yellow Fiesta bobbing and sinking in the waters of the quarry with Michael's deceased corpse tightly strapped in the driver's seat.

Shane was at a complete loss, looking from me to the road in front of him and back again. "What—*happened?*"

"She was in head-on collision with a propane tanker," I said, trying to keep the rehash brief.

"But then why did you and Michael say—"

"There were extenuating circumstances," I cut his query short. "I believe she left some undeveloped film in my house for safekeeping when she stopped by after our brother's wedding. I found it under my couch. I took it to have it developed, but before I could pick it up, the photo shop was robbed."

"No shit?"

"No shit," I said flatly. "The employees were killed, and every single roll of film was taken. Michael showed up at my house shortly afterward. He said something happened down here, but he didn't know what. Gina seemed ruffled, and that was totally unlike her. He thought maybe she saw something that might have gotten her killed, and *that's* why we came."

Shane took a long moment to process my words. "My God! I'm so sorry, Mr. Dwayne. I'm so sorry for your loss. I can't even imagine—"

Ah, shit, here came the standard condolences for the bereaved, and I was just too wrung out to hear them again, despite Shane's obvious sincerity. "Thank you," I said, waving him off before he could offer anything more. "But after everything that's happened in the past couple of days, I can't help but feel that Michael was really onto something, and now *he's* gone. I really think it has something to do with the Academy. What do you know about it?"

"The Academy? Shit, I don't really know much," he said. "I mean, students are recruited from Briarstaff and other communities, but it's not like you put yourself up for consideration. There aren't flyers circulating telling you what it's all about, nothing like that."

"Okay, sure, but Rusty's going, right? Doesn't he talk about it at all?"

Shane scoffed. "Rusty only hangs around with us because he's got it bad for Rose. He's a creepy little fuck, pardon my French. He doesn't talk to me about *shit*. He knows how I feel about his brother."

"His brother?"

"Yeah," Shane nodded. "Jimmy Perkins—the guy you pounded on. The guy I would *love* to pound on."

I blinked. I hadn't made the connection, despite obvious physical similarities between the two. Their nasty dispositions had been pretty similar, as well. Now that I knew, I couldn't believe I had missed it.

"So, once these kids go off to the Academy, you don't ever see them again?" I asked. "Not even during summer break?"

Shane thought about it. "You know, I honestly don't think they get a summer break. I mean, I know they are required to live on campus."

"Sounds very military," I noted. "Do they recruit both boys and girls?"

"Uh-huh," confirmed Shane.

"Do you have any idea at what age they start recruiting?"

He shrugged. "Mostly junior high, but I remember one kid in my class who was recruited out of the third grade. She was freaky smart, though."

"Do you think the teachers have any input on selection?"

"Maybe," he said. "I don't know."

"Is there a particular *type* of student that seems to attract the Academy's attention?"

"Wow, Mr. Dwayne, I really don't know," he said, rubbing his tired eyes. "I've never really thought about it."

"Of course, Shane. Sorry." I realized I had been grilling him and it was time to back off. There was only so much I could reasonably expect a high school boy to know about a secretive facility to which he had absolutely no connection. The horrific events we had just escaped had undoubtedly traumatized Shane, and I needed to give him a little breathing room.

I stared through the windshield at the dark road ahead, trying to guess how much longer we had to go. Maybe thirty miles? Time and distance lost all meaning when the scenery had barely changed. The reflectors in the faded line dividing lanes grew hypnotic, and my eyes were beginning to get heavy.

"Mr. Dwayne?"

I lifted one eye to glance at Shane. "Yeah?"

"I really *am* sorry about Ms. Gina. I hope you catch the fuckers who did this—pardon my French."

My smile was tight. "Me too, Shane. Me, too." I closed my eyes and felt myself drift away.

·····•••••◦◯•••••····

I was abruptly awakened by the urgent sound of a palm striking flat against the back glass. It took me a moment to get my bearings. It seemed more reasonable that the previous day should have been a nightmare, and what I wouldn't have given for that to be the case, but as my surroundings came into focus, I realized it was only wishful thinking. I could have only been asleep for a few minutes. What had I missed?

I looked over my shoulder as Trevor hammered on the back panel again. I slid it open.

"What's wrong?" I asked. I quickly scanned the truck bed to make sure all parties were unharmed and accounted for. On first pass, nothing seemed out of the ordinary.

"I think we've got trouble," said Trevor, pointing behind us, far into the distance.

I squinted, straining to see what I was missing. The road was flanked on both sides by tall trees, and we were traveling a relatively straight pass, but after careful inspection, I thought I caught sight of a blue and red undulation painting the treetops far, far in the distance.

But it was getting closer.

Shit.

I listened for a siren but couldn't hear anything over the roar of the truck's exhaust. Overwhelmed by frustration, I wanted to scream. I had no time to deliberate, but the decision before me was absolutely clear. I grabbed my backpack from the floorboard and began rummaging through its front pockets.

"Pull over," I said to Shane as I retrieved one of my IT Consulting Services business cards and a pen. He looked unsure, but understood the tone of my voice, easing right and stopping the vehicle. I flipped the card over to its blank side and hurriedly scribble Melanie's name and phone number. Almost as an afterthought, I also jotted down Nina Crockett's name. Next, I pulled my wallet from the main compartment and grabbed all the cash I had left. I handed it all to Shane, who was totally perplexed.

"Take this," I said. "When you get to Claymore, call the number on the back of that card. Tell Melanie what you can about what's happened and tell her I'm in real trouble. Tell her to call Nina Crockett. I don't have time to find her number in my phone, but Melanie can get it from my things at home. Nina's with the FBI, and she'll know what to do. You have to make Melanie understand she is not to come here by herself. She's hard-headed, so you really need to make her understand how dangerous it is."

Shane nodded numbly. "Got it. What are you *doing?*"

I opened the passenger door and hopped out onto the roadside, hitching my backpack up over my aching shoulder. The red and blue lights were brighter now, but headlights weren't quite visible yet. Now, I could faintly hear the approach of the shrill siren.

"After what we just went through, I bet they probably want a piece of all of us, but all they're going to get for now is me," I said through the open door. "Get back on the road and step on it, do you hear me? Get these folks to safety and make those phone calls just as fast as you can." I slammed the door closed and slapped the truck's side as if it were a horse I could coax into a gallop.

Shane nodded grimly, shifting into gear and speeding away, the roar of his engine fading faster than the approach of the siren. I could see headlights now, beams pulsing from high to low and back again. I kicked at the ground and uttered a creative string of obscenities as I awaited the inevitable.

I had almost gotten away.

CHAPTER TWENTY-FOUR

"Well, look what we have here."

Sheriff Charley Daniel was all smiles as he got out of his cruiser. He silenced the siren but kept the lights pulsing, no doubt to irritate, and I shielded my eyes against them, wincing. I had placed my backpack on the ground at my feet, keeping both hands completely visible; I didn't want to give him any excuse to shoot me.

"How can I help you, Officer Daniel?"

He slowly bridged the distance between us, hands flexing at his sides. "Seems to me the last time we spoke, I told you not to even *think* about leaving this town." His hot breath was in my face, entirely too close for comfort, but I forced myself to stand my ground and match his glare.

"I was just—"

His right fist lashed out like lightning. I barely detected the motion and was suddenly on my hands and knees, staring at the gravel pocked berm of the highway beneath me. The world tilted precariously as a thick, bloody strand of saliva stretched from the split he had reopened in my bottom lip to where my outstretched hands had instinctively kept my face from bouncing off the pavement.

"So, where are your friends, Mr. Morrow?" asked the sheriff as he paced a lazy circle around me.

"What friends?" I asked thickly, blood continuing to ooze from my split lip.

He reared back and kicked me in the side with his steel-toe boot, and even though I tried to roll with the momentum, I was pretty sure I felt a rib throw in the towel. I yelped as the pain sucked the breath right out of me.

Sheriff Daniel straddled me and leaned down, grabbing my hair and pulling my face close to his. "I've had about enough of your smartass horseshit," he said, and my eyes widened as I caught the faint scent of gasoline on his shirt collar. He glared at me expectantly with bloodshot eyes still irritated from their earlier exposure to the accelerant. "Where...are...your...*friends?*"

He flung my head backward against the pavement, and everything went dark for a second before a curtain of stars parted to reveal his angry face staring into mine, waiting impatiently for my response. His miles-wide smile was long gone. This man had been a willing participant in a mob intent on murdering an entire family—I had no delusions about my own personal safety now. I blinked, trying to keep my vision from doubling.

"I don't know," I said, and he immediately clenched his teeth, drawing his fist back. I flinched and raised my hands to shield my face. *"I really don't know!"*

He paused, giving me a moment to think while he decided whether or not he believed me. Since I wasn't the greatest liar, I figured it behooved me to adhere as closely to the truth as possible. I tried to draw a deep breath and was rewarded with a sharp, stabbing pain in my side.

"They dropped me off. Told me I was on my own," I said, continuing to shield my face. "Said they were sorry, but people around me kept getting hurt. Or worse."

Sheriff Daniel straightened, looking impossibly tall from my vantage point. A full moon shone brightly over his shoulder, shrouding him in shadow. He stared at the highway running north, listening for any trace of Shane's truck. "How long ago?" he finally asked.

I shook my head, trying not to gag on the coppery taste in my mouth. "Fifteen—maybe twenty minutes ago?"

"Dammit!"

He stepped over me and kicked at the ground while clenching and unclenching his fists. I went for a fetal position, rolling over to protect my face and fractured rib as best as I could while he raged over whatever thoughts were running through his mind.

"He let that Van Buren boy see his goddamn face," he muttered, pulling at his own face, and I knew he was talking about Tommy Pruitt. I lay as still as I possibly could, letting him process while hoping to avoid his wrath. "I *knew* it was a mistake to bring him. Spineless little shit has likely fucked us *all*. Okay, fine. *Fine*. We'll just have to cut him loose. Emmitt won't like it one bit, but we'll have to stick together. It ain't like we all haven't had to make sacrifices."

His attention shifted back to me. "We're going to have to deal with you once and for all."

My blood ran cold. Was he planning to off me, executioner-style? In my head, I could hear Delphine Bartlett recounting the fate of her Ohio neighbors, and my mouth was running before I could prepare a script.

"You can't just kill me," I said. "That won't be the end of it. People know I came here with Michael Arthur. You can't just—"

That prompted a laugh. "Michael Arthur. Jesus!"

I surely didn't like the sound of that. I tried in vain to scuttle backwards as he reached down and hooked a hand through my elbow and began to hoist me up. I cried out as white-hot pain jolted through me, my position adjusted without my consent.

"This will probably be a whole lot less painful if you work with me," sighed Sheriff Daniel. "C'mon. Get to your feet."

I followed his instruction, and he promptly spun me around, pulling my hands behind me to bind them together with a zip tie. He stooped to collect my backpack and walked me back to his cruiser, where he popped the trunk. For a second, I thought he planned to stash me back there, but he merely tossed my backpack inside and slammed the lid. He guided me to the backseat and made sure to crack my head against the door frame as he shoved me inside.

Panic had taken hold, and I was completely out of ideas.

We rode back to town in uncomfortable silence. I knew the sun would be rising soon, but I couldn't check my watch with my hands bound behind me. We approached the town square, and there was no sign of activity. Cleanup crews had come and gone, and the Ferris wheel stood tall and silent, ready for another day of family frivolity; it seemed completely obscene under the circumstances. I'm sure the news of Hattie's death spread through the town like wildfire. Just the thought triggered a fresh wave of anguish and guilt. I should have *never* allowed her to get involved in this!

Sheriff Daniel followed the detour bypassing the town square's perimeter, cruising through the sleeping neighborhoods that bordered the square and eventually arriving at the jail. He pulled to the curb and turned the car off, rolling the windows halfway down. It was still quite warm outside, and I guess the same rules that apply to pets applied to me as well. He turned around and glared at me though the steel mesh that separated law enforcement from detainee.

"Don't go anywhere," he smirked, opening the door and getting out of the car. He lit a cigarette as he crossed to the jail and went inside, leaving me alone with my imagination, which was busily constructing various scenarios of exactly how they might kill me. I tested the strength of the zip tie, but I could barely move my hands at all, much less gain leverage against the tie's locking mechanism.

Across the street and straight ahead was Madame Phalange's fortune teller booth. Almost all the ornamentation had been removed from the front, replaced with a series of handwritten cardstock notes:

CLOSED – FAMILY DEATH

DO NOT FRET! MADAME PHALANGE
WILL EMERGE SOON!

But most tellingly:

KARMA IS A MOTHER
VENGEANCE WILL BE REALIZED…

I was startled when the driver's door suddenly opened, and the dome light flared bright. Nick Pollard poked his head in and began fumbling with the instrument panel, squelching the overhead light. "Hey, Mr. Morrow," he said with a quick grin.

"*Nick?*" I craned my neck to look through the window on the opposite side of the car and saw Sheriff Daniel deep in animated conversation on the phone, pacing back and forth past the jail's window. "What in the hell are you doing here?"

"I knew something was wrong when Shane was gone so long," said Nick, unlocking the rear doors from the switches on the driver's side. "He was supposed to be back just as soon as he dropped Trevor and Audrey off up to the Andersons. He called me when they got to Claymore and told me all the shit y'all've been through—"

320

"Did he call Melanie?" I interrupted. "Was he able to—"

"*Yes*, he got through to your lady," said Nick, pushing my shoulder forward to inspect how I was bound. I yelped when my wounded rib jabbed me from within, and he jumped back. "Sorry! Are you hurt?"

I bit my bottom lip, getting a handle on the pain and nodded. "He either cracked or broke a rib, I'm not sure."

Nick tried again, exercising a little caution this time. I kept an eye on the window of the jail, watching as Sheriff Daniel continued to pace as far as the phone cord would allow. He looked even angrier than before, and whoever was on the receiving end of his call was surely getting an earful.

"Hell, yeah." Nick sounded pleased as he found the zip tie that was taut around my wrists. He pulled a knife from his pocket and opened it, exposing a blade that looked razor sharp at its point with a serrated portion nearer the rubber-coated black handle. "I can get this off pretty quick, but I don't want to cut you. Can you shift to your right? I don't want to cause you any more hurt."

It wasn't pleasant, but I maneuvered around enough to provide better access. Nick went to work on the zip tie, but no sooner did he begin than I saw Sheriff Daniel slam the phone down and turn toward the door.

"*Shit!*" I yelped. Panic welled, and I scooted back to my original position, much to Nick's consternation. "You need to go. *Now.*"

"But I'm not done—"

"The sheriff's coming back. *Go!*"

Nick waffled for a second before folding the knife and tucking it into my hand. Then he was off, using the sheriff's car as a shield and keeping his profile low to the ground as he rounded the corner and disappeared in the direction of the IGA. I could feel that the zip tie was looser, but I didn't attempt to test it quite yet. Sheriff Daniel was already beside the door of the car, fumbling with his keys, and my panic kicked into overdrive when I realized Nick hadn't relocked the rear doors of the car. What if he noticed the switch was in the unlocked position? And the knife? I was torn about the knife. I was glad to have it—certainly better than nothing—but what if the sheriff noticed I was holding something in my hand? I could imagine his furious reaction upon discovery.

But I needn't have worried. His phone conversations had him so agitated, he didn't even look in my direction as he passed my window and opened the driver's door, sliding in behind the wheel. He was also too agitated to notice the dome light didn't turn on when he opened the door— thank God! He wasn't in the mood to chat, either. He fired up the engine and put the car in gear, executing a three-point turn before taking us back through the detour from which we had come. He muttered to himself, occasionally lashing out at the steering wheel. He wasn't having a good night, but mercifully for me, it was making him careless. With just a little effort, I slipped the knife into my back pocket and out of sight.

· · • • • ● ⌒◯⌒ ● • • • · ·

Sheriff Daniel parked his cruiser parallel to the doors of Dr. Morris's clinic. In the distance, I could see a helicopter approaching, and I worried what *that* was all about. Was I being flown away to some private yet undisclosed location to meet my fate? The sheriff pulled my door open and grabbed me roughly by the elbow, dragging me out of the car. I tried not to let him see the agony he caused, knowing it would only give him satisfaction, but it was mighty fucking hard. It felt like that rib was floating around, poking freely at every internal organ I had.

To my surprise, instead of guiding me toward the helipad that was on the lawn beside the clinic, he marched me back through the automatic doors and inside. The sterile lobby was completely empty, so Sheriff Daniel pulled me toward the semi-circular reception desk where he leaned on a buzzer

322

that echoed throughout the building. He slammed his hand down hard on the desktop and bellowed, *"Morris!"*

Dr. Morris's wife, Patricia, hustled in through the hallway, her eyes pinched and her silvery hair escaping its disheveled bun. "What is the meaning of this, Charley?" she demanded in a no-nonsense tone. "Don't you come charging in here acting—"

"Get me Jeb," he said, cutting her off.

"He's busy getting—"

"I don't care!"

He slammed his hand down again and leaned across the desktop, matching her steely glare for a full five seconds before she finally looked away.

"I'll see what I can do," she mumbled, and her next few words were choice but unintelligible. She pushed through the swinging door that led to the examination area—the same examination area where we had taken Hattie. I wondered if she was still back there.

Sheriff Daniel shifted his focus back to me, eyeing me up and down with pure disgust, and I decided silence was my safest option. The noise from the helicopter was louder now, and I could see its searchlight scanning portions of the parking lot as it sought out the helipad.

Dr. Morris blustered in from the examination room, clearly upset with the interruption. "What the hell is this all about, Charley? I told you on the phone that I won't do what you're asking, and there's no two ways about it."

"Goddamn it, Jeb, we don't have any *choice!*"

Dr. Morris crossed right to a short hallway containing his and hers lavatories and a glass emergency exit, through which he could see the helicopter landing.

"You need to get him out of here," Morris said, indicating me without actually looking my way. "I can't have these paramedics or anyone else seeing him here."

"Then you better show me where I can stash him, because I'm not leaving here until we come to an understanding," countered Sheriff Daniel.

"Fine! Dammit!" Dr. Morris turned to his wife, who has observing intently from behind the safety of the reception desk. "Patsy, will you take Mr. Morrow back to Exam Room 2, please?"

She looked at me uncertainly.

"It's fine, dear. I don't think we have anything to fear," reassured her husband. As an afterthought, he added, "At least not from Mr. Morrow. Now, as for *you*, Charley, you may as well take a seat, because I'm not even discussing this until we get these folks on their way."

Sheriff Daniel clearly didn't like being told what to do, but the paramedics from the helicopter were hustling across the lot from the helipad and would be inside the building shortly. He plucked the Stetson from his head and sat down in the waiting area in a huff, reluctantly forced to comply.

Mrs. Morris came around from behind the desk and approached me, indicating the swinging doors. "If you'll just follow me, Mr. Morrow," she said, as if I was just another patient being called back into triage. It was nothing short of ethereal.

I complied, following her through the swinging door and wincing as the door swung back and bumped my wounded side.

"Are you hurt?" she asked, and it seemed pretty ridiculous considering the state of my swollen bottom lip which had only recently stopped bleeding, but her sincerity was genuine, and I had the feeling she and her husband were not exactly willing accomplices to whatever was going on.

"It's nothing," I said through clenched teeth. It wasn't like Sheriff Daniel was going to wait for them to patch me up.

She led me down a short corridor with a total of four examination rooms, two on each side. None had actual doors, only curtains on rings to provide some semblance of privacy, but the curtain for Exam Room 1 was partially opened, and I peered in as we passed by. A man lay on his stomach on the bed, his face turned toward the gap in the curtain. He was either asleep or unconscious, dark-ringed eyes closed in a face gone startlingly pale. Pinpricks of blood seeped through the dressing that had been applied to his right shoulder, from the base of his neck to just below his armpit.

When Audrey Peterson had used the pitchfork earlier that night to protect her boyfriend, it was her own father she had impaled.

I sat in the examination room on the edge of the bed, slumped slightly forward as that position seemed to provide the most relief. I listened as best as I could, but the paramedics were boisterous, and Dr. Morris's voice was a low, steady monotone. While I didn't catch many specifics, the long and the short of it was that Audrey had inflicted some pretty serious damage to her old man. The paramedics were flying him over to Kanawha County where he could receive treatment beyond the capabilities of Dr. Morris's clinic. The prognosis didn't sound great.

After they had transferred Troy to a wheeled gurney and made their way back to the helicopter, I listened as its rotors began to churn the night air with more urgency. Soon, I could follow the sound as it ascended and began its journey, fading quickly into the distance.

My mind was racing.

I could hear Dr. Morris arguing loudly with Sheriff Daniel in an outer office. They were too far away for me to hear what they were saying, but I knew it was about me, and I knew it wasn't good. I could tell that the zip tie had given even more as I had been dragged from one location to the next. I briefly considered tugging at it to see if I could get it to snap, but where would I go from there? The only exit would take me right past the office in which Sheriff Daniel and the doctor were quarreling. Even if they didn't notice me, I had no idea where Patricia Morris was, and while I sensed that she and her husband weren't in perfect alignment with whatever cause the sheriff was championing, I couldn't guarantee she wouldn't sound the alarm if she saw me making a break for the door. Besides, in my present condition, I wouldn't get very far. Sheriff Daniel was so agitated he probably wouldn't even chase after me; he'd just shoot me in the back as I ran.

One slim chance remained.

I tried to tabulate how long it had been since Nick told me Shane had spoken to Melanie. It seemed like hours, but my sense of time was shot all to hell. It would take time for Melanie to contact Nina Crockett, time for Nina to organize any sort of FBI response—if she even believed Melanie. I wished I'd told Shane to have Melanie call Brady Garrett for Nina's phone number instead of sending her scurrying across town to try and find it on my computer. He used to date her in the not-so-distant past. Assuming, of course, Brady was even out of the hospital yet. *Dammit!* Every glimmer of hope was met with a promise of despair. I couldn't rely on being rescued. I was going to have to find my own window of opportunity and seize it, and I could only hope that I'd get the chance.

The argument between the doctor and sheriff grew louder as they exited the outer office and headed my way. Words began to emerge, and I didn't care for any of them.

"You're going to pay for this, Jeb, I promise you that," warned Sheriff Daniel.

"Don't you threaten me, Charley Daniel. I've been here longer than you've known words, and I will be here long after. I mean, who do you think you *are?*"

There was an abrupt clatter as metal hit the cold tile floor, and Patricia Morris screamed. I couldn't stay still any longer, sliding off the edge of the examination table and crossing to peek around the privacy curtain.

Wild-eyed and face flushed, Sheriff Daniel had Dr. Morris in a headlock from behind, restricting the doctor's airflow while his wife looked on in horror, tears streaming down her cheeks. A tray of medical instruments lay scattered across the floor, apparently sent flying during the scuffle.

"What are you *doing*, Charley?" begged Patricia. She was practically bowing in supplication as she tried to simultaneously reach out to her husband and yet remain at a safe distance. "You're hurting him! You let him go right *now!*"

"I will," said Sheriff Daniel, his tone calm and ominous. "But not before you give me what I came here for."

"Don't do it, Patsy," warned the doctor, his voice constricted. "We both took oaths to heal not harm, and I take mine seriously. I know you do, too! We are good Christian folk! We know better than this! If Charley Daniel is willing to gamble with his eternal soul, then so be it."

I held my breath as I watched fury and frustration mount in Sheriff Daniel's expression. I fully expected him to snap the good doctor's neck. Patricia Morris was literally on her knees, begging for her husband's release, and the tension in the room was underscored by the loud ticking of a clock in the lobby.

Finally, Sheriff Daniel threw his head back and took a deep, steadying breath, letting it out slowly. The angry red flush to his face lessened, but his grip remained firm around the doctor's neck.

"If you insist on this...this...*conscientious objection*," he said. "I don't have time to argue over values. Just get me the compound. I'll do it myself."

Patricia hesitated only an instant before getting to her feet and crossing to a small refrigerator, where she thumbed through some metal trays before extracting a couple of syringes nearly half full of a pale-yellow substance.

327

She walked back to where Sheriff Daniel held her husband and held them just out of his reach. "Let go of my husband," she said coolly.

The sheriff relaxed his grip as his trademark grin slid menacingly into place. He grabbed the syringes as the doctor stumbled toward his wife, coughing and pulling for air. "I wish I could say I thank you, but you have made this far more difficult than it needed to be, and believe me, the town council won't forget about it." He bundled the syringes in gauze and stuffed them into his shirt pocket.

"If you're going to kill that young man, I don't want to know anything about it," Dr. Morris croaked. "But if you're still trying to learn something from him, you better take it easy with that. Doesn't take much to put a man out, and only a bit more would put him out permanently. Preliminary tests are all over the place."

I slipped away from the curtain and returned to the examination table before the sheriff headed my way, which I knew would be in any second. My heart was racing. I didn't want the sheriff practicing medicine on me without a license. Despite Dr. Morris's warning, I didn't believe it mattered all that much to Sheriff Daniel if he overdosed me into the Great Beyond. Was it time to try and make a break for it? It seemed much less likely that the doctor and his wife would intervene if I did, but I would still have to get past the sheriff, and he was furious and just looking for someone to pound. I wouldn't be much of a challenge.

The metal rings sang out against the curtain rod as the privacy screen was abruptly pulled aside. Sheriff Daniel filled the entrance, his ugly grin still in place.

"C'mon, Morrow," he said. "Let's get this over with."

He grabbed me by the elbow and led me out into the hallway and through the outer office, where Dr. Morris and his wife clung to each other, watching our progress with fear in their eyes. I couldn't even beg them to call for help—who could they call?

We stepped through the sliding doors and into the parking lot, heading back toward the sheriff's cruiser. The tiniest hint of daybreak had crept into the eastern horizon, signaling this horrific night would soon be over.

But even in this new day, people just weren't quite done dying.

CHAPTER TWENTY-FIVE

"Where are we going?" I asked tonelessly. I had moved beyond panic and was simply numb.

"Am I making you late for an appointment?" sneered Sheriff Daniel, and I turned toward the window. It really didn't matter. I'd rather not know.

We headed back toward Briarstaff, reversing the course that had brought us to the clinic. The darkened festival looked abandoned…maybe even haunted. We looped around through neighborhoods before resuming an eastward path on Route 5 toward the quarry.

Clearly, the sheriff wasn't working alone. He had made several phone calls from his office before we had headed out to the clinic. So, who else was involved? I knew for a fact Tommy Pruitt and Troy Peterson had been participants in the burning of the Anderson home. Sheriff Daniel had suggested the town elders would be displeased with the doctor and his wife for not complying with his requests, so it was safe to assume most of them were involved. But after witnessing Jeb and Patricia's outright defiance of the sheriff's demands, I wondered exactly how fragmented this town's leadership might be. And what was the deal with this 'injectable compound?' What kind of information could they possibly be trying to get from me? I felt like I had mostly been spinning in place, save for the discovery of the server farm with Hattie. My heart ached as the recollection of her empty, open eyes flashed before me, and it was an image that would haunt me for quite some time. But the purpose of the server farm remained elusive. It could be the world's largest collection of recipes, for all I knew.

Still, that had to be it. They wondered exactly how much I had seen and exactly what I knew about it. They would be sorely disappointed to learn I knew next to nothing. On second thought, it was probably their greatest hope. I couldn't tell what I didn't know. Of course, I had seen the location, and that was likely enough to seal my fate.

As we neared the track that led through the woods and back to the quarry, I spotted another vehicle already waiting on the path. I had grown accustomed to all the road-worn trucks so commonplace in Briarstaff, but this one seemed somewhat familiar with its bed filled with boxes, plastic gallon containers and other assorted junk. It wasn't until Sheriff Daniel pulled to the side of the road, perpendicular to the truck's tailgate to block access from the highway that its driver emerged from behind the wheel, and tumblers fell into place.

Jimmy Perkins. Well, why not?

Sheriff Daniel got out of the cruiser and opened my door, pulling me to my feet. He tipped his Stetson, and Jimmy nodded before turning to me and giving me the once over. His eyes held nothing but hatred for me. I really *had* done a number on him. His lips were split, and it was difficult to tell where the swelling stopped and his wad of chew began, but it didn't impede his ability to release a gnarly brownish stream that came within inches of splattering my shoe. He wore saggy jeans and a ribbed, sleeveless t-shirt that couldn't hide the bandages wrapped tightly around his scrawny midsection. Our nearly dueling injuries were not lost on me, although he also wore an Ace bandage on his right wrist, so I supposed I could claim victory. For now.

"Anybody been out this way?" asked the sheriff.

"Not a soul," said Jimmy.

"Good. Let's try and get this thing done fast."

Jimmy headed back for the driver's side while the sheriff tugged me around to the other. He opened the door and held it expectantly, waiting for me to hop in and slide in next to Jimmy. "I don't suppose I could have the window seat?" I asked, but the look on his face told me seating had already been assigned.

I was barely situated when Jimmy drove an elbow hard into my abdomen, knocking the breath from me and triggering an alarming wave of nausea. I was thankful it hadn't been on the side with my broken rib. I would have likely passed out.

"Pardon me," he said, smirking. "I was just tryin' to fasten my seatbelt."

He wasn't. The truck didn't even *have* seatbelts.

He shifted into gear, and we began our final trek through these woods.

The sun was moments away from making its dazzling entrance as we reached the dusty cliffside, and Jimmy maneuvered his truck to block passage to anyone curious enough to bypass the sheriff's cruiser at the other end.

"Keep your eyes and ears open," Sheriff Daniel instructed Jimmy. "I don't anticipate anyone bothering us this early, but I don't want no more of those damn kids up here, seeing things they shouldn't be seeing. We're going to have a hard enough time containing what's already gotten out."

Jimmy nodded and got out of the truck, assuming a position near the hood with his arms tucked behind himself in his best imitation of parade rest. He looked like little more than a boy playing soldier.

Sheriff Daniel led me around the other side of the truck, and as we emerged from the tree line, I was startled to see a bright yellow Ford Fiesta parked near the rim of one of the rocky outcroppings. Troy Peterson had said it could never navigate the off-road terrain, but it was apparently nimbler than he realized.

Michael Arthur?

The car appeared to be empty from where we stood, but I supposed there could be a body stashed somewhere inside. But as the sheriff directed me toward the caves, I spotted Michael near the middle entrance, slumped on the ground with his back against the craggy rock wall, his head lolling off to one side while his arms appeared bound behind him.

"You've had him here this whole time," I observed, but the sheriff wasn't feeling particularly talkative. He walked me over to join Michael and let go of my elbow.

"Have a seat," he directed, and I awkwardly complied, my rib complaining the whole way down. I glanced at Michael, and he stirred, his eyes fluttering. He was filthy and rumpled with a couple days' worth of thick stubble across his face but seemed otherwise intact. I watched as the sheriff pulled the syringes from his shirt pocket and freed one from the gauze. "Now, I really wish Dr. Morris was here to do this, but—"

He stooped over and pulled me sideways, jabbing me in the fleshy part of my right shoulder and injecting what appeared to be half of the first syringe's contents—there was no real measurement involved. I tensed up reflexively, and the shot burned like fire as the chemicals spread through muscle tissue. He allowed me to drop back against the wall and stepped over to Michael, kneeling beside him. He pulled Michael forward by his left arm and aimed for his shoulder with the same syringe. Sharing needles was apparently of no concern, either. Michael winced, but the sheriff just grinned. "Aw, now, it's just a little shot, big fella. Ain't nothing to worry about." He pulled the empty syringe back and capped the needle, patting Michael roughly on the shoulder before returning it to his pocket where the other syringe waited.

"What in the hell is that shit?" I demanded. I wasn't sure if it was attributable to the shot itself or just the knowledge it had been administered, but my heart was beginning to race, and I felt flushed.

"Just a little something they cooked up over at the Academy," said the sheriff, rising to his feet. "It's not exactly FDA approved, but it's proven useful upon occasion. I think it may have also killed a couple of subjects, but I might be confusing that with a different experimental drug—I'm not really sure. They're working on quite a few."

I swallowed hard.

"Doesn't really matter," he continued, pausing to light a cigarette. He took a deep drag and blew the exhaust in our general direction. "We all know how this is going to end."

"What is it you want?" I asked.

"The truth, Mr. Morrow," he said, taking another hit from his cigarette. "I'd really like to start there, and let's face it, y'all haven't been truthful since the moment you got here."

I attempted shocked indignation, but my words disintegrated into a stammer.

Sheriff Daniel held up a finger. "Let's just stop right there, okay?" He looked at his wristwatch. "We're going to give it another fifteen minutes or so for the medicine to do its thing, and then we'll talk. 'Til then, you're just wasting my time."

He flicked his cigarette toward my feet and wandered back toward the truck, where Jimmy appeared to be transfixed by a pair of dancing lightning bugs.

"Michael," I whispered as loudly as I dared through clenched teeth. "Are you in there?"

He nodded blearily, and one eyelid opened. He attempted a laugh, but it caught in his dry throat. "I think we're fucked, buddy."

334

"Maybe not just yet," I said, focusing on the zip tie that bound my wrists. I twisted them in one direction then the other, feeling the tie loosen a little more, but still not quite enough to pull a hand through. I tried to pull my arms apart and was only rewarded with a sharp pain in my side. I bit my bottom lip to keep from crying out and slumped forward in frustration.

And suddenly I caught a break. Behind my back, the tie snapped, and my hands abruptly dropped away from each other. I could feel blood rushing back into my fingertips. I bit my lip again, this time to suppress a giggle. I looked up and saw Sheriff Daniel was still occupying Jimmy's full attention, his back to us.

I reached into my back pocket and fished out the knife Nick had left for me. I flipped the blade out and reached behind Michael, locating the zip tie that bound his hands together. "Give me just a sec," I said, focusing on sawing through plastic and not flesh. "I can free us, but I don't know how long we have before whatever that was kicks in."

Michael nodded. "They know Gina's dead," he said. "They've known all along."

"I gathered that, and I'm pretty sure you were right. This was no accident. But other than Sheriff Daniel, who are 'they?' And what is it they think *we* know?" I cut through the last of the tie binding Michael's wrists, and he flexed his fingers.

"The sheriff. The Petersons—I don't know who all else. They think Gina told us something about what she saw. They've been interrogating me for days. I don't know any other way to tell them I don't know anything!"

I slipped the knife back into my pocket. "For now, we've got to get out of here."

"How?" asked Michael incredulously. "We'd have to go right past them!"

"Not necessarily," I said, carefully shifting position so I could attempt to get to my feet. "We could use the entrance to the cave and go out through a path Hattie—" I winced as her image flashed before me and backed up.

335

"—go out a different way." I was having trouble getting my legs to cooperate. They felt sluggish and heavy.

"What's wrong?" asked Michael.

"Oh, no, no, no—" I groaned, trying to force my feet to support my weight, but my ankles wanted to roll, and I flopped back against the rock wall, eliciting another jab of pain from my side, but the pain was dull, and that wasn't a particularly good sign. "Whatever he injected me with is starting to kick in."

 Michael tucked his hands behind his back. "Looks like Sheriff Daniel is heading back this way, anyhow. Think *hard*…is there anything at all that Gina told you when she visited? Any names, any dates—"

I shook my head, watching our future prospects dim as the sheriff sauntered our way, his shit-eating grin back in place, masking his true intent. "We didn't talk about her work at all. She wanted to hear about Melanie and her daughter, and what I had been up to, and—"

A ripple of inappropriate laughter burbled out of me, and I had the weirdest sensation that I could actually feel my hair growing. There was no doubt the drug was working now. My laughter ended in a hiccup and a snort, and I leaned toward Michael conspiratorially. "Matter of fact, she didn't even mention you at all."

Michael's focus intensified. "How about the film? Did she say who or what was on that roll of film?"

I cocked my head to the side and sat back, the entire evening playing back in out-of-sequence segments. We had reminisced. We had eaten pizza. We had made fun of our brother. All the normal things siblings might do when they haven't seen each other in a while. Then, like a needle jumping across the grooves of a vinyl record, I recalled my various conversations with Michael as we had traveled here and concocted our backstory. More importantly, I remembered what *hadn't* been said.

"I never mentioned the film to you," I said, my voice sounding far away. Sheriff Daniel was practically upon us now, but I was having trouble determining the exact distance. Jimmy Perkins had nearly faded into a hallucinatory fog behind him.

"Sure, you did!" urged Michael. "It was either at Ida's Diner or—"

"No," I said flatly. "I'm sure of it."

Michael sighed and leaned forward, resting his forearms on his knees, his unbound hands dangling in front of him. Inexplicably alert, he glanced up at Sheriff Daniel and shrugged.

"Well," he said, rising to his feet. "So much for *my* cover."

CHAPTER TWENTY-SIX

I stared stupidly at both men towering above me. My tongue was thick in my mouth, but my breathing remained unrestricted, so I was irrationally calm—almost nonchalant. I wasn't really sure I cared whether they killed me or not, but I desperately wanted one of Sheriff Daniel's cigarettes. It was all about priorities.

"What did you say to him?" the sheriff demanded, whipping his hat off his head with one hand while running the other through his sweat-drenched hair. Then, as an afterthought, "And how did you both get loose?"

"What difference does it make what I said?" asked Michael, dusting himself off. "He knows. And you'll want to check his back pockets. He's got some sort of switchblade."

I continued to stare at Michael while the sheriff pulled me forward, cursing under his breath and searching until he found the knife Nick had given me. I could feel my rib shifting, but it caused no discomfort whatsoever. "So, who are you?" I asked.

"Michael Arthur," he said, smiling smugly. "I didn't lie to you about *that.*"

"You never dated my sister." It wasn't a question but a statement of fact.

"No," he said. "And luckily for you, I'm not a particularly cruel person. Otherwise, I would tell you how devastatingly beautiful Gina was, and how much we enjoyed each other's—company, if for no other reason than to cause you great discomfort. But the truth is, she was the biggest pain in my ass imaginable from the moment she showed up in Briarstaff. Always with the questions, questions, questions!"

"What kind of questions?" I asked.

Michael laughed and pointed at me. "Questions about the questions! Now, *that's* funny! She kept digging into the affairs of my Academy, and well—that's just not something that's done. Every time I thought I'd thrown her off the scent, there she was, trying a whole new approach."

"So, you're with the Academy?" I had entered the rhetorical portion of my questioning because all I was really focused on was the pack of cigarettes in the sheriff's front pocket. *Man*, did I want one!

"I *am* the Academy," he replied, swelling with pride. "I have been the Academy's chancellor for the past seven years. Not a thing goes on there without my knowledge and approval."

"Okay," I said, and I couldn't have sounded less interested. I pointed to the sheriff. "Can I have a cigarette, please?"

The men exchanged a puzzled glance before the sheriff shrugged, pulling a pack of full-flavor Camels from his pocket. He handed me one and stooped to light it. Although more robust than my preferred selection, I relished the warmth of the smoke and the rush of nicotine that followed.

"Can we get back on topic?" Sheriff Daniel asked Michael, tucking the cigarettes and lighter away. "I think it's safe to say he's under the influence now."

I agreed with that wholeheartedly. For a fraction of an instant, I wondered why Michael wasn't feeling the effects as well before realizing I had fallen victim to a little sleight of hand. Sheriff Daniel had never actually injected Michael with the compound. I was more than a little slow on the uptake.

Both men leaned in close enough for me to pull my head back, and I rewarded them by blowing a plume of smoke in their faces. Michael recoiled, fanning away the smoke with his hands while the sheriff continued to bore holes through me with his eyes.

"We really need you to concentrate, Mr. Morrow," said the sheriff. "Did Gina tell you what she had on that film?"

I shook my head slowly. "No idea."

Michael stood. "Well, this is pointless," he said. He stepped away, picking up a long-range two-way radio he had hidden amongst the rocks nearby. He began an earnest conversation largely comprised of unintelligible code words while the sheriff continued to keep watch over me. I was mainly content to take another hit from the cigarette, thinking how nice a shot of whiskey would be right about now.

"HELL-O-O-O-O-O?"

A woman's voice rang out, echoing throughout the woods, and Sheriff Daniel turned in disbelief while his useless guard, Jimmy, scrambled like a frightened rodent to determine the source. I had no problem at all identifying the affected lilt. Caroline Peterson emerged a few yards behind Jimmy, carrying what appeared to be my partially unzipped backpack in one hand and Jimmy's gun in the other. She must have discovered it while rooting through my pack, which she held out before her as if it were the filthiest thing she'd ever laid hands on. The gun, however, seemed entirely at home. She pushed past Jimmy, clearly startling him as she teetered toward us on ridiculously high wedge hiker boots, but the cracks in her carefully constructed façade were on full display. Her auburn hair was no longer perfectly coiffed, and the lines on her face had deepened decades in a matter of days. She scowled at the sheriff, shaking the backpack at him.

"What is the meaning of this, Charley?" she demanded.

"What are you talking about, Caroline?"

"You didn't even *try* to hide your cruiser," she said. "You may as well have put a sign on the road pointing this way. You know, sometimes we *do* actually get some traffic to the festival from surrounding counties. You didn't lock it and look what I found in the trunk. Didn't you even go through it?" She held the gun up and gave my backpack another shake before dropping it at the sheriff's feet. I heard a sound suggesting my expensive camera contained within was probably broken, but I couldn't muster any righteous indignation. I was still marveling at her ability to navigate the terrain in her ridiculous boots.

"What about it?" asked Sheriff Daniel with nerves that continued to fray.

"Well, to begin with, he could have shot you," she said incredulously. "And besides, it's *evidence!* Good Lord, Charley! This is all supposed to be disposed of! Did you even remember it was there?"

The sheriff sighed. "Shouldn't you be with your husband, Caroline? I mean, how's it going to look if you're not there by his side?"

"How *can* I be there, Charley? Everything I've left to you boys has all gone to shit, hasn't it? The debacle with the Andersons, and now Audrey is gone—" She pursed her lips and placed her hands on her hips, suddenly recognizing that Michael was earnestly in conversation on his radio near the rocky edge of the plateau's outer rim. "What's this? What's going on?"

"He knows about Michael," muttered the sheriff, indicating me.

"Well, for *shit's* sake!" she exploded, throwing her hands into the air. "Can't anyone do anything right? Did you at least get him dosed? Did you at least find out if she told him what was on the film or what she saw or what she heard? *Charley?* Are you *listening* to me?"

Sheriff Daniel stood with his head cocked in perplexity, staring in Caroline's general direction but not really seeing her or focusing on her tirade. Unaccustomed to being anything less than the center of attention, she turned to follow his gaze.

"What in the hell is *this?!?*" she screeched, her shrill voice completely losing its practiced, modulated cadence.

I leaned to my left and struggled to focus on two figures in animated conversation near Jimmy's truck. One was Jimmy—his bandaged hand gave that much away—but it took a bit longer to recognize the other as his little brother, Rusty. He was clearly upset, his hands gesticulating wildly while Jimmy tried to calm him down. They both froze at the sound of Caroline's harpy shriek, turning toward her as one.

"James! Russell!" she called out, waving them over with the waggle of a single pink fingertip. "Bring yourselves over here right this instant!"

Like troubled students called before their principal, the Perkins boys ambled in our direction, dragging feet the whole way. Even in my current state, I could see they were both clearly scared to death of Caroline. Who wouldn't be?

"What is the meaning of this?" she demanded.

"I was watching the woods like the sheriff told me to, ma'am," sputtered Jimmy. The color had drained completely from his face. "Rusty ain't s'posed to be here."

Caroline nodded slowly, deliberating before turning expectantly toward Rusty. "Russell?"

"I—I—," stammered Rusty, his eyes darting in every direction that wasn't Caroline's.

"Yes?" she tapped her foot expectantly, burning holes in the boy with her own. "Stop fidgeting, Russell, and use your words."

Rusty abruptly burst into tears, blubbering, "I didn't mean to shoot her—I mean, it was supposed to be *him*—" He pointed toward me. "—but then she-she-she stood up, and-and-and—"

Caroline's face veered toward sympathy, and she reached forward to place a reassuring hand on Rusty's upper arm. "Oh, Russell. I'm so sorry. I can only imagine how you feel, but you needn't worry about any trouble. Sheriff Daniel has everything well in hand. Do you see this?" She held the gun up to show Rusty.

"Hey! I think that's my gun!" interjected Jimmy. "That asshole stoled it from me!"

Caroline shot the elder Perkins a warning glare before refocusing on Rusty, who was both nodding and shaking his head, tears streaming down his freckled face. "No one's going to know you shot that girl, Russell. Between the doctor and the county coroner, the bullet that will be recovered will be from *this* gun. Do you understand me, Russell?"

But Rusty was beyond basic comprehension. "But-but-but—*Hattie*—"

"*Shhh*," said Caroline, her pale pink fingertips lightly stroking his upper arm. "It will be all right, Russell. Sometimes in conflict, sacrifices have to be made. Hattie was in the wrong place at the wrong time, that's all. You were only doing what Sheriff Daniel told you to do. Mr. Morrow will be identified as the shooter, not you. Above all else, we protect the Academy, yes?"

Rusty nodded uncertainly.

"We protect our own, and we protect our agenda," she continued, her voice set to soothe. "We are preserving our way of life for ourselves and our future generations. We can't allow these outside influences to undo everything we believe in, now, can we?"

Rusty shook his head, his breath now hiccupping in and out, and I thought I heard the vague rumble of thunder, although the lightening sky appeared cloudless. I was beginning to question the accuracy of my own senses. I took another drag from the cigarette, absorbed in the drama unfolding before me and completely oblivious to my own imminent peril.

Caroline licked her lips in a gesture that seemed weirdly serpentine. "I say all that to say this. What I need you to do now, Russell—are you listening to me? Good. I need you to go back home. Let us finish what we're doing here. You've done an *excellent* job, and you'll be rewarded for your efforts, I promise you! And really, I believe Hattie—"

Apparently, that was one 'Hattie' too much.

343

Rusty pulled away from Caroline, devolving into a hysterical mess. He doubled over, hugging himself tightly and fresh sobs erupted, startling everybody but me—I was transfixed, currently unable to be startled.

"Oh, my-my-my, *God!*" he screamed. *"Hattie!"*

Caroline was flustered, not even remotely used to losing control. She looked from the sheriff to Michael for support, but the sheriff was just as stunned as she was, and Michael continued to bark orders over his two-way radio, pacing back and forth. I heard another rumble of thunder and thought I smelled smoke, but I was too invested in what was playing out before me to even look around.

Rusty's expression had morphed into anger, and he backed away from Caroline, his finger wavering between her, the sheriff and Michael, who paid no attention whatsoever. "Hattie was my *family!*" he screamed. "She was the *only one* who was nice to me! The *only one* who didn't want something from me! The *only one* who didn't treat me like I owed her something! And you let this happen! *YOU LET THIS HAPPEN!*"

Caroline cast a final glance toward the sheriff, rolling her eyes before turning back to Rusty, raising the pistol and shooting him in the forehead.

There was a collective gasp as we all watched Rusty crumple to the ground, his hysterics permanently silenced.

Jimmy was frozen in place, showered with remnants of his little brother's brains, his mouth hanging open in shock. Sheriff Daniel leaned down, clasping his knees in his hands, looking like he might be sick at any moment. Even Michael's attention was diverted from his radio. He stared at Caroline in stunned disbelief.

"You shot my little brother," Jimmy eventually said, his voice small and hollow.

"Caroline," Michael said, looking disappointed. "Was that really necessary?"

Caroline's eyes widened as she pivoted toward him. "Was that *necessary?!?* That boy was never going to keep his mouth shut! Never! Did you *hear* him? Of course, you didn't. You were busy over there on your radio. And doing what, exactly?"

"You shot my little brother," Jimmy repeated, blinking rapidly as he began to realize the source of the mess he wore. He started flicking at pieces of particulate on his hands and arms with growing horror, trying to rid himself of the carnage.

"It's over, Caroline," said Michael. "I've initiated the Exodus protocol."

"You've *what?!?*" Caroline staggered as if she had been dealt a physical blow.

"You shot my little brother!" Jimmy screamed, his hands turning to claws as he fixated on the distracted woman before him. She was too preoccupied with her own outrage to notice the change in Jimmy's demeanor, the aggression in his stance, but at the last second, she did, swinging the gun back around in Jimmy's direction.

She was a fraction of an instant too late.

He dove at her, throwing his arms around her midsection. She screamed as she went down, her arms knocked high and to the left. The gun discharged once more before skittering out of her hand as she hit the hard ground. I watched as it slid in what seemed like slow motion toward my feet. I thought I might be able to grab it if I could just get my limbs to cooperate, but they were so heavy, and it was difficult to focus or retain my motivation. I was sure I smelled smoke now, more than could possibly be emanating from the fraction of cigarette I continued to nurse, but I also seemed to recall olfactory impairment was a possible sign of stroke. Was I having a stroke? Whatever they had dosed me with was certainly doing its thing.

"Charley!" Caroline screamed, struggling to keep Jimmy's hands from tightening around her neck. "Get this idiot off of me!"

345

I turned toward the sheriff, wondering why he just stood there with his mouth agape, staring at Caroline and leaning against the barricade which mostly covered the entrance to the cave. His hand was clamped to his stomach, just above his belt buckle. It took a moment to notice the dark stain spreading from underneath his hand.

"You shot me," he said, stunned. "You actually—"

He slid down the barricade, plopping onto the ground six feet away from me, his feet thrust forward, and his hand fell away to reveal the entrance wound created by the stray bullet. His eyes rolled back and closed, his head lolling on his shoulders.

"Charley!" Caroline screamed again before turning on Jimmy and digging her well-manicured fingertips into the sides of Jimmy's face, raking them down and pushing him away from her. She scrambled to her feet and joined Michael as they raced to Sheriff Daniel's side. Jimmy seized the opportunity to flee, scurrying back along the tree line before darting into the woods and leaving his own truck behind.

"We've got to get him to the doctor," said Caroline, using the sheriff's own hand to try and apply pressure to the wound.

"We don't have time for that, Caroline," said Michael. "We have to cut our losses and get out of here while we still can. The Academy has been evacuated. It's being demolished as we speak. You need to go to your husband, and I need to catch the Perkins boy before he can run his mouth to anyone else."

The anguish on Caroline's face was palpable, and the faint glow in the eastern sky seemed to vaguely pulsate. While daybreak may be near, this was the ambient light of a campus on fire on the crest of the far ridge. The smoke wasn't hallucinatory, and I saw tendrils of it seeping out through the cave's entrance where it had found escape through the underground tunnels Hattie and I had investigated only hours beforehand.

"But what about my town?" she asked sullenly.

"We always knew this was a possibility," said Michael, helping Caroline to her feet. "You've had a good run. Now, we do as you said. We protect our own. We protect our agenda. First, I need to catch Jimmy. He's not the most credible, but he'll sure make a lot of noise. Start getting everything else loaded into the car as best you can. I'll help you load the bodies when I get back. Then, we'll nudge it into the quarry and be done with all of this."

The bodies. I certainly didn't like the sound of that.

Caroline nodded, bending to scoop up my backpack, while Michael took a final look around, mentally compiling a checklist of things to tend to upon his return. His eyes widened and locked on mine as realization dawned that I held Jimmy's gun in my right hand, pointing it in his general direction.

"You're not going anywhere, you son of a bitch," I said, and I squeezed the trigger.

Nothing happened. Not even a click.

I brought the gun closer and saw the safety was engaged, probably as a result of Caroline dropping it when Jimmy bowled her over. Michael wasted no time, charging forward while I fumbled with the safety. I thrust the gun ahead, but Michael was right on top of me, his hands outstretched and trying to wrench the gun away from me. I closed my eyes and squeezed the trigger, feeling the gun jump in my hands as it fired. Michael collapsed on top of me, doubling over and screaming in pain. I managed to push him to the side where he rolled into a fetal position and rocked back and forth. He appeared to have the misfortune of being crotch shot, and I couldn't have planned it better.

Caroline stood before me, wavering in a rare but grand display of indecision. Her hair danced in whisps all around her head, her tear-stained face streaked with runaway mascara. All of her accomplices were down, and she looked completely lost. Black smoke continued to roll out through the cavern entrance, thickening as the eastern horizon continued to brighten. I felt the need to cough. I could hear a *whump-whump-whump* both near and far, the natural acoustics making it impossible to pinpoint. The gun felt heavy in my hand, and I could hear chattering inside my head. My eyelids were growing heavy, too, and I longed for sleep. Should I shoot Caroline while I still could? I looked at Rusty's ruined face, staring vacantly forward and decided there had been enough gunplay. I let the gun drop to my side, coughing and rubbing smoke from my eyes.

Caroline's eyes brightened, focusing on the gun and taking a step toward it just as the chattering in my head morphed into a familiar keening I recognized. It was very close now. Caroline took one more step, and I lifted the nub of cigarette I still held in my left hand, bringing it to my lips to pull one last hit from it, causing its tip to flare bright. I flicked it in her general direction as the colony of bats burst angrily through the cavern opening, driven from their resting place by the billowing smoke of the burning Academy. They followed the cigarette as if it were an insect, flocking around Caroline before diverting at the last second, cocooning her in a veritable cloud. Her scream was pure terror as she whipped her arms around, trying to both shield her face and shoo the bats away. She staggered backward, finally betrayed by her outrageous footwear, tripping on her own feet and stumbling toward the edge of the rock precipice. I was transfixed by her progress, unbelievably calm in the presence of so many bats. With a final cry, she went over the edge as the bats shifted direction and headed into the woods.

Then silence, save for the steady *whump-whump-whump* which continued to draw closer. I recognized that sound, too, but my eyes couldn't stay open for a second longer. I allowed them to close for just an instant but found it too difficult to reopen them.

I slid away.

CHAPTER TWENTY-SEVEN

My eyes were heavy, but I finally managed to open them a slit. I strained to recognize my surroundings. I was strapped to some kind of gurney, and an intravenous drip was attached to my arm, clear liquid siphoning down through a tube and into my veins. A clear mask was strapped to my face feeding me a stream of cool oxygen. I could feel my rib again, and I could have done without that. I seemed to be in the back of an ambulance, but the interior was dark, illuminated only by the various displays of equipment that had been hooked to me. Resting in shadows against the opposite compartment wall was a woman, her features indistinct save for a cascade of long hair clasped in ponytail and pulled forward over one shoulder.

"Melanie?" I croaked, my throat still full of smoke, both cigarette and otherwise.

"No," she said, leaning forward and taking my hand. "Not Melanie. *Shhh.*"

I gasped. Gina's beautiful face hovered before me, visible in the translucent glow of the portable heart monitor. I had to be dreaming. Or worse.

"Am I—dead?" I asked.

She laughed, a sound I thought I'd never hear again. "No, little brother. You're not dead."

"But-but-but—"

"*Shhh,*" she said, putting a fingertip over my oxygen mask and smiling with such bittersweet concern. "I am so, *so* sorry. I didn't mean for you to get dragged into all of this. I didn't mean for *anyone* to get dragged into all of this."

"All of this—what?" I croaked, completely perplexed. I was afraid to close my eyes, afraid she would disappear, and everything would go back to as it was.

"*Shhh,*" she repeated, taking one of my hands into hers. "I don't have long, but I think you need a little bit of explanation or you're likely to just go stirring everything up all over again. You're kind of a pain in the ass that way, you know?"

I giggled and nodded dumbly, before pulling her toward me and hugging her fiercely despite a sharp protest from my rib and the challenging entanglements of various medical apparatuses. She hugged me back as best as she could before leaning back and wiping tears from her eyes. She cleared her throat.

"A little over a year ago," she began. "I was approached by a gentleman named Joseph Greene about doing some field work for the government, Homeland Security to be exact. I'm pretty sure the name was an alias—it might as well have been Colonel Mustard. I'm not sure if anyone I've met so far has given their real name.

"My reputation for photography provided a perfect cover for me to be here. On the surface, it was a photo essay of small-town life after the main source of revenue for the economy dried up. What they were really looking for were pictures of any prominent people in the vicinity of the Academy."

She took a sip of water from a bottle before pulling my mask back and helping me with one. Water has never tasted so sweet in all my life.

"This Academy," she continued, "is just one of several throughout the country. They are all interlinked, and they all have the same agenda. They

350

are carefully selecting and grooming an army. Not just soldiers, but scientists, doctors and software engineers. They believe technology is a scourge that's ruining this country—the world, actually, and they are determined to put a stop to it."

"But wait a minute," I said, the water soothing and restoring my voice. I tried to raise up on one elbow only to be helped back down by my sister, who then lightly smacked my arm. Bad Dwayne. "Why software engineers if they think technology is the enemy?"

"The only way to fight a fire this big is with more fire," she said. "The internet has changed the world in ways that weren't even imaginable not so very long ago. It's pervasive, completely intertwined with our everyday lives. Online banking, social media, eBooks and online news outlets replacing print media—it's completely changed the way we do everything. To bring that sort of juggernaut to its knees, these people have software engineers developing viruses, malware—anything and everything you can imagine. They hope to eventually destabilize the entire internet. The server room you saw was just one of several network clusters they have situated around the country. They've destroyed this location to prevent its content from being discovered, but the data is all backed up to other facilities at different sites."

"Data redundancy," I said. "It's at the foundation of every good disaster recovery plan. But that's lunacy!"

"You'd be surprised at how much momentum this movement has going for it," she said. "I know I was. It's easy to rankle at the suggestion of Big Brother watching and listening to everything we say or do, but isn't it equally terrifying to think of the awful sorts of things that can happen in a vacuum? You've had a pretty good taste of that yourself in these past few days. And that is exactly what these people aim to achieve. They want to restore the vacuum, preserve their power. It's elitist, racist and far more organized than you'd ever believe."

I shook my head, trying to understand what sounded like great science fiction. I squeezed Gina's hand, still expecting her to evaporate before my eyes, but her hand was solid, and she squeezed back. I had so many questions but couldn't find words.

Gina continued, "Most of the people in Briarstaff are good, honest folk, raising their families with the same set of values and the same conveniences they grew up with. They can't miss what they've never had. And the kids are amazing. Smart, open-minded in surprising ways considering their surroundings."

She paused, biting her lower lip.

"I'm just sick about Hattie," she said, her voice hitching. "She was such a free spirit. She was driven by curiosity, and it's a wonder she didn't run into trouble long before we got into town, little brother. She was in and out of those caves all the time. I don't think she was ever perceived as a threat." She sensed my guilt and was attempting to assuage my feelings—likely hers, as well. I couldn't think about it just yet. The pain was too fresh and would last a lot longer than that of any broken rib.

"On one of my first days in town, I met Shane and the others out by the quarry," she continued. "I was trying to find a good vantage point to observe the Academy, and there they were, enjoying the summer sun and each other's company. I asked them what they knew about it, but it was just background noise to most of them. Always there, but no real curiosity. They hadn't been invited and would probably never set foot inside. Except for Rusty, of course, because he would be attending in the fall, but he was never very talkative. It intrigued me. It was like the elephant in the room that no one discussed. So, I started asking around town about it, and it was sort of like poking at a hornet's nest. Next thing I know, Caroline and Troy Peterson are going out of their way to track me down. They offered to arrange a lunch for me with the Academy's chancellor—"

"Michael Arthur," I croaked, and she nodded. "Please tell me you weren't—you know—*with* him."

She tossed her head back, laughing richly. "Oh, he *wishes!* No, although he sure was giving it his all. Very sure of himself, but he came across as smug and evasive, and that's never really done anything for me. I wanted a tour of the facility, but he only agreed to meet me in Shawnee, some little Olive Garden wannabe. It was the closest thing to fine dining around. I began to catch on that Michael didn't like to be seen in town. He had contacts within the town council and a few people I call gatekeepers—for example, that Shepley woman who runs the motel where I stayed, and Dr. Morris and his wife. They ran interference and kept most outsiders away. But Michael didn't want his connection to the Academy to become widely known. He wanted to preserve a sense of anonymity.

"Lunch was nearly comical. He tried to dispense with any questions I had about the Academy just as quickly as possible. What is the Academy? An accelerated learning program for specially selected students. Selected how? By secret criteria. By whom? A panel of experts. What kind of experts? Experts in all areas of study. His non-answers were absolutely infuriating, and he did it all while making eyes over me and making passive-aggressive remarks about how off-putting it was to be interrogated by such a pretty girl. I figured if he wasn't above flirting, I wasn't either, so I tried to sweet-talk him into that tour, but he wouldn't budge there. Said it was against Academy policy. Said he'd rather give me a tour of his private residence.

"I was pissed off by then. I was getting nowhere, and although he offered to pay for lunch, I insisted on treating. Told him I would write it off as a business expense. Imagine my surprise when the waiter said my card was declined. I tried a different one. Same thing."

I had a sense of déjà vu as I recalled my own experience in Shawnee.

"I was completely mortified when he had to come to the rescue and pay the bill instead," she said. "I insisted I would repay him, although he tried to assure me it was no big deal. It was a big deal to me. I didn't want to feel indebted to him for anything. He said we could square up over dinner some other time, and I just *knew* he was pulling something so he could see me again, but for the life of me, I couldn't see how.

"I made a trip to Elkins the next day, hoping they might have a Chase branch, and I was in luck. The customer service rep couldn't understand why my cards had been declined because their system didn't show any attempts for authorization. He noticed the chips had been gouged, but the magnetic strips should have worked unless the card had gotten completely fried. He thought it was highly improbable that both things had happened, but thinking back, I had gone to the restroom before the waiter took my card to cash out the first time, and I left my purse at the table with Michael. He could have done anything he wanted.

"I decided to withdraw enough money so I wouldn't have to worry about it again for the rest of my stay, and on the drive back to Briarstaff, it occurred to me that I could take the ball right out of Michael's court. Rather than suffering through another pointless meal, I decided to go directly to the Academy under the pretext of reimbursing him. I knew he'd say no if I gave him any warning, so I just went straight there."

My eyes were beginning to droop again, but I needed to hear the rest. "You made it inside?"

"Oh, hell no!" she laughed. "That place is surrounded by an eleven-foot fence and with armed security guards manning a cinderblock bunker near the only entrance. It looks far more like a prison than an educational institution. The main building is barely visible from the security checkpoint, only a single paved lane that veers back onto the property.

"When I told the guard why I was there, he wasn't buying any of it. I was asked to accompany him back to the security booth while he called for further instruction, and believe me, he wasn't asking, he was ordering. About fifteen minutes later, Michael showed up at the gate in a Jeep. It was the first time I'd seen his smooth exterior crack. He didn't expect to see me there, and he didn't like that I was on his turf. I'm pretty sure that was when he first saw me as an actual threat. He couldn't get me out of there fast enough, although I did manage to repay him for our previous lunch. I had a feeling he wouldn't be reaching out for dinner."

I yawned beneath the oxygen mask. Every time I blinked, my eyes were harder to open.

"I hadn't really found a way to get close enough to see anything on the Academy's grounds, and Michael was done being gracious, so I was running out of ideas," continued Gina. "Besides, Matt and Sheila were getting married the next day, and I had already allowed myself to take the weekend off. That's when Hattie showed me the bunker entrance embedded in the cave wall. I couldn't believe it! It was like a Cold War leftover or something. I found out later that the property had once been a regional fallout shelter in case of nuclear emergency but had been decommissioned. The whole thing had been accessible from within the main building, long before it housed the Academy, but those areas were walled off when the Academy took possession. Somehow, they missed the ductwork when they were sealing the area off, and that's how I found—"

"The server room," I interrupted, stifling another yawn.

She nodded. "Yes, and it made sense. Lots of data is maintained in underground facilities because it doesn't require nearly the same amount of energy to keep the rooms as cool as they need to be. But that wasn't all I found. I pressed on through the venting and was suddenly looking into an enormous—I don't even know what you'd call it. A war room? Fifteen, twenty people were hunkered around a giant wooden conference table, clearly planning something big. I was scared to get too close to the opening of the vent, afraid they would hear me or see me up there, but there was so much commotion going on, I was probably being overly cautious. And that was when I recognized a few of the folks at the table."

Gina told me their names, two men and a woman, and my eyes widened. These were long-term members of Congress whose names would be familiar to anyone even remotely aware of current affairs. On the surface, they ideologically represented both political parties, but in reality, they served an entirely different master. How surprised their constituents would be if this affiliation were known.

"That's when I got my pictures," said Gina, uncapping the water bottle and taking another sip before sharing with me. "And got the hell out of there. I was really spooked, and that's where I think I screwed up."

"How so?" I asked.

"I went straight back to the motel and started loading up, just as quickly as I could. I could say it was because I was behind schedule to leave for Matty's wedding, but I still had plenty of time. Honestly, I wanted to put some distance between me and what I'd just seen." She glanced at me and placed a hand on my cheek. "I think I may be only marginally better than you at telling lies, little brother. My default tactic is never to overshare. I didn't want these people to know anything more about my personal life than need be, so I had never mentioned I was planning to be gone that weekend. I had originally planned to return after the wedding to get photos of the Apple Festival and tie up my cover story, but I was in such a hurry to get going, it caught Mrs. Shepley's attention. She wondered why I was in such a hurry to get on the road, and couldn't I join her for lunch? I tried to calm myself, but my heart was beating so fast I could practically hear it myself. It started to feel like she was stalling me, and my imagination was having a field day with that. It felt completely paranoid and yet entirely justified to put some distance between me and that town. I told her I'd meet her back in the motel office after I loaded the last of my car but took off just as soon as she was out of sight. It took a hundred miles or so before I started to feel like I wasn't being followed."

"But you were," I said, and she nodded.

"Michael must have had a tracker put on my car," she said, lowering her forehead into her hands. "And I led him straight to our family. He called me that night at your house, and it sure wasn't to ask me out again. He demanded I meet him right away at a rest area near Lancaster. He made sure I understood that no one in our family was safe until he saw me. Not you, Matt, Mom, Dad—anyone close to me. He said he just wanted to talk, but I knew I wouldn't walk away from any meeting we had.

"I called Joe Greene right after I left your house, and he arranged for someone from his team to intercept me at a BP along the way, taking me into protective custody while another agent, Chloe Devereaux, took my place for the rendezvous with Michael. We resembled each other a great deal, although she was far more proficient with a gun. She planned to take Michael into custody for questioning while Joe's team determined how legitimate the threat to our family actually was. And that's where everything went wrong."

She took another drink and swallowed hard, looking toward the ceiling, avoiding my eyes.

"Michael never intended to meet me. He planted something in my car, probably while we were at the wedding. Something blew beneath the hood and the car ended up plowing through the median before colliding with that propane tanker. Killed Chloe instantly and burned her beyond recognition, and I'm still having a whole lot of trouble with that. From that moment forward, I was effectively dead. It was the only way to protect you all until Joe's team got enough evidence together to blow this scandal wide open."

"The film," I said.

Gina nodded. "I didn't realize it had fallen out of my bag, and it was the only proof I had placing those congressional officials on Academy

357

premises. Joe sent an agent to your house to look for it, but he came up empty-handed. You must have already found it."

I was startled by how casually my house's defenses had been penetrated. I had no idea that anyone had been inside. It sent a chill down my spine. "I came across it after your…"

I couldn't finish the sentence.

"The funeral," she said, finally looking back at me. "And that's where I really screwed up. I shouldn't have gone—"

I attempted to sit up. "I *knew* I saw you!"

She smiled wistfully. "Your reaction startled me, and I was hundreds of yards away in the woods. Not much gets past Michael—he thought he saw me too, but he couldn't be sure. I never *dreamed* he would attend the funeral! I mean, everyone believed I was dead, and I should have just left well enough alone, but— I needed to see that everyone was all right. It was the closest I could come to saying goodbye." She looked away.

"He was actually following you," she continued. "You had just been all over the news again for solving a murder and saving that reporter's life. Michael wondered if my visit to you had been more than just social. He thought I may have been consulting you about the things I had discovered in Briarstaff. And now he wasn't even sure if I was really dead. He used you as bait, figuring he could lure me out of hiding if I thought you were in danger. Joe almost had to sit on me to keep from doing exactly that. His team was planning to extract you today—I wouldn't let it go on any longer, but things unfolded more quickly than anticipated. No one could have predicted the sheriff would send Rusty out into those woods with a rifle. And while I knew the town was incredibly racist, I never expected Caroline to exact such vengeance on the Andersons because their children had the audacity to fall in love." She shook her head.

"But it's *over*, now," I said. "You can come home! I can't wait to see Mom's and Dad's faces! And you'll be able to meet your niece or nephew when—" I stopped mid-rant as I registered her expression. She bit her bottom lip and looked skyward, a trickle of fresh tears spilling down her cheeks. "What? What's the matter?"

"I can't do any of that," she said.

"But *why?*"

Her smile was a tight line. "Because without the film that Michael recovered from the photo shop, I am the only eyewitness that can place those members of Congress on Academy grounds. Joe doesn't have quite enough evidence to make his case airtight. I have to remain in protective custody for the time being while Joe's team does their jobs. I only convinced him to let me tell you because I don't think you would have left it alone." She attempted to chuckle. "You're kind of bull-headed."

My eyes burned as fresh anger triggered belligerence. "What makes you think I'll leave it alone now? I could help, you know? Speed up the process somehow—"

"No!" Her hazel eyes finally fixing on mine. "You will do no such thing, and I mean it! Michael could never completely convince them I had survived that car crash, and when I didn't come riding to your rescue, even he's willing to admit he was mistaken. The Academy's board is doing a lot of damage control to explain away what you witnessed, and they're pulling up stakes entirely from Briarstaff. But if they believe for a second that you're still poking around, no one in our family will be safe. No one."

It was difficult not to scream in frustration. "But how long will this go on? Our parents don't *deserve* this—"

"Don't you think I know that?" she interrupted, her own anger flaring. "There isn't a single thing that's fair about any of this. And I don't know how long it will take. I pray it won't take long, but I have no way of knowing."

"This is utter bullshit," I said, this time managing to sit up. "I can't just—"

I started to fumble with the IV line in my arm when Gina stood and forcefully pushed me back down, pulling my hand away from the tube.

"You will do exactly what I'm telling you to do," she said. "You are going to leave it alone. It's not like when we were kids. You can't just turn a stupid horse head lamp on in the window to let me know it's safe to come home. I'll let you know when I'm able to come home. But in the meanwhile, you can't tell anyone. Not Dad, not Mom, not Matt—not even Melanie. Everyone's safety depends on it."

"But—"

"But nothing," she said, standing and tracing my IV line back toward its saline drip. "I know how well you lie, little brother, but I'm really counting on you this time. And I know it's not fair, but neither is what happened to Hattie—or to Chloe." I was startled to see her pull a syringe from the pocket of her dark sweatshirt.

"What are you doing?"

"We're about to make a pit stop," she said, flicking the tip of the needle and pushing air bubbles through. She inserted the syringe into a port in the IV line and depressed the plunger. I began to panic, tired of being on the receiving end of medical treatment from folks without proper training, but almost immediately I felt the surge of adrenaline dissipate, my eyelids instantly gaining heft. "It's time for me to get off this ride. You just remember what I told you. Leave this alone. Promise me that. I'll be back just as soon as I can. I promise you that."

I tried to protest, but my mouth no longer cooperated. I just stared back at her, slack-jawed with tears streaming from the corners of my eyes. She wiped them away with her thumbs before leaning down and kissing my forehead. I simply nodded, unable to deny her request.

I blinked for what seemed an instant, but when I opened my eyes, she was gone.

EPILOGUE

"You're worrying me," said Melanie from behind the wheel of my SUV. She brought my newly acquired used car to afford me a little more comfort than I would have had in her own little Mazda, and I appreciated her consideration. I would normally be white knuckling the armrest and sending up prayers to St. Christopher for safe passage but couldn't find any enthusiasm. If I had made it through the last few days, I could surely survive the various tailgating, lane-hopping and general disregard for speed limits that distinguished Melanie's particular style of driving.

"Why do you keep checking your cell phone?" she asked.

I looked at the screen once more before dimming it and shrugged. I aimed for nonchalance, but I couldn't fight the compulsion to keep checking for service. It felt important.

The concern was evident as her eyes kept shifting my way in the icy blue reflection of the dashboard light. The sun had set shortly after we crossed the Ohio border on US 35 near Gallipolis, and we glided across a ribbon of asphalt beneath the incandescence of a full moon. After an initial outpouring of relief at seeing one another, we had traveled much of the distance in near silence. Melanie tried several times to engage, but I was deep in my own thoughts and didn't feel quite up to it. My head throbbed in the aftermath of the chemical cocktail that had largely debilitated me, and a handful of Excedrin had yet to kick in. Uncomfortable silence was relatively new territory for us, but I couldn't manage much more. Despite intense curiosity, Melanie didn't push, granting me space as I stared out the window, watching reflective mile markers whip by as we made our way back to a home I wasn't sure I'd ever see again.

I had awakened in an emergency room in Morgantown with no recollection of the ambulance ever making an additional stop for Gina to disembark. Whatever she had given me knocked me out fast, and the rest of the journey had happened in between the rise and fall of extraordinarily heavy eyelids. In fact, the entire memory of our conversation had attained an ethereal, dreamlike vagueness, and I was starting to question whether it had really happened. Could it have just been the byproduct of wishful thinking? Once awake, I was examined by an attentive medical staff before being released into Melanie's care with detailed instructions for how to treat my fractured rib at home.

Shane had followed my instructions to the letter, calling Melanie at his first opportunity. In turn, she contacted Nina Crockett with the FBI, and Nina and a few other agents had flown in via helicopter. I realized its propellors were the source of the steady *whump-whump-whump* I had heard as I lost consciousness at the quarry. She had airlifted me down to Dr. Morris's clinic and from there, I had been transported to Morgantown by ambulance. I still don't know how Gina got into the vehicle, and if Nina knows, she isn't talking.

It would be quite some time before I heard any satisfactory resolution to the events of that evening, pieces trickling in from a variety of sources over the next several months. I was forced to be patient, keeping a promise only reluctantly made to probe no further.

Fortunately for you, I won't make you wait.

It was touch-and-go for Troy Peterson for quite a while. He suffered a series of infections at his wound sites that resulted in the partial removal of one lung and permanent damage to his spinal cord. He will require the use of a walker for the rest of his days. He will stand trial alongside Tommy Pruitt for the destruction of the Andersons' home as well as for perpetrating a hate crime. Audrey Peterson, Trevor Anderson and Shane Van Buren will be star witnesses for the prosecution. The men have refused to acknowledge anyone else who was present that night, save for Sheriff Daniel, whose death was the only thing keeping him from standing trial as well.

Sheriff Daniel succumbed to the accidental gut shot he received courtesy of Caroline Peterson. He was already gone by the time Nina and her team landed. State police would discover crimes of astonishing magnitude both committed and obscured by the late sheriff, including complicity in the murders of the Conley family from Ohio. Their bodies were recovered from the bottom of the quarry where they had been submerged for nearly two decades. I wondered if the town's teens would ever swim those waters again. The sheriff had unlimited authority to do as he pleased, and what pleased him most was to tend to the needs of the F.O.E. and support the Academy in any way he could. His office was seized by state authorities, pending election of a new sheriff by county residents.

Caroline Peterson survived her tumble over the edge of the rock cliff, breaking an ankle as she landed on a narrow ledge nearly eight feet below. Nina's team rescued Caroline and took her into custody to stand trial for the murders of Rusty Perkins and Charley Daniel. Jimmy Perkins would be testifying for the prosecution in this case, having not only witnessed Caroline's lunacy but only narrowly escaping the same fate himself. I still don't care for the man, but he didn't deserve to die. Needless to say, Caroline didn't take home her seventh blue ribbon for winning the Apple Festival Bake-Off that Sunday.

Michael Arthur survived the wound I inflicted without specific intention yet neither with regret, a messy castration via small-caliber firearm, and was taken to a nearby medical facility for treatment under the watchful eye of the FBI. Sometime between his condition stabilizing and yet before he could be transferred into the custody of Homeland Security, he disappeared without a trace. No one saw anything and security video had been compromised. Entirely off the record and over a thank you dinner Melanie insisted on hosting in her honor, Nina Crockett shared her belief that Mr. Arthur had been eliminated by his own organization, deemed entirely too risky to remain in custody, where he could be interrogated endlessly. Dead men tell no tales, but the uncertainty is proving difficult; there are still moments when I'm sure I see his face in a crowd, ready to exact vengeance on me or my family. I'm still mortified I ever bought that load of shit he was selling. I thought I was a better judge of people than that, and it was a sobering realization. Amongst the many voicemails that were waiting for me on my phone was an interesting one from Jacko Pierce, my friend at *The Columbus Dispatch*. While he hadn't discovered anything particularly noteworthy about Briarstaff, he had discovered that *The Washington Post* had no record of Michael Arthur on staff. If only I had gotten the message sooner—but I could lose myself entertaining a game of *ifs*.

The rest of the town elders slithered back into the woodwork, escaping any sort of responsibility for misdeeds past or present. They had successfully shielded themselves behind those who had no choice but to take the fall, and unless new evidence emerged, it would very likely stay that way. Even facing lengthy incarceration, they remained loyal to one another, lips tightly sealed. Dr. Morris and his wife, Patricia, were cooperating with authorities to the best of their ability, and it didn't look likely they would be charged with anything. They had never actively participated in anything, but were duty bound by their obligation to heal when the occasional mess was brought into their clinic by the others. The clinic was currently up for sale, and the Morrises were looking for a nice place to retire in Florida.

Audrey and Trevor both took their GEDs, bypassing their senior year in high school and graduating early. They attend a community college in a small coastal Virginia town, playing coffeehouses on the weekends where they are occasionally joined by their friends, Shane and Nick, whenever time and gasoline allows. The foursome is processing the logistics of a small-scale summer tour along the eastern coast, and I plan to take Melanie and Jasmine to at least one of their performances once the specifics are hammered out. Traveling is a little more difficult for Shane these days. He and Joy Beth have been seeing quite a lot of each other, and Shane is taking the responsibilities of helping raise a toddler very seriously. Surprising absolutely everybody, Jimmy Perkins had the good grace to offer no objection when she filed for sole custody of their son, although the poor child's name would forever be a reminder of a life she had almost endured. Jimmy was currently living with Penny, the waitress from Ida's Town Diner. Apparently, she gave as good as she got, and they seemed blissfully happy beating the shit out of each other on a regular basis. I can only shake my head.

When I think about Briarstaff—and often I do, whether I want to or not—I recognize a cautionary tale of how evil can thrive when kept in the dark, and the odd isolationism that was championed by town officials helped maintain a status quo entirely undeserving of most of the town's residents. In Shane, Nick, Trevor, Audrey, Joy Beth, Delphine (Madame Phalange, she would likely prefer) and most especially Hattie, I realize there is always hope, even when things are at their most desolate.

I've even heard that internet may finally be on its way...

"Are you awake?"

Melanie's voice startled me, and I straightened in the passenger seat, my rib reminding me for the thousandth time it was still there, still unhappy. "Yeah," I said blearily. "I must have dozed off for a second. I don't usually do that."

"I'm pulling in your drive," she said. "We'll get you inside, and I'll stick around for at least a few hours anyway. I need to get a little bit of sleep before I pick Jasmine up from the Caudills."

I rubbed my eyes as the sight of my old farmhouse loomed to our left, gravel crunching beneath the tires as Melanie parked beside her own car. She shifted into park and turned the ignition off, the sound of crickets swelling around us. Dexter's silhouette was visible in the front window, and I saw him peep, a figment from a silent movie, jumping down and heading toward the door to greet us once we let ourselves in.

"Well, shoot," said Melanie, squinting up at the house and frowning.

"What?"

"I've tried to be energy conscious," she said. "But it looks like I missed a light upstairs."

I followed her gaze to the second story window of my bedroom that looked over the front lawn. Framed in its center, bare bulb blazing was the gawdy horse head lamp I had made in high school ceramics, the one I always used to let Gina know it was safe to come home.

This time, the message was for me.

THE END

AFTERWORD

The family into which Richard Dwayne Morrow was born was modeled closely after my own. It's been said you should write what you know, and for me, I've used it as a crutch to help me remember "who was who" in a fictional world I was only just beginning to explore. Most of the names were changed to protect the innocent—save for one, the eldest Morrow child, Gina. Unlike Dwayne's older brother, Matt, Gina was always mentioned but never present, and that was very intentional. Even after more than three decades, I still have difficulty staying on topic for long.

Gina Lee Miller was born on March 21, 1964, to Donald Richard and Nancy Jo Miller in Portsmouth, Ohio. She was their first and only girl and came into this world with spina bifida, scoliosis, and hydrocephalus—quite a learning curve ahead for these new parents. Although the hydrocephalus would resolve shortly, mercifully leaving Gina's mental capabilities intact, the other conditions would set limitations on every other aspect of her life. Her first mode of ambulation came courtesy of braces and crutches, which she embraced enthusiastically. Unfortunately, her enthusiasm was not equaled by her balance, and after multiple spills and many broken bones, a wheelchair was deemed—safest. In a time before handicapped accessibility was ever a thing, the smallest journey outside of our home was an enormous undertaking. She was home schooled by some of Clay Township's finest. She was a reasonably good student with a propensity to slip into daydreams with little to no notice, and who could blame her? Within her imagination, she was free to do the things her earthly body wouldn't allow. She read voraciously, precious books fueling her imagination, and she loved music, namely ABBA, Blondie and Queen. She preferred both to watching television, although she would do that upon occasion, too.

She loved her younger brothers, Wesley and Darin, and was never resentful of the things they took for granted that she could not possibly do. Neither of them was afflicted in the ways that she was. There was no doubt we loved her, too, although at the time, it was completely lost on us how fortunate we were by comparison. We could come and go as we pleased, and she would patiently await our return, hoping we might occasionally bring along some of our own friends, all of whom she enjoyed thoroughly. Sometimes we did, and sometimes we didn't, never fully understanding how much that brightened her day and expanded her world. I wish I had been more aware at the time, but hindsight is 20/20, and I don't believe we were gifted with any special enlightenment just because our sister was born with a debilitating birth defect. It was how we grew up, and at the time, it just seemed normal.

We lost Gina when she was 23.

I was 19 when I received my first real "wake-up call," a sharp slap in the face reminding death is not just reserved for the elderly. The circle of life is a best-case scenario, not a guarantee, and the Grim Reaper can come a-callin' when you least expect it. Sure, I had experienced death before. I had lost my paternal grandparents, both of whom were quite elderly. I barely even remember my grandfather. My grandmother lived with us for a time, but I was also very young, and when her health began to deteriorate, it just seemed the natural progression of things.

While I remember the general sense of grief at the time of her passing, it was not at all the same as that awful evening in November 1987 when I learned my sister would not be returning from the latest of her many surgeries. She was at Children's Hospital in Columbus, an extraordinary facility that continued her care into adulthood because their specialists were so intimately involved in her unusually lengthy medical history. Scoliosis aided by gravity had worsened to the point that Gina's oxygen supply was slowly being cut off. Her only real chance for survival was a risky surgery to straighten her spine, something my father was staunchly against.

Several years prior, a similar surgery had been attempted during which doctors discovered Gina's bone density was abysmal, bones crumbling upon manipulation. During the procedure, she had stopped breathing, and doctors were barely able to resuscitate her. She spent countless months in a body cast, rolled around our house on a makeshift wooden bed my dad built from a Pepsi dolly, a hand cart modified to lay flat on four wheels, with a hinged section to allow her head to be elevated, and an area below to store a ready supply of her ample medical accoutrement.

But Gina had no intention of dying a slow, cruel death, and she was, after all, an adult. At this point, I was always her biggest advocate, taking her side and championing her cause although my father would probably only go so far as to say I had a great, big mouth. The choice was hers, and when she made it, I was just *certain* it would be like all those other surgeries. She would be recovering at home in no time.

Until that evening when Aunt Ginny came into the shoe store where I was working. One look at her face, and I knew. And while the blow landed in slow motion, I vividly remember being unsure if I should finish ringing up the sale I had just made or simply go—it was both absurd and surreal, the beginning of things that would never again be quite the same.

Life is full of wishes unrealized. I wish my sister could have experienced more in her all-too-brief time on this planet. When I started this book almost twenty years ago, it was my intention to take her along on a mysterious adventure. Earlier this year, I revisited what I had written and was resolved to finish it, but remembering the original direction I had envisioned, I thought it might be too dark and considered changing my approach. But after reading what I had put to paper all those years ago, it felt exactly right, and so, I chose to stay the course. It might not be what friends or family would have expected, but I think Gina would have approved.

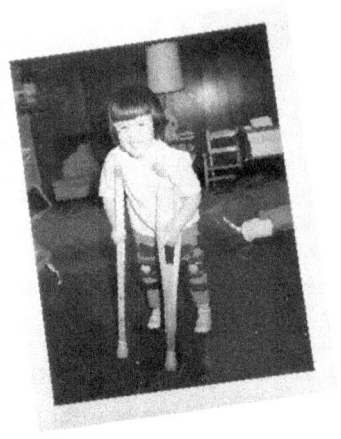

There is this *thing* that happens when I am writing a story. I won't prattle on about it for long, I promise. I may *think* I know where a story is headed, but on more than one occasion, my characters have informed me otherwise. I know it sounds like lunacy, but the characters always know better than I do what should transpire. Members of my Grove City Writers' Group nod when I speak of it, so I'm pretty sure I'm not the only one who experiences this phenomenon.

As such, I would be completely remiss not to mention the biggest surprise of this book came when the Shane Van Buren character waltzed right in with his easy, cockeyed grin and plopped himself down right in the middle of things.

The setting for this story is *extremely* loosely based on my experience in a quaint little Kentucky town in the early 1990s. My family was trying its hand opening a pizza restaurant, and everyone was thoroughly enthused but me. I went along grudgingly, afraid I was abandoning a burgeoning career with an office supply chain that would, soon enough, get swallowed up by its larger competitors, but what did I know? I didn't want to be the reason my family didn't take their shot at an American dream, but I was resentful I had to give up what felt like mine. I was miserable, and it unfairly tainted everything about that time and that town for me.

Except for the teens.

These teens were the most curious cats I'd ever seen. We were the new kids on the block, and they wanted to know what we were all about. Eager to run deliveries or make pizzas, they earned a little spending money while hanging out in the newest "hot spot" in their little town. We had video games and pool tables in the lobby—it was unlike anything they'd ever seen, and they couldn't get enough. They were good kids, raised well and hard-working. Funny, optimistic and exuberant, they also worked well together.

One of those teens was Christopher Shane Vanderen, although we knew him as Shane.

I didn't know him very well, but he was the type of guy who brought light into any room he entered. Seemingly never in a bad mood, he lifted people up when he sensed they were down as if it was entirely effortless. At a time when I found very little to smile about much less laugh, he had me in stitches with his various schemes to overthrow the management of our little pizza shop so we could assume complete control, rechristening the establishment, "Darin & Vanderen."

Tragically, Shane lost his life only eight days into his 18th year in an automobile accident. The tight-knit community reeled in shock as the news made its way back from the University of Kentucky hospital in which he died despite intensive efforts to save him. I have never seen a funeral so large in a community so small. He was loved by many, and the collective grief was heartbreakingly palpable.

The character of Shane Van Buren was written with the deepest respect and is intended to honor and remember a young man who, like my sister, was taken from his friends and family far too soon. It felt like he deserved an adventure, too.

As always, thanks for reading,
Darin Miller
Grove City, OH
August 18, 2022

NEXT UP...

ISOLATION

Dwayne Morrow Mystery #5

CHAPTER ONE

I spent most evenings on my front porch, moving slowly back and forth on my glider, watching day trade places with night.

I couldn't admit it, but I was struggling. Everything I knew had been turned inside out, and even though I was back home, I couldn't just pick up where I had left off. The world had stopped making sense, and the urge to sleep was almost overwhelming.

My name is Dwayne Morrow, and I don't know what the hell I am anymore. Once upon a time, I was in a comfortable little rut, operating a one-man PC support service out of my two-story farmhouse in Grove City, Ohio. Never much of one for organized education—or organized religion, for that matter—I gained my skills courtesy of YouTube and good old-fashioned trial-and-error. Hardware upgrades, software installation and network configuration—those are my specialties. I have built a small but steady client base that keeps the bills paid and the lights on, but the work is redundant and ultimately unfulfilling.

Almost a year ago, I had a Major Life Event. MLE, for short. I was nudged out of my comfortable rut by the temptation contained within an invitation to my high school reunion. As my primary social circle had been comprised of me and my cat, I thought it might be time to check in with some of the old classmates and see what life had tossed their way. Before I even made it back to my hometown of Lymont, I learned that my best friend, Ryan McGregor, had been murdered, and the suspect remained at large. His mother, Sarah, had been like a second mom to me, and there was no way I could refuse her request for me to ask around, see if any of our old mutual acquaintances might have some information that would help. Before I knew it, I was in so far over my head I could barely stay afloat. It was terrifying and exhilarating in equal measure, and in the process of finding the truth behind that horrible event, I began an entirely unexpected new relationship with Ryan's estranged widow, Melanie. She and their daughter, Jasmine, have since moved to Columbus so Melanie could pursue better employment opportunities and college courses, and who was I to argue? Long distance relationships are hard work.

I also started getting the first nibbling of discontent in my own career trajectory and decided I might be better suited for private investigation. I had renewed an acquaintance with an old schoolmate, Doug Boggs, who ran his own PI agency in Lymont and convinced him to open a satellite office off West Broad in Columbus so I might work as an apprentice, logging field hours as I worked toward my own license. In its original version, my plan had me taking cases in Columbus while Doug and his overbearing office manager mother, Loretta, remained in the southern part of the state. None of that had gone exactly to plan, and both of them were underfoot far more often than I liked. But they had me over a barrel. Even after stumbling through and solving two more fairly high-profile cases, I needed them as much as they needed me.

Then I had to go and have another Major Life Event. Er, MLE.

These things never ask permission, they just barge right in, upending everything around you. My brother, Matt, got married, and I lost my sister, Gina, in a matter of days. The particulars are fully detailed elsewhere, but the aftermath has left me in an unfamiliar and uncomfortable state.

I'm not entirely sure I can trust my own memory, and that has destabilized me in a way I'd never imagined. And it's not like I can talk about with anyone. If my memory is sound, I grudgingly made a promise that I wouldn't discuss it, not even with Melanie, and ain't that some shit? Trying to grow a relationship under the constant shadow of a lie isn't where I want to be. And if my memory *isn't* sound, then I'm probably bound for an institution, anyway.

I glanced over my shoulder as a persistent thumping sounded against my front window, punctuated by the occasional screech of claws on glass. My black cat, Dexter, stared at me from inside, his head cocked, unaccustomed to being anything other than my constant companion when I was home. I had never spent so much time in sight but out of reach. Seeing that he had my attention, he paused long enough to issue a silent peep before resuming his two-handed assault on the glass. I rapped a knuckle at face level, startling him and prompting a hiss before he jumped from the sill and back into the living room.

Whoops.

I had attracted unwanted attention. I heard footsteps approaching the front entrance from within, and soon the screen door opened. Brady Garrett poked his head out, dangling two beers in front of him.

"Hey," he said with a grin. "Want some company?"

He didn't wait for an answer as he closed the screen door behind him and joined me on the glider. I took the beer he offered and nodded, thinking this whole evening had been a bad idea, but Melanie wouldn't budge. Brady is a reporter with the Columbus Dispatch who has inserted himself into a couple of my escapades, the last of which nearly cost him his life. Initially,

I couldn't stand his smarmy disposition and relentless determination, but I have to admit, he's been a valuable resource and maybe isn't such a bad guy after all.

I decided to steer the conversation before he attempted to try.

"So, it's Diane, is it?" I asked.

"Dina," he corrected.

"Sorry," I grinned. "I was close. That was fast work. How'd you manage that?"

He ran a hand through his dark curly locks. "She was a nurse at my rehab facility. Worked with me three times a day, and I dunno—" He shrugged. "I guess she's just into me."

I nodded as laughter spilled out from inside the house. Whatever Melanie and Dina were discussing was amusing to both parties, but I wasn't curious enough to investigate. I took a long pull from my beer, preferring liquor, but I was less picky about my alcohol these days.

"Thanks for inviting us over," he said.

"All the credit goes to Melanie. Where are the kids? They're suspiciously quiet." Brady had brought along his son, Billy, and his temporary ward, Scott Nichols, to keep Jasmine occupied while the adults had their little dinner party.

"They're holed up in your office playing Xbox. I told them if they got bored, they could mess around with any of the shit on your desk. You wouldn't mind."

"You're an asshole, you know that?" I wasn't really concerned. All three of those kids had better manners than Brady.

"Yeah, well, it's good to see you, too, buddy. I mean, you look like shit, but it's good to see you."

We floated into uncomfortable silence, sipping our beers, and just as Brady started to open his mouth, I thought of another distraction to pursue. "How's your recovery coming along? Are you back at work yet?"

"Soon," he said. "I'm taking a couple more weeks' disability just because I can. My benefits are good, and so are my savings. I pretty much feel back to normal, though."

"Good, good," I nodded, adding, "I'm glad."

As if to reinforce how genuine my feeling actually was.

And back into uncomfortable silence.

Now, I wanted a cigarette. I quit smoking years before, but alcohol seemed to trigger that weakness in me. I didn't have any cigarettes, and no one else in the house smoked, so I was shit out of luck.

"How 'bout them Bengals?" I said, aiming for the inane.

"The season is still a few weeks away," he said. He finished his beer and sat forward, placing the empty bottle on the porch before clasping his hands together between his knees. "You know, if you ever—"

"I don't."

"But you might—"

"I wouldn't."

"You never know—"

"I'm positive."

"*Hey!*" Brady sat back, throwing his hands up in surrender. "Can I even finish a thought, here?"

I sighed, closing my eyes tightly and rolling my head from side to side, trying to loosen the knots that seemed to have taken residence in my neck.

"You know how sorry I am about your sister," he said. "But you can't just keep going like this. You need to talk to someone."

I threw my head back and laughed. "And that someone should be *you?* That's rich, Brady. Next thing I know, every single thought I shared would be all over tomorrow's *Dispatch*. I mean, you have no *idea* what this is like—"

My words caught in my throat, and I mentally kicked myself as I watched his expression drop. Brady's entire life had been punctuated by grievous loss, every bit as cutting as my own, if not more so. He lost his wife in an automobile accident, his parents in a plane crash and a recent girlfriend to a psychopathic killer. What in the hell was *wrong* with me? He shook his head, rising from the glider while I stared, slack jawed and gobsmacked at my own callousness.

"Oh, God, Brady," I said, getting to my feet. "I'm so sorry, man. That was a horrible thing to—"

He held up a finger, stopping me. "I didn't deserve that," he said quietly. "But I'll let it go, because believe it or not, I *do* understand. And while I don't particularly want to do it right this moment, I *am* here when you're ready to talk."

I nodded, rightfully feeling like a fool.

"I'm going to collect the kids and my date, thank Melanie for a wonderful evening and get out from underfoot," he muttered, picking up his empty bottle before going back inside. Under his breath, he muttered, "Dickhead."

Dexter stared at me from the window. There was no mistaking his expression. He was extremely disappointed in me, too.

········•••••◦⟨◦⟩◦•••••········

"I've got Jasmine settled upstairs," said Melanie, sliding in beside me on the glider and tucking herself underneath my arm. Four more empty bottles of beer had collected near my feet. "I thought I might take her to a movie tomorrow afternoon. There's a new Pixar playing. Wanna come?"

I stared at the stars visible in the distance from beneath the porch roof and shrugged. "I don't know," I said. "Maybe."

She nodded, taking my hand in hers. "Might be a nice distraction, but you know—whatever you want to do. Just wanted you to know you're welcome."

"Mmm-hmm."

"Brady took out of here kinda fast, didn't he? Did something happen between the two of you?"

I smiled wistfully. "I need to work on my manners."

"Ah," she said. "I'm sure it will be fine. Brady's a good guy. He thinks a lot of you."

"I know. I just wish he'd use a whole lot less words. It's—triggering."

"What did you think of Dina?" she asked, and when I glanced, her eyes were floating toward the heavens, and she looked like she'd just smelled something revolting.

I laughed. "I can't say I paid that much attention, but apparently you have some thoughts on the matter."

"I don't understand why Brady doesn't just go back with Nina," she said, referring to Nina Crockett, our FBI friend. She and Brady had dated briefly when we were all pursuing—and being pursued by—a serial killer. "He keeps going for these fake blondes with fake tits and minimal brain cells. It's so high school."

"I thought she was a nurse."

"A nurse's *aide*," she informed me. "A custodian of bedpans. A changer of linens and trash liners."

"That isn't what a nurse's aide does."

She scoffed. "I can't believe they'd trust her with much more. She thought a uvula was a type of birth control, and I won't even tell you how we got onto *that* topic."

I tightened my arm around Melanie and kissed the top of her head. I didn't know how much slack she was willing to cut me or for how long, but I appreciated her patience and understanding more than she could possibly know.

"You wanna watch a movie?" she asked, looking up at me.

I shrugged and shook my head. "I think I'll sit out here for a bit longer—if you don't mind. I'm just trying to—"

7

She placed two fingers against my lips. "Say no more. It's a little after ten. I'll go up and fall asleep to some TV in our room. But you better spend a little time with that cat of yours. He's starting to take out his displeasure with you on me, and he never liked me that well to begin with."

She leaned in and kissed me softly before standing.

"I love you," I said. She winked, blew me another kiss and went inside. A moment later, the living room light winked out.

Our room.

It warmed my heart that she thought of it as such. We didn't live together, although we may as well for all the time she had spent fawning over me lately. She was doing everything she could to prop me up until I could figure out a way out of this funk. I honestly don't know if I would have had the patience.

I didn't deserve her.

I caught the sound of an engine in the distance, drawing nearer, which was a little odd for the hour. Orin Way is a narrow, gravel lane that runs straight as an arrow east to west, and I have no neighbors within visible range on either side of my property. A large part of the appeal to my farmhouse was the relative solitude while still remaining within easy driving distance to Columbus. I watched a pinprick of headlights pierce the eastern horizon, propelled by an engine that would soon need a new muffler.

It sounded vaguely familiar.

The oddly shaped silhouette slowed as it neared the mouth of my driveway, its presence activating a motion-detect security light mounted at the apex of the roof of the old barn across from my drive. I recognized the Pontiac Aztek immediately and groaned.

Doug Boggs.

Shit.

His driver's door shrieked in protest as he opened it and hopped down. It positively screamed when he slammed it shut. I made a mental note to get him some WD-40 for Christmas. His expression was unreadable at that distance, but he held his camouflage hat in his hands, and I took that as a good sign. I squinted at the passenger side and saw no trace of his mother, Loretta. That was *definitely* a good sign. He was short, stout, and I couldn't believe I had missed the parallel to a teapot in all these years. The buttons of his red-checkered flannel shirt strained to contain his barrel shape; his neck alone had the top button on life support. He chewed on a soggy, unlit cigar as he bridged the distance between us, rotating his hat through thick fingers.

"It's a little late, don't you think, Dougie?" I called as he ambled up the wooden stairs to my porch. "Maybe you could have called?"

He paused on the top step, sighing as the security light winked out behind him. For a moment, we were both plunged into darkness. "I've been *trying* to call," he said. "For *weeks*."

"Is the phone proving a little too challenging? It's not that hard. You just enter the number and press the green button. You could have your mommy add me to your contacts, and you wouldn't even have to remember the number." I gasped. "These newer phones? You can even *talk* to the Google. Ask it to call me for you!"

It's entirely possible that alcohol makes me mean, but there's absolutely no doubt that Doug Boggs does.

A light flicked on upstairs, casting an oblong rectangular glow over my front yard from above my porch roof. I heard a window slide open, and Melanie called out, "Is everything all right down there? I thought I heard voices."

"Yes," I said. "It's just Doug."

"At this time of night?" She wasn't amused. "Douglas Boggs, I told you I'd have Dwayne call you just as soon as he possibly could."

I covered my grin while Doug squirmed uncomfortably. She had been running interference for me!

"It's okay," I said. "He won't stay long."

"N-n-no, ma'am," he stammered, and it was everything I could do to keep from bursting out laughing.

After a brief silence, Melanie replied, "See that you don't." The window closed and the light winked out.

"Talk about mommies," Doug grumbled, before resuming the nervous rotation of his cap. "Look, um—I, uh—first, I want to tell you how sorry me and Ma are for you and yours. It's just an awful thing. I wanted to say something at the—um, you know—um, service, but I ain't good with words and you had all those people around you. I didn't want to butt in."

I stared at him for a moment and nodded.

"Well, see—I've been trying to call you, but I either get the answering machine or your lady won't patch me through. I didn't have no choice but to come out here and see you face to face." He was rotating that cap so fast I expected it to suddenly break loose and fly across the yard.

"What's this about, Doug?" I asked.

"I already told you I ain't good with words, so don't get mad when I ask this," he hedged.

I nodded, unconsciously clenching my hands together. Lord only knew what would come next, but I would be damned if the next chapters of my life revolved around my exploits in prison. "Go on," I said.

"I need to know when you're coming back to work," he said, each word running into the next. "I mean, I need to know *if* you're coming back to work."

I cocked my head and stared at him, counting to ten. Then twenty.

I took a deep breath, leaned back in my glider and exhaled slowly. It wasn't an unreasonable question. I had been equally negligent in tending to my consulting business. My savings were dwindling and soon enough, utilities were going to start winking off, one by one.

"I don't know," I finally said. "Soon. I think."

Doug sighed and began pacing the length of my porch. "I'm gonna need a little more than that."

"What do you want from me, Doug? I'm doing the best I can."

He stopped pacing and looked down at me. "I know. I hate like hell to be standing here putting you on the spot like this. But we're circling the drain, here."

"What do you mean?"

He resumed his pacing. "I only opened the office on West Broad to help you get your hours in. You know? Help you get your PI license. Did you change your mind? Did you decide this isn't what you want to do after all?"

"No," I said. "That isn't it. It's just that with everything that's happened, I'm—I'm—"

He stopped pacing and held up a hand. "I get it. I really do. But the truth is, I can't keep this office open if you aren't a part of it. I can't afford to pay another associate, and let's face it, Ma is an awesome office manager, but not so good in the field."

I had my doubts about both, but I kept my mouth shut.

"My bread-and-butter is in Lymont, and if we can't figure out a way to make this work, I'll have to close the West Broad office next month," he said. "And that won't benefit either of us. Remember, you're on the lease as a responsible party, too."

I bit my tongue and started counting again. Ten. Twenty. Thirty. Forty...

I had stupidly signed a contract indebting myself to Boggs Investigations in a way I had never imagined. Doug must have sensed my escalating rage because he was quick to continue.

"But that isn't all I'm here to talk about," he said, attempting a smile but looking as though he may have shat himself a wee tiny bit. "I've got a real opportunity to share with you while you make up your mind what you want to do."

11

I weighed my options. Throw him off the porch or let him wade in a little deeper? I chose the latter.

"What?"

Doug relaxed, seemingly pleased he had overcome this latest obstacle. "Boggs Investigations has been offered an all-expenses paid pass for six—next weekend—Labor Day weekend!—to partake in a trial run of a new murder mystery weekend on Marble Toe Island!"

I stared at him vacantly, uncomprehending.

"Marble Toe Island!" he repeated, clapping his hat back onto his head. "Out on Lake Erie!"

I shook my head, still not sure where he was going with this.

"It's a team building exercise!" he enthused. "It's exactly what we need!"

I groaned. "Are you *kidding* me?"

"Not at all! I mean, look," he said, and the pacing continued. "Let's face it, you and Ma need a whole lot of work. You and me—well, you have a little problem with authority. I think it's exactly what we need to figure out if this is even worth it."

I chewed the inside of my jaw. I had counted to nearly two hundred and thought I might be able to speak without devolving into violence. "You, me, and—" I shuddered. "Your mother. That's three of six. Who else?"

Doug paused, spreading his arms wide. "Entirely up to you."

I raised an eyebrow. "Really?"

"Absolutely!"

I sighed. "I don't know, Doug. How soon do you need to know?"

He clapped his hands and headed for the porch stairs. "No rush! No rush at all!" He turned as he reached the bottom of the stairs and the security light winked on again, casting him in silhouette. "Just let me know by end of day tomorrow, okay? Or our tickets will go to the next in line, and I'll have to close our Columbus branch."

I stared at him devoid of expression. I let my middle finger do all the talking.

ISOLATION
Dwayne Morrow Mystery #5

AVAILABLE NOW

ACKNOWLEDGEMENTS

I am thrilled to have Lynne Hobstetter, Teri Lott and Traci Steele return once again to provide a first line of defense against my poor choices—grammar and otherwise—in the composition of this story. For a moment, things looked a little iffy for Teri; she managed to break multiple bones, including her dominant hand, in the weeks prior to me finishing this book, so I wasn't sure she would be up for the challenge. But like the trooper she is, she came to my rescue without hesitation. Without feedback and input from these talented ladies, these books would certainly suffer. I can never thank them enough. As always, any mistakes, factual or otherwise, are completely my own.

Never underestimate the power of your Facebook network! As I started piddling around with Facebook Ads after the release of *Retribution*, I got a FB message from a former school friend, Susie Hart, offering advice and hands-on expertise in designing my promotional materials. She currently teaches graphic design, and her background is in that and advertising. She is extraordinarily talented and has been so generous with her time and ideas. She has elevated every single bit of marketing I've attempted to do, and the results have been immediate. Susie, you are the *best!* Thank you!

The cover photo was a lot trickier this time around. I knew it had to be one of two things: either a rock quarry filled with sparkling blue water and caves around its perimeter—unlikely given its very specific requirements—or a Ferris wheel, the centerpiece of the Briarstaff Apple Festival. We opted for the second choice, but getting that photo was no small feat. State fairs and many county fairs would be too large to 'stand in' for our little hometown festival. We had a false (yet costly) start at a small county fair in Ohio. Admission, food, drinks and gasoline were through the roof, and despite promotional photos from the previous year's fair prominently displaying one, there was no trace of a Ferris wheel once we got there. So, we began to map out the remaining nearby county fairs, prepared to hit the road for as long as necessary to find what we were looking for. The very next Saturday, my nephew, Scott Bennington, casually mentioned he had passed a street fair in Grove City just miles from my house, and it might do the trick. And indeed, it did! No dead body parts this time, just a series of magnificent photos taken by my daughter, Nicki Miller, capturing exactly the right tone for this story. I think it's the best cover yet!

Most of all, thank *you* for reading. I am truly humbled that people are responding to these characters that have come to mean so much to me. I can't wait to see what Dwayne and Melanie get into next!

Darin Miller
Grove City, Ohio – September 2022

ALSO AVAILABLE

REUNION
Dwayne Morrow Mystery #1

CIRCUMVENTION
Dwayne Morrow Mystery #2

RETRIBUTION
Dwayne Morrow Mystery #3

ISOLATION
Dwayne Morrow Mystery #5

ABDUCTION
Dwayne Morrow Mystery #6

DECEPTION
Dwayne Morrow Mystery #7

DELUSION
Dwayne Morrow Mystery #8

OVER CONSUMPTION
*A Dwayne Morrow and Jane Bond
Novella
(Co-written with V.R. Tapscott)*

OTHER WORK

BROKEN BITS AND BOBS
*A Collection of What Ifs, What Was,
and What Never Should Be*

HOUSE OF SECRETS
*Every Room Holds a Story
(Contributor, "Redemption")*

EQUILIBRIUM

THE LIBRARY
CENTENNIAL
ANTHOLOGY
*Celebrating the Lives and People of the
SPL Community
(Contributor, "Meredith's Bad Day")*

DID YOU LIKE ME?

☐ Yes! ☐ No ☐ Maybe?

May I ask a favor?

If you enjoyed reading this book as much as I enjoyed writing it, won't you please consider leaving a rating and/or review on Amazon, Goodreads, Barnes & Noble, BookBub, or anywhere else you might see fit? It only takes a moment to leave a rating and a maybe a couple more for a short review—even a simple 'I would recommend this book!' will do nicely.

Word of mouth is the single most powerful tool in an Indie author's toolkit, and ratings and reviews help more than you may realize in growing our audience. Think of it as a gratuity you might leave a server after an evening of fine dining, but this gratuity doesn't cost a thing—only a few moments of your time.

Thank you for your kind consideration.

Amazon

Goodreads

Barnes & Noble

BookBub

ABOUT THE AUTHOR

Darin Miller was born in Portsmouth but currently resides in Grove City, both of which are located in Ohio. While he has worked in Information Technology for three decades, he has *not* solved a single, solitary crime to date. He is the BookFest award-winning author of the Ohio-based *Dwayne Morrow Mystery* series, as well as an unrelated short story collection, *Broken Bits and Bobs*, and a standalone psychological horror thriller, *Equilibrium*. With equal parts action, humor, suspense and mystery, the *Dwayne Morrow* series features characters you're sure to love—and in some cases, loathe.

Stay current with updates, short stories, and other special promotions at www.darin-miller.com.

www.ingramcontent.com/pod-product-compliance
Lightning Source LLC
Chambersburg PA
CBHW070618260626
47161CB00007B/2488